Praise for the l...
of Su...

Laird of the Wind

"This lavishly crafted love story brilliantly combines history and romance. Mysticism, passion, beauty, treachery, intrigue, and unforgettable characters . . . spellbinding."
—*Romantic Times* (4½ stars)

"The intensity of emotion and lush writing style . . . combined with King's expert plotting and eye for fascinating historical detail make *Laird of the Wind* an exceptional read." —Amazon.com

Lady Miracle

"Strong sense of time and place, masterful plotting, compelling love story—and more. . . . Extraordinary . . . mythically lovely . . . King's brilliant storytelling and painstaking historical research elevate this tale."
—*Publishers Weekly* (starred review)

"The latest treasure from a writer whose star is in ascendance. . . . Riveting . . . superb . . . marvelous. . . . Truly a treat, like savoring fine Belgian chocolate, reading her work is almost sinfully delicious."
—Paintedrock.com

The Raven's Moon

"A marvelous Scottish tale. Absolutely wonderful characters, breakneck pacing, and a great setting. I couldn't put it down."
—Patricia Potter

"A wonderfully dark and delectable read. Susan King evokes the Lowlands as few writers have—with all the passion, intrigue, mystery, and beauty of the land—and tells a unique, well-crafted romance." —*Romantic Times*

The Angel Knight

"Magnificent . . . richly textured with passion, and a touch of magic."
—Mary Jo Putney

"Ms. King, a visual writer extraordinaire, has blended a mystical and historical tale so precise that the reader will be drawn in and won't ever want to leave."
—*Romantic Times*

"A romance of tremendous beauty and heart. Readers will not be able to put this one down. . . . Her books will stand the test of time."
—*Affaire de Coeur*

ALSO BY SUSAN KING

Laird of the Wind
Lady Miracle
The Raven's Moon
The Angel Knight
The Raven's Wish
The Black Thorne's Rose

The Heather Moon

Susan King

A TOPAZ BOOK

TOPAZ
Published by the Penguin Group
Penguin Putnam Inc., 375 Hudson Street,
New York, New York 10014, U.S.A.
Penguin Books Ltd, 27 Wrights Lane,
London W8 5TZ, England
Penguin Books Australia Ltd, Ringwood,
Victoria, Australia
Penguin Books Canada Ltd, 10 Alcorn Avenue,
Toronto, Ontario, Canada M4V 3B2
Penguin Books (N.Z.) Ltd, 182-190 Wairau Road,
Auckland 10, New Zealand

Penguin Books Ltd, Registered Offices:
Harmondsworth, Middlesex, England

First published by Topaz, an imprint of Dutton NAL,
a member of Penguin Putnam Inc.

First Printing, April, 1999
10 9 8 7 6 5 4 3 2 1

To Audrey LaFehr and Karen Solem—
heartfelt thanks for constant faith and support

Prologue

"Fore me! A dainty derived gipsie."
—Ben Jonson, *Masque of the Metamorphosed Gipsies*

Scotland, the Borderlands
February 1526

"Your father is a thief," her grandmother said, drawing Tamsin close. "A Scottish rascal and a *gadjo,* a non-Romany. He wants you to live with him in his great house of stone, and he'll come to fetch you this day."

Tamsin had never been inside a house of stone, and wondered what it would be like. Cold and dark, she thought, without the warmth of the sun and the fresh smell of the greenwood that she loved so well. She was not certain that a thief was desirable in a father, either Romany or Scot, but she smiled up at her grandmother, trusting her, knowing that her grandparents would not let her go with her Scottish father if he was a bad *gadjo.*

Nona Faw smiled, her wrinkled, high-boned face handsome and tawny, framed in a turban of purple silk. Her eyes were deep black, unlike Tamsin's green eyes, which she had inherited from her father, a man she had seen only a few times in her life.

"Archie Armstrong has a good heart," Nona went on. "Who are we, the Romany, to judge a man for thieving, if he cares for his family and avenges his enemies that way? He has always been generous to our people, though we travel as strangers and pilgrims through Scotland. And he has paid us well to raise you, my little Tchalai, after . . . the one who bore you went away six years ago."

Tamsin knew that her grandmother still grieved for her daughter, who had died birthing Tamsin. Nona would never again speak her daughter's name, nor would she wear red, her daughter's favorite color. Such gestures were part of the Romany way of mourning. Tamsin was not allowed to wear red either, although she loved the color well and did not remember her mother at all.

Her grandparents would not even use the *gadjo* name that her mother and father had agreed upon when she was born, for it was yet another reminder of her mother's death. Her father called her Tamsin when he visited the gypsy camp, and she thought of herself by that name. She liked the sound of it, and cherished the knowledge that her parents had chosen it together.

Tamsin nodded. "*Avali*, yes, Grandmother," she said. "I will go with the man my father, if you wish it so." In truth, the thought of leaving her grandparents frightened and saddened her, but she had always done as they had asked.

"Your father wants to take care of you, his girl-child," Nona said. "I suspect, now that his two grown sons have died, he needs some happiness in his stone house, which he calls Merton Rigg. You will live there to please him, and to please us."

"I must stay there always?" Tamsin asked uncertainly.

"We promised your father to let you go with him, though you are small yet, and the brightest star in our lives. And so we called you Tchalai, for the pale green stars in your pretty eyes," she added. "But we will see you as often as we can on our travels, my dear. Now, I want you to remember one thing well."

Tamsin looked up at her. "What is that?"

Nona bent close. "Your little hand may frighten some, Tchalai. You must take care to hide it well. Many there are who will not understand what they see."

Tamsin nodded. She tucked her strangely formed hand behind her, curling it into an awkward fist. "I will, Grandmother."

"Some Romany believe you have the evil eye, that you were born with a curse." Nona Faw brushed Tamsin's dark curls out of her face. "I think the *gadjo* are even more foolish than our Romany brothers and sisters about such things. How could a small babe, born of love, bring a curse into the world? How could this face, these beautiful water-colored eyes, carry bad luck?"

"I know that some say I am *wafri bak*, bad luck," Tamsin said, nodding solemnly. "Grandfather gets angry with them."

Her grandmother stroked Tamsin's cheek and sighed. "Fate has marked you with a flaw for some reason, and we must trust that fate will look after you. But you must be strong in your heart to bear what comes to you. One day, I hope, you will see your hand as a gift instead of a burden."

Tamsin nodded again, though she did not understand what her grandmother told her. She saw no gift, only a small, ugly hand, different from any other hand she had ever seen, and not nearly as useful as others. She wished it were pretty, but she knew that the most fervent wishes could not change her hand.

Later that day, when her father rode into her grandparents' camp, Tamsin thought that he was the largest man she had ever seen. Archie Armstrong was tall and big and very handsome. Even his teeth were large when he grinned at her. She smiled up at him shyly, and his answering laugh was loud and pleasant, making her laugh, too. He was blond, green-eyed, and rosy-faced, and reminded her of a shaggy golden bear.

She waited quietly while he spoke with her grandfather in the Scottish tongue, which she did not understand. Her father handed her grandfather a heavy bag of silver coins. Tamsin knew that John Faw was an earl in his own land, a foreign place far from Scotland. She was sure that he would be happy to have another bag of coins to hide under the floor of his wagon. She hoped he would give her a silver piece to wear on a string around her neck. Her grandmother wore so many coins that they jingled and glittered on her full bosom whenever she moved.

Finally her father mounted his horse and held out his arms to Tamsin. Her grandmother kissed her repeatedly, hugging her until they both were damp with tears.

Her grandfather, who always smelled of smoke, horses, and the metals that he worked, touched her head gently and told her that they would come to see her whenever their wanderings took them near Archie's stone tower. Then he looped a leather thong, strung with three silver coins, around her neck, and handed her up to her father's arms.

"All will be well," her grandmother said. "You will go there, and you will see. All will be well."

Tamsin nodded, clutching her small bundle of belongings in her good hand, hiding her left hand under her cloak. As they rode away, tears slid down her cheeks, even though she tried to stay silent and act proud.

After a while, she wiped the tears away clumsily with her hand, fisting it so that her father would not see its strangeness. She feared he might decide not to take her to his great stone house, where her grandparents very much wanted her to be.

In her heart, Tamsin knew that she wanted to stay out under the sky and the stars, to travel through wind and sunshine and rain with her grandparents. She did not want to be shut inside a *gadjo* house as dark and smelly as a cave.

But her father's smile, and his nice laugh, made her feel safe. Her grandparents had promised to visit her as often as they could. If she proved unhappy, she could ask Nona and John Faw to take her back into their Romany band.

Besides, she admitted to herself, she was curious to learn what Scottish thieves and stone houses were like.

"Sweet Savior! Will ye look there," Archie growled. He turned to the man who rode beside him, and pointed down to a narrow glen at the base of the hill on which they sat their horses. A group of men rode alongside the burn far below.

The movement of his arm jostled the small girl in his lap, and Archie steadied her with one hand. She looked up at him, still silent, as she had been in the few hours since he had fetched her from the camp of the wandering Egyptians, called gypsies.

He smiled slightly. She trained her wide, limpid gaze on him, green as glass and framed in thick black lashes, set like jewels in her small, honey-colored face. The child was too serious, too quiet, he thought. Her trust and willingness, and her dark, delicate beauty, pulled at his heart, endearing her to him more than he could admit to anyone.

She reminded him much of her mother, but for those eyes—his

own, light green—and her tawny skin, paler than her mother's darker tone. Her mother had been beautiful and kind, and he had never cared that she was a gypsy lass. He had loved her well, and she him. If she had lived through this child's birth, he would have had fine sons of her, and gentle nights.

Archie glanced at Cuthbert Elliot, his mother's brother, who had ridden out to meet him not long before, bearing tragic news. "There's a party o' men down there, wi' a lad between them," Archie said to his uncle. "Those would be them, then."

Cuthbert nodded, his thin face grim beneath the frame of a steel helmet. "Aye, heading away from Rookhope Tower, as I told ye. They ride for the earl o' Angus, who lately holds our young King James in his power. And there's young Master William Scott between them. Puir lad, he's the Laird o' Rookhope now, since those de'ils hanged his father just this morn."

"Aye, for the theft o' two cows from the English, ye said. By God!" Archie shook his head sadly. "Allan Scott, hanged without trial. 'Tis muckle hard to believe it."

"A wicked sort o' justice, to hang a man within sight o' his own tower, with his wife and bairns at the window," Cuthbert said.

Archie shivered in the cold winter wind, which held a damp hint of snow. But more than chill disturbed him.

Last year, he had lost his two strong, beloved sons to the gallows, hanged for reiving crimes. He thought the grief might never leave him. Now the cruel death of Allan Scott, the notorious Rogue of Rookhope and his dearest comrade, brought a pain almost as deep, and just as bitter.

He wrapped his arm securely around his small daughter and hugged her to him without a word. He knew that she could not yet understand his language, but he wanted to let her know that he would keep her safe.

She glanced up at him and smiled a little. So innocent, he thought, so pure and trusting, untouched as yet by the pain and the injustice in the world. He wanted her to stay that way, but knew that life would take that innocence from her, with or without the good care of a father. She had been marked by grief before she had even left the womb, he thought, with but half a wee hand.

He returned her smile, and her small, sweet face brightened. He felt the sorrowful pain in the region of his heart ease a little. Then she turned her head to look down into the glen, where the lad and his captors rode along the edge of the burn.

Archie sighed. Tamsin might be a waif and a gypsy, but she was his child, his only child now, and he meant to honor his obligation to her. Her brothers, whom she had never known, were gone. Their mother, his first wife, had died long ago. Six years ago, Tamsin's mother died after a year of marriage. With sons to inherit Merton Rigg, and the gypsies willing to care for his infant daughter, he had not felt the need to find a new wife.

But last year, his life had changed with the tragic deaths of his sons. All he had left to him now was this half-blooded daughter, crippled and small, who did not even speak Scots.

"The Rogue o' Rookhope was the best of all the Border rogues," Cuthbert said. Archie looked at him, reminded of his presence. "He were the finest reiver in all the Scottish Border-lands."

"Aye. I'll mourn him like my own brother," Archie said. "Like my sons."

"The earl o' Angus has done a black deed, and his men wi' him, including that knave Malise Hamilton. See him down there, like a dark vulture, riding beside the lad." Cuthbert scowled. "Bastard half-brother to the earl o' Arran, the regent himself, and so he thinks himself finer 'n a king. Bah."

Archie frowned, watching the man who led William Scott's horse through the glen. A light flurry of snow began, obscuring the view, but Archie saw William's proud, straight carriage. The lad turned his face up toward the falling snow, his dark hair winging out in the breeze.

"Will Scott is scarce thirteen, but look at him," Archie said. "Rides proud as any Border rogue, as if he's unafraid o' those bastards, as if he knows he's equal to any man. He minds me well o' his da. Where will they take him, do ye know?"

"Angus has decided to make him a hostage o' the crown, and a pledge for the good behavior o' the surname, 'Scott.' "

Archie sighed. "Poor lad. I wonder what will become o' him

now. God's blessing upon him, and his mother too. Lady Emma has lost both her man and her eldest bairn this day."

"But even in her grief and shock, she thought kindly of yer friendship, and sent a man to Merton Rigg wi' the sad tale o' the hanging. Did I tell ye that Malise Hamilton gave her four gold coins in recompense for her husband's death, one for herself and one for each bairn?"

"And they have the cheek to call us scoundrels!" Archie shook his head. "But see ye, that William Scott is a bold one. He'll be a braw, handsome man one day, as his father was."

"I hear he's to be confined with young King Jamie himself, as a companion. Angus wants it so. He says 'twill keep the Border lords in check to have one o' their own pups hostage wi' the king. William Scott will learn fancy speech and writing and dancing, and wear silks and gewgaws. He'll forget he ever was Rogue's Will, the son o' Allan Scott o' Rookhope."

"He willna forget," Archie said fiercely. "And when that lad's a man, Hamilton and Angus had best beware. They'll regret what they did this day."

"I hope so." Cuthbert gathered his reins. "We'd best get yer wee Tamsin home. My mother is there, wi' a hot fire waiting, and she's made a fine stew. Though she frets that she doesna ken wha' wee 'Gyptian bairnies eat."

As Archie watched, William Scott looked up. Archie raised a hand in silent salute, his throat tightening. Even at some distance, through a veil of snow, the lad seemed to recognize his father's friend. He lifted a hand in reply.

"A braw lad," Archie murmured. "Cuddy, what will we do now, my lass and me?"

"What?" Cuthbert asked.

"At the new year, Allan and I discussed a marriage between his Will and my Tamsin. I promised to fetch my lass from her gypsy kin, who nursed her through her infant years. We agreed 'twould be a good match. I told him—" His voice broke.

He remembered his friend, tall and dark-haired, lean as a whip, a wickedly clever reiver and a loyal comrade, yet a man with a gentle manner for his lady and his bairns. "I told him Tamsin was a bonny lass," he said. "I said she would grow into a fine lady for his lad. Despite her hand, and her dark blood."

"Despite that, hey," Cuthbert said, glancing at the girl.

"Aye. Allan dismissed her gypsy blood and her wee hand as naught. He said she was an Armstrong o' Merton, and 'twere good enough for him were she a troll wi' my own fearsome face."

Cuthbert smiled a little. "Did ye get that marriage promise doon in writing?"

"Nah," Archie said. "Our word was all the bond we needed."

"And should hae been. But ye lack proof o' the promise, and now ye lack the bridegroom. Ye'd best forget that marriage promise, Archie. We may never see that lad again."

Archie felt a crushing disappointment. He looked at the lad who rode proud and unafraid through the glen, and glanced at the child in his lap, who watched the scene below. Archie wondered how much she understood of what she saw. All of her attention seemed fastened on the boy.

The two bairns were somehow alike, he realized suddenly. Dark and slender, proud and straight, they matched like brother and sister, like twin souls. He frowned, for his poetic thought only increased his sadness.

" 'Twould have been a strong match, a child o' mine and a child o' Rookhope's," he said.

"Aye so. But young Rookhope will be raised a ward o' the crown and in the court. He'll become book-ruined and full o' silly manners." Cuthbert shook his head. "Find yer lassie a fine reiver to run livestock out o' England wi' ye, and to take care of Merton Rigg when ye're gone. Or find yerself a new wife, and get new sons on her. I've a cousin ye might fancy."

"I've had two wives, and three bairns, and I am weary o' death visiting me," Archie answered. "I have one bairn left to me, and I'll keep her close. I may never risk the taking of another wife. Losing kin is too hard, Cuddy. Too hard." He lifted the reins. "Let's get the lass home."

"Look. Yer wee Tamsin looks as if she knows Will Scott herself," Cuthbert remarked. "She seems sad, like."

Archie glanced down. Tamsin leaned forward, a frown creasing her brow. He saw the glint of tears in her eyes. She lifted her right hand, just as Archie had done moments earlier.

The boy in the glen looked up and waved at Tamsin. Then he turned away. Archie felt a sharp tug deep in his heart.

"Och," Cuthbert said, as if he too felt the same pain. "D'ye think she understands who he is? That he was meant for her, and now she's lost him? That we've all lost him?"

"How could she know that? I willna tell her, nor will you. There's nae point in burdening her wi' this sad tale."

"Aye, she will never meet that lad." Cuthbert heaved a long sigh. "This day has made my heart full sore. I will have to make a ballad about William Scott and the gypsy lass."

Archie groaned. "Yer ballads are the worst I ever heard."

"Will-yam Scott," the child said softly.

"I thought ye said she doesna have the Scots tongue," Cuthbert said.

She looked at Cuthbert. "Tongk," she repeated.

"She's quick, this one." Archie patted the girl's silky head. "John Faw said she speaks the gypsy tongue and some French, which he taught to her."

"And just how are we to teach her Scots?" Cuthbert asked. "Wi' much pointing o' fingers and repeating o' words?"

"I will find her a tutor who has French and Scots both." Archie watched the party of men with the lad disappear into a passage between two hills. He sighed deeply and turned his horse away from the lip of the hill.

"God's own wounds, Cuthbert," he muttered. "Allan Scott o' Rookhope was the best of rogues. I will never forget the injustice that was done this day."

"Nor I. If that lad ever decides to avenge his father, he will have Armstrongs and Elliots riding at his back."

"Aye." Archie sighed. "Rogue's Will Scott might have been my own good-son, wed to my lass."

"Archie man, what must be, must be," Cuthbert said. "Ye'll find the lass a husband. Ye have time. Years, yet."

The child stirred in Archie's arms and settled against his chest as they rode. Soon she drifted into sleep. Her left hand slipped free: a fingerless wedge, curled like a claw, though the thumb was normal enough. An odd little thing, Archie thought, and startling to see, but soft and smooth and plump as any child's hand. He tucked it gently under her cloak, and held it for a moment while she slept.

As he rode toward home, he wondered if he would find a husband for her at all when the time came, let alone one to equal the son of the Rogue of Rookhope.

Chapter One

Your pardon, lady, here you stand
(If some should judge you by your hand)
The greatest felon in the land
Detected.
  —Ben Jonson, *Masque of the Metamorphosed Gipsies*

July 1543

Her eyes were a cool, delicate green, even in torchlight, but her gaze was hot and furious. If her gloved hands and booted ankles had not been bound, William thought, she might have thrown herself at him in a rage.

Of the men gathered in the dungeon cell watching her, William Scott stood closest. He had advanced toward her, while his English host, her captor, stayed by the door with his guardsmen in trepidation.

She watched William warily, nostrils flared, eyes narrowed, breath heaving beneath the old leather doublet she wore. Despite men's clothing and the agile strength of her resistance, not one of them had mistaken her for a lad. She was clearly female, with well-shaped curves beneath doublet, breeches, and high boots.

Besides, William thought wryly, only a woman could cast a glare that would make several armed men hesitate.

She reminded him of a cornered wildcat: lithe, tawny, eyes blazing. Still, he saw a flicker of fear in her gaze. He remembered too well what it was like to be confined, bound, watched like a mummer's animal. Though he had been a lad at the time, the day of his own capture—the day his father had been hanged—still burned clear in his memory.

He edged closer. "Be calm, lass," he murmured.

Her glance darted from him to the others, sparking like green fire. She looked down at the man who lay collapsed at her feet. Large, blond, bearded, and considerably older than the girl, he seemed barely conscious, blood seeping from a wound on his brow. She stood over him, William realized, like a fierce guardian.

William advanced steadily, his palm held out. "Be calm, lass, we only want to talk to you."

She shuffled backward, keeping her balance even with bound ankles. Long tendrils of dark, curling hair spilled over her eyes. She shook the silken veil back, glaring.

"Take care, man. If you go closer, she will attack," Jasper Musgrave, his host and her captor, warned behind him. "I know her. A savage—half Border Scot, half gypsy. A wild girl, that one. 'Tis said no man will wed her, no matter how her Scottish father bribes and begs them."

William noted the understanding, and a flash of hurt, in her eyes. "She's no savage," he murmured over his shoulder. "She defends herself and her companion. She thinks we mean harm."

Musgrave laughed harshly, shifting his great bulk a step or two closer. "And so we do! She and her father, and the rest of their comrades, took four of my horses."

"The man is her father?" William frowned. He had first seen the prisoners only moments ago, after his host had led him down to the dungeon. The hour was past midnight, but he and Jasper Musgrave had sat late by the fire, drinking Spanish sherry and negotiating a complex matter of couched bribery and cautious acceptance. But the mellow flavor of good sherry had not disguised the sour taste of the discussion.

Jasper Musgrave's men had come into the great hall to inform their lord that they had captured two Scottish reivers who had stolen some horses. The rest of the thieves had fled, but they had imprisoned the two in the dungeon. Musgrave had asked William, as his Scottish guest and a member of a reiving surname himself, to witness their interrogation.

"Aye, they are father and daughter," Musgrave said now. "Border scum from the Scottish side. They and their kin have plagued me for years. My land lies just south of his land, and but six miles separate our towers. I might see them hanged for this, now that I have them in my keeping at last." Musgrave gestured toward the man on the floor. " 'Tis our good fortune that he took a sore hurt. We would have had a struggle indeed, had Archie Armstrong kept hearty this night."

"Armstrong!" William glanced at him. "Of what place?"

"Merton Rigg," Musgrave said. "Half Merton, some call it, because the tower sits directly on the—"

"Directly on the Border line, in the area called the Debatable Land," William supplied, remembering. "Merton sits half in Scotland and half in England, since the house was built before the current border was shifted."

"Aye," Musgrave muttered. "And the English part of that land is mine. The case has been in the Session courts since our fathers' time. No judge will settle the boundaries of our portions, since that would entail a change in the national borders." He looked closely at William. "You know Armstrong of Merton Rigg?"

"My father knew him long ago. They rode together."

"Your father was a notorious scoundrel. You had the favor of your Scottish King James once, but he's dead now, and a mere infant girl the heiress of his kingdom. You do not have your king's favor any longer, William Scott. You're naught but a rogue yourself now." He smiled and folded his hands over his belly. "And just the sort of rogue we need—a canny Scot who still has ties to the crown, and yet has sense enough to join our cause."

"Aye, I've sense enough," William muttered bitterly. He saw that the girl listened, her eyes keen, her breath heaving beneath the old frayed leather doublet. He glanced down at her father, a brawny heap on the earthen floor, blood smeared over the man's face and blond head.

Despite the wound, and the whitening of the man's once-reddish whiskers, William recognized those strong, handsome features. Archie had been a close comrade of his father. William remembered the man as huge, blond, often laughing. He had been young when Armstrong had lost his two sons to execution by hanging, but he remembered his own father's distress over the incident. Archie's daughter was much younger than her brothers would have been, he thought, younger than his own thirty years.

As he stood watching the girl and her father, waiting while Musgrave muttered some orders to the guards behind him, William remembered something further about Archie Armstrong. An image came back to him with a near-physical shock.

He had seen Archie on the day of his father's death. While he had ridden through a narrow glen, his horse led by the men who had taken him prisoner for the Scottish crown, he had looked up to see Archie seated on horseback on the crest of a hill, watching the party ride past. His father's friend had lifted a hand in a faithful salute.

A dark-haired child sat in Archie's lap that day. She, too, had waved to William, and he recalled waving back. He remembered, with a deep pang of emotion, how desperately he had wanted to break free from his escort and ride toward the refuge and welcome of his father's friend.

He stared with sudden wonder at Archie's daughter. She would have been no more than five or six the day William had been taken. Surely this half-gypsy was that dark-haired little girl.

Her solemn salute, and her father's, had meant a great deal to him. In the midst of the grief, fear, and anger that he had endured that day, their silent, respectful farewell remained in his memory as a shining moment of precious value to him.

"And Archie is another scoundrel dropped into our laps," Musgrave was saying. "I'll convince him to lend us his support, too, for our little scheme, or I'll offer him a noose. What say you to that?"

William drew his breath, summoned himself out of intense memories and back into the dungeon cell. "Archie? He's naught but a minor laird and a midnight raider," he said in a deliberately casual tone. "I doubt he will be of any use to us. Were I you, I would let him go."

His immediate instinct was to discourage Musgrave from involving Armstrong in this scheme. He would not see this particular Borderman brought low if he could help it. William resolved, fists clenched, to do whatever he could do to set these two free. He owed them something, he thought. He owed them that much.

"Ah, he is just the sort of scoundrel we need," Musgrave countered. "Besides, Armstrong and his daughter have ties to the Egyptians that wander the Borderlands. That could be quite useful indeed."

"Egyptians?" William asked, startled. He caught the girl's quick frown, saw in her glittering green eyes that she listened intently. He turned and lowered his voice. "Gypsies? What use could they be?" Impatience surged through him. "You had best explain this cause to me in full, Jasper, if you want my help in your plan."

"I told you," Musgrave said smoothly, remaining in the shadows. "King Henry needs a Scotsman such as you, with influence at court and respect among the Bordermen. But we can make good use of a common marchman like Archie."

"I am curious to learn the whole of your plan," William said. He sensed the girl watching, listening, though he did not look at her just then.

"You will learn all in good time. Rest assured, 'tis a grand scheme."

William was weary of Musgrave's elusive games. He had been trying to learn the truth of the plot for two days. He had heard only a few vague references to King Henry, the eighth of that name, and some mumblings about the good of Scotland and the infant queen, Mary Stewart. But he had heard enough, and suspected enough, to make him determined to find out the rest.

"I will hear this grand scheme soon or I am gone," he replied. "And with me, my influence at court and in the Scottish Borders."

Musgrave shot him a dark glare. "First I'll learn what Archie Armstrong was doing on my lands at night, and with my horses in his grip." He moved forward, breathing heavily. He was thick-jowled and huge, his width more remarkable than his height. He could have made two of any man easily, William thought, watching him.

"See you," Musgrave said, "Armstrong may not be able to confess his crime just now, judging by that head wound. The girl is our only source if we want to learn what happened to my horses. Untie the cloth over her mouth so she can answer my questions.

That vixen would attack me, but she'll not go after you, a Scotsman, and a friend to her father."

William cast Musgrave a sidelong look, careful to keep it short of a glare. He had been cultivating the man's good opinion, and he would not undo it now. His own reputation had led him into this. Most Bordermen knew that William Scott had been a captive of the crown, and then a friend of King James of Scotland.

Now, though, he was currently in deep disgrace at the royal court, headed by James's queen dowager, Marie of Guise. Musgrave believed that William Scott was bitter enough to be disloyal as well as disgraced. William had encouraged that impression.

When Musgrave had approached him a few days ago with a covert offer of gold and hints of a secret English plot, William had shown great interest. He had visited the man's castle on the English side of the Border to discuss certain possibilities. He played the good comrade, and the foul Scot.

Most Scottish Bordermen in Liddesdale, where his own Rookhope Tower was situated, and in the Debatable Land, where Armstrong's Merton Rigg lay, knew Jasper Musgrave, whose castle lay within a moonlit ride over the border. The man had a reputation as a clever English scoundrel, not above treachery and thievery. William did not know him well personally, although his cousin Jock Scott was enamored of the English girl who was betrothed to Jasper's son.

Earlier tonight, William had dined with both Musgraves, listening to flattery and increasingly blatant attempts at bribery. William had agreed, finally, to support King Henry's cause in Scotland. He had not put his name in writing, but the unsavory verbal promise he had made had left him with a cold feeling in his gut.

But Musgrave had come to him with the bribe, and he felt an obligation to his queen, and to himself, to pursue it. He sensed a deeper, darker plot beyond King Henry's probable interest in stirring war between the two countries. William was determined to discover what the full scheme might be.

He glanced again at the Armstrong girl and her father. Although he had convinced Musgrave to regard him as an ally, William could not condone taking down a laird's daughter like a common thief. The reiving incident had nothing to do with politics and intrigue, and needed to be resolved quickly.

Frowning, he moved toward the girl. She shuffled back. "Easy, lass," he murmured, and took her by the shoulders. She stiffened under his touch but allowed him to turn her. He felt the fine make of her through leather and padding, strong bones and lean muscle beneath his hands. Tension seemed to thrum through her like drawn lute strings.

When he loosened the knots behind her head, her hair tumbled over his fingers, jarring his senses. The softness and heathery scent were distinctly out of place in a cold, dank dungeon. She turned her head to stare up at him, and he saw the delicate gleam of small gold rings in her earlobes.

She was lovely and fierce, yet he sensed her uncertainty. Sympathy surged through him. She reminded him of himself, years ago, in the first days of his royal captivity: bound, chained, grieving, and defiant, spitting like a cat but as terrified and vulnerable as a babe.

"Untie my hands!" Her voice was hoarse.

"Just the gag," Musgrave said. "I think her tongue is all we must needs deal with just now."

She ignored Musgrave and stared at William. "I must see to my father!" William realized that much of her intensity sprang from panic on behalf of her father. Her gaze pleaded with him, begged him to listen. "Loose the right hand. I dinna need the left. Please, sirrah."

He looked at the man lying in the shadows at her feet, fair head dark with blood, face pale and still. Without a word, William began to undo the ropes around her wrists. The hemp was twisted and the knots were firm.

"Rookhope, leave her be," Musgrave said.

"The man is sore hurt," William snapped. "You should have had someone tend to him sooner. Let her help her father." Musgrave lifted a brow at his sharp tone, but subsided.

William worked at the stubborn knots, and finally slid his dirk free from the sheath at his belt. He slipped the blade carefully between the rope and the girl's gloved hands, easing the edge into the knot.

She twisted to look over her shoulder, jerking her arms slightly, enough to throw off the course of the blade. The sharp edge sliced into her wrist and into the heel of his hand where he held the rope taut. Both winced, a shared intake of breath.

"Pray your pardon," William murmured. He slit through the knot and freed her hands. She circled her right hand around her left wrist protectively. He noticed blood on her skin, and reached out to take hold of her arm.

She yanked, but he held firmly. "Let me see," he said, and turned her gloved left hand to see a small cut on her wrist. The thin slice on his own hand stung and dripped, and spotted her wrist. He swiped at their mixed blood with his thumb.

She gave him a startled look, wide-eyed and almost frightened, and jerked her hand from his. Then she dropped to her knees and stripped the glove from her right hand.

With tapered fingertips and a gentle touch, she smoothed away her father's hair to examine his wound. Then she lifted her hand toward William. "I need a cloth. The gag will do." He gave it to her, and she wadded the cloth against her father's head wound, pressing firmly.

William turned. "Water," he said to one of the guards. Musgrave scowled but did not interfere. Within a minute or two, the guard came back with a sloshing wooden bucket, which William took and set down on the floor by the girl.

She dipped the cloth into the water and bathed Armstrong's head and face. When he shifted and groaned, she gave him a sip of water from her cupped right hand. "Da, easy, now. There."

She bandaged his head, though William noticed that she held her gloved left hand stiff and awkward, half fisted. He wondered if she had been injured in the raid, but she did not seem to be in pain.

After a few moments, Armstrong sat up and leaned against the wall. "Damned headcrack," he muttered. "Hurts like the de'il! Where are we, lass?"

"In an English dungeon—Musgrave's own," she told him. She kept a hand on his shoulder, curling her legs under her as she sat beside him.

"And about to pay for the crime of stealing my horses," Musgrave said, stepping toward them. "Tell me, Archie! How many were you altogether? My men reported four horses missing from my barn and the lock broken. Yet my men found only two horses and took down just the two of you. You could not have done this with only a girl. Where are the rest?"

"Rest o' what?" Archie asked, putting a hand to his brow.

"The rest of my horses," Musgrave said. "You took them."

"Horses? All I remember is snatching a few leather halters, and here ye accuse me o' stealing horses? What do ye take me for?" Armstrong huffed indignantly.

"I take you for a horse thief!" Musgrave snapped.

"We snatched halters," the girl said. " 'Tis as he said." Her temper had calmed. She looked up at Musgrave and kept a protective hand on her father's shoulder.

Musgrave had said the girl was half gypsy. William could see that heritage in her smooth, honey-colored skin and in her thick dark hair. Her pale green eyes were remarkable in contrast. Archie had eyes of a similar color, though ordinary in his broad, handsome face.

He watched them, intrigued. A bonny young gypsy with an old scoundrel for a father, he thought. Thieves all. But he knew that his father had loved this particular rogue like a brother. He owed it to Allan Scott's memory to do what he could to help Archie Armstrong and his daughter.

Within a day or so, Musgrave might bribe Armstrong to help the English cause, or he could hang them both. But the Armstrongs did not need to be sucked into the mire of deceit in which William himself had stepped. He frowned, wondering how he could convince Musgrave to release them.

"Halters!" Musgrave sputtered. "Halters!"

"Aye, a few leather bridles, three or four sets," Archie said. " 'Tis hardly worth the taking doon o' a man and a lass in such a naughty manner as this! But do ye let us go, we'll return them, if indeed they belong to ye. Where did ye put those tethers, lass?"

"I let them go along the highway," she answered.

"By 'swounds—" Musgrave raised a fist. "Tell the truth!"

Archie rubbed his head. "I dinna quite recall what we did this even. After that fine supper we shared, Tamsin, what then? A peaceful game o' cards, as is our habit at eventide? Some music? How did we come by this place, lass?"

"We went for a ride by moonlight. Just you and me."

"Aye, 'twas a bonny night for that. Just ye and me."

"Liars, the both of you!" Musgrave shouted. "You took my horses, you rascal, Archie Armstrong! As you have done before!"

"Before?" Archie asked blankly. "Who are ye, did ye say?"

"Bastard! You know me as well as I know you! You've plagued me for years!" Musgrave lunged forward. The girl kicked both feet out at Musgrave's thick leg, her ferociousness returned like a burst of flame.

"Hold!" William reached down and took her by the arms, lifting her to her feet so that he could keep her still, though she tried to shake off his grip. "And Jasper, calm yourself."

"See you, Armstrongs," Musgrave snarled. "I am lately named a deputy to Lord Wharton, the warden of the English Middle March. And this is William Scott of Rookhope, whose name you surely have heard on your side of the Border. You had best tell the truth, or I will see you both hanged. How many horses did you take, who was with you, and where have they gone? Men and horses both."

"Eh, I took halters, Jasper, though yer men snatched eight sheep from my lands two nights past," Archie growled, struggling to sit straight. "Unhand my daughter! I know ye, William Scott. Rogue's Will, they called ye as a wee lad. Yer father was a fine scoundrel—the Rogue o' Rookhope, and none like he!"

"But his son favors the English," the girl muttered.

William was silent, distracted by his effort to hold the tenacious girl, who twisted against his grip. Her head scarcely cleared his shoulder, but she was strong and supple.

"Keep her in hand, Scott, or I'll have my guards take over the task," Musgrave snapped. "Behave, girl! You and your father were caught reiving in the red hand. You are a half-blood gypsy, and likely even more a thief than your father. I'd beware my fate, if I were you. Archie!" Musgrave looked down at Armstrong. "Think of your daughter, man! Do you want to see her taken by the hangman's rope, too, like your sons?"

The tension in the small cell was steel-sharp as Armstrong

glared at Musgrave. Then he closed his eyes, his cheeks growing more pale. Within a moment, he heaved a sigh.

"Well," he said. "I do have a crack in my pate. Tamsin, did ye see a horse or two attached to them halters?"

She stared at her father. "I—I might have."

"Tamsin and I went for a wee ride by moonlight, and we found a few fine tethers," Archie told Musgrave. "Can we help it if 'twas a horse or two attached to 'em in the dark? Och, ye should watch yer property better, man, if it wanders about at night."

William kept hold of the girl and turned his head to smother a smile. He remembered that his father had delighted in Armstrong's antics and wit. A quick, unbidden memory, of his father and Archie laughing uproariously, warmed him, made him want to widen his smile. He frowned instead.

"Well enough," Musgrave snapped. "Well enough, you have had your jest, Archie Armstrong! Spend the night in this dark cell, the two of you, and we shall see how you plead in the morn."

"I'll note this well, I will," Archie said. "A sore wounded man and a fair young lass, held in a foul pit! I'll send word o' this to the queen o' Scotland!"

"Your queen is a squalling infant," Musgrave retorted.

"Aye, well, I'll complain to her mother," Archie grumbled.

"And her father before her, King James, was never fond of Armstrongs," Musgrave went on. "He hanged a gang of your surname a dozen years ago, and 'tis a pity he did not take you with them! But he's dead now, and the Scottish crown and the queen dowager will show you even less sympathy than you would have had of King James. Complain, man—if you can even pen a word!"

"My lass can pen well, for I had her tutored," Archie said. " 'Tis true King James didna love Armstrongs. When he was scarce more than a lad, he hanged thirty o' my kinsmen, along wi' the greatest scoundrel of them all, my uncle Johnnie Armstrong." Archie paused and shook his head sadly. "But King James loved gypsies well. He gave a safe-conduct, and royal favor too, to Tamsin's grandsire, Johnnie Faw o' Lesser Egypt." He looked at his daughter, who nodded.

"Damned thieves," Musgrave said. "But I can use a few

thieves. Tomorrow I will have an offer for you, Armstrong. You had best accept it, or you and the girl will sing neck psalms before dusk tomorrow." He turned to stomp out of the cell. "Rookhope, come ahead!" he roared from the corridor.

"I'll question them further and be with you shortly," William called. He turned back, still holding the girl's arm. "Armstrong, listen well to Musgrave. He doesna make jests."

"Bah," Archie mumbled. "He has naught to say to me but 'beg yer pardon.' I should remind him how many sheep and horses his men have taken from my lands in the past months." He leaned his head against the wall and touched a hand to his brow, which had begun to bleed again through the bandage. "I'll tell him that, when I can think proper-like." He winced and closed his eyes.

William looked down at the girl, who had ceased to tug against his grip. He had been aware of her warmth and strength all the while the others had been talking. Now he let go of her, half expecting her to snarl at him, shove at him.

Instead, she tilted her head and looked at him without fear or resentment. "Tell Musgrave that we took only halters, as my father said. Taking horse gear isna a hanging crime. Tell him that, so he will let us go."

He watched her for a long moment. "I would, if I believed you," he said.

Chapter Two

"I think ye maun be my match," she said,
"My match, and something mair . . ."
—"Proud Lady Margaret"

"You dinna believe me?" Tamsin asked, as she looked up at
William Scott. Torchlight spilled through the doorway, flickering in a bright halo around his dark hair and his wide, square
shoulders. He leaned close, his gaze grim. She leaned slightly
back.

" 'Twasna that dark, my lass, and you and your father are not
that stupid," he murmured. "Nor am I. Musgrave thinks the pair
of you are simple fools, but I see differently."

She widened her gaze, hoping to feign innocence, but his
steady gaze affirmed that he meant what he said. He did not believe her innocence for a moment. Likely those clear blue eyes
never overlooked anything, she thought. He was not the least like
Jasper Musgrave.

This man was lean and hard, strikingly handsome, and keen-
witted, much the opposite of her father's old enemy. But she had
never regarded beauty or intelligence as an outward reflection of
good character. She had learned to seek true worth within each
person. Otherwise, her own flaws would have persuaded her long
ago that she had scant worth herself.

She could not allow herself to be charmed by William Scott's
pleasing outward appearance, nor would she favor him based on
his father's character, as her father was likely to do. She had
heard of this man through her father, a tale of a lad taken long ago
by the Scottish crown to stand as imprisoned pledge for the good

behavior of his kinsmen. He may have been friend to a king, but his deeds, so far, told her that he was not to be trusted. And she had to be honest with him now or risk worse trouble.

"My father delights in annoying Musgrave," she finally admitted. "He and Jasper have been enemies since they were young. Usually my father manages to escape harm. But this time he was caught." And for now, she was left to face it alone, she thought, glancing at her father, who appeared to be asleep.

"And you with him," William Scott said. He folded his arms, watching her. "What happened? And how is it that Archie rides with his daughter?"

"I dinna ride with him by custom," she said. "He asked me to come along because he was scarce of able men." She shivered a little, remembering the harrowing moments last night when she and her father had been taken down. "Two nights ago, Musgrave's men snatched eight sheep from our lands. My great-uncle Cuthbert saw the deed and knew the men, but couldna catch them. My father swore to return the favor. But most of his kinsmen and comrades were gone to Kelso, to the market fair, and there was no one to ride with him but Cuthbert and me."

William nodded. "I sent men and livestock to that fair myself," he said. "Go on. Why would he want to endanger his own daughter? Reiving is no game. 'Tis a serious and risky matter."

"I am a nimble rider, taught by the Romany—the gypsies— who know horses better than most," she said. "My father knew I could help in the herding of beasts taken in payment for our sheep. So I rode with him and Cuthbert into England, and we were caught."

"With Musgrave's horses in hand," he said.

She shrugged and nodded. "We found a few horses pastured on Musgrave's land. My father thought 'twould be a good thing to sell Musgrave's horses at the market fair this week, since Jasper is likely going to sell our sheep there. So we took them. As we came back over the border, we met an ambush."

"Musgrave's men were waiting for you?" he asked.

"Aye. We nearly escaped, but my father was struck down and fell from his horse. I turned back to help him, and I was brought down too. They took us here." She looked away. "My uncle got away. At least I hope he did," she murmured.

"He did," William said. "With the rest of the horses."

She let out a breath of relief. "They waited for us, I see that now. They knew we would come after them for taking the sheep. Musgrave must have set those horses out to trap us. He doesna leave horses pastured like that at night by habit."

William nodded his understanding. "This feuding has gone on a long while between your father and Jasper."

"Since they were lads," she said. "Their fathers fought too, over the land boundaries. But 'tisna a deadly feud, just one of harassment. My father delights in finding ways to annoy Musgrave, but he wouldna truly harm him. There would be no pleasure in that. Jasper will let us go in a day or so. After a rest, they will go after each other again."

"I wouldna be so certain. Jasper lacks your father's humor. And he is under the scrutiny of his King Henry just now. He may react differently than you think. Step carefully with him."

She frowned. "Why does a stranger take trouble to warn us?"

"I dinna want to see a hanging," he said quietly.

"Hanging is naught to a rogue like you."

"You are wrong," he said, brisk and low.

"Besides, Jasper wouldna dare."

"He would," he said. "This time, I think he would."

She scowled, feeling wary. "Why should you care?"

He shifted where he stood, facing the door. The torchlight spilled over his clean profile, his firm jaw, the long, wide column of his throat. "I remember your father, though I was a lad the last time I saw him," he said. His voice was quiet, calm. She watched him, and felt oddly warmed, in that chill, dank place, by the timbre of his voice, the steadiness of his presence. "My father thought well of Archie Armstrong. For the sake of that old loyalty, I offer you what advice I can. Take it or not, as you please."

"Why should I trust you?" she asked. "You are a comrade of Musgrave, who is English, and my father's enemy."

"You have no reason to trust me," he said simply, glancing at her. "But you can believe that I want you and your father well out of this matter, where neither of you belong. Tell Archie to say aye to whatever Musgrave suggests to him. Say aye, and he will let you go your way. Else you may both hang."

Her heart pounded, but she revealed none of her dread. She tipped her head to watch him. "I heard you and Musgrave. I know there is some plan between you. My father will never agree to be part of an English scheme. And Jasper willna hang us. He will let us go in the morn."

He slid her a glance. "Horse thievery is no light crime, lass. He could hang you both and be within his rights. Or he could keep you here for months, even years. Dinna be a fool."

She frowned at the unbearable thought of lengthy confinement in a cold, dark dungeon. She would sicken in such a place, without her freedom, without the air and the sun. Like a plant plucked from the earth, she would wither and dry up. The thought terrified her.

"I want to be free." She shrugged to mask how desperately she meant that. "Who wouldna?"

"Then take freedom, no matter the price, when he offers."

"What price? What will he offer us?"

"A bribe of some sort. He will ask you to join the English in some cause. Agree to it."

"What cause?"

"I dinna know."

"And yet you agreed to help him, I heard you! You are more a rascal than I thought. You took a bribe from him!"

"What I did isna your concern, lass," he said. He leaned close, his voice so low that only she could hear. Soft and deep, its power thrilled through her body as if he had touched her. "I only suggest that you tell your father to accept the offer and take the reprieve that comes with it."

She would not flinch from his steady gaze, or the closeness of his body. Warmth radiated from him, and his breath, wine-sharp, air-soft, drifted over her face. She wanted to show defiance, but she felt a sudden urge to lean toward him and accept the help he seemed to offer.

She resisted that urge, although his presence captivated her. She told herself that he was not trustworthy, nor would he care what happened to a reiver and a gypsy.

But her heart pounded as she remembered, unwillingly, what had happened earlier between them. When he had set her hands free, his blade had cut her, and him. And had set her heart and thoughts into a spin from which she had not yet recovered.

The edge of a knife, a turn of a hand, a moment of shared blood: those elements were part of the Romany custom of marriage.

The realization once again sent her thoughts reeling, made her knees weak. She could not think about that now, with his gaze intent upon her as he waited for her to speak. Her mouth went dry, and she looked away. She must say nothing of the situation of marriage, though her heart seemed to trip over it.

"Did you hear me, lass?" he asked. "I want you to agree to whatever Musgrave tells you to do."

Taking a deep breath, she looked up at him. "Neither my father nor I will agree to help the English."

"I suspect your father is a thorough rogue," he said. "Once he's free, he'll avoid Musgrave entirely until this matter is done. Tell Archie to agree, but tell him to take no coin, to give Musgrave no true hold over him."

"Why should I tell my father any of this?"

"Because, lass, you care more for your father's welfare than for your own," he said in a near-whisper. She caught her breath at the mysterious, sensual power his voice held. Her body seemed to melt at the sound. She drew back. "Heed me well. Tell him to listen to Jasper. 'Tis more important than you can guess."

She sighed and glanced at her father. "Da, do you hear the man?" she asked. Archie did not move. She frowned, leaned over him. "Da, speak to me. Are you well?"

Her father mumbled, shook his head. Alarmed, she knelt beside him, despite the restraints around her ankles. "Da, what do you need?"

Archie groaned softly. She touched his head with her folded left hand, snug in its leather glove. More a mitten than a glove, the casing had a pattern of stitches that imitated four fingers held together, cleverly concealing her deformity. She dipped her bare hand into the cold water in the bucket and offered her father a drink.

He sipped awkwardly, turned his head away. The bandage, wet with blood, slipped over his brow. Tamsin attempted to adjust it with one hand, while Archie slid sideways along the wall.

"Da!" she cried, catching at him.

"Eh," he mumbled. William dropped to one knee beside her and took her father by the shoulders.

"Armstrong," he said in an urgent tone. "Archie Armstrong."

Archie grimaced. "Eh . . . let me sleep. . . ."

William shoved some straw into a makeshift pillow and helped Archie to lie down. He lifted the man's eyelids, slapped at his cheeks gently, and received an irritable response. "He just needs rest. He'll be fine," he told Tamsin.

With her bare hand, Tamsin tugged at Archie's bandage. "I need to tend to this again," she said. "I made poor work of it before." She pulled at the tucked end with her bare fingers.

"What's wrong with your other hand?" William asked. "Is it hurt? Here, let me do that." He took over the task of loosening the bandage.

His touch was warm and gentle. Tamsin snatched her fingers away as if his had been flame. At the same time, she dropped her left hand out of sight.

"My hand is fine," she said stiffly.

William grunted skeptically and unwrapped the bandage, revealing the swollen, split lump on Archie's brow. He sopped at the blood with the bandage and glanced at Tamsin. "We'll need another cloth."

She nodded. "I'll rip the hem of my shirt, then." She began to unfasten the hooks down the front of her leather doublet with the fingers of her right hand.

"Let me help," William said, touching her wrist. She batted his hand away. "I meant no insult, lass," he growled. "Your left hand is obviously hurt—"

"My hand is fine," she snapped again. William raised a brow and turned back to press the wet cloth to Archie's wound.

Tamsin resumed her task. One by one, the hooks flew free as she worked them, fast and capable, accustomed to using one hand. Her doublet fell open, and she pulled at the tucked hem of her linen shirt. "Here—cut a strip with your dirk," she told him.

He did. Within moments, he wrapped and secured the strip around Archie's head. Tamsin removed her leather doublet and folded its bulk, handing it to William. He shoved the garment under Archie's head to serve as a more comfortable cushion than dirty straw.

"He will be fine by morning," William said, as Archie began to snore. "Just make certain, in the night, that he sleeps sound and isna faint. Jostle him now and again to awaken him."

She nodded, aware that her father could slip into unconsciousness with such a head wound. Then she realized that she too would have to lie down and sleep in the cavelike dungeon. She shivered and wrapped her arms around herself. "I'll stay awake the night."

William sighed. He knelt close beside her on one knee, the other leg bent, and looked at her. "Listen to me," he said. "I dinna agree with imprisoning women. But this is Musgrave's house, and I willna interfere so long as you are well kept. I will have blankets and food sent in for both of you. First let me look at your wounded hand."

"I am not hurt." She tucked her gloved hand under her arm.

"You lack the use of it," he said. "Is it broken? Did you hurt it in the raid?"

" 'Tis fine," she said, this time through her teeth. She was not about to show him her small, misshapen hand.

"If you canna admit to a weakness, so be it, lass," he said. "I have been guilty of that myself. But I thought women werena subject to such fits of pride."

She did not reply, rubbing her arms in the chill.

"You're cold," he observed calmly.

She glanced down. Through the pale weave of her linen shirt, she could see—as he had—the globes of her breasts and stiffened nipples. She covered herself with her forearms and sent him a sour glance.

William loosened the pewter buttons that fastened his brown woolen doublet, drew it off, and held it out. "Take this."

She hesitated, then slipped her arms into the sleeves. The garment was still warm from his body. He shifted and reached out to lift the doublet over her shoulders. He tilted her chin out of the way and fastened the button on the high neck, then proceeded to the next one.

She did not try to stop him. Buttons were more difficult for her to manage than hooks and loops. She stayed silent, watching him as he worked.

He was pleasant to gaze upon, his shoulders wide and his neck strong, revealed by his loosely shaped shirt. The torchlight highlighted the clean structure of his face and his glossy, thick hair. Kneeling face-to-face, she was aware of his warm, comfortable smell: smoke, maleness, and something spicy-sweet, like cinnamon.

As he worked the buttons, he stirred odd sensations in her, as if she were a small bit of iron pulled by a lodestone. He had shown kindness toward her and her father, but she was wary of him. He was, after all, a guest in Jasper Musgrave's castle and a comrade in some English scheme.

"Tell me," she said. "Why do you support Musgrave's plan, whatever 'tis?"

"And why should I not?" he asked. He pulled the placket close over her breasts to fasten the buttons. A subtle sensation spun through her as his hands lingered and then moved down. She told herself it was just the welcome warmth of the thick woolen doublet.

"I . . . I have heard stories of your father," she said, her breath curiously affected by the movement of his hands. "I have heard ballads sung about his deeds—the Rogue o' Rookhope, they called him."

"Aye," he said gruffly, concentrating on a stubborn button.

"Allan Scott was a bold reiver, they say. Yet no matter what trouble he stirred up, he never took from Scottish Borderers, only English."

"I know my father's history. What is your point?"

"I wonder how the son of such a man can take up with the English in a black scheme."

"Since neither of us knows the full scheme, we canna judge if 'tis black or white."

"Jasper Musgrave would do naught but wickedness. What have you agreed to do for him?"

"That," he said, moving his hands below her waist, "is none of your concern, my lass." He drew the doublet together over the juncture of her thighs. The sensation that blossomed in her lower body was so strong and immediate that she wanted to leap away from him.

"It is my concern," she said, her tone sharpening, "if it affects my father and myself."

" 'Twill affect neither of you if you heed me, agree to Musgrave, and get you gone from here quick as you can." He slid the last button through and got to his feet. He stood looking down at her like some mythic warrior god, his hands resting light on his hips, his shirt loose over his chest, his legs widespread and powerful in long, gleaming leather boots and black breeches.

"Musgrave has a right to arrest you and Archie," he said. "The Scottish council willna protest if he executes you both. The lives of a petty reiver and a gypsy, even a female gypsy, are minor compared to peace in the Borders."

" 'Twould be more honorable to hang," she snapped, "than to side with those you support, Rookhope."

"Aye," he murmured. "It might be so. But you will see that you have no choice in this."

"I'll wager you had a choice!"

"I did," he said. "I did indeed." He held out a hand to her, palm outspread, to help her stand.

She looked at his wide palm and touched a fingertip to the long line that sloped across its center. "I see here you have a keen mind," she said. She leaned closer, peering in the low light. "And these lines tell me that you are strong in many ways—in will, in heart, in body. So I dinna understand why you have taken up with a naughty man like Jasper Musgrave."

He closed his hand. "What nonsense is this, gypsy?" he asked softly. "I gave you no leave, nor coin, to read a fortune in my hand."

She sat back. "Consider it payment for your good advice."

He watched her for a long moment. "See that you take that good advice on the morrow." He turned and left the dungeon.

Her father snored and the guards paced and murmured in the corridor outside. In the cocoon formed by those sounds, Tamsin sighed and leaned her head against the wall. She closed her eyes, but she could not still her thoughts and emotions.

Above all, William Scott lingered in her thoughts. She remembered his face, his voice, his touch, and his kindness, as well as the moment when he had sliced through the ropes that bound her wrists. The cut on her wrist was small and had bled only a little. But its importance was great.

She rubbed the cut with her finger and sighed. William Scott had turned her hand over, inadvertently touching his skin to hers, mingling his blood with hers. She had nearly gasped in astonishment, uncertain how to react. Scott, she was sure, did not know what he had done, but she had known immediately.

According to Romany custom, shared cuts and the mingling of blood, said with a vow, created a marriage between two people. She had witnessed the ceremony many times in the gypsy camps. Archie had married her mother that way, she knew.

To have it happen spontaneously stunned her. She did not know what to think. Her father and her grandparents, had they witnessed the incident, would regard it as meaningful, a marriage made by the hand of fate.

Tamsin alone knew that a marriage bond had been created between her and William Scott. And she must keep her silence.

The irony of the incident struck her like a blow. She had never thought to be part of a marriage union. For years, both her father and her grandfather had searched for a husband for her. Among Scotsmen and Romany, one man after another had refused to risk marrying a girl with dreadful imperfections—that hand, that tainted blood.

At first she had felt the humiliation keenly. As time went on and the refusals continued, she had decided that she did not want to wed. The man did not exist who could accept her and love her for what she was, and she would marry no man who had to be bribed or begged.

William Scott would be no different than the rest. Had her father approached him, he would have reacted like the others. He might have shown greater horror, knowing that part of the wedding ceremony had actually taken place, decided by fate.

She squeezed her eyes shut against stinging tears and told herself that the moment was unimportant, an accident, nothing more. But she felt a sense of loss and rejection. She knew that her father would treasure a union between his daughter and the son of his comrade. The realization that the accidental marriage could never be real made her infinitely sad.

Then she drew a deep breath and told herself that she could never let her father, or William Scott himself, learn about the marriage ritual that had taken place between them.

Chapter Three

"To seik het water beneath cauld ice,
Surely it is a greit folie—
I have asked grace at a graceless face,
But there is nane for my men and me!"

—"Johnie Armstrang"

The ropes that bound her wrists were uncomfortably tight. Tamsin bit back a wince and shifted her shoulders where she leaned, seated, against the cold stone wall. Two guards had come into the cell that morning with more bread and ale, having brought food and blankets late last night. They had tied her hands and her father's again before leaving.

Now she flexed the left, still encased in its glove, and glanced at her father. He sat beside her, his eyes closed, but she knew he rested rather than slept. Shadows filled the cell, though daylight leaked through a high window slit. Torches flickered on the wall beyond the slatted iron door, and she heard the guards talking quietly.

Archie had roused earlier to eat some bread and sip the ale. His forehead was bruised and his movements were slow, although he spoke with spirit and made light of his injury. Tamsin was certain that the blow to his head, from the flat of a sword at the time of their capture, had drained his strength more than he would admit.

Surely fate had ridden with them, she thought, shivering. She felt as if a shift had occurred in the fabric of her life, as if a wind moved past, heavy with storm and promise. Somehow she felt as if she might never be the same after this. She could only hope that whatever destiny awaited her, and her father, was not the most final of fates. William Scott had been correct in saying that Jasper

Musgrave could exercise his power as a deputy warden. Tamsin was not prepared for death. Nor, she suspected, was Archie.

"Da," she said, looking at him. "You're tired. Rest on my shoulder. Here." She sidled next to him.

"Go on, ye wee bit, ye canna hold me up," he grumbled affectionately. "Ye fret like an auld woman. I'm fine."

"Your forehead is purple. You look like you fought with Auld Nick himself, and lost."

"Tch! Insults! Would I lose a fight w' the de'il? And I am a bonny-looking man. Well," he said, flashing a weak grin, "but for that young Rookhope, hey."

"Oh," she said. "He isna so bonny."

"He's much like his da, tall and dark as a raven, but with his mother's blue eyes. A man pretty enough to make a lassie's heart go all soft-like." He smiled. "Hey? What think ye?"

She made a face. "I think you've heard too many ballads."

"Och, ye must like him some, hey?" She heard a hopeful note in his voice and knew she must convince him otherwise.

"Scott of Rookhope wouldna suit me," she said, a little flippantly. "Besides, he's a friend to Musgrave. And likely wed. Did you even consider that? Your constant search for a husband for me—and thus a reiving comrade for you—is tiresome. You ask near everyone we meet. I wonder that you didna ask Musgrave if he needed a wife!"

"Hey, I have my limits, lass," he muttered. "I did wonder about his son Arthur, but they say he's newly betrothed." He smiled mischievously, and she knew he teased her. He would never want a Musgrave for a good-son.

"I dinna want a husband," she whispered fiercely, hearing the guards outside the door. "None want me—why should I want one of them? You've offered me to so many by now—"

"But twelve or so," he said. "I've hardly begun."

"Hardly begun!" An indignant squeak. "You've been searching for years, and each man has turned down the offer! Oh, some would like to bed a gypsy fast enough, but none will wed one, particularly one marked by evil at her birth!"

"Tamsin," he said, sighing. "I wed a gypsy lass, and was happy with her, though 'twas brief. 'Tis sad, what some think about ye. Ye're a bonny lass, and we'll find ye a man."

"Nay! 'Tis done! I willna wed any man who needs bribing or begging. Besides," she added, "we may well hang here."

"I wouldna like to see ye hanged a maiden."

"Oh, Da," she said in dismay. "What does it matter?"

"Ah, but to see young Will Scott o' Rookhope again," he went on, as if he had not heard her. " 'Twas nearly worth being caught!" He slid her a glance. She made sure to scowl at him.

"And just what do you think Rookhope is doing here?" she asked crisply. "No holy day visit, I assure you! And dinna dare to ask him if he wants a wife," she added hastily. "We are in muckle trouble, Da. Think of that, and naught else."

"I do think of it. If my life is forfeit, then I want someone to look after ye, and after Merton Rigg, when I'm gone."

"If we live through this, then I will take care of Merton Rigg. And I will take care of you and Uncle Cuthbert. Just give up your notion that some man will take me for a wife."

"There was a lad for ye, once," her father muttered.

"What did you say?" She peered at him.

He stirred. "I'll see what I can do, is all. I'll see."

"Oh, aye. The executioner will put the rope on you, and you'll ask if he's wed, and would he take a one-handed gypsy."

"I might do that," he said, and winked at her, though it made him wince. "Tamsin, listen to me. What I want for ye is this—a man who doesna care about yer small hand, or the hue o' yer skin, but who warms yer heart and ye his, like a hearthfire." He grinned. "And he must be as fine a rascal as yer own father."

"Da," she said, touched deeply. "Thank you. But there's no rascal like you." She gave him a fond smile. "I wonder—perhaps we can get out of this after all, by agreeing to Musgrave, as Rookhope says we must."

Archie grunted. "I'd rather hang. I'll be dead by down of sun, and pray yer pardon."

"You will be safe." Tamsin touched his wrist, which was bound like hers. He opened that hand. "The line of your life is long and deep-cut." She hoped to reassure him, and herself.

"Och, 'Gyptian tricks again? Ye spend too much time wi' yer

gypsy granddame. I let ye travel wi' the gypsies, and ye learned some wicked heathen ways." His tone teased her again.

" 'Tis hardly wicked to read a life story in the lines in a hand, if God put the story there Himself. The Romany know how to read the lines, is all," she said.

"Many pay good silver to have their palms read. Though I never saw much use in it, myself—or wickedness, to be true. But I will say, yer gypsy kin taught ye a knack wi' the picture cards. Hah, and no one can beat ye at card games. A good skill, that one." He smiled.

She tapped his hand with her fingertip. "You will outlive us all. You're too stubborn—and too lucky—to go so soon."

"Eh, my luck willna last forever." He sighed. "Tamsin, if I'm truly about to die, ye must know this," he said solemnly. "My dearest dream is that ye should wed Rookhope's son. I have wanted that since ye were born and he but a wee bit lad. Allan wanted it too."

She had never heard this before, and she wondered if his head injury, and their dilemma, made him sentimental toward his beloved friend's son. "Da," she said gently, "dreams are fine at night, but they come to naught in the day. Let this one go."

"Dreams can come to much, if ye never give them up," he said. "This is my fond dream, which I've kept close for years. I never thought 'twould be possible, but now the lad is back from the royal court. So if they hang me this day, you must remember what I said, and go to Rookhope to tell him what I wished."

She bowed her head. Guilt slipped through her, for she knew that she could never tell her father about the accidental bond of blood between her and William Scott. Archie would put far too much value on it. She stayed silent, uncertain how to reply.

"Seems to me," Archie said, "that Will Scott is just the sort o' rogue ye want, lass. A fine rogue, with a good heart. He did help us last night."

"But I dinna really know him," she said. "Nor do you."

"He's Allan Scott's lad," Archie said stoutly. "He's another Rogue o' Rookhope."

"But the son isna like his father. You told me that William Scott was taken hostage as a lad and raised at the royal court."

"I know he had a gentile confinement, educated beside King James himself, sharing his tutors, learning foreign languages, letters, books, and such. And I know he was a friend and an advisor to King James too. A fine lad, that Will Scott. He didna return to Rookhope until last year, I heard."

"He isna the Border rogue you wish him to be. He's a man of the court, and a friend to the English. I know you were a loyal friend to Allan Scott, and he to you, but that may blind you to the truth of his son. We dinna know him. He might indeed be treacherous, Da."

Archie sat in silence. Then he grunted. "He might be a foul rascal, true. But then again, he might be a bonny scoundrel like Allan. We dinna know yet. Do ye look at his palm, and ye can tell if he be a bad or a good rogue."

"Palmistry isna for spying on a man's character," she said. She could hardly tell her father that she had already seen William Scott's palm briefly, and that the qualities she saw there only affirmed what her father saw in the man.

"I dinna need to see his hand," Archie said. "I know he's a braw man, and a trusty one. Rogue's Will, we called him, though he was but a scrap o' a lad and the shadow o' his father." He smiled a little to himself, as if lost in memories.

Tamsin sighed in exasperation. "He is in agreement with Musgrave on some secret matter!" She glanced toward the door as a guard walked past, and lowered her voice. "I told you what he said to me. Accept whatever Musgrave offers you, no matter what, or we will both be hanged."

"See, Rookhope tried to help us. He's a good rogue."

"He wants us to side with the English!" she insisted.

"Hey, guard!" Archie called. The guard reappeared and looked at them. "Tell me. Is Rookhope wedded?"

Tamsin sighed and shook her head in frustration.

"What? Wed?" The guard frowned. "Nay, I dinna think so."

"Hah!" Archie looked at Tamsin triumphantly.

"Promise me you will say naught to him about a wife!" she said. "Da, you must promise me!"

Archie mumbled reluctant agreement and closed his eyes.

* * *

Later, Tamsin and her father followed the guards out of the dungeon and up a narrow winding stairway. Archie stumbled, alarming Tamsin, but he recovered his balance. They emerged into a dim corridor, walking along until the guards stopped at an arched oaken door.

"In here." One of the guards knocked and opened the door.

Tamsin entered the chamber, which contained a large curtained bed and several pieces of furniture. A window, its lower shutters opened, spilled golden sunlight into the room. She walked past the bed and stood in the middle of the wooden planked floor, her father just behind her.

Three men watched them. William Scott stood by the window, leaning a shoulder against the wall with taut grace. Nearby, Jasper Musgrave and a third man, younger than the other two, sat in chairs beside a table.

In daylight, Jasper Musgrave was huge, with pale, doughy skin, sparse gray hair, and a quilted maroon doublet stretched tightly over his belly. By contrast, William Scott was lean and striking to look upon. Long-limbed and raven-haired, his jaw darkened with the smudge of a few days' beard growth, he wore clothes that, while simply cut, were far more elegant in their plain quality than Musgrave's elaborate satin doublet. Quiet strength and simplicity made him seem like a portrait of a dark, intense angel beside Musgrave's representation of gluttony.

Despite his natural and appealing beauty, despite his kindness of the night before—she still wore his brown doublet—Tamsin let herself see only the scoundrel. His association with Musgrave made her suspicious of his character. She wished her father would see that also.

The third man was a young, slimmer version of Jasper Musgrave, his features pleasant. The young man seemed vague, as if he faded beside the power of William Scott and the massive presence of Jasper Musgrave.

The guards murmured with Musgrave and took their leave, shutting the door behind them. William Scott watched Tamsin steadily, his blue eyes flashing in the sunbeam that cut through the window glazing. She glanced away—and gasped.

A thick, knotted noose lay on the table with papers, a few goblets, and a wine jug. Musgrave played with the hempen tail that spilled down to the floor. He watched Tamsin and Archie through narrowed eyes.

She drew a breath and raised her chin. "From the rafters, Jasper Musgrave? You think to hang us, here and now?"

"Quiet, gypsy, lest I tell you to speak." Musgrave let go of the rope and took up a goblet, sipping noisily. Beside him, the younger man sifted through the parchments.

Scott folded his arms across his chest and remained silent. His remote manner set him apart from the others, but Tamsin saw a small muscle pulse in his jaw. A rosy stain crept into his cheeks as he watched the other men.

Dark as a raven he might be, she thought, but he had fair, telling skin. What tapped at his conscience or roused his anger to produce that blush, she could not guess.

"Hey, Arthur," Archie said to the younger man. "Come to protect yer father from the likes o' me?"

"My son is here as my deputy," Jasper said. Arthur nodded.

"Yer lad is a fine reiver," Archie said. "He's taken sheep and horses from me, I know that. And now he's a deputy. What a braw lad!" His false heartiness edged on sarcasm.

Tamsin sent her father a warning glare. He ignored her.

"I have an offer for you, Archie," Jasper said.

"I am nae yer man in any matter," Archie replied stiffly.

"As a laird who can summon a hundred horse—" Arthur began.

"Two hundred," Archie interrupted. "Scoundrels all."

"Exactly what we need," Jasper said. "You may be a scoundrel, but your name is respected among the Scottish marchmen. There are many men who will follow your lead."

Tamsin frowned at William Scott, whose expression remained impassive, although the pink hollows of his cheeks gave a glimpse into his thoughts. Something angered or bothered him greatly about this interview, she realized. She wondered if he was displeased with the Musgraves or the Armstrongs—or if his own conscience troubled him.

She narrowed her eyes. His insistence that they accept Musgrave's offer might come from Scott's own need to trick them or to be rid of them. She was not certain. He was clearly not like the

Musgraves. He was intriguing, mysterious, and wholly compelling. And she could not seem to stop looking at him, her gaze stumbling over the glances he slid toward her.

Jasper Musgrave tapped a parchment sheet that lay beneath his hand on the table. "I could hang you for horse thievery. But we may be able to bargain, you and I."

"I willna bargain wi' ye, Jasper. So hang me." Archie straightened to his full and considerable height.

Tamsin felt her heart sink at her father's words. She feared that Jasper Musgrave would lose his temper and hang Archie without further questions. The noose lay on the table like a coiled, sleeping snake. She suddenly wanted to run, to be free of this place at any cost.

She saw William Scott slide another glance toward her. His blue eyes conveyed a silent, intent message, and she remembered his words from last night: *Say "aye" to whatever Musgrave offers, else you will both hang,* he had told her. *I want you both out of this.*

Now he said nothing, but she was sure that he still wanted them away from here. A subtle sense of danger spun in her gut. She edged closer to her father.

"Da," she whispered, "listen to Musgrave. We must get out of this however we can." Archie growled in full temper. She looked at William Scott, but he had turned his head, breaking the gossamer bond between them, dispelling the fragile hope for his support that she had begun to feel.

"You are a captured criminal, Archie," Musgrave said.

"Ye tricked us last night, Jasper," Archie answered. "Those horses— er, halters we took were laid out a-purpose to lure us into yer trap. I willna bargain wi' ye."

Musgrave slapped the table. "I'll trap you further, with a noose around your neck, if you don't shut up! King Henry will be generous with all Scots prisoners to honor Scotland's new queen, out of the grace of his great heart. You will be pardoned, if you cooperate."

"There is nae grace from a graceless heart! Think me a fool, man? Henry wants to conquer Scotland! Our queen is a wee babe. The noblemen squabble for power, and argue whether a lass of any age should sit the throne. Henry seeks to purchase Border support so he can take Scotland in his grip. Ye willna have treachery o' me!"

"King Henry will expect support for his cause in Scotland, in return for pardoning you and your daughter!"

"Fine!" Archie shouted. "Go tell yer king we wish him well! That's all the support he'll get o' Archie Armstrong! Now leave me be—or hang me high!"

William Scott stepped forward as Musgrave began to sputter. "Tempers serve no purpose here," he said calmly. "Jasper, explain your offer to the laird of Merton."

Musgrave grunted. "I have been instructed by Lord Wharton, who takes his orders from King Henry, to find Scottish Bordermen to help advance a plan formed by the king himself."

Aware that her father's temper had not yet cooled, Tamsin stepped forward before Archie could retort in anger. "Say out what you want of us, Jasper Musgrave," she said.

"You keep a woman of the Egyptian race in your house, Armstrong," Musgrave said, ignoring her.

"Ye know Tamsin is my daughter," Archie replied.

"But her mother was one of the Egyptian race. Does she have contact with roaming gypsy bands?"

"She has kin among one band. That doesna concern ye."

"Gypsies have been banished from England and from Scotland." Musgrave scowled. "Harboring them breaks the law in both lands."

"My daughter," Archie growled, "has been in my house since she was six years old, and ye will leave her be."

"Where was she born?" Musgrave persisted.

"I was born in Scotland, and baptized in a parish kirk," Tamsin answered.

"She is a proper Scot," Archie said. He towered protectively beside Tamsin. Even with bound hands, he radiated a rough power. "Ye canna punish her for her gypsy blood. Leave her be, and say what ye truly want."

"King Henry and Wharton, with others, have designed a plan to further the king's cause in Scotland. We need men to support that."

"Ye need lairds wi' loyalty to the English, nae such as me," Archie said.

"We also want common Bordermen," Musgrave answered. "The success of our plan depends on help from men like you, Archie."

"Men who would never be involved with the English," Tamsin said, "will be hard to convince."

"Coin heals a variety of political ailments," Musgrave answered, though he did not look at her. "And we could also benefit from the help of gypsies, who never turn down coin for any task. I hear that once they give their word, they keep it."

"Of course they keep it!" Tamsin snapped. "You can leave your spoons out around the Romany."

Musgrave lowered his brows. "And what does that mean?"

"She means the gypsies are trustworthy," William said.

"But you willna get their promise for this plan," Tamsin said.

"Will I not?" Musgrave growled.

"Gypsies and rogues!" Arthur Musgrave, who had been listening intently, looked at his father. "Dinna listen to her—we take too great a chance in dealing with such men."

"They are exactly what we need for this," Jasper said. "Rascals all, eager for coin, without Scottish loyalties but with Scottish ties. With Rookhope, Armstrong of Merton, a few Border scoundrels, and a handful of gypsies, this plan will succeed nicely."

"What is your scheme?" Tamsin asked.

"A plan to benefit all, north and south," Musgrave said.

"War?" Tamsin asked, horrified.

"Nay. I cannot say as yet." Musgrave glanced away.

"King Henry wants only good for Scotland," Arthur said. His father nodded. "Our king is greatly concerned for his northern neighbors, who lack a strong ruler. The little queen of Scotland needs his guidance."

"Aye, he sees a chance to take over Scotland!" Archie said. "I willna help ye." He set his jaw stubbornly.

"Think of your daughter, man. She could be hanged for a tawny and a thief. And you, gypsy"—Musgrave looked at Tamsin—"will you dance at the end of a rope?" He picked up the noose that lay on the table, and drew its loop through his thick fingers. "Will you watch your father dance there?"

He handed the rope to Arthur and murmured to him. Arthur stood and came forward. In a quick and surprising movement, he stepped toward Tamsin and dropped the loop over her head. He slid the knot tight, jerking her head back.

Tamsin cried out as she felt the wrenching pressure at her throat. She raised her bound hands to the rope and clawed awkwardly at it with the fingers of her right hand. Arthur tightened the knot again, until she felt dizzy, heart pounding, knees growing weak.

Through a haze of shock and fear, she heard Archie bellow at Arthur, and saw William Scott stride toward her.

"Stay where you are!" Jasper Musgrave said. "Arthur, if either of them comes near, pull the knot hard. Now, Archie," he said smoothly, "tell me again that you refuse to help us."

"She has naught to do with this!" Archie shouted.

"Leave her be," William said. His voice was quiet, a growl of thunder in the room. Tamsin saw him step closer, saw Musgrave throw up a hand to stop him.

"Archie only needs convincing. She will not be harmed." Musgrave smiled. "We can use the skills of a gypsy—this one, or another of her acquaintance, if she will not cooperate. Archie will know who to hire for us."

William ignored him and looked at Arthur. "Let go of her."

Arthur paused, and Tamsin pulled helplessly at the rope. Musgrave heaved himself to his feet and walked toward her. With one finger, he traced her throat. Waves of dizziness and fury washed over her.

"A fragile neck," Musgrave murmured. " 'Twill snap quick."

Swift and sure, William Scott swept past Musgrave like a bird of prey to grab Arthur's arm. He slipped his other arm around Arthur's neck and pulled back. Tamsin felt another tug as Arthur kept his grip on the rope.

"Let go, Arthur," William growled, "else your own neck will snap!"

Chapter Four

"Have you any gold, Father?" she says,
"Or have you any fee?
Or did you come to see your own daughter hanging
Like a dog, upon a tree?"
                    —"The Broom o' the Cathery Knowes"

Time and breath seemed to stop for a moment while William waited, heart pounding, the crook of his arm around Arthur's neck. "Jasper," he said. "Tell your son that I mean it."

"Eh, let go of her, lad," Musgrave rumbled.

Arthur released the rope. William flung him aside, scarcely noticing as Arthur stumbled to the floor and regained his feet.

The girl struggled for breath and clutched at the rope with one bare hand. William widened the noose and slipped it over her head. He whipped the rope away, and it smacked into the wall and slid into a heap. The girl coughed, and William touched her shoulder, his fingers trembling.

She looked up at him. Her green eyes had a startling clarity, as if her unguarded soul glimmered there, as elusive and shining as the shadow of a fish slipping past underwater.

A moment passed, no more, while he wondered at what he saw: innocence pure enough to tug at his heart, a precious spark of trust. Then her eyes clouded and she looked away.

"Th-thank you," she murmured, her voice hoarse.

"Tamsin," he whispered. "Are you hurt?" He cared only that she was safe. He scarcely noticed the three men who stared at him, one in gratitude, two in anger. They were dim candles beside her eloquent flame. He felt her heat beneath his hands, spreading into him.

"She's unhurt." Jasper Musgrave waved a hand casually as if to dismiss the incident.

"Tamsin?" William asked again.

She nodded, her bare fingers easing over her throat. "I am fine." Her voice was faint, strained. William merely nodded, though he felt a raging impulse to throw a Musgrave or two through a window. Silent, deliberately calm, he lifted his hand from her shoulder.

"Lassie, are ye sure ye're unharmed?" Archie asked beside him. The girl nodded, and her father turned to William. "I thank ye, sir, I do," he said gruffly. His eyes were as light and vibrant a green as his daughter's, William noticed. Relief and gratitude, and something more, seemed to shine there.

"I did what was necessary to stop a cruel thing," William said, looking at Musgrave in disgust. He walked away, turning his back on the others to stare out the window.

"Eh, she's fine," Musgrave muttered. " 'Twas but to make a point with Archie."

"The devil's own point, Jasper," William snapped over his shoulder. "Ill thought and ill done."

" 'Tis a mighty fuss over a gypsy," Jasper replied in a low voice.

"Over a woman," William corrected.

"Aye! And a bonny woman she is, and shouldna be treated thus! Rookhope knows it, hey!" Archie said.

William heard Jasper snarl at Arthur, blaming his son for a cruel act that had been his own suggestion. Arthur slammed the door as he left.

William stared unseeing through the thick window glass. He fisted his hands and took in a breath as he mastered his temper. The sight of the noose around the girl's neck had shaken him deeply. Such a threat meant little to men like the Musgraves. Hanging was a common punishment dealt out by reivers, lawmen, and kings alike. But William did not regard the act of hanging so casually.

Even the sight of a noose could bring a cold sweat upon him, could make his heart pound and edge his temper toward boiling.

He would carry the gruesome memory of his father's death forever.

Seventeen years had passed since that day. He had learned to
cool his anguish, to bury it deep, suffering the occasional dreams
and memories in silence. But nooses, ropes, and cruel acts such as
Musgrave favored could draw the pain and the anger to the surface in an instant, challenging his usual calm.

When he had seen the rope around that fragile, beautiful throat,
a well of fury and fear had gathered within him. Control alone
had kept him from exploding into a savage act. Now his temper
still rocked, his legs still trembled. He flexed his hands and stared
through the window in silence.

"She's a fine lass," Archie said, capturing William's attention.
"Some man will be fortunate to have her to wife. And nae Musgrave is worthy to speak her name! Ye're the de'il's own, Jasper,
and yer son. I willna forget this."

"You and your damned tawny stole my horses, you scoundrel!"
Musgrave shouted. " 'Tis a hanging crime!"

William turned. Though he did not look directly at the girl, he
felt her gaze, full and luminous, on him. Since the moment she
had walked into the room, she had claimed a steady thread of his
awareness. Now he felt the thread strengthen to a cord, as if his
act of protection had truly bonded them.

"Jasper," he said. "If you want my cooperation, deal with these
people honorably."

Musgrave drew a breath. "Armstrong, your girl's life will be
spared . . . or not. That depends on what you decide now."

" 'Tisna necessary to threaten me through my daughter! 'Tis a
coward's way. Eh, maybe 'tis yer way, ye blackhearted dog."

"I willna hesitate to hang her! There are laws against tawnies
wandering free in England. I have the full right of this, and you
know it. Make your decision. Agree to help me, or watch her
hang, and then be hanged yourself."

William saw Archie sigh, saw his shoulders slump in visible
defeat. The girl watched her father with wide eyes.

"What will ye have of me?" Archie asked, sounding resigned.

"Gather men who will follow me, and gypsies as well," Musgrave said. "I will supply coin for you to pay them all, but I want

a list of willing names and signatures, or their marks, and how much you paid to each. I want the list in a fortnight, and then you will learn more."

"I must know more now," Archie said. "Borderers and gypsies are a suspicious lot. They will ask questions."

"Just use coin, man," Musgrave said. "Or threats. As you choose. See it done within a fortnight."

"This secrecy and intrigue speak ill of your scheme, and of your king," Tamsin said hoarsely.

"If Henry Tudor means to start new wars along the Borders," Archie said, "I willna help ye. I will turn the Bordermen against ye, Jasper Musgrave. And that will cost ye nae coin at all!"

Musgrave gestured toward William. "Rookhope sees the sense of this scheme! And he is a man of reputation in the Borderlands, and at court. If you have any sense at all, you will see the advantage in joining us."

"He clearly knows more about it than I do," Archie said. "Ye keep yer secrets close, Jasper."

"Just trust that this is a wise and necessary action, which can prevent years of war between England and Scotland," Musgrave said. "I will see you in a fortnight, Archie."

"If the Borderers refuse . . ." Archie shrugged.

"Then I have plenty of rope," Musgrave said. "See you, more than Armstrongs will hang if any Scotsman sets foot on my land or acts against me. I will come to Merton in two weeks, with your daughter. I will release her then."

"You canna hold her here!" Archie said.

Tamsin gasped. "I must go with my father!"

"The gypsy will act as your pledge, Armstrong, until the signed promises of willing Bordermen and gypsies are delivered to me. Trustworthy gypsies—if any exist."

"Holding a pledge for good behavior," William said coldly, "is part of Scots law, not English."

"True," Archie said. "The English dinna take honorable pledges. They take hostages, and mistreat them. Ye canna keep her here and get my word on anything."

"I can. I am a deputy in this march. She is my prisoner for crimes committed last night and on other occasions. As are you,

Archie. But I will release you for a fortnight only. Do what I want, or your daughter will suffer for it."

"I need the lassie's help to speak to the 'Gyptians," Archie said. "They willna listen to me if I come to them without her." Tamsin knew he lied for her sake.

"Aye, he needs me to talk to the Romany," she said. "He canna find them without me, unless they travel over his lands."

"She speaks their foreign tongue, which they teach only to their own kind," Archie said. "If ye want the help o' the gypsies, then ye must let her go wi' me. I will return in a fortnight. Ye have my word on it."

Musgrave waved a hand loosely. "I cannot let you both go free on the strength of mere promises. She'll stay."

"What d'ye want? A ransom fee? I'll pay it, whatever 'tis. I have gold aplenty."

"Plenty of gold to a Scot is a pittance to me!"

"Ye bastard, I misdoubt ye'll keep her safe!"

"I'll keep her as safe as I please, you old field bull!"

"Cur! Ye willna—"

"Enough!" William said. "I will take her into my custody."

The others turned to stare at him. He had spoken on impulse, weary of the battling of two stubborn enemies who tugged the girl's fate between them.

He knew his offer made good sense. "I will keep her as a pledge at Rookhope for a fortnight," he said. " 'Tis common practice for a Scotsman to take custody of a Scottish prisoner, even when the accuser is English."

"Aye! Let Rookhope have her," Archie said. The glare that Tamsin shot her father would have melted a lesser man, William thought. Archie looked unperturbed.

Jasper Musgrave frowned. " 'Twould be acceptable. The gypsy would still be under my supervision, in a way."

"You have no authority on Scottish soil," William pointed out. "But I can hold her, and put a stop to this squabbling—for a while, at least," he added.

"I dinna want to go with Rookhope, nor stay here," Tamsin said to Archie. "Da, I must be free."

"Tamsin, 'tis Rookhope," Archie said. "Ye'll be safe."

"He—he means to keep me prisoner!"

"We are not offering you a choice, gypsy," Jasper said. "One dungeon is as good as another. You are my surety, so you must be confined somewhere. Do not forget about the charge of horse thievery."

"One dungeon is as dark as another," she said fiercely. "And prison is no different than death to a gypsy."

Jasper waved a hand. "Take her out of here. I will waste no more time with this lot. Archie, I want that list of names and promises within a fortnight."

"Ye'll get yer list," Archie growled.

"Come ahead," William said. The girl turned her glare on him, still sparking like green fire. Taking a lesson from her father, he gave her a calm little smile and turned away.

"Will Scott," Jasper Musgrave said behind them. "Make sure that Archie meets his promise to me. Go with them when they visit those gypsies, and oversee Archie's damned list. I do not trust these two."

"Very well," William agreed. He ignored the girl's continued glare.

He opened the door and beckoned to the two guards who stood in the doorway. "Wait here in the hallway with these two prisoners until I come out," he said. He ushered the Armstrongs through the doorway, resting a hand on the girl's arm to guide her when she shot him a recalcitrant look. Archie followed her, looking grim. William gave him a somber nod and shut the door.

He spun toward Musgrave. "Tell me what this scheme is about," he said. "Or lose my influence entirely in this secretive matter of yours."

"Secretive," Musgrave said. " 'Tis the word, aye, or we will all lose in this scheme."

William folded his arms. "Tell me."

"For now, I can only reveal to you the most basic of our intentions," Musgrave said. "Until I have the Border scum and the gypsies bound by signed oaths and payment in gold, I cannot discuss the details of the plan with anyone but Lord Wharton and King Henry."

"I might understand how Bordermen's promises could help King Henry," William said. "But gypsies?"

Musgrave sat back and twined his fingers over his belly, where the pewter buttons pulled tight. "What are the gypsies most known for, eh?"

William frowned. "Wandering in caravans through England, Scotland, and Europe . . . keeping to themselves, horse training, tinsmithing, basket weaving, palmistry to earn silver . . . of what use is any of that to you and your king?"

"Sleight of hand, fast-and-loose, clever tricks to take coin from a purse. Lying, stealing, horse thievery," Musgrave detailed. "Fortune-telling, dancing, singing, juggling—even at the royal courts, mind you! The wearing of strange attire, and a tiresome claim of descent from Oriental kings, so that the best among them say they are princes and earls, when they are in reality but vagrants and heathens." Musgrave smiled. "Now think you. What worse is said of the gypsies? How do English mothers frighten their children into obedience, hmm?" He looked pleased as he sat back.

"I believe that the gypsies," William said, forcing a casual tone, "are known for stealing children."

Musgrave nodded. "And how fortunate for us that they have earned a repute for that sort of thing."

William frowned as a realization struck him, bringing with it a cold chill. *You bastard,* he thought, staring at Musgrave. There was only one child whom King Henry would want in his custody. The king of England had already secured a promise from the Scottish crown to wed Queen Mary Stewart, eight months old, to Henry Tudor's little son Edward. But William had heard that Henry was not content with a promise for a future wedding. He had requested that the queen be raised at the English court, and he had been soundly refused. King Henry would not accept that refusal lightly, William knew.

"And what child," William went on, "would you hire gypsies to steal for you?"

"I think you can guess. And I think you know how much benefit both Scotland and England would take if a certain poor babe were raised by her kindly English uncle, who sits upon the English throne." Musgrave smiled.

William stared at him, eyes flat, expression mild. He dared not speak in that moment, for the fury that gathered in him.

"I do not trust gypsies well enough to do what King Henry wants done," Musgrave said. "I am not certain they would comply, in truth," he said. "My most trusted men will do the deed. Once I have my little band of thieves in compliance, the blame will come to rest on the gypsies. Clever, hey?" He grinned. "You are among the men I will trust. 'Tis said of you that you keep your word. And 'tis said that you are no longer a friend to the Scottish nobility. You will earn land and privilege, and more gold than you can dream of, in England."

William drew a long breath, schooling his outrage, seeking a countenance of reason and compliance. If he revealed his true reaction now, he would lose a unique chance to destroy this threat to the little queen of Scotland.

Not only was he loyal to Mary Stewart, but he was a father himself. His own daughter was near the queen's age. In the pit of his stomach and the core of his being, he felt a deep urge to protect Mary Stewart, as he would have done were his own child threatened.

A stroke of fate had included him among the conspirators. He was in place now on the board of play, a pawn—more nearly a rook, he thought wryly—who could see the game undone.

"I gave you my word to be involved in this scheme of yours," William said, choosing his answer carefully.

Musgrave nodded. "Good. I knew you for a scoundrel, Rookhope, just like your father. Now take those troublesome Armstrongs with you, and see that they obey their promises to me as well."

"Well enough." William put a hand on the door latch.

"Will Scott," Musgrave murmured. He turned over a parchment sheet and dipped his quill in ink. "You have a daughter of your own, do you not?" His mild tone gave William another spiraling, icy chill. "Under a year, born about the same time as your mewling, weak Scottish queen, I think. Your poor babe lacks a mother, does she not? Gone in childbirth, I heard. An unwed Scottish noblewoman. A pity." He shook his head slowly. "But if I were you, I would tread carefully for that child's sake."

"You wouldna dare," William growled.

"Of course not." Musgrave looked up and smiled, but his eyes were like shards of ice. "See this done, Will Scott," he said. "Each step of the way. I have your promise."

William stared at him silently.

"Break it, and I cannot guarantee the safety of your daughter."

He wanted to kill the man where he stood. But he could not, or he would lose track of this damnable plan. He did not yet know the whole of it. Heart pounding, William yanked open the door and slammed it as he stepped outside.

"Send a page to ready my horse," he ground out to the two guards who waited with the Armstrongs. "And tell him to saddle the horses these two own, as well."

"Hey, add one or two more while ye're at it—good English stock," Archie said. A little grin bloomed on his bruised face.

William, distracted from his simmering thoughts by Archie's boisterous tone, looked at the blond man thoughtfully. He and Archie had more in common than anyone suspected, now that both their daughters—and their queen—had been threatened by Musgrave. William sighed sharply, and remembered again how much his father had liked this man.

He liked him very well himself now. And he did not want to see Archie Armstrong, or Tamsin Armstrong, endangered because of his own situation. He smiled, quick and flat, at Archie, who grinned.

The girl, though, scowled at both of them before turning to stride down the corridor behind the guard.

Chapter Five

A pair of days in a dungeon had reminded her how essential the sky and the earth were to her well-being. Tamsin inhaled the fresh, breezy air and gazed at the green Border hills, dotted with grazing sheep, and at the bright summer sky, where clouds sailed fat and low. She patted her dapple gray horse's thick neck and smiled. She was glad to be free of walls and dark confinement, glad to feel the wind stirring her hair, and the gray's steady power shifting beneath her.

No matter her secret objections, she could not deny that William Scott was a far better jailer than Musgrave. Soon enough he would confine her inside his tower. But for now, she could feel air and sunshine again. Her Romany blood, and years spent with a wandering people, made physical freedom so necessary to her that she could not thrive without it.

She glanced at William Scott, who rode beside her. He sat his dark bay with easy grace, his gaze watchful beneath the sloped rim of his steel helmet. He was as stoutly armed as any Border rider, with a pair of wooden, brass-trimmed pistols and a crossbow, and an upright lance strapped to his saddle. He wore high leather boots and a back-and-breast of shining steel, the two-piece armor commonly worn by Bordermen who could afford it. Most Scottish Bordermen, like Archie, wore the more economical protection of thickly padded, iron-reinforced leather jacks.

Tamsin noticed that his gear was of excellent quality, the possessions of a wealthy man, though none of it was elaborate. A man could show his wealth and upbringing by unnecessary decoration, but William Scott did not. Even his speech was the Scots of a Border laird, rather than the English-influenced Scots of a courtier.

Intrigued and fascinated, she glanced frequently toward him as they rode and wished she knew more about him. He blended kindness with what she was sure was treachery. And he seemed perfectly at home among Border lairds and reivers, although he had spent years at the royal court as a friend to the king.

"Look there," Archie said. William turned his attention toward Archie, and Tamsin did too. "Merton Rigg." He halted his horse and pointed to the east.

Tamsin and William steadied their horses and gazed over a peaceful vista of hills and valleys. In the distance, a stone tower, surrounded by a wall, topped a rocky outcrop that jutted up from a bleak, uneven hill. Thick green trees surrounded the base of the hill, the whole forming a strong and pleasing picture from where they sat. Tamsin lifted her chin in pride as she sat beside her father.

"Half Merton, we call it," Archie went on. "The borderline between England and Scotland runs under the foundation, dividing the tower nearly in half. The kitchen and lesser hall, and two bedchambers, are actually in England, ever since the last treaty, a generation ago."

"I remember hearing about Half Merton when I was a lad," William said. "As I recall, my father said that you yourself were born in England."

"Aye, well," Archie grumbled. "My mother had a fast travail, and couldna make it to the Scottish bedchamber in time. But I'll trust ye to keep yer mouth closed about that."

William smiled, a subtle lift of his firm mouth that Tamsin thought attractive. His blue eyes sparkled like the sky, making her want to smile too. But she resisted.

"You can trust me," he told Archie. "And your daughter? Is she Scottish or English, by the location of her birth at Merton?"

"I was born in a gypsy wagon. In Scotland," she said.

"A Scottish lass for certain." He gave her another of those quiet little smiles and turned to scan the hills.

She looked along the earthen road, which split a hundred yards from where they sat. One fork would take her to Half Merton and familiar surroundings. The other road would lead her to Rookhope and the unknown, with a man she did not wholly trust.

But her father seemed eager to trust him, and especially eager to see his daughter go with him. She sighed, knowing exactly why Archie liked the arrangement.

Now that he knew William Scott was not wed, her father probably planned to offer her hand in marriage to him before long. She frowned, fisting her left hand, feeling the slight sting of the healing cut on her wrist. She could not tell anyone the secret that she carried.

Even if William Scott was a loyal Borderman—which she knew he was not—he would never prefer a half gypsy to the ladies of the court, who had beauty and refined manners. She fervently wished that her father would hold his tongue, but she was sure that he would pursue the matter and distress all of them.

Sitting there, she made an impulsive decision that would serve both her father and herself—at least for a while. She looked at William. "I intend to stay with my father," she said firmly. "Farewell, William Scott. Thank you for the escort." She turned her horse to head for Merton Rigg.

William reached out a swift arm to snatch the bridle. "You'll go home in two weeks," he said firmly.

"I'll go home when I will!" she replied.

His blue gaze was sharp. "You'll come with me now."

"Och, let the lass go to Half Merton for a bit if she likes," Archie said. "We needna tell Jasper, hey? We'll have a good supper, and ye can ride to Rookhope wi' her later."

"Nay, Da," she said. "I want to stay at Merton."

"He's given his word to keep ye, and he will."

"Da, how can you—"

"Hush!" Archie said brusquely. Tamsin stared, for her father rarely scolded her. "She'll need her gear," Archie told William.

"Lassies like their baubles and things. Let her get what she needs, and have supper wi' us before ye go on to Rookhope wi' her."

"I do need my gear," Tamsin said quickly. At Merton, she could dig in her heels and stay. Even if her father insisted she go to Rookhope, she could appeal to Cuthbert and his mother, her great-grandmother, who also lived at Merton. A little time under the scrutiny of Cuthbert and Maisie Elliot might render William Scott eager to escape on his own.

If she had to, she would slip away and seek her gypsy kin, she thought, determined to stay out of Rookhope's dungeon.

"Gear? I thought gypsies traveled with naught but the clothes on their backs and the cleverness in their souls," William said. He looked at her and lifted a brow.

"There's another reason I want ye to come to Merton first," Archie said. "If ye will have the keeping of my bonny unwed daughter"—Archie emphasized the words, and Tamsin shot him a dark scowl—"for a fortnight, she will need a companion. 'Tis proper, see ye. I'll send someone from Merton along wi' ye."

"Oh? Who might that be?" William asked.

"My uncle, Cuthbert Elliott, or my own granddame, Mother Maisie," Archie said.

"Cuthbert and Mother Maisie are both far too old to sit in a dungeon for a fortnight," Tamsin said. "Cuthbert is threescore and ten, and Maisie is nearly another score older."

William lifted his brows in surprise. "I wouldna expect them to ride with us to Rookhope. Let them stay at Merton."

"But they're still sprightly," Archie argued. "They wouldna be much of a bother to ye. Tamsin needs someone there to see that all is proper, see ye."

"Your lass is safe with me. I willna disgrace her," William said, his previously friendly tone hardening. Tamsin saw his jaw clench, saw his eyes flash, blue and hard. "My mother and sister are at Rookhope. They can act as Tamsin's guardians, if you think she needs protection from such as me."

"Nah, nae protection," Archie said. "Just witnesses."

"Will you make your mother and sister spend time in the dungeon to keep me company?" Tamsin asked. She knew she sounded sarcastic, and did not care. "Or will you let me out for a little each day, to take in sunlight and air for their benefit?"

He sent her a sour glance. "A few days in a dungeon might tame that tongue."

" 'Twould likely make it worse," she retorted.

Archie smiled indulgently at them. "Tell me," he said after a moment of tense silence between Tamsin and William. "Your mother, Lady Emma, is at Rookhope again? I know she left there, years ago . . . after ye were taken away as a lad. A fine, bonny lady, yer mother. I didna know she had returned. I heard she had married Maxwell o' Brentshaw."

"She did, fifteen years ago. He died last year, and she came to live at Rookhope again."

"Ye stayed away from Rookhope a long while, lad. Years more than the span o' yer confining."

"I had a place at the king's side," William said. "I went to Rookhope Tower only occasionally, until last year. Now . . ." He shrugged. "A few of my kin live there with me." He slid Tamsin a glance. "Though we rarely use the dungeons."

"Then you must get someone to sweep them out," she snapped.

"Indeed I will," he growled.

"A fortnight might nae be long enough for you two," Archie observed. "Ye may have to keep her longer, Rookhope . . . er, until Musgrave and I work out our differences."

"I think not," William said.

Tamsin leaned toward her father. "I know what evil scheme you have in mind," she said between her teeth. "Stop."

Archie blinked at her innocently.

William looked out over the hills, his hand still on the bridle of Tamsin's horse. She tugged at the reins, and he let go easily, surprising her. But he sent her a warning glance.

Swiftly, acting on impulse, she leaned forward and kneed her horse, surging along the road in the direction of Merton.

William swore and shouted her name, echoed by Archie. She heard the steady thud of hooves behind her. If she had her way, neither of them would catch up to her. She was a skilled rider on a swift horse, and lighter by far than her pursuers.

She guided the gray off the road, urging him to a long, easy gallop across a flat meadow. Then she tucked low and let him sail over a hedge. She knew the land here, knew the swells and slopes, and veered the horse toward another track that would take her around behind Half Merton. A quick glance over her shoulder revealed her father and Scott riding toward the hedge.

Galloping low and swift along a straight track, she soon neared a forking of the path. She saw something in the earthen crossing, and reined in so quickly that her horse whickered and turned. Tamsin leaned over to look at the ground.

A few stones lay in the dust, along with some scratchings in the earth. The stones outlined a small heart, with several long intersecting lines, one ending in a arrowed point.

The design was a *patrin,* a sign left by Romany to indicate the direction they had taken, and understood by their kind. Such signs were hardly noticed by unpracticed eyes, and made little sense except to the Romany. Tamsin could read the symbols as clearly as she could read English, French, and Latin.

The heart referred to a specific location, more than a dozen miles from the crossroad, in the territory of Liddesdale. And the straight lines, with one angled point, showed the direction the group had taken.

Tamsin circled her horse in the road and glanced toward Merton, so close that its crenellated tower roof rose into the sky, separated from the road only by a wide swath of trees. Then she looked back at the men riding behind her. She saw Archie point toward her, and saw William Scott lean low to urge his horse faster along the track.

Tamsin turned the horse and took the left fork.

She was gone by the time they reached the crossroad. William cursed under his breath and circled his horse.

"She's off to Merton," Archie said, pointing to the right.

"I saw her ride left," William answered impatiently.

"She has nae reason to ride that way. If she did, likely she means to circle around to Merton along that road."

William looked down at the ground, as he had seen Tamsin do just before she rode off. An arrangement of stones and lines in the dust caught his eye. "What is that?" he asked.

Archie peered down. "Stones, Will Scott."

"More than that. Gypsies leave signs for other bands of gypsies to recognize. I have seen similar markings in the road before, though each one differs. Tamsin surely knows what this one says. She took the left fork for a reason." He looked up. "I think I'll find a gypsy camp in that direction—and your daughter as well."

"That could be, though I dinna know what those markings mean. She does have some canny 'Gyptian tricks." Archie glanced at William. "As ye may find out."

"I have scant tolerance for gypsy tricks just now," William said. "But I must find the lass."

"Go to, then. I've just been treated to two days o' Musgrave's sorry hospitality. My belly is empty, and my headcrack pains me sore. I'm riding on to Merton. If she's gone to Johnny Faw and that gypsy lot, she'll return home to Merton when she's ready. She does what she wants, that lass, but she always comes back to her da." He smiled. "Be patient, lad."

William sighed and looked along the empty road. "I dinna have the leisure to wait upon her whim," he said.

"But ye gave yer word to Musgrave to hold her for a fortnight, and ye'll do it, hey?"

William thought Archie looked oddly hopeful. "You seem eager to obey Musgrave's wishes of a sudden."

"Jasper knows I'm a disobedient sort, 'tis why he threatened my lass. I dinna want her in his keeping. But yer custody o' my Tamsin is a different matter."

William looked at him. "Why?"

"Ye said ye would keep her safe."

"Aye," William said slowly. "Why do you want me to keep her at all? She's run from me. I would think you'd applaud that."

"I do applaud her spirit. But I have my reasons to want her in yer custody." Archie paused. "I dinna know why ye support a man like Musgrave, but I'll wager 'tis secret games o' some sort. Politics, and suchlike, which I dinna care for, myself."

William eyed him steadily. "I have my reasons as well."

"And I'll ask nae questions. I trust ye for a man o' yer word and I'll hold ye to it. Ye said ye'd keep the lass well."

William inclined his head, studying Archie. The man's eagerness in this made him wary. "I think you might have some plan of your own, Archie Armstrong."

"Me? Och, my thinking is simple, man. If ye keep Tamsin, Musgrave will think I'm doing what he wants," he said blithely.

"Ah," William said. "And will you?"

Archie paused. "I willna do what that coney orders. But I want my lass safe, so I want her wi' ye."

"You intend to break your word to Musgrave."

"Word given under force and duress is meaningless. When I give my word in honor, I keep it. But I willna do what Musgrave demands. Nor that sneakbait rascal, King Henry."

"You take a great risk."

"Aye. And I will trust ye to say naught to Musgrave." Archie watched him. "I see yer father strong in ye, lad. Nae just in yer bonny face, but in the help ye gave to me and my lass. And I think yer heart is as loyal and good as was Allan's. Am I wrong?" he asked softly.

William looked away, his throat tightening. He felt gratitude wash through him, sudden and deep, bringing him to the surprising brink of tears. Archie, who had known Allan Scott better than most, had given William a precious part of the father he had lost with but a few honest words.

He strove for his voice. "If you wish to go against Musgrave," he finally said, " 'tis your matter, and I'll say naught of it. And I'll keep your lass safe at Rookhope for so long as must be."

"Aye, then." Archie nodded. "I'll take her back when Musgrave loses his interest in keeping a hold over me."

"That may never happen," William said wryly.

"True," Archie said with a little grin. "Then ye needs must keep her, hey." He grew solemn. "Musgrave may go after me when he finds I dinna support King Henry's secret matter after all."

"Aye. He wants that list."

"Och, now, I didna say he wouldna have a list."

William frowned. "What do you have planned, Archie?"

"If Musgrave doesna have to tell his scheme," Archie said, "then I willna tell mine." He grinned.

"You're an auld scoundrel." William smiled reluctantly. "And your daughter is a troublesome lass. I had best find her, I think."

"Oh, I think that would be wise," Archie said.

William sighed. He had few enough threads to follow in unraveling the English plan. The Armstrongs, father and daughter, were his best link just now to the whole truth of the scheme. But now Archie and Tamsin had gone in unexpected directions, the girl quite literally.

He knew now that Musgrave meant to organize an English effort to steal the Scottish queen. But he did not yet know how, or when. More details were necessary if the attempt was to be thwarted, and the girl and her father could lead him to those details.

His obligations were coming together like paths in a crossing, he thought, looking down at the road. In addition to the promise he had given Musgrave to remain involved in the scheme—and he would, he thought bitterly—he had also promised Archie to watch over the girl.

"Go on to Half Merton," he told Archie. "I must go home to Rookhope first. But then I intend to ride out in search of your daughter."

"Good. I'll send word to ye if she's at Merton. Otherwise, you can ask any farmer or Borderman in this area if the gypsies have passed through here, and so find them fast enough. But be warned, the gypsies can be a naughty lot if a man tries to take away one o' their women."

"Then I'll have to convince her to come with me willingly."

Archie studied him for a moment. "I will give ye one caution, Will Scott, from a father," he said. "Treat my lass wi' courtesy. Or ye'll find me as stout an enemy as a friend."

"You have my word on it." He paused. "I too am a father. I have a daughter but eight months in age."

"I thought ye had nae wife!"

He looked away. "Katharine's mother died at her birth."

"Ah. Then I will wager," Archie said softly, "that ye would give up yer life for that wee bit lassie o' yers."

"I would," William said.

Archie nodded as if satisfied with something. He gathered his reins and turned his horse toward Merton Rigg. "Luck be wi' ye," he called over his shoulder. "I dinna envy ye the task o' bringing back Tamsin if she doesna want to come wi' ye. But if any man can convince her, Will Scott"—he grinned—"I think ye are that man."

As William watched him ride away, he had the disquieting sense that Archie had spoken of far more than finding and keeping a gypsy lass for a fortnight.

Chapter Six

"What news, what news, bonny boy?
What news hes thou to me?"
"No news, no news," said bonny boy,
But a letter unto thee."

—"Bonnie Annie Livieston"

For several miles, William followed a drover's track along a ridge that skimmed the hills like a raised spine. The track provided a fast northeast route between the disputed area on the edge of the Border, called the Debatable Land, where Merton Rigg was located, and the territory of Liddesdale, which contained Rookhope lands.

The Debatable Land was an area along the western part of the border line, disputed by England and Scotland alike. The territory was a lawless land where outlaws and scoundrels hid from authority, and free and honest men scarcely dared to leave their animals pastured. Merton Rigg lay on the easternmost tip of the debated area.

Liddesdale, whose boundaries began a few miles farther north, was scarcely more lawful, filled with scores of Scottish Bordermen who made a sound living on the basis of borrowing good livestock and gear in the dark of the night. Generations of burning and looting at English hands had brought parts of the Scottish Borders to a wild, ungoverned state. Constant complaints from the crowns of both England and Scotland, and continual efforts to establish order there, had been by tradition either ineffectual or far too harsh.

Reivers and thieves as well as cattle drovers often took the ridge road, and William kept his gaze wary as he rode. He knew the track was most dangerous on moonlit nights, when reivers brought livestock secretly over the hills, either heading out of England or out of Scotland. But now all seemed quiet along the route, and the bay covered the distance with long, fast, efficient strides.

Within an hour, William rode over moorland and hills that belonged to him, all part of Rookhope Ryde, as his property had been called in his grandfather's day. Daylight faded and the sky took on a dense pewter cast, edged with indigo along the horizon. The wind grew strong and cold, and the air heavy, as if a summer storm approached.

Soon he saw the stark silhouette of Rookhope Tower, situated on the crest of a hill. Backed by acres of dense forest and fronted by a steep slope that led to a narrow glen, the stone keep was naturally protected by its setting. From the rooftop a wide view could be had of the surroundings, and access to the tower could be difficult.

As he rode, he noticed the portcullis in the outer wall slide upward. Two horsemen streamed out through the opening and headed down the western side slope. A path had been worn over centuries there, since the incline was the most gradual of the slopes that surrounded the tower property. One of the men saw William coming along the road and hailed him with a wave.

William narrowed his eyes and recognized them both. One, the younger of the two men, was a friend whom he was glad to see. The other, an older man, was closer to a personal enemy than any man he knew, though they had always maintained a veneer of chill politeness when dealing with one another.

He frowned, and halted his horse along the road to wait. The men headed toward William in the failing light, clods of earth spitting away from the horses' hooves.

"Will!" The man in the lead lifted a gloved hand in greeting. His handsome features were framed by a neatly trimmed auburn beard and cropped hair, and he smiled as he rode closer, halting his horse a few feet from William.

"Good day, Perris." William nodded toward his friend, his greeting cool only because of the presence of the older man who pulled his mount to a stop beside them.

"We were just leaving Rookhope," Perris said. "How fortunate to meet you out here. We thought we would miss you altogether, and have to return later this week." William smiled, flat and tense. He regarded Perris Maxwell as a kinsman as well as a friend, for his mother had married Perris's uncle, Maxwell of Brentshaw, years before. Bound by marriage kinship, they also knew each other within the royal court, where Perris, schooled in the law, acted as a royal advocate for the king's widow, the queen dowager, Marie of Guise.

William looked at the man beside Perris and inclined his head. "Malise. Greetings."

"William," Malise Hamilton said. His dark blue eyes and closely cut silver hair gleamed in the low light. "How fortunate, as Perris says."

As always, when he saw Malise Hamilton, William felt tension infuse him. He and Malise were linked by tragedy and resentment, even hatred. Not only had Malise Hamilton been a member of the escort who had taken William away from Rookhope Tower the day his father had been hanged, but Malise was also the father of the woman William had loved and lost, the mother of his child.

Because of the bitter, unresolvable bond between them, William found it wisest to simply avoid the man whenever possible. He summoned control over his anger now, as he faced the man but a hundred yards from the site where William's father had died and Malise had taken a young lad prisoner.

They were further linked by the existence of Katharine. The thought of his infant daughter's welfare gave him reason to school his hatred for her grandfather.

"We arrived at Rookhope this morning on official crown business, but you were away," Malise murmured. "Your sister Helen acted as a gracious hostess in your absence. Poor lass."

William sucked in a quick breath at Malise's condescending reference to the scarring that his younger sister Helen had endured after a smallpox attack years ago. He began to utter a hot reply, but Perris leaned forward to interrupt him.

"Lady Helen is hardly a poor lass," Perris said. "She is blessed with an abundance of charm and grace. I find her lovely and delightful. I confess, your remark surprises me. Do you find something to pity in her?" The smooth question was a dare.

William joined Perris in staring at Malise, who cleared his throat and shrugged. "Not at all, of course. Your mother was ill and kept to her bed," Malise went on. "She never came down to offer hospitality."

"Perhaps she had an ague," William murmured. He realized why his mother had kept to her chamber, and suspected Malise knew, too. Lady Emma could not tolerate Hamilton's presence on the rare occasions that the man visited Rookhope.

"Katharine is beautiful," Malise said. "She reminds me of her mother at that age."

"Aye." William nodded brusquely. "You said you are here on official crown business. You could have sent a footrunner."

"Madame the Queen Dowager sends her personal regards to you," Perris said.

William stared at him, astonished. He had been shunned at court for months. During that time, he was sure that Marie of Guise, King James's widow, shunned him along with the rest.

"She wanted this private message delivered to you, written in her own hand." Perris reached into his doublet and pulled out a folded parchment closed by a red wax seal.

William accepted it warily, unsure if it boded ill or good.

"I told her that I would seek you out and give you the summons, since you and I have business between us," Malise said. "And I wanted to see my granddaughter, of course."

"Madame wishes to see you immediately, at Linlithgow Palace," Perris said.

William tucked the parchment away to read later. "Good," he said. "I have something to discuss with her myself."

"And what might that be?" Malise asked sharply. "We both are privy to whatever news is brought to Madame's attention, as you know."

William crossed his gloved hands on the pommel of his saddle and felt his horse shift restively beneath him. "I will keep the details private until I have spoken with Madame," he said. "Since you are riding back to Linlithgow now, though, I hope you will deliver a message to her for me."

"What is that?" Perris asked.

"Tell her that I will ride there tomorrow, so soon as I see my family. And advise Madame to consider moving the queen to a place of greater safety as soon as possible."

"Why? Is there some danger to Her Grace?" Malise demanded.

"I have heard disturbing rumors," William said cautiously.

"Rumors that King Henry wants to snatch the wee queen?" Malise made a scoffing sound. "There are always such rumblings. He blows hot like a boiling kettle, and says what he likes for all to hear, but does not follow through always. He suggested to his advisors that they take her father, King James, years back, but they were too cowardly to try, any of them."

"Or too wise," William murmured. "Nevertheless, until the truth is discovered, Queen Mary's safety must be of paramount concern. Linlithgow Palace isna as defensible as Edinburgh or Stirling."

"Madame already plans on moving the queen to Stirling Castle," Perris said. "Her coronation will take place there next month."

"Next month is a long while away," William said. "She should be moved before then, I think, either secretly, or under a substantial force of men. Convey that message to Madame. I will bring the particulars to her myself."

"Very well, then," Malise said. "If you think she will listen to you. I do not know why she wants to speak with you. It might very well be a reprimand, which you only deserve."

"I will take my chances," William murmured. "Farewell to you both." He lifted his reins.

"There is one other matter between us," Malise said. William looked at him. "I sent you a lengthy letter a fortnight past, and was displeased with your reply."

"I will say it again, then, if you didna understand, Malise," William said. "I have no interest in marrying either of the Hamilton ladies you suggested for me in your letter."

"You must marry, and soon," Malise said in a fierce tone. "I will not tolerate my granddaughter being raised without a mother. You have no reason to refuse either one of my nieces. One is a widow with good property, the other her unmarried sister. 'Tis kind of my kin to allow the offer to be made to you. We all know the circumstances of your . . . relationship with my daughter."

William narrowed his eyes and waited for his temper to cool before he spoke. And he wondered, as he often had in the past, how Jeanie could have been the daughter of this man. But in Malise's dark blue eyes, and in his narrow, handsome features, he saw fleeting hints of Jeanie's laughing blue eyes and lovely face. The memory of her made him draw in his breath.

Just before she died, while he had held her hand and prayed silently for her strength to return, he had promised her that he would come to peace with her father. In his heart, he did not know if he could keep that oath. But for the sake of Jean's memory, and for the sake of their daughter, he had to try.

"I thank you for your concern," he said in a cool voice. "But when I wish to take a wife, I will choose her myself."

"You could have made that choice last year," Malise barked. "My daughter died unwed."

"Had you allowed her to contact me, you would have no grievance with me now," William said through clenched teeth.

Malise glanced away, his face set hard and pale. "I didna think she would die," he murmured.

William let out a hard sigh. "We all would have lost her, either way, to a hard birth."

"Will you dishonor my granddaughter now? Katharine has royal blood in her through the Hamilton line. Her uncle is the Regent of Scotland, and second in line to the throne. She requires a home and a mother befitting her blood."

"She has a fine home. And she had a fine mother."

Malise thinned his mouth, flared his nostrils. "I want Katharine raised in a Hamilton household. Rookhope Tower is naught but a den of thieves."

"I was raised in that den of thieves," William said between his teeth. "And flourished there, until you and the earl of Angus's men took me forcibly away from my kin. I wager my daughter will flourish among rascals just as well."

"I did not order your father's death," Malise said. "Angus was the one who gave the order. I came after 'twas done."

"You werena far behind," William said.

" 'Twas long ago," Perris said quietly. "There is no need to argue it today, or ever. Tragedy was done that day. Neither of you can change it." His interruption was an attempt to pacify, William knew, offering the respite William needed to calm his spiking temper.

"A sad day for many." Malise smiled in the sour way that was peculiar to him, as if the only kindness or apology he could manage was a bitter turn of his lips. "But another death is between us, more tragic than the loss of a horse thief."

William stared out over the hills, jaw tense, hands tight on the reins, and did not reply. He could not look in the direction of the oak tree where his father had died.

"Agree to wed one of my nieces, and give my granddaughter the home I want for her," Malise said. "And perhaps I can begin to forget and forgive what happened."

"Neither of us will forget. Or forgive," William said.

"Jean made her choice when she went to you. She begged me to love you like a son," Malise said. "I have vowed for her memory's sake, and for my granddaughter, to fulfill that promise, though I would rather see you hanged for your lewd behavior." He narrowed his eyes. "Understand that what I do is for the child. Wed one of my kinswomen, and raise my granddaughter as befits her bloodline. I will see that you benefit from your status as kinsman by marriage to the Hamiltons."

"Oh, I will wed," William said, in as mild a tone as he could muster. He cared little to gain any status that would bring him into Malise's company. "I canna promise to whom, or when. Nor can I promise that you will be pleased by my choice. But you may be assured that Katharine will someday have a mother. And you can be assured that she will always be safe and well in my keeping."

"In your keeping," Malise repeated. "That is the question, is it not? Wed soon, and to a Hamilton woman who can provide my granddaughter with the upbringing she deserves, or I will take my complaint to the Court of Sessions. I have lately hired an advocate in Edinburgh to look into the matter."

William looked at Perris, who nodded grimly. "I know the man," he said. "A capable procurator."

"Hamilton's claim is not valid," William said.

"My advocate thinks otherwise," Malise said.

William looked at Perris, who nodded. "A child of a mother who is still under the guardianship of her parents can be interpreted as belonging to the grandparents rather than the father," he explained. "The civic court can settle this if Malise decides to pursue his complaint. They could decide for Malise. Or for you," he added.

"Jean's child is illegitimate," Malise said. "Katharine rightfully belongs to me. I want her raised in my household."

A chill slipped down William's back. "She is mine," he growled.

"Malise, the child should be with her parent," Perris said. "You know the moral side of the issue."

"The moral side is that Scott should have left my daughter unspoiled," Malise said. He looked at William. "I want Katharine, and the rights to the property her mother left her. Otherwise, you will wed the lass I choose for you, and sign over the guardianship of the property to me. If you do that, you may keep the child." Another of those flat, sour smiles that only darkened his eyes further.

"The land," William said. " 'Tis what you want. You think to control it by taking custody of Katharine. As her father, I have the right to protect that property until she is of age."

"That land is too valuable to leave to the care of the son of a rogue," Malise said.

"Usually in such cases," Perris said, "a price is agreed and paid for the privileges pertaining to the land until Katharine comes of age. 'Twould always remain hers in ownership."

"He's asked a price," William said. "Though not in coin."

"What most concerns me is Katharine's welfare. She is left to a pack of shifters and thieves," Malise said.

"I will believe that concern," William said, "when the moon is proven to be of green cheese." He glanced at Perris and nodded a silent farewell, receiving a nod and a wry glance in return, as Perris conveyed his opinion of Malise's position.

"Make no attempt to claim my daughter, Malise," William said. "Or you will regret ever making my acquaintance those years ago on the day you and your comrades hanged my father."

Without looking back, he guided the bay horse forward along the path that led to the tower. Behind him, he heard Perris and Hamilton canter away, their hoofbeats fading within moments.

He spurred the bay forward, his heartbeat heavy and hard, as if suddenly the hounds of hell pursued him. Reason told him that all was well inside Rookhope, but Malise's threats had stirred uneasiness and fear in him. He had to see that Katharine was safe, regardless of what reason said.

He thought, then, of Marie of Guise and her own threatened child, the queen of Scotland. He suspected, when she learned of the English plot against her daughter, she would react as a mother first and a queen next. His sympathy and understanding as a parent himself gave him a stronger motivation than even steadfast loyalty to the little queen of Scotland.

Earlier, he had hesitated over whether to pursue the gypsy lass or to ride home first. He was deeply glad that he had gone back to Rookhope. After he had seen Katharine and his mother and sister, he would obey the queen dowager's summons. He hoped she meant to offer him clemency, even forgiveness, for the tragedy of Jean's death, which had affected them both.

Regardless of what she wanted of him, he meant to take the opportunity of a private audience to tell her of the plot that he had uncovered. He knew he would have to follow her wishes regarding the scheme, once she knew of it.

He would need two or three days to ride to Linlithgow, seek an interview with the queen dowager, and ride back, he thought. The journey could be made in a day if he pressed his horse's pace. When he returned to Rookhope, he would set out to find the gypsy girl.

He would ask his cousins Jock and Sandie Scott, who often came to Rookhope, to accompany him to search for a gypsy camp. They might even know the whereabouts of one. William preferred a moonlight ride, as did most Bordermen, who were accustomed to riding through the night on reiving errands and sleeping well into the day. A few nights from now, he thought, would be a perfect time for such an outing.

As he approached the high stone wall that surrounded Rookhope Tower, he heard a shout from a man who stood watch on the rooftop. Likely one of his cousins, he thought, raising a hand to wave. He bypassed the small, easily defended side entrance, which was still closed, and followed the outskirts of the wall toward the open main entrance.

He rode along a wide, grassy shelf between the stone wall and the steep slope that fronted the tower. For a century and more, that difficult access had discouraged hostile visitors. The tower crested a forbidding wooded slope, at the base of which lay a narrow, turbulent burn.

Opposite the tower, separated by the narrow chasm, a rounded hill soared into the evening sky. One widespread oak tree topped its bare upper curve.

Nearing the portcullis, William glanced across the gap at the bleak hill. The oak tree stood alone, branches silhouetted against the sky like hundreds of gnarled hands and fingers. A small mound, a single grave, was sheltered at its foot.

The hill had grown barren over the years, sustaining only sparse grass, tufts of heather, and the dominant, twisted old tree. Many believed that the hill and the oak were haunted, and no one went there, William knew—but for his mother, his sister, and himself.

William glanced there, and gave a grim nod of respect for the memory of Allan Scott, buried beneath the oak. As he came toward the portcullis, he saw that the iron grille, and the massive wooden doors behind it, stood open.

As hc rodc through the gate, his sister Helen crossed the width of the bailey yard, carrying a small, bundled child in her arms. William looked down as she approached.

He scarcely saw his sister, his gaze hungry to see the small face beside hers, now turning up toward him: wide blue eyes beneath dark curls, cheeks chafed pink, a round little mouth.

He dismounted, aware of an upsurge of the sweet, easy joy that he felt only for his daughter, and he opened his hands to lift her high.

Chapter Seven

Sum speikis of lords, sum speikis of lairds
And sic lyke men of hie degrie
Of a gentleman I sing a sang. . . .

—"Johnie Armstrang"

Hooves rang in hollow rhythm on the cobbled street as William approached the south gate of Linlithgow Palace. He greeted the royal guards with a brusque nod and reined in his dark bay, which sidestepped and tossed its black mane, echoing his master's haste.

" 'Tis the laird o' Rookhope!" one of the guards called. Within moments, the portcullis creaked upward and a guardsman waved William into the entrance tunnel. He dismounted and handed the bay's reins to a page, then strode toward the square court at the heart of the palace.

Summer sunshine warmed the rosy stone of the inner facade, with its tiers of glazed windows. Through an open shutter in the northwest tower, where the royal apartments were located, the irritated cry of an infant floated down to the courtyard.

"Ah, the queen of Scotland herself, fussing for her supper," a man remarked. William heard footsteps behind him, and turned to see Perris Maxwell, now looking less the reiver and more the well-dressed gentleman in a black velvet doublet, short breeches, and black hose on his muscular legs. Perris grinned and extended his hand to William, who smiled, glad of the chance to speak openly with his friend, without Malise Hamilton's dampening presence.

"Greetings, Perris." William clasped his hand, and then nodded toward the west block of the palace. "Queen Mary Stewart herself, is it? She sounds strong and lusty."

"Aye, as you will see. And well you should know the sound of a bairn. Your own wee daughter is a bonny bairn."

"And she was wailing a lusty fit when I left Rookhope Tower early this morn. I was glad to have a reason to be away."

"Hah, she melts her father's heart like butter in the sun. Must be that toothless smile."

"Aye." William tapped Perris's arm. "What's this? Velvet? And slashed sleeves? You look like a Spaniard."

Perris grimaced. "Lady Margaret Beaton convinced me to order this from her father's tailor. Mourning black, for the king. I confess she fitted me out in things too fancified for my taste. I complained that Will Scott always wore plain gear at court, no matter the fashion, and the ladies loved it well." Perris scratched at his beard. "Lady Margaret insisted 'twas Will Scott, not the gear, the ladies loved so well. That quiet charm you have is apparently sweeter honey to bees than this silly gear."

William smiled, then grew solemn. "Perris, you know that I return here only to please Madame, and for the sake of Her Grace, the wee queen. I wouldna come back to Linlithgow otherwise. And I have no wish to see Malise just now."

"I know. He is not here. Some will be displeased to see you at court, Will, and others might show you pity. There is still much talk of the bonny laird o' Rookhope, and his misdeeds and tragedies."

"I am certain that my visit to Madame the Queen Dowager will provide new fodder for wagging tongues," William drawled.

"Madame herself summoned you here, so 'twill stifle some of those tongues. She doesna hold the scandal against you, Will, though I know you believe she might."

"I know it distressed her greatly, and I am sorry for that. But I willna apologize for what was a private matter between Jeanie Hamilton and myself. I ask no one's forgiveness."

Perris nodded. Among his friends, William thought, Perris was one of the few who had not borne him an ill prejudice based on rumor. "But I think you can be certain of her friendship, after all. Madame still regards you as one of the few she can truly trust.

You earned her friendship when she arrived in Scotland knowing no Scots, and the king scant French. You showed much patience in teaching her our language. I vow she values your hand at playing cards, and that bonny face as well."

"I will always honor Madame. I hope she knows that," William said quietly. They passed an elaborate stone fountain at the center of the courtyard, and both men paused beside it. "But I wonder why Madame sent for me. Her letter only mentioned an urgent matter," he said. "She doesna need me, a Border laird, to comment on issues. She has advisors and judges, priests, and lawyers—like you."

"I dinna know what 'tis, in truth," Perris said. He grasped William's hand. "And I must go attend to a matter for Madame. Not legal work this time, but important, nonetheless. I am to find a local miller to grind oats into the finest powder. Her Grace the queen spits up her porridge."

"Go to, then," William said, chuckling. Perris grinned and hastened toward the south gate.

William turned back to look up at the carved stone fountain, and recalled a day five years ago when its spouts and basins had overflowed with red wine and rose petals, a display ordered by King James in honor of his new French bride, Marie of Guise. The stone spouts were empty now, the basins green with lichen, the water levels low and murky. Wine might never flow there again, William thought grimly. His hand went to the folded parchment tucked inside his leather doublet, written in Marie of Guise's own elegant italic script.

He had been surprised by the summons. The queen dowager's display of friendship touched him deeply, and he would strive to do whatever she wanted of him. He owed that much to her. He owed it to Jeanie's memory too. As one of Marie's ladies-in-waiting, Jeanie had loved her royal mistress and friend dearly.

Standing beside the fountain, he recalled sweet late evenings nearly two years past, when he and Jeanie Hamilton had met near this fountain. Those clandestine and passionate meetings had led them both along a tangled and tragic path.

She had been lovely and young, and the only child of the one man he truly hated. William knew that rumor claimed he had shamed her deliberately. Few knew the real tale, he thought bitterly. Nor would he enlighten the curious.

He turned and strode toward the northwest tower.

The echo of his pace was rapid and strong as he headed up turnpike steps and down wide, vaulted corridors until he reached the royal presence chamber. The guard outside the door lifted his halberd to allow William passage.

"Rookhope, sir, welcome back." He opened the thick oak door. William thanked him and handed over his long sword, aware that Marie of Guise disapproved of weapons worn in royal audiences. The guard waved him inside.

Sunlight poured through two tall windows, pooling on red brocade window-seat cushions and wall tapestries, and spilling in bright bars over the floor tiles. Music filled the air, emanating from the far end of the huge room, where the royal dais stood empty. Nearby, several men and women gathered in a circle around a man strumming a lute. All were finely dressed in costly fabrics, gowns and doublets gleaming with pearls and jewels. He could smell a blend of musky perfumes from where he stood.

William glanced at his own clothing and brushed at the dust from his ride. His garments were good quality but simple in style, as he preferred: a sleeveless doublet of supple Spanish leather, pierced for coolness and comfort, over a finely woven linen shirt; breeches of black serge, and high leather boots, as were worn by soldiers and reivers, rather than courtiers. He wore his dark hair longer than was stylish, and did not keep a shaped beard, though he sometimes let his whiskers grow out. He did not polish his nails and wore no jewelry.

He knew that most of the women at court favored his appearance. The rest, male and female alike, scoffed at his plain gear as more suited to a Border thief than a sophisticated man of the court. William was both, but he cared as little for the niceties of fashion as he did for the opinions of others.

No one glanced at him as he walked into the spacious chamber. The courtiers surrounded a man seated in their midst who sang a ballad. His voice was vibrant above the soft twang of the lute strings. William paused to listen, leaning a shoulder casually against the oaken paneling.

> The bonny laird went to his lady's door
> And he's twirled at the pin
> "O sleep ye, wake ye, Jean my lass,
> Rise up and let me in."
>
> Fair Jean rose up and let him in
> For she loved him best of a'
> He's ta'en her in his arms twain
> And she let her kirtle fa'.

A chill trickled down his spine. His heart slammed, his jaw tightened, and he remained outwardly calm by sheer effort.

The singer was a young man in an elaborate black satin doublet. William recognized the queen dowager's assistant secretary. He listened, and decided not to interrupt. Yet.

> "O Jeanie, what ails ye?" her father spoke.
> "Does a pain cut in yer side?"
> "I have nae pain, but a lover's gift,
> And my laird willna wed me for pride."
>
> Fair Jean went to the wood that day
> And took with her some silk
> She leaned her back against an oak
> And bathed her bairn in milk.

William had heard enough. He pushed away from the wall and crossed the long room with such purpose that his wooden-soled boots echoed.

The others turned. Nearly all gasped, the women flattening their hands against their stiffened bodices. The secretary struck a dissonant chord and jumped to his feet.

"Sir William!" he cried.

"Greetings, Francis. And to the rest." William inclined his head and walked forward. A path appeared for him as they moved back, gowns rustling, shoes scuffling.

"Lady Margaret, Lady Elspeth. Fleming, Randolph. Lady Alice," he listed grimly as he plunged through the gap. "Seton, Lady Mary. Sir Ralph." He nodded to a tall, handsome man.

William pushed past them as they murmured greetings and backed away. A few had the grace to look embarrassed as he passed. He was glad to see some display of conscience.

He halted, fisting one hand at his waist. "Interesting ballad, Francis," he remarked.

"I—I did not write it, Sir William," Francis stammered. He stood. "I—I had it from a black-letter broadsheet."

"Indeed. Already circulating in broadsheets, is it?"

"Aye, the song has become quite popular. I've heard it sung in Edinburgh, and I hear 'tis sung in England, too."

"I see. And what is it called?"

" 'The . . . The Bonny Laird—' " Francis said. He looked down at his wide-toed leather shoes as if he wanted to sink into oblivion. " 'The Bonny Laird o' Rookhope.' "

"Ah." William let the silence linger.

Francis swallowed, his cheeks red. He glanced at the others, who had strolled across the room. "What—what brings you to court after so long, Sir William?"

"Madame sent for me. Kindly tell her that I have arrived, and that I await her pleasure." He extracted the folded note, displayed its seal and ribbon, and tucked it away again.

"She sent for you?" Francis blinked in surprise.

"Aye." William stared evenly at him.

"Sir William, I—I am most sorry. I would not have sung the ballad had I known Madame sent for you. I am your friend, sir."

"Then I wonder you sing the song at all."

" 'Tis often requested during musical suppers. Many enjoy it, for the melody and for the tale, which is well-known now."

William glared. "I dinna care what is said about me, Francis. But Jeanie Hamilton is dead, and canna defend herself against chatter and gossip. If you wish to act the friend, then respect her memory."

Francis nodded, coloring deeply. "Ce-certainly." He stepped

away. "I will announce you. But Madame has many interviews scheduled this afternoon."

"I will wait," William said. Francis sped past the dais, which was fitted with two empty throne chairs beneath an overhead canopy. On the end wall hung an embroidered tapestry. Behind the cloth, a door led to a small audience room and a short corridor that provided access to the queen's private apartments. Francis hurried through the doorway.

William turned. The circuit of his gaze took in the presence chamber, without acknowledging those who stared at him and murmured among themselves. He walked to one tall window and leaned a hand on the side of the niche, turning his back on the room. He had nothing to say to the others. Nor did they, he suspected, have much pleasant to say to him.

He looked out over the serene surface of the loch that spread behind the palace. As he watched a pair of swans glide there, he felt, rather than saw, the curious and accusing gazes that fastened on his leather-clad back.

"Sir William." Her voice was just as he remembered, low-pitched and gentle, with a marked French accent. "Come in."

"Madame." William bowed his head and stepped farther into the royal bedchamber. He glanced past the carved bed curtained in violet damask, and past fine pieces of furniture, toward one long window. A tall woman stood silhouetted by the northern light, her hands folded in front of her.

She had grown thin, he thought immediately. But the last time he had seen Marie of Guise, she had been great with child. Since then, she had given birth and had been widowed, and now bore part of the responsibility for her late husband's country on her square, capable shoulders.

"Thank you for responding so quickly to my message, Sir William." She was tall, nearly six feet, her carriage naturally elegant as she glided forward. Light glinted over the pearls edging her black cap and black damask gown, and revealed the dusky shadows beneath her eyes.

William bowed over her extended fingers, barely touching her hand, and straightened. She was nearly of a height with him, and he met her gaze boldly, as he always had done, though she was a queen and he was but a Border laird.

"You look well," she said. "I have missed you, William."

He bowed his head again. "And I, you, Madame."

She smiled. "How does your family? And your daughter?"

"All fine, Madame. And Her Grace?"

"Quite well. Come and see." She turned, and he followed.

In a shadowed corner, a young woman in a dark gown sat in a chair, her arms full of a bundled, quiet infant swathed in pale, trailing silks. A small hand lay tucked against her chest while she crooned softly to the babe. The nurse lifted a fold of silk, and William gazed down at Scotland's queen.

Her face was lovely, peaceful, eyelids closed, full lower lip moving slightly as she dreamed. Pale golden-red curls covered her head, and her skin was delicate and translucent.

"I have scant knowledge of infants, other than the one who dominates my own household," he murmured. "But I know enough to judge a confection of a creature in this small queen."

"*Merci,*" Marie of Guise murmured, and continued in French. "She has been fitful. The first teeth cause her discomfort."

"Ah." He went on in French without effort. "Katharine has had the same trouble. My mother gives her a remedy for pain."

"*Oui?* What remedy does she use?"

"I do not know, Madame. I will have her send the recipe if you like. It does provide us some peace." He smiled.

The queen dowager dismissed the nurse with orders to set the queen in her cradle in the adjoining chamber. The girl carried the sleeping infant through an open door, closing it behind her.

Marie turned, her gown whispering over the floor, and sat in a chair. "Before you leave, you must play a few games of the cards with me. You always give me a challenging game, monsieur."

"Madame, I would gladly play at the cards with you. But you would win all my gold and turn me out with an empty purse."

She tilted her head on her long neck. Her fine brown eyes grew serious. "You and I, we have had our losses," she said after a moment. "But we go on. What choice do we have?"

"Indeed, Madame," he said quietly. He had experienced grievous loss, but Marie of Guise had endured devastation. She had been widowed months ago, and less than two years earlier her two tiny sons had died of illness within days of one another. He could only admire her resolute strength and calm.

"I summoned you here for two reasons," she said in French. "I have had long meetings of late with Malise Hamilton."

Tension grew in him, but he bowed calmly. "I spoke with him myself just yesterday."

"He tells me that he urges you to wed, and soon."

William frowned. "He demands that I provide a suitable mother for his granddaughter. He wants me to wed a woman chosen by him. I have refused."

"He has always regarded you as a son, despite the tragedy you caused. He wants to be forgiving, and is concerned for his granddaughter's welfare."

"Did he tell you that he may take the matter to the civic courts and make a complaint for custody of Katharine?"

"I tried to dissuade him from that. But he wants the best upbringing for the child. If you do not wed soon, he will do what he can to gain *la petite* from you. He is much devoted to your daughter."

"He is devoted to the land that she inherited upon her mother's death. He seeks to control that property. His advocate will undoubtedly name the land in Malise's complaint against me."

"Do you think Malise so cold a man?"

"I do."

She frowned. "He is aware of your enmity toward him."

"Enmity!" He nearly laughed. "Madame, the man had a hand in the murder of my father, and controlled my life according to his wishes until I was a man."

"He feels the same about his daughter. He thinks your actions, and misdeeds, and lack of morals, caused her death. Rumors say that you sought revenge on Malise through Jean."

He looked away. "I regret her death, Madame," he murmured.

"I know. William, Malise asked me to speak with you about taking a wife. Regardless of your dispute with him, you must believe that he loves his granddaughter."

"As do I. And I will see to her welfare myself." He folded his arms. "Madame, you are a gracious diplomat. I apologize if Malise has pressed you to intervene in this."

"But you do need a wife. Your daughter needs a mother."

"My mother and my sister dote on her. Katharine does not suffer for the lack of her *maman*. She is cared for in all ways."

She sighed. "And what of you? Such a vigorous man needs a wife, a companion."

"I am flattered by your concern, Madame. Your kind heart melts for the child's sake, I think."

"*La pauvre petite*. Her mother was my cherished friend."

"I know. Please understand that I am in no hurry to marry." He drew a breath. "Someday, but not . . . so soon, Madame."

"I will tell Malise not to worry about his granddaughter's welfare. But you must promise me to find a wife to content you." She gazed at him solemnly. "I speak as a friend, William. I have never seen you *joyeux*. Always you seem to have a sadness in your heart."

He smiled, shrugged. "My daughter's existence eases any sadness I feel. As does your friendship, Madame."

"Give me none of your charm, monsieur, but truth now. Promise me to seek true contentment for yourself."

"I will do my best," he said. "Now, Madame, is that truly why you summoned me here?"

"There is another matter. My husband valued your advice regarding the Borders."

"He did not always follow the advice I gave him."

"But I will. You understand the ways of the Scottish Border, and you can help me now."

"I am honored, Madame. I will try to help."

"Word has come to me that Scottish Border lords have been approached by English, on behalf of King Henry, with offers of gold," she said.

"Madame," he said. "I have recently been approached myself. And so I intended to speak to you about this matter."

"Do you know who has accepted these bribes, and why?"

He shook his head. "Not yet. A certain English lord made the offer discreetly."

"The regent and Malise Hamilton believe that King Henry

plans to attack Scotland again. Henry may think to purchase support from the Scottish Borderers. He favors bribery, abduction, and intrigue as methods of statesmanship."

"I have accepted this bribe, Madame," William said quietly. "I think you will understand why."

She paused. "Ah. You have decided on your own to act as a spy for me . . . when I was about to suggest the same to you."

He inclined his head in acceptance. "The English think all Scotsmen are in need of money, so they offered me a good sum. Now that I am in their favor, I intend to discover their plans."

She sighed in relief. "King Henry claims to support my daughter as the rightful queen of Scotland, but I fear that he means to harm her. The regent and my advisors do not believe that King Henry is heartless enough to take an infant from her mother." She fisted a hand in her lap. "But I cannot rest at night for fear over my daughter's welfare." Her voice caught.

William understood, utterly, the queen's need for assurance. "I know little of the scheme just now, Madame, but I will tell you what I suspect. As soon as I learn the rest, I will bring word to you."

She nodded gratefully. "That is all I ask. The regent will see to the consequences for those involved."

He leaned forward and spoke in low, urgent tones, explaining what he knew of the situation. Finally, he bowed his head. "I promise, upon my very life," he said, "that the little queen will be made safe."

Chapter Eight

"A poore saffron-cheeke Sun-burnt Gipsie."
—Dekker, *Satiromastix,* 1601

Tamsin stood beside an oak tree, outside the reach of the firelight, and watched the dancing. Her Romany kin whirled and laughed as the wild, poignant music of a viol, played by her cousin, rose into the treetops that encircled the clearing.

She swayed her hips while she stood in the shadows, and tapped out the rhythm with her right hand against her thigh. She hid her left hand behind her out of habit. In the Romany camp, she never wore her concealing glove, for her grandmother thought it an unnecessary and foolish vanity.

Nor had Nona Faw approved of the immodest doublet and breeches that Tamsin had been wearing when she had arrived in the camp. Tamsin had dipped quickly in a stream before donning a woolen skirt and thick plaid shawl over a loose linen chemise, her feet and legs bare. In the camp, she looked much like the other Romany women, but for the uncovered hair that showed she was as yet unmarried.

She glanced around and saw her grandfather talking with one or two men near the area where the horses were penned by ropes slung between the trees. Beyond them, the Border hills were silent and stark in the moonlight. She was relieved that neither her father nor William Scott had followed her here. The camp was tucked in a hollow between high, rugged hills, a difficult location to find unless one knew the site, as she did.

Earlier, she had told her grandfather that she and Archie had been out stealing horses in recompense for sheep Musgrave had taken. She explained that she and her father had been held by Musgrave, and that she had heard Musgrave talk of a plot against the Scots that would somehow use the Romany people, forcing Archie to help him.

She implored her grandfather to make no agreement to help Englishmen or Scots, including her father, until the matter had passed. John Faw had listened, promising to think about what she had told him and discuss it with his kinsmen.

Then her grandmother had called her away, asking Tamsin to help prepare a feast, since that night was the eve of a wedding. The festivities, celebrated by John Faw's band with another band of Romany, had begun several days before, as was the custom.

The bride, Tamsin's young cousin, and groom had not yet exchanged vows. Tamsin's grandfather, as one of the leaders of the Romany in Scotland and northern England, would perform the marriage ceremony that night.

Near the bonfire, the bride, barely fourteen, flashed her dark eyes and her red skirt, and danced flirtatiously around her sixteen-year-old groom. He grinned and took her hand.

Tamsin, seeing the joy and the desire on their young faces, felt a twist of regret and yearning for the husband she would never have, for the wedding feast, the dance, the vows that would never happen for her. Her father's efforts to find a husband for her had failed; her grandfather too had tried among the Romany. She was unwanted and unmarriageable, that much was proven.

Or seemed so. The secret knowledge that she had, indeed, exchanged the precious Romany token of shared wounds, shared blood, with a handsome, desirable man made her heart leap within her. She scowled at her own fancy and folded her arms as she watched her Romany kin around the bonfire.

The music swirled again, and more people came forward to expand the circle of dancers. Tamsin tapped a foot rhythmically in the grass, accustomed to being on the outside of such festivities.

"Join them, girl," a voice said behind her. She turned to see her grandfather approach. He looked at her with solemn black eyes above his long nose and gray beard. "Go on, join them."

"*Kek,* no, Grandfather," she said in Romany. "They will not invite me to dance with them. They think I am *wafri bak,* bad luck, especially at a wedding feast. You know they think I am born under a curse." She half smiled to show him that their opinion did not hurt her. But the truth was not so simple.

"If dancing would bring you joy, I will tell them they must invite you," he said gruffly. He stood beside her, scarcely taller than she was, wide-shouldered and muscular, a strong, dark man who radiated an earthy sort of power.

She shook her head. "No one wants to touch my hand in the circle dance," she said. "Many of them—especially those from the other Romany band—think that I carry ill fortune and will thus give it to them. Some of them even think I possess the evil eye because of my light-colored eyes."

"They are idiots," he said bluntly. "I called you Tchalai myself, for your eyes that remind me of stars. Though your father gave you a Scottish name, after his own kin." He shrugged. "You know that the Faws have never believed that you are cursed, Tchalai."

"I know, Grandfather," she said. "I thank you."

He grunted. "Tchalai, I have thought about the news you brought. We want no trouble with the *gadjo,* nor will I aid any man who mistreats my granddaughter or her father. We will break camp and leave after the wedding, so that no one will find us."

"I am glad," she said. "My father does not want to bring harm to your people. He only agreed so that I could leave that English castle."

John Faw nodded. "Your father is a good man, for a *gadjo.* Though he has not found you a husband." He slid her a glance.

She sighed. "He has tried, Grandfather."

"I know of a man who wants you."

Her heart thumped fast. The face that came to her mind belonged to William Scott. She frowned. Her grandfather did not even know the laird of Rookhope; and she was glad he did not know what had happened between her and that laird. She must be very tired from the ordeal of the last few days, she thought, to let such foolish thoughts distract her.

"What man?" she asked.

He pointed with his thumb toward the bonfire. A man stood on the opposite side of the fire, gaunt but handsome, with a large black mustache. "That is the groom's uncle, Baptiste Lallo. He wants three horses in trade for the two fine ones he brought with him. Or he says he will trade them for you as his wife."

Tamsin gasped. "You would trade me for horses?"

"I have not accepted his offer. I am thinking about it."

"But Grandfather, Baptiste Lallo's father argued with you, and split his band away from the Faw band. All Romany know that the Lallo group are thieves and rascals in England, where they roam! How can you expect me to go with him? How can you sell me to him, like a horse?"

He frowned. "Baptiste's father was a renegade, true, but Baptiste is sincere in his wish for peace with the Faw band. And he is willing to take you, girl. He wants you."

She glanced up, and saw Baptiste looking at her across the clearing. He smiled, his eyes gleaming black points. "But I do not want him!" she said.

"You need a strong Romany husband to tame the unseemly boldness you have learned at your father's knee," John Faw said. "I am thinking it was not good to let you go with Archie Armstrong those years ago. You are not the modest Romany girl you should be. But a Rom husband will teach you to behave with respect and modesty. I do not want you to become the unmarried girl among our people. It is not a fitting state for the granddaughter of the leader."

"I have decided not to wed." She folded her arms.

"Unless you marry, you will grow old scrubbing cooking pots and tending children who are not your own. Your father has not found you a husband, as was his duty. I will now do my best for you."

"Please, not that man," she said.

"This feast, this happy celebration tonight, could be for you, Tchalai. I will give you gold and silver and many fine things when you wed. We will dance for a week."

"I do not want to marry that man!" she cried.

"It is time to heal old differences among our two Romany bands. And I have not yet decided the matter," her grandfather added.

Tamsin bit her lip anxiously. Across the clearing, Baptiste Lallo nodded to her. "Grandfather," she pleaded. "The Lallo band has made a bad name in England for all the Romany."

"That was his father," John Faw said. "I will ask others what they know of Baptiste. And I will consider what you have said. But you will never have a marriage celebration unless we do something for you soon."

Tamsin listened while she watched the Romany whirl about the fire. The pace seemed to quicken her heart, but she felt the burden of her lack of welcome. Suddenly she knew that she did not belong here, where she could be sold to a man for a few horses.

She rubbed her left wrist, feeling the sting of the small cut there. The irony of that tiny wound sliced deep into her heart. She had a marriage, she wanted to shout at her grandfather. Fate had found her a husband, had bonded her to him. He was more kind, more handsome, more skilled and daring than any man John Faw or Archie could find for her.

But in truth, she had only a sad mockery of a marriage, a sacred token made without meaning, without love. No man would truly love her in her life, would willingly marry her, unless he had been paid well to do it.

Despite her proud protests against marriage, she was deeply lonely. That realization crashed through her, heavy and hurting. She too wanted someone with whom to share the small joys and difficulties of each day, each year. Her small hand and mixed heritage did not make her any less a woman, or give her fewer needs and desires.

She stifled a sob, turned on her heel, and fled into the night. Her grandfather called out to her, but she did not glance back. Behind her, the dancers' laughter and the music echoed toward the stars.

She ran on through thick grass, her legs pumping. The wind lifted her hair, ruffled her skirt. All she wanted was to put her own thoughts and anguish behind her if she could. All she wanted was a measure of peace and love in her life.

The full moon, slung high and opalescent in the darkness, lured her up a long slope. The incline was dense with heather, and she slowed to walk through the deep, tufted plants. The tiny blooms were thick and fragrant in the night air, and she broke off a tough stem, covered with fragile bells. She inhaled their sweet, light, calming perfume, and walked onward.

The music faded behind her, replaced by the whisper of the wind and the burble of a stream that cut a tumbling path down the hill. The fragrance of the heather, the cool moonlight, and the steady rush of the burn soothed her emotions as she ascended the slope.

The Romany would not provide the refuge for her that she had hoped. If she disobeyed her grandfather, she could not easily stay with them. But she could not return to her father's home for fear of what the English lord would do.

Besides, she thought, Archie's newfound adulation for William Scott made her feel that, for the first time in her life, she could not rely on Archie for complete support.

He wanted her to marry Rookhope. That thought made her laugh, soft and bitter, as she stood knee-deep in the moonlit heather. The last place she could go for refuge was to Rookhope Tower itself, where another dungeon awaited her.

The breeze rippled through her hair as she walked with no clear idea where she went, lost in her thoughts. The Romany never wandered aimlessly, and always knew their next destination. Tamsin did not.

But then, she reminded herself, she was only half Romany, just as she was half Scot. Now she had begun to wonder, for the first time in her life, where she truly belonged. The answer did not come to her.

At the top of the hill, the wind swept over the peak, stirring her skirt, whipping her hair across her face. She spun to look down over the dark moor below. Tents and wagons dotted the open field, and the bonfire glowed like a hot yellow star fallen to earth.

She thought about her grandfather's words, remembered his criticism of Archie. Her father loved her well, she knew, but he had raised his daughter to be a reiver, not necessarily a lady. She had been given a book education by a dull, kind male tutor, so that she could write and read, even knew French and Latin. But she could not run a household as well as she could play at the cards or coax a flock of sheep from a moonlit pasture.

From the Romany, she had learned a love of freedom that had spoiled her for life in a restrictive manor household. Nature, to her, was teacher, shelter, provider, and a source of constant delight and wonder. The Romany had taught her tricks of cleverness, sleight-of-hand, and how the nuances of the voice could make a lie bright as truth. She could cook hedgehog stew, steal chickens, and weave baskets. She knew how to decipher the map of life in an open palm, could read messages in the picture cards, and knew how to convince people to part with good silver for both services.

But she did not belong fully in either culture. Did a man exist somewhere who could love her for what she was, who could admire what she knew of two cultures? Did a man exist who could love her with her flaws?

William Scott came insistently to her thoughts. She closed her eyes, shook her head to dispel his image.

She walked up the hill, distracted by her thoughts. The stream to her right sounded like soft thunder, and the wind buffeted her as she stepped onto the crest of the hill. The thunder was even louder here, an insistent pounding. She turned. And gasped.

A few feet away, a horse rose over the rim of the hill like a dark vision. The animal bolted toward her, a demon in the night, dark and strong. A rider hunkered low on its back, armor glimmering in the cool moonlight.

Tamsin screamed and stepped back, stumbling as the horse bore down upon her. Behind it, another horse soared over the hilltop, and then a third, rising in the night like dark ghosts. The fierce sound of beating hooves mingled with the howling wind.

"Out of the way!" someone shouted. "Move!"

Her foot struck a rock and she fell hard, slamming to the earth. She scrambled to get out of the path of the oncoming horses, instinctively raising her arm in front of her face.

The front rider shouted again as his horse streamed past, leaping over her as she crawled free. An iron hoof caught her a glancing, painful blow in the thigh. She half dragged herself away and curled in terror as the other horses thundered by within inches of her.

The first rider circled and came back, drawing the horse to a restive halt beside her. As Tamsin struggled to her knees, the horse whickered and bucked. The rider spoke calmly, then looked down at Tamsin.

"Are you hurt?" he asked.

She looked up. He was silhouetted against the white moon, and at first she saw only the massive horse and its wide-shouldered rider. The man's steel helmet glimmered in the low light. Beyond him, the other riders turned and waited.

She tried to stand, but her injured leg buckled under her. She half collapsed with a low cry.

The man leaned down, held out a gauntleted hand, and swore.

"Tamsin Armstrong," she heard William Scott growl, "what the devil are you doing out here?"

Chapter Nine

"... wretched, wily wandering vagabonds calling and naming them selues Egiptians ... delyting ... with the strangeness of the attyre of their heades, and practising paulmistrie to such as would know their fortunes."
—Thomas Harmon, *Caveat of Common Cursetors*, 1567

William stared down at Tamsin in the moonlight. She plainly gaped at him. Then she whirled and took a step. Her leg seemed to collapse under her, and she half fell to the ground.

"You canna walk far like that. Come up here." William leaned toward her and held out his hand, intending to lift her up behind him. The bay, already agitated by the sudden appearance of the girl in his path, sidled nervously under him. William tightened his knees to control his mount, and stretched to grab the girl's arm. "Come up, and hurry. They'll be after us soon!"

"Who?" She pulled, resisting, as he tried to haul her up.

He glanced over his shoulder. The steady beat of horse hooves, an incessant, faint sound that he had heard for too long now, grew even louder. "Up, lass, or be trampled for certain!"

Bless her for quick wits, he thought. She gasped at the increasing thunder of approaching horses and reached up in the darkness. William lifted her, his fingers closing over her left forearm. Her feet cleared the ground, and she rested one bare foot on his leg to vault neatly into position behind him, despite her injured leg. She wrapped her arms tightly around his waist.

"Nicely done," he commented, and let the bay launch forward. He hunkered low, and felt the girl do the same, her arms secure about him. Ahead, his comrades—his cousins Jock and Sandie Scott, who were in turn cousins to each other—galloped ahead.

A backward glance showed their pursuers clearing the rim of

the hill. The riders' armor and weapons caught a cruel, cold gleam in the moonlight. William urged the bay ahead, down the long, gradual slope toward the moor. As the ground leveled, William gave the bay full rein, and they overtook his cousins within moments.

One of William's cousins whooped as the bay passed him, and both spurred their horses to a faster gallop, barely managing to catch the bay. Behind them, William could hear the other horses pounding in fierce pursuit.

In one direction, he saw the golden sparks of several campfires. In another, the hills rose high and dark against the moonlit sky. Unwilling to risk the horses farther in the hills at night, he veered for the campfires. His cousins followed him down the slope.

He glanced at the girl when they reached the base of the hill. "Hold tight," he said, and urged the bay forward.

The horse had a powerful, long stride at full gallop. A cousin rode to either side of him, steel bonnets gleaming, lances and pistols at hand. The rhythm of the horses' hooves seemed to match the pace of his heart, seemed to stir, in that meter, his pride and his power.

He felt exhilarated, his spirit heightened within him by the speed and the danger and knowledge of who he was, what he was. A reiver and a rogue, as his father had been, and his father before him, a long, uninterrupted line of Scotsmen who fought, in their way, for freedom of land, of heart and spirit, though they were called scoundrels for it rather than warriors.

Jock drew even with him, a smile on his handsome face beneath the steel helmet, his long blond hair fanning out. Jock felt the same thrill, William realized. The reason for the pursuit—the theft of a few English cows, and a kiss stolen from an English girl—was forgotten in the heady risk of the chase.

William turned and saw Sandie's face, lit by a bright grin. William knew that his stocky, red-bearded cousin took pride and delight in the knowledge that some English had been harried and aggravated that night.

William smiled to himself as he rode onward. He felt the weight of the girl at his back, felt the press of her thighs to either side of his own. She was calm and bold, which pleased him. He was not surprised that Archie Armstrong's daughter took a fast chase over a dark moor in stride.

Behind them, four Forsters and Arthur Musgrave were determined to apprehend them. Jock and Sandie had taken advantage of the moonlight to ride into England to visit with an English girl. Anna Forster was betrothed to Arthur Musgrave, according to the wishes of both fathers, but she and Jock had met and fallen in love a few months ago. William knew that Jock had been riding out to meet Anna secretly for quite a while.

He had accompanied his cousins, planning to venture out in search of the gypsy camp, since Sandie and Jock had said that they knew where it was. While Jock had met with Anna, Sandie had snatched a few Musgrave cows and had herded them onto Forster land for a prank. This, and Jock's clandestine meeting with Anna Forster, had brought a host of Forsters, and Arthur Musgrave as well, on their tails for the remainder of the night.

William knew his own risk in this night's endeavor. If Arthur Musgrave recognized him, his arrangement with Jasper Musgrave would be jeopardized, and a feud started between them.

He glanced back. Their pursuers had fallen behind. A line of trees edged the moor, and William veered toward those, slowing the bay to a canter. His cousins followed, and they made their way between thick birches, slowing under cover of the trees.

William watched over his shoulder. Their pursuers might have lost the trail in the darkness, but he would make no assumptions. He urged the bay ahead, guiding him cautiously toward the other side of the wooded area.

He turned to look at the girl, who gripped him hard around the waist. She lifted her head. "Who rides after you?" she asked.

"English," he said. "Forsters. Arthur Musgrave."

"Musgrave! Why would you run from him, or any English?" she asked in a bitter tone. "I'd think you would be eager to meet with them."

"My comrades—my cousins—brought them on our tail, after a ride south to visit a certain English lass. As it happens, Arthur is her betrothed. He and her brothers gave chase."

"Why are you part of this?" she asked. "When last I saw you, you were on your way to Rookhope." The false sweetness in her tone made him want to grind his teeth.

"I would not be out here if you hadna run off," he said.

"You didna need to go after me."

"Indeed I did," he drawled. "Ho! Jock! Sandie! This way!" He waved to the others to follow.

Sandie drew alongside of him. "Will, ask your gypsy if she belongs to that camp across the moor."

"Gypsy?" William looked at Tamsin in mock surprise. "I thought we'd picked up a wildcat on the hill." She made a face at him, and he smiled full at her.

"Is this the lass you told us about?" Jock looked at her. "The one in your keeping?"

"I'm in no one's keeping," she snapped.

"Hey, Archie Armstrong's lass!" Sandie peered at her. "I've heard tales o' this one. A wild one, they say."

"Wild enough," William drawled. He looked back, and saw the dark forms of the English riders through the trees. "Come on!" he said quietly, and cantered toward the open field at the other side of the trees.

Within moments, the pursuers saw them, and shouted. William urged the horse over another fast stretch of moorland.

The girl lifted a hand to point. "Ride that way, toward those trees," she called. "There's a bog there, but you can avoid it if you keep to the far side of the trees. Lead your cousins in a single line. If the English follow, they willna see the bog in the dark."

William nodded and rode cautiously over the soft ground. The treacherous surface was little more than a subtle gleam among the thick, tufted grasses.

As he reached the far end of the pass, with Sandie and Jock behind him, he heard splashes and turned to see the Forsters and Musgrave floundering in the shallow bog. Four of their horses had stepped, whinnying and protesting, into the dark, slimy pool. A fifth rider stayed on solid ground and halted his horse. William turned to guide his bay toward the camp as Jock and Sandie glided ahead.

Tamsin tightened her grip on his waist. "A pistol!" she said. "I saw the flame of a matchlock!"

William reacted quickly, spinning the bay, aware that Tamsin's back was a direct target for a pistol shot. He lifted a crossbow from a saddle loop and aimed it at the rider behind them. He too could see the spark now. He loosed the crossbow bolt.

The explosion of the matchlock echoed over the bog. William heard a buzz like that of a bee, and felt a sharp pressure in his arm. He knew he had been hit, though he felt no pain. He knew the quarrel he had released found its mark. One man shrieked in the darkness and fell backward.

Pressing his wounded arm close to his side, William jammed the crossbow into the saddle loop and gathered his reins to take up a ferocious pace, while the pain seared and grew. The bay seemed to sail over the soft ground. Ahead, the glow of the gypsy campfires grew larger.

He turned to glance at Tamsin. "Are your kin here?"

"My grandparents," she answered. She briefly rested her left hand on his upper sleeve. "Oh! You're hurt!"

In the moonlight, a dark stain filled her curled palm. As William turned, Tamsin hastily wiped her hand on her shawl. "You've been shot!"

"Aye." He lifted his arm a little and winced at the burning pain. " 'Twill be fine. We need to ride on."

"We must stop here and tend to it," she said.

"We canna take the risk. They will soon shake loose that bog and be after us again."

"The bog slowed them, and one of them is wounded. Stop here and let me look at your wound," she said firmly. She touched his sleeve. "There is a great hole in your arm, and much bleeding. It needs attention now."

He shook his head. "Later. We will ride on."

"We?"

"You," he said, looking down at her, "are coming with me to Rookhope, as was agreed."

"Oh, nay, I willna," she said, and began to slide her leg over the horse. William caught her arm.

"You will," he said. "Dinna forget you canna walk far on that leg. You're wounded yourself."

"Then we both need to stop here."

"If we stop, you stay with me," he said firmly. "I said I would keep you for a fortnight. Your own father wants it."

"Hah! I'm sure he does," she said.

He looked at her, puzzled. A shout sounded, and William looked up to see his cousins riding back toward them. "We heard gunfire," Jock said. "What happened?"

"A pistol ball caught William," Tamsin said quickly.

Jock rode closer. "By God!"

"The bleeding must be stopped," she said. "My grandmother and I can tend to it if he comes into the camp."

Jock glanced at William. "Let her take care of it—'tis a long ride back to Rookhope. 'Tis said the gypsies are fine healers."

"This gypsy has no care to heal me, only to get her distance from me," William said, looking steadily at her through the dark.

"I can remove a pistol ball, if need be," she said. "I've removed many balls from men. Pistol balls."

Sandie hooted. William twisted his lips to keep from smiling. "I dinna doubt that," he drawled.

"Sandie and I will lead the English away from here," Jock said. "You can safely ride to the camp and beg hospitality of the gypsies."

William sighed in reluctant agreement. "Only long enough to get my arm tended," he said. "Ride on to Rookhope and tell my kin to expect me home soon."

"Aye, then," Jock said, gathering his reins. "Keep him safe, gypsy. There's a wee lassie who canna do without him back at his tower." He grinned at William.

"See you keep that lassie safe," William said.

"Always," Jock said in a serious tone. He turned his horse, and he and Sandie galloped away.

Tamsin lifted her right hand to point. "There—that great bonfire in the center of camp is near my grandfather's wagon. He is the leader of these people. My grandmother and I will see to your wound, and then you can be on your way."

"And you with me," he growled.

As they drew near, he heard music and laughter. He saw a large group of people clustered near the bonfire, many of them dancing, most of them smiling as they talked, or ate, or watched the dancers. Music swirled throughout the campsite, a rapid meter and intriguing melody. The tempting scent of roasting meats filled the air.

A few dogs barked as William and Tamsin rode into the camp. Some of the gypsy men called the dogs back and stepped forward. The dancing stopped and the music faded into silence as fifty or more people watched them warily.

William halted the horse near an oak tree at the edge of the campsite. Some of the gypsies walked closer, their gazes suspicious. The sudden silence, filled only by the crackling bonfire and the wind, seemed eerie. William was aware that he was a conspicuous, and probably unwelcome, outsider.

"They look displeased to see us," he murmured.

"Since I am the one bringing you here, your arrival may be regarded as an ill omen." He glanced at her, wondering what she meant.

"Is this a Romany feast day?" William asked. They had interrupted some sort of celebration, he realized. Beneath the shelter of a grove of trees, in the golden glow of a bonfire, the tawny-hued gypsies stared at him with clear distrust.

"My cousin's wedding feast," she answered. He felt her tense behind him and sit straighter. Her arms fell away from his waist. Oddly, he missed their pressure.

An older man came toward them, his eyes an onyx gleam in his high-cheeked face, his beard long and gray above his barrel-chested torso. He stopped and glared at both of them. Then he spoke sharply to the girl in a strange language, the sounds blunt, rapid, and rhythmic; William realized he spoke Romany, the tongue of the gypsies.

"*Rya,*" Tamsin answered, bowing her head. She began a rapid stream of the same language. William knew the word *rya*. Other gypsies, whom he had infrequently encountered in the past, had used it as a term of respect for gypsy men as well as nongypsy gentlemen.

The old man looked angry, and William tensed. He was also aware of the suspicious gazes of the men who gathered a few feet behind the old man. He must be her grandfather, William thought, for he had the confident look of a leader. The others waited quietly while he spoke.

The bay shifted beneath them and William soothed him, reaching out to pat the broad neck. Pain seared again when he moved his arm. Glancing down, he saw blood soaking his sleeve, and he covered the wound with his other hand. Warm blood seeped through his fingers.

The old man stepped forward and held his arms up to the girl, clearly ordering her down from the horse. She slid down, limber and quick despite her injured leg, but William heard her intake of breath as she stood beside the horse. Her grandfather spoke to her in low tones while she shook her head.

Unwilling to let the girl bear the brunt of her grandfather's anger, William vaulted down from the saddle to stand beside her. In armor and steel bonnet, he towered over both the old man and the girl. She was of medium height, for the top of her dark head was even with his jaw, but she seemed slight without the bulk of the jack, doublet, and boots she had worn before. He glanced down at her while she spoke earnestly to her grandfather.

Her profile was delicate and exotic, the nose straight, the lips full, the chin fine, her eyes large beneath dark brows. Her dark hair spilled past her shoulders, rippled and silky. Thin golden hoops sparkled through the black curtain, while silver gleamed at her slender throat.

She was a comely lass, William thought, born of a people known for natural beauty. When she glanced up at him, he was amazed once again by the color of her eyes, cool and green in her warm, dusky face.

He studied her, fascinated, while she spoke with her grandfather. Her clothing was soft and simple, her feet bare. She wore a dark skirt and bodice over a linen chemise, and a tartaned plaid as a shawl, with her hair loose. The other women, except the girls, all wore cloths wrapped snugly around their heads.

While Tamsin spoke to her grandfather, holding one hand tucked under her cloak, some of the gypsies came forward to stare at William. The dogs continued to bark, and a few children cried, comforted and held, he noticed, by women and men alike.

The grandfather glanced at William, his eyes keen and cautious. Then he nodded and crossed his arms flat over his chest, bowing his head to William.

In the few times he had met with gypsies in the past, William had seen this form of gypsy greeting. Unable to fold both arms over his chest in a proper return greeting, he bent his right arm over his heart, bloody hand folded, and bowed his head.

"Welcome, *rya*," the old man said.

"My thanks, *rya*," William said. "I apologize for disrupting your celebration. May I beg hospitality of you?"

"My grandchild, Tchalai, says you saved her life when she was beneath the feet of a horse," the man went on. His English was heavily accented. "And you have taken a hurt in your arm. Because Tchalai owes you, her grandmother and myself owe you too. You are welcome to join our feast."

"I thank you. But your granddaughter owes me naught, nor do you. 'Tis I who owe my life to your granddaughter." He glanced down at the girl. "I might have been killed if she hadna warned me in time to avoid a pistol shot to the back," he said, keeping his gaze linked to hers. She lowered her eyes. "I must beg help of a healer. I will offer you coin in return."

The old man shook his head. "No coin! We owe you, good *rya*. I am John Faw, earl of Lesser Egypt, and these are my retinue." His hand swept toward the other gypsies. "We are pilgrims traveling through your fair Scotland. What is your nom, Border *manús*? Where do you come from?"

"My name is William Scott. I am the laird of Rookhope Tower, in Liddesdale."

"Rookhope! We know that stone tower." The old man frowned. "I remember a man called Allan Scott of Rookhope."

"He was my father," William murmured.

John Faw placed a hand over his heart and inclined his head. "*Rya*, your father was generous to the Romany. He gave us shelter and food, though we heard it said he was a fierce thief."

"I remember, as a lad, that he allowed gypsies—ah, Romany—to camp on his lands, and to tend his horses. If you come to Rookhope lands, be assured that I will do the same."

John Faw smiled. "You have our thanks! The son of Allan Scott is welcome here. He was a good friend to our Tchalai's father."

"Aye, he was," William said quietly.

Faw spread his spatulate fingers in a welcoming gesture. "You will stay, and share our food, and let my countess heal your hurts. Nona! Nona!" He headed toward one of the wagons, and William followed.

A cloth lifted from a doorway at the back of the gypsy van, and light spilled forth. A flood of Romany poured out with it. Nona Faw stood in the doorway of the wagon and flapped her hands at her husband. She pointed a finger toward William, and both Faws spoke in low, fierce tones.

"She doesna want me here," William murmured to Tamsin. "Perhaps I should leave, after all."

"When they finish arguing, they will let you in. But they will take their time. They enjoy quarreling."

"They enjoy it?" He looked askance at her.

"Aye, my grandfather says. Nona's anger fires him up to passion like a young bull." She smiled, a quick flash of white, and William stared at her. "Be patient, William Scott. The gypsies dinna rush any matter."

"I can be patient as a stone," he muttered, taking his bloodied hand away from his sleeve, "but not when I am bleeding."

"Ah, men, they are weak like kittens," Tamsin said, her tone imitating her grandfather's rhythm of speech. William saw a teasing glitter in her eyes. She pushed at his back. "See, they are waving toward you now. Go in," she urged. "My grandfather says he will see to your horse. Go in."

He gave her a skeptical glance, looked with even greater doubt at the old woman who scowled at him from the wagon steps, and stepped forward when Tamsin gave him another light shove.

Chapter Ten

"The idle peopill calling themselves Aegiptians . . . that have knowledge of Charming, Prophecie, or uthers abused sciences . . ."

—Acts of the Scottish Parliament, 1579

William entered the wagon, dipping his head low to clear the canvas doorway. Behind him, he heard the music start again, and heard John Faw call out to someone. Tamsin mounted the steps too, stepping into the wagon after him.

Nona Faw gestured a welcome. She was a wizened elf of a woman, brown and wrinkled as a dried apple, swathed in a striped shawl and a pale headcloth. A necklace of gold and silver coins gleamed on her bosom. Her eyes glittered like jet, intelligent in their creased settings. She pushed him toward a cushioned bench that lined the opposite wall of the narrow space.

The wagon, he saw, was a tent erected on a long cart bed, somewhat like a traveling van used for noblewomen. Overhead, wooden struts supported a canvas covering. Inside, the space was snug and smoky, crammed with cushions, benches, and baskets. Coals glowed in a brazier on the floor. Smoke curled out of a hole in the canvas cover, and the low ceiling was draped with swaths of cloth, making the interior quiet and cozy.

William edged around the brazier, while Nona let forth a spate of Romany directed at him. He looked at Tamsin.

"She says to sit," she said.

"She said more than that. Tell me exactly what she said, if you will," he murmured. He eyed the old woman warily as she continued to ramble on in Romany and wave her hands.

"Very well. She says to sit, sit, sit, bleeding and wounded

Scotsman who saved her granddaughter's life from thieves and murderers in the moonlight," Tamsin translated. "She says she is not afraid of blood, show her your gory wound, she will not faint. She says she is a woman, not a weakling man."

"Thank you," William drawled.

Tamsin's eyes were bright with humor. "Sit."

He sat, and the girl stepped past him, tripping over the wide toe of his boot. She winced and her cheeks turned pale. Her grandmother spoke to her, and she answered, shaking her head.

"You hurt your leg when you fell on the moor," William said.

" 'Tis a bruise. I will be fine. You are the one bleeding to death, after all."

"Ease that tongue of yours, I am cut to the quick already." He took his hand from his sleeve, his palm filled with blood.

"Aiieee," Nona said, and whirled to fetch some cloths.

Tamsin peered at his arm and touched his sleeve. " 'Tis deep, I see now," she murmured. "I didna mean to mock you." She turned to speak to her grandmother.

Nona came toward him and clapped a folded cloth to his arm, pressing it tightly. He sucked in a breath, and the pad grew red with blood.

When she poked at the gash with strong fingers, bright spots swam before William's eyes. He drew a long breath to resist the power of momentary agony. Nona spoke to Tamsin.

"The pistol ball is gone," Tamsin translated. "It tore through your arm. The wound has bled out, and looks clean."

"Good," he said. "I think she would have dug the ball out with her fingers if it had still been in there. Your grandmother has an unforgiving touch."

Nona knocked hard on his breastplate and snapped at him in Romany. William looked at Tamsin.

"She says to take off that metal shirt and your doublet."

He nodded and removed his helmet, shoving his fingers through his dark hair. Then, while Nona worked at his arm, he began to unfasten a shoulder buckle awkwardly with one hand. Tamsin reached out to assist him with her right hand, her left fisted at her waist.

"Two hands would help most here," he said. "Does your left hand still hurt you?"

"I told you before, it isna injured. My left hand . . . isna good for small work," she said. He nodded, concentrating on the task. Together they undid the buckles and lifted the back and breast pieces away. Nona stepped away to fetch something else, and William held the cloth over his wound.

Tamsin knelt before him. With the nimble fingers of one hand, she undid the long row of hooks and loops that closed the front of the leather doublet he wore beneath the armor. He recalled doing the same task for her not long ago. His subtle surrender as he waited gave him a pleasant feeling of intimacy.

When she leaned close, he sensed a subtle fragrance about her, like heather on the wind. She worked her way down the row of hooks, her breathing soft. Her lashes were thick and black against her cheeks, and her eyelids half hid the clear pools of her eyes. He noticed too the lush curves and swells beneath her clothing. A rush of desire flooded unexpectedly through him, hot and fast. He cleared his throat.

"Ah," he said. "What is it your grandparents call you? Chahl-i?" He tried to pronounce it.

"Tchalai," she murmured, softening the sound. "It means 'star.' They dinna use my Scots name, Thomasine, which my father gave to me for his father, Thomas Armstrong of Merton Rigg."

"Star," he said quietly. He understood the name. " 'Tis fitting. Your eyes . . ." A wave of weakness swept him, and tiny spots floated past his eyes. The wagon interior grew dim. He shook his head slightly and leaned his shoulders against a crude wooden panel behind him.

Tamsin frowned. "William Scott? Will?"

He watched her as if in a dream. Her eyes were green and liquid, like moss seen through a shimmer of water. He had never seen eyes so luminous. All else around him began to fade.

"William," she said sharply. He stirred, tried to answer, but felt slow and heavy, as if he swam through thick fog. "You look pale as the moon," Tamsin said. Nona handed her a cup, and she held it to his lips. "Drink."

He swallowed the liquid, wine sweetened with honey. Tamsin

watched him, her hand on his shoulder. Within moments, he felt clearer. Tamsin pulled at his doublet, and he shrugged it off. "Press hard on the wound," she said.

She tugged at his wide-sleeved linen shirt, grasping the cloth in that odd way he had noticed, with her fisted left; the hand was bare, and he noticed that the back of it was small and fine-boned. She drew the shirt off of him and set it aside. Cool air drifted over his naked back, but heat from the glowing brazier warmed his chest and arms.

"You have lost a lot of blood," Tamsin said. "Lie down." She pushed gently at his chest, her right palm a pool of heat on his skin. He leaned back onto a pile of pillows.

A few feet away, Nona stirred the contents of a small clay jar with a finger and spoke to Tamsin, grinning in an elfin way. She came over to sit beside William on the bench.

"What did she say?" William asked.

"She thinks you are a beautiful man. As pleasing as the Romany men, who are well-known for their handsomeness." Nona spoke again. Tamsin replied. "She says she will use a healing ointment on your wound, but there will be a scar. She says your wife will like it. A man looks good with a scar or two to show his bravery, my grandmother says."

"I dinna have a wife. And I have scars aplenty."

"I told her that. These look like they were once fierce wounds," Tamsin said softly. She touched a nick on his chin, and a long, shiny scar across the front of his shoulder. Her touch was soft, smooth, warm.

"Swordplay, as a lad," William explained.

"I hope you have improved since then," she remarked.

"Aye," he said, with a little laugh.

Nona clucked her tongue as she applied a damp cloth to his wound, and spoke again. "My grandmother says I must not touch you," Tamsin explained. "And she says your scars are small flaws." Her wide eyes were deep and serious. "Some have far greater flaws, believe me. Be proud of your beauty, and the perfection of your body."

He knew somehow that those were her own words rather than her grandmother's. He suppressed a groan as Nona slathered oint-

ment over the deep gouge and pinched the edges of the wound together, then wrapped it in snug cloth strips. She fashioned a sling
for him with some cloth, and cleaned the dried blood from his
arm and hands.

"My thanks, madame," he enunciated to the old woman, half
sitting up. She pushed him back, not gently.

"You be welcome, Border *manús*," Nona replied. She gave him
a toothless, charming grin. William lifted a brow in surprise.

"She knows some English, when she wants to use it," Tamsin
said. She picked up his leather doublet. "My grandfather can
patch the hole in the leather. This is a fine garment. Spanish
make, I think, with such an ornate pierced pattern and rolled
shoulder caps."

"Aye. I bought it in Edinburgh from a tailor who had purchased
cloth and leather goods from a Spanish trader."

Nona leaned forward and stroked the leather, exclaiming in her
language, clearly admiring the garment. "She likes fancy gear,"
Tamsin said.

"I will send her something fancy as a gift of thanks," he said.
"What would she like best? Silks or jewelry? Spanish leather? I
owe her a debt for tending to my arm."

"She would like that, William Scott. Anything that sparkles
would please her."

"I will send her some precious baubles and a bolt of silk."

"Not red," Tamsin said quickly. "She never wears red."

"She would look fine in red." He watched her. "As would you,
lass," he murmured. More than fine, he thought; she would glow
in that color. Even the reddish light of the brazier touched flame
to her cheeks and brightened her eyes.

"I never wear red either," she said. " 'Twas my mother's favorite color. We will never wear it again, out of grief."

"My condolences. Did she die very recently?"

"When I was born," she said.

William gave her a quick, bemused look. "What was that,
twenty years ago?"

She blushed, her cheeks growing deep pink. "More than that,"
she said. " 'Tis the Romany way of mourning, to remember loved
ones forever," she explained. "Her name is never spoken. Even if

another person has that name, we do not say it. Her favorite foods are not eaten by her family, her favorite song is not sung. My grandmother does not wear red, nor do I, and my grandfather will no longer eat honey, since his daughter loved it so well. You may think it odd, but 'tis the Romany way to show grief."

"I understand, lass," William murmured. "I do." He glanced away, thinking of his father, and of his own abhorrence for nooses, and how the sight of an oak tree could bring back memories both sad and fine. And how his daughter's smile could remind him so keenly of Jean that sometimes he had to turn away.

"The Romany love with passion," she said, as if she needed to defend the customs of her mother's people. "They dinna give up their dead easily. And they love forever."

" 'Tis the best way to love," he said softly. Her words seemed to echo in his head, in his heart, touching a current of passion and pain that still streamed through him, the result of the deaths of his father, and recently, of Jeanie Hamilton. "No one gives up memories of the dead easily, lass," he said.

"I have been fortunate," she said. "The only one I have lost has been my mother, and I didna know her at all."

"Fortunate indeed," he murmured. "Tell me, what will you have for yourself, Tamsin the gypsy? Nona will have silks and baubles. What would please you? I owe you for helping me too."

"You owe me naught. You saved my life at Musgrave's castle." She touched her fingers to the slight bruises at the base of her throat. The sight made his blood simmer with anger again.

"Nevertheless, I pay my debts. What will you have?"

"The only thing I want of you is my freedom."

"That," he said, "I canna give you."

"You can," she whispered. "None would know but you and I. You can ride to Rookhope, and tell Musgrave you lost me."

"But I wouldna want to lose you," he said in a low voice. "I have given my word to keep you well, and I will do that." She looked at him silently, her eyes crystalline green. A curious thrill coursed through him.

While he spoke, Nona sat beside him. She took his right hand in hers, turning it palm up, and smoothed her fingertips over his skin, tracing the lines of his palm with a yellowed fingernail. None spoke quietly.

"She says you have good luck in your hand," Tamsin said.

"Of course. Good luck, a long life, wealth." He shrugged.

Her brow furrowed. She clearly disliked his response. "My grandmother doesna tell lies for silver, as some might think. She sees your life written in your hand. She sees your past and your future, and all that is in your heart and your head."

"Did you see that, when you looked there?" he asked.

She frowned. " 'Twas dark," she said curtly. "But if I looked again, aye, I could read your life."

"But I like my secrets," he murmured.

"What you truly want to hide canna be revealed to us."

"I once read something about the art of palmistry," he said. "An Italian treatise, a book that King James had in his library. Palmistry has a reputation in Europe as a science rather than as divination. Many physicians there use that, and the art of phrenology, to help them understand their patients."

"Wise men," she commented. She nodded when Nona spoke again. "My grandmother says you had a tragedy as a lad, and after that you were surrounded by wealth and power, and you are wealthy now. She says you still feel poor and lonely, an outcast." Nona spoke, and Tamsin nodded. "She says you have lost two whom you loved. A parent. A lover. She says . . . that you are a father yourself." She looked at him, questioning.

"I am," he said gruffly. She tilted her head in curiosity, but did not ask, and he did not offer.

Nona spoke again, and Tamsin listened. A little frown creased her smooth brow. "She says," she began, "that a deep love, a love that is destined to be fulfilled, will be part of your life. You know this woman, she says." She lowered her eyelids and glanced away. "You must claim her or you will never be truly happy."

He withdrew his hand quickly from Nona's grasp. Though he doubted such a love would ever come to him, he did not know how the old woman had discerned the other details about his life. But he would listen to no more. He liked his secrets and his privacy.

"Tell her that I will give her coin for her tricks."

"She doesna do tricks," Tamsin snapped. "She isna a monkey or a bear. You said yourself 'tis a science. A person doesna have to be a university-trained physician to practice this and do it correctly." Still holding his leather doublet in her hands, she went to the doorway of the wagon.

Nona, oblivious to their exchange, smiled at William and walked over to stand beside the girl. They spoke quietly, and Tamsin shook her head, murmuring.

William stood, bringing on a wave of dizziness. He ducked his head beneath the low cloth-slung ceiling. "Lass," he said. "My doublet, if you please. And ready yourself. We must leave for Rookhope."

She did not look over her shoulder. "You will stay," she replied. "You need to rest. And in the morn, when you leave, I willna go with you." She spoke again to Nona, who turned and strode toward William, chattering in Romany, and then shoved at his chest. He sat, and Nona nodded. She pointed to the pillows until he stretched out with reluctance.

"She says you will sleep here, as our guest," Tamsin explained. "My grandmother and her husband will sleep beneath the stars so that the fine gentleman can recover on their bed."

"I willna take their bed," he muttered, sitting up again. His head spun, and he admitted to himself that he might benefit from a little rest. "Tell her I can sleep on the ground beneath the wagon."

"I canna tell her that! 'Tis where I sleep." Nona spoke again. "She says you must close your eyes. She wants to tend to my leg now."

William complied, leaning back and closing his eyes. He heard murmuring, heard Tamsin wince, heard Nona scold her, then a long silence. Thinking they were done, he opened his eyes.

Tamsin stood with her back to him, her skirt pulled high on one side, left leg extended, knee slightly bent. A large purple bruise darkened her thigh. Nona applied the same ointment to it, with a far gentler hand than she had used on William.

He closed his eyes quickly. But he could not easily dispel the sight of that long, gracefully shaped leg, with the red light of the brazier sliding along the smooth, slender curves. His blood heated within him, rousing his body to a pleasant state, not quite arousal, but a kind of definite awareness.

A commotion sounded in the camp beyond the wagon. William opened his eyes, seeing Tamsin drop her skirt hem and turn toward the door. He sat up, recognizing the fast beat of horse hooves. Tamsin and Nona peered through the doorway, talking in low, agitated voices.

"Aiiee!" Nona said, and flapped her hands, pointing at William, chattering rapidly to Tamsin. She bent to rummage through a large basket and pulled out a bundle of clothing.

"What is it?" William asked.

Tamsin turned. "Arthur Musgrave!" she hissed. "He and another man have just ridden into the camp!"

He grabbed his shirt and strode toward her. "Give me my doublet!" Rest be damned, he thought. He needed to get to his horse and his weapons, which were slung on the saddle.

If Arthur Musgrave saw him, there would be trouble, but he could lead the riders away from the camp. The gypsies had helped him when he needed it, and he wanted no harm to come to them in return. He would have to come back for Tamsin, he realized.

Nona thrust the bundle at William, talking insistently. He took it, puzzled, and looked at Tamsin.

"She says you must put those on and stay here!"

"Nay. I must go out." He pulled on his shirt, suppressing a groan as he put his arm in the sleeve, then took the doublet from her and tried to do the same, but Nona shoved hard at him.

"What the devil does she want?" he demanded. He pulled on the doublet, catching his breath in agony, and lifted his helmet to jam it on his head. He hoisted his steel breastplate with one hand, and Nona smacked the armor, spilling a flood of Romany. The sound of horses, and men shouting, grew even louder.

"Please, William Scott, listen to her," Tamsin said. She came toward him and pulled at the armor he was trying to fasten. "My grandmother says you must hide in here until these men are gone. We willna let them know that you are with us."

"Hide? Dinna be foolish."

"Do it, or you will bring trouble to this camp! These men mean to take you down! They tried to kill you!"

"I willna hide from scoundrels."

"If anyone is killed in this camp, or nearby, the Romany will be blamed and punished! Put these on!"

He stopped, hampered by her, and by his own clumsiness, unable to don anything with two angry females determined to stop him. "What alarms you so?" he asked Tamsin.

"They hang gypsies for naught, you know that!"

"No one will be hanged," he bit out, working the buckles of his armor.

"And if trouble occurs at my cousin's wedding, 'twill curse her marriage! Bad luck will always follow the bride and groom."

"Nonsense," he said firmly. "I will lead the riders away from the camp, and no one will have bad luck of them but me. I can shake them loose without trouble." He turned to lift the door flap. "And then I will come back for you," he added.

Nona yanked at his arm. He nearly yowled in pain. She mumbled in rapid Romany, waving the ragged bundle she held.

"Please," Tamsin said. "Please, William Scott. You dinna understand—this is very bad."

"Why?" he asked, breathlessly, fighting pain, trying to shake loose Nona's insistent hand on his arm.

"Dinna go out there. If anything happens at all, I will be to blame. I couldna bear that. I am . . . *wafri bak* among these people," she said quietly. "Bad luck. Some of the Romany believe that ill fortune comes to them when I am around."

"Why so? Because you are part Scots?"

She shook her head, clenching her left hand into a tight little fist, putting it behind her back. "Please just wait here. Let my grandfather and the others send these men on their way." She glanced up at him, her eyes like green pools. He saw a need reflected there, so genuine and surprising that he ached in his heart to see it.

"What is it, lass?" he asked. "What bothers you so?"

She shook her head. "Please, William Scott. You said you owed me a favor. Pay me, then, by staying here."

William sighed, and took the cloth bundle from Nona's hands.

Chapter Eleven

But I'll a fortune-telling go,
And our fortunes make thereby
Well said, my little gypsy girl,
You counsel famously.

—English Gypsy Song

"Your grandfather is leading them this way," William whispered a while later. Standing beside Tamsin, he peered through a slitted opening in the closed canvas doorway.

John Faw strolled toward the wagon with two men in helmets and leather jacks, and paused to speak with them. "They may know me, despite this gypsy gear I'm wearing." William indicated his borrowed clothing. "If they see me, I canna guarantee peace. They will know 'twas I with Jock and Sandie."

"Grandfather has told them that we have seen no Bordermen all evening. But now they ask to have an Egyptian woman tell their fortunes before they leave."

"I heard. Your grandfather could have refused."

"They offered coin," she said, shrugging. "And my grandmother is well known among the *gadjo* for fortune-telling." She turned and spoke to Nona, who sat in the back of the wagon. The old woman waved her hands and whispered rapidly.

"What does she want?" William asked.

"She wants me to go outside and talk to the men and tell their fortunes for silver." While she spoke, she reached into a basket and withdrew a pale silken scarf, which she wound around her left fist. "Since I speak their language, I can read their palms more quickly than Nona, so they will leave sooner."

"Arthur Musgrave will know you," he said quietly.

"Aye," she said simply. "He may. But I am protected here. By the time he tells his father, I will be gone."

"Aye, to Rookhope."

She shrugged and did not answer.

William peered over the top of her head at the men who spoke with John Faw in the flickering light of the bonfire. "Very well, then," he said decisively. "We'll go out."

"We? They mustna see you!"

"I look like a gypsy in this gear, if I keep my distance." He glanced down at his clothing: a brown woolen tunic, a bright silk scarf around his neck, a wide-brimmed woven straw hat, and a striped cloak that covered the sling on his left arm. Nona had insisted that he remove his boots and nether stocks, so he stood barefoot, his breeches hemmed at the knee.

"They willna notice me among the others," he said firmly.

"You are dark-haired like a Romany—but you are taller than most, and your skin is pale. Grandmother wanted to rub walnut juice and grease over your skin to darken you, but we didna have the time."

"I might have let *you* do that, lass," he drawled, "but your grandmother has the gentle hand of a blacksmith. I'm going out."

She reached up and tugged the hat brim over his eyes. "If you must go out, keep those blue eyes hidden."

"You have green eyes, and you are a gypsy," he murmured.

Nona uttered an abrupt command, and Tamsin turned to give her grandmother a meek reply, as if in apology.

William lifted a brow. "She doesna want you to talk to me."

"She says I shouldna stand so close to you, or speak so privately with you. Nor should I touch you. 'Tisna proper, unless we are courting." Nona spoke again, shaking a knobby finger. William looked at Tamsin.

"I mustna speak to you again, except to translate, unless you go to my grandfather and ask for permission to court me. She says . . ." Tamsin drew a breath and looked away, while Nona mumbled on in an insistent tone.

"I think those reivers out there are less a threat to me than yon granddame," he said lightly. "What does she say?"

Tamsin peered through the slitted door flap. "She says no Romany man will ever want me for a wife if I act so improperly. She says no Scotsman will have me either. Not only am I bad luck, but I am poorly behaved." Nona spoke again. William looked at Tamsin expectantly.

"I heard my name, lass. I think I should know what was said of me."

"She says not even you, William Scott, would wed me, for all you need a wife; she saw that in your hand." She lifted her chin defiantly. "There. You wanted to know."

"Pray pardon, lass," he murmured. "I've brought this trouble upon you. Tell your grandmother I am to blame."

" 'Tis I who must apologize. My grandparents follow Romany traditions, and there are strict rules for women. I dinna keep to those customs very well, and my grandmother sometimes gets impatient with me. She seems to like you, though, for she has allowed us to talk. I shouldna speak to you at all, except when she bids me."

"Ah," he drawled. "You are a rebellious lass, I see."

Standing in the dark beside her, he saw a small movement through the doorflap. She tucked her left hand, swathed in silk, behind her. He realized that she hid her hand as often as she could. He wondered what was wrong with it; some childhood injury, he thought, for she had admitted that the hand was weak. But she did not allow it to be seen. Scarring, perhaps, he thought. He could not imagine why she would be ashamed of it.

Nona came forward, shouldering between William and Tamsin. She draped a dark, soft cloth over Tamsin's hair, wrapping and tying it. Then she took her arm, murmured a few words, and tugged her down the steps.

William peered out at the firelit clearing, watching while Tamsin and Nona joined John Faw. John spoke to Arthur Musgrave and his companion, then walked away.

Arthur pointed around the camp, clearly questioning Tamsin about any reivers who might have come to the camp. She shook her head repeatedly.

Casually, William stepped down the wagon steps and strolled around the clearing. He kept his hat pulled low, and the striped cloak provided good cover. He nodded to some of the Romany as he passed. A few glared at him, but John Faw nodded, willing to play the ruse for the sake of peace in the camp.

William made his way toward the trees, where Tamsin and Nona stood with the Englishmen. He leaned a shoulder against the slender trunk of a birch tree not far from them, and watched the dancing, which now resumed. He angled his head slightly beneath the guise of the old dark hat, and directed his attention to the conversation behind him.

"They can deny it till Judgment Day, but one of these gypsies must have seen them," Ned Forster said. He was wide and heavy-set, and no taller than Tamsin. "I could swear I saw a gypsy riding with one of them—was it you, girl?"

"Not I, *rya*," Tamsin said smoothly. She kept her voice calm with effort. "I have been here at my cousin's wedding. If reivers rode through this camp, we would have seen them."

"I know you!" Arthur Musgrave peered at her. "Armstrong's gypsy daughter! Why are you here? What evil scheme is this?"

"No scheme," Tamsin answered stiffly. She could not look at Arthur just then, remembering the choking feel of the rope around her throat. But she drew a deep breath and forced herself to lift her head proudly. "I came here to talk to the Romany, as your father suggested."

"He told Archie to do that, and Archie whined he needed your help. I told my father we ought to gather our own help, and not rely on Border thieves and tawnies. So where, then, are Armstrong and Rookhope? William Scott was to keep you in his custody. Where the devil is he?"

"Those were Scotts we chased this even," Ned said. "Could one of them have been Scott of Rookhope?"

"If 'twas, my father will be furious at his betrayal," Arthur answered.

From the corner of her eye, Tamsin saw William Scott saunter toward them, his identity shielded by her grandfather's cloak and hat. She nearly caught her breath in alarm when she saw his pale bare feet—surely those feet would give him away as a nongypsy. But the two men with her did not seem to notice him.

She watched with a sense of relief as William leaned against a birch, hidden by shadows and the wide sweep of his cloak and hat.

She exchanged a glance with her grandmother, who stood beside her, now holding a fat, blazing tallow candle so that Tamsin would have light for the palm reading. Tamsin looked at Arthur, who had asked to have a Romany woman tell his fortune.

"If you want me to see your future, I must hold a piece of silver that you have held in your own hand. Then I will be able to see your fortune clearly."

"Do not think to fool me, for I can see your fortune clear too," Arthur said in an ominous tone. "You'll be hanged."

She kept her eyes lowered though anger simmered in her. "You asked to have your fortune told, and my grandfather summoned me to do it. Do you want me to continue?"

"Aye," he grumbled, and took a coin from his belt pouch.

She accepted it in her right palm. The silk scarf was securely wrapped around her left hand, leaving only her thumb exposed. She knew from experience that no one wanted to see her strangely shaped left hand, let alone be touched by it.

Nona watched them with hawklike intensity as she held the candle. Tamsin knew that her grandmother was also there to act as a guardian in case the men tried to act rudely toward her. Except for purposes of palmistry and healing, Romany women were permitted little contact with men who were not kin, husband, or betrothed. Young women were closely watched by their elders.

Tamsin had overstepped the boundaries of conduct with William Scott, but Nona had been lenient in her supervision. Tamsin suspected, since Nona found William charming and beautiful, he was allowed more privilege than was customary.

Arthur and Ned, on the other hand, had not earned Nona's approval and were subjected to her unrelenting and suspicious glare. The men edged away from her, but the old woman stayed put, her candlelight and her guardianship a necessary part of the circle they formed.

Tamsin was keenly aware that William now sat beneath the tree, probably able to hear most of what was said among them.

She had to keep herself from constantly glancing his way, afraid she would call attention to him.

She took Arthur's hand, cradling it in her silk-swathed left hand. Holding the coin in her fingers, she traced its silver edge over the lines in his palm, peering carefully, tilting his hand to see it in the yellow light of the bonfire, and in the brighter glow of the candle flame.

"Who is that man?" Ned Forster asked, pointing through the trees toward William. "Why does he sit near to us like that, instead of dancing and singing with the rest?"

"He is . . . my husband," Tamsin said impulsively, hoping to give his close presence a reason that the men would not question. Once the words were out, she almost winced at what she had said, for that was far too close to a truth she meant never to reveal.

She saw William tip his head beneath the old hat as he listened. "He willna disturb us," she added in haste, to discourage him approaching.

"I thought you were unmarried," Arthur said, frowning.

"If I have a gypsy husband, you would have no reason to know about it," she said.

"Aye, she has a husband who's eager for his woman to earn some silver." Forster laughed. "He sits there to make sure she gets her silver, hey. These Egyptian people are lazy and shiftless. Look at them dancing and singing—the men never do work, but make baskets and play music. The women do the chores, earn the money, and even steal the food, while the men sit idle."

"If you could sit around idle, you would," Arthur said. "Now be quiet and let the chit tell my future."

"Foolishness," Ned grunted. "Worthless heathens, they are."

"I am a baptized Christian, as are many of the Romany," Tamsin snapped.

"Our King Henry banished all of 'em from England," Ned said. "But then the gypsies came into Scotland. Back and forth over the border, from one country to the next, each time a law is passed banning their existence, like vermin chased out of the kitchen and scuttling back in again by another hole."

Tamsin nearly dropped Arthur's hand as she glared up at Ned

Forster. "Scotland's kings have shown the Romany royal favor," she said in angry defense. "King James himself visited my grandfather, when the king made his progresses in commoner's disguise through the countryside. The king himself gave my grandfather a note of safe passage and letters of favor."

"Think you I believe that?" Ned asked. "The gypsies are full of easy lies."

"I will show you that note if you dinna believe me! King James summoned gypsies to entertain at his court, and he sometimes sent for a gypsy man to nurse his horses through illness and injury. We had the respect of Scotland's king, and we are allowed the freedom to wander this country so long as we are peaceful."

"No more, now that King James is gone," Arthur said.

"So long as the gypsies are on this side of the Border, you are Scotland's trouble," Ned said. "The Scots have bigger concerns than gypsy wanderers, with an infant for a queen and no true ruler. None of you have been deported, as you should be."

"Rya," she said, making an effort to stay calm against their infuriating prejudice, "dinna try to tell me where I should be. You happen to be an Englishman in Scotland after midnight. You commit March treason just standing here on Scottish soil!"

"Hah, what does a gypsy girl know of March treason!" Ned elbowed Arthur and laughed harshly.

"My father is an Armstrong," she said.

"Aye. She's but half a gypsy, this one," Arthur said.

"Huh. Armstrong scoundrels! You'll get but half the worth of your coin from her, then," Ned muttered. "If that."

"Be quiet," Arthur said. "I want my future told."

Ned grunted and leaned against the tree trunk. Tamsin tilted Arthur's hand toward the light and examined the pattern of lines and crisscrossings in the man's broad palm, using the edge of the coin rather than her fingertip.

"Ah," she said after a few moments. "Long life is here. And good health. But you must be careful of your stomach." She touched the edge of the coin to a crease. "This line shows a weak stomach. You must stay away from wines and rich foods."

Ned sniggered. "Aye, Arthur, stay away from French wines. Too dear in cost. Drink good English ale, eh?"

Arthur rubbed his slightly plump belly. "I do get pains when I eat rich food."

"And you had a serious head wound as a lad," Tamsin went on. She was certain of that, for her grandmother had taught her well. "This tiny island along this line, and the bar above it, tells of an injury to the head," Tamsin said. "You were about fifteen years old, I think. You lay ill for a long while."

"That is amazing," Arthur said. "Ned, remember when I was thrown from a horse as a lad and stayed in my bed for weeks?" He leaned forward eagerly. "You've earned some of your silver. Now tell my future."

Tamsin considered the minor grooves etched along one major line. "I see . . . a marriage for you, and many sons."

"Ah," Arthur said, pleased. "With Anna, my betrothed."

She hesitated. She tended to be honest when she looked at a life in a palm, or when she spread out the picture cards, unless she saw a short life span, or tragedy.

The line of Arthur's heart was shallow and etched, showing Tamsin that he did not listen to his heart or his conscience often enough. She already knew that he was capable of meanness, and of not thinking for himself. His line of fate, running up the center of his palm, was broken and weak in places.

She frowned. A flaw in the fate line, just at the point she estimated as his current age, told her that he would endure a heartbreak soon. Farther along, the line strengthened, indicating another love within five years, which would lead to marriage and children.

Nona leaned forward and peered too. "He will lose a love," she muttered in Romany. "But look at that square. The one he will lose does not love him. There is another, later, who will love this ox, and turn him into a sheep, I think. That would be good for this one. Tell him."

Tamsin nodded. "If you are betrothed now," she said, "I see another love for you, a better love. You will marry well and live content, but not with the lady you choose now."

"What? I will marry Anna Forster! I already have her father's promise of her hand."

She shook her head. "Let that one go, *rya*," she said kindly. "I see a better match for you later." She closed her eyes and felt a firm certainty. "That is what I see."

"Anna," he insisted. "You see Anna for me."

"Hah," Ned said. "The tawny wench is right!"

"Anna likes me well!" Arthur argued.

"She likes Jock Scott well. 'Tis why we were out riding after him this night, blockhead."

"If I find Jock Scott of Lincraig, or his kinsmen who rode with him, there will be none left of the Scott surname for Anna to favor," Arthur muttered. "Gypsy, you are wrong."

"Anna told her father she would not wed you," Ned said. "He locks her in her room, but her mother lets her out. Anna had another rendezvous with Jock Scott—you saw that this very night! You've already lost the girl."

"I'll kill Jock Scott for cuckolding me! Gypsy," Arthur said fiercely, "tell me how to make her mine. You must know some spells. Make me a potion, or tell the old hag to do it. I will pay you any amount of gold."

"I know naught of magic," Tamsin replied. "Nor does my grandmother." Nona frequently used spells traditional to the Romany, but Tamsin was not about to admit that.

"The gypsy chit cannot see the future in a few skin wrinkles," Ned said. "I told you 'twas a waste of good silver. Palmistry is for fools and women."

"Every hand holds a tale of past, present, and future," Tamsin said. "Even yours, Ned Forster."

"Bah!" Arthur pulled his hand away. " 'Tis said that Egyptians know the secrets of the future. But this is folly! You did not foretell me what I wanted to know!"

"If you dinna like what you hear, I am sorry," Tamsin said.

Ned took Tamsin's right hand. "Here, girl, look at my palm now," he said. "I will give you pretty coins, and more, do you tell me what I want, hey." He chuckled low. "You're a fine wench, though you be part gypsy." He pulled her closer.

Tamsin pushed at him. "I dinna want your coin. Be gone!" Nona reprimanded him in Romany, but he did not look at her.

Ned held her arm in a tight grip. "I have a pouch full of coin, and a codpiece that's full too." He grinned and Tamsin shuddered.

She glanced toward William, who placed a hand on the ground, readying to stand. Anxious to prevent him from coming closer, she tried to jerk away from Ned. "You must let go of me!"

"*Gadjo* pig!" Nona said in Romany. She held the candle high and purposefully spilled hot tallow, and though she missed Ned's arm, he yelped.

"Ned, stop," Arthur warned. "Her husband is just there. He'll defend her. We'll have trouble with this whole tribe!"

"Her man will not care what she does, if he sees silver of it," Ned replied. "Come with me, girl. We will find a quiet place— and you can look at my palms." He was breathing heavily as he tugged at her arm.

"Bad *manús*!" Nona said in awkward English. She shook the candle, and the flame blew out. Neither man looked toward her. Tamsin flung her grandmother a desperate look, and Nona reached out to snatch the silver coin from Tamsin's hand before hustling off, calling for John Faw, who had disappeared among the guests.

As Nona passed William Scott, who had stepped away from the tree and was moving toward them, she muttered to him in Romany and waved him toward Tamsin. He nodded beneath his hat.

"Be gone before there is trouble!" Tamsin urged Ned and Arthur. She glanced back at William.

"Trouble, hey," Ned said to Arthur. "We'll be off with her. We'll make a game of it! The gypsies will chase us into England, and give us reason to hang one or two of them for vagabonds and thieves." He dragged her another few steps. Arthur muttered a weak protest, but ran toward their horses, which were tied on the other side of the trees.

Tamsin glanced wildly over her shoulder. William advanced between the trees, silent and ready as a wildcat. Tension hardened the long, agile lines of his body. Neither of the Englishmen noticed him.

If Arthur recognized him, Tamsin thought frantically, there

would be violence in the camp. She had to get free on her own. Struggling against Ned's grasp, she cried out and faltered as her bruised leg twisted painfully beneath her.

Ned slowed, and Tamsin kicked his booted shin with her bare foot. He let go of her right and yanked on her left arm. The silk cloth slid free, exposing her hand. The light from the bonfire fell across its small, odd shape.

"Huh! What is that?" Ned stopped abruptly. "God be with, 'tis a devil's claw!"

Chapter Twelve

". . . Catiffe, witch!
Baud, Beggar, Gipsie: Any thing indeed,
But honest woman."

—Ben Jonson, *The Magnetic Lady*

Firelight illuminated the shape of her left hand. Instead of separate fingers, a curved wedge of flesh rose from the top of her palm, narrowing to a tip with a single, delicate oval fingernail. In Ned's grimace, she saw revulsion and fear, a look she had seen too often in her life.

Ned stepped back. " 'Tis a sign of evil!"

His fear gave her a sure weapon, the only one she had. She held the hand high in the yellow glare of the firelight. Regret flashed though her, but she had no time to think, had no other choice. Her hand could not be hidden now.

Ned stumbled into Arthur, who had run toward him. "God's bones!" Ned cried. "Look! She's a witch! She means to curse us—look at her hand, man!" He grabbed Arthur's sleeve and pointed at Tamsin. "She's part demon!"

She held her hand up like a threat. She stared at Ned, making her eyes wide, hoping their odd color would alarm the men further. She took a step forward, and they backed away.

"Be gone from here—or I'll curse you with the evil eye!" she said. Arthur gasped.

"God in heaven, she can do it too, look at her," Ned muttered.

"The devil in the shape of a woman," Arthur said. "She wore a glove when I saw her before. 'Twas to hide that demon's hoof! By God! My father should have hanged her for a witch!"

She sensed William behind her in the shadows like a protective presence. Yet she was aware that he watched her, that he knew, now, the truth about her. A sob curdled within her. While she could endure what these brutes thought of her, a tender, wounded part deep inside of her did not want William Scott to see her flaw, her weakness, her ugliness.

She sucked in a breath. No matter how much she hurt inside, she would not let it show. She was the granddaughter of an earl of Egypt, and the daughter of a great Scottish scoundrel. Lifting her chin to raise her pride, she held her left hand high, unmoving.

"Arrest her, man," Ned said, looking at Arthur. "You have the authority! Your father made you a deputy warden of the English Middle March!"

"Ah," said a deep, sure voice behind her. "But we are in Scotland, lads. Arthur has no authority here."

Tamsin caught her breath as the sudden, welcome warmth of William's hands rested on her upper arms. He guided her behind him, and she went without protest, her heart beating fast. She peered at Ned and Arthur around the width of his shoulder.

"Her husband!" Ned said.

"I told you!" Arthur hissed. He blinked. "By God! What? William Scott—guised as a gypsy!"

William inclined his head. "Very good. Now get out," he ordered. "You disturb a wedding."

"Yours?" Ned sounded confused. "Did you wed the gypsy this evening? Is that what this celebration is all about?"

"There are easier ways to bed a tawny than to wed her!" Arthur said. "That one's a witch! And you must be a fool to want her! Though she's a pretty little tart. I wager you did not know about that claw either, hey?"

William slithered free the dirk sheathed at his belt. "Guard your tongue," he growled.

"She took our silver and put a curse on Arthur!" Ned said.

Arthur looked startled, but nodded. "Aye!" he said. "She put an evil eye on me—both of us—and she took my silver, telling me lies!"

"She told no lies," William said. "Palmistry is regarded as a science among scholars and physicians, though I doubt you know that. And she knows a good deal about your true character, Arthur.

Certainly more than you would want anyone to know," he added in a low drawl.

"Did you truly wed that gypsy?" Arthur demanded. "My father will want to know what the devil you are up to!"

"If I were to wed a gypsy, 'twould be my concern, and not yours or your father's," William said. "If I were to wed a gypsy"—he twirled the dirk and caught it, swift as a spinning star—"your father should be pleased, for he wants a contact among these people for his own purposes. Now be gone from here. Or the evil eye will be the least of your troubles."

"I will tell my father what I saw here!" Arthur said.

"Tell him that you saw Tamsin Armstrong and me meeting with the gypsies. Tell him too that Ned insulted the lass in a lewd manner, and you both were sent out of here as you deserved."

Ned snarled and drew his own dirk, launching toward him. William stepped aside with easy grace, his arm sweeping back to shield Tamsin.

Ned stopped abruptly, staring past them. Tamsin turned to see her grandfather and several Romany men walking toward them. John Faw held a whip and lashed out with it, cracking the supple length.

William looked at Ned and Arthur. "Be gone," he ordered.

Wordlessly, the men turned and ran toward their horses. Within moments, they vaulted into the saddles and rode away, vanishing into the darkness of the moor.

Tamsin whirled to see John Faw nod silent thanks to William Scott, who nodded in return. Her grandfather looked at her.

"Are you harmed, girl?" he asked in Romany.

"I am fine," she replied, rubbing her left wrist with her right hand. Her small hand was open to view, but she did not care. The damage had been done.

John Faw stared from her to William for a long moment. Tamsin was sure that he had heard Arthur asking William if he was indeed her husband. She swallowed nervously and waited for John Faw to ask for an explanation or to show his anger.

But her grandfather only swiveled his black, intense gaze from one to the other, as if he tried to divine what they knew and he did not. She realized that he would say nothing to her of his private thoughts, or the matter of her behavior, in front of his people. After a moment, he turned to walk toward the bonfire, followed by the men. The camp was quiet. Just when the music and chatter had stopped, Tamsin could not have said.

John Faw gave the signal for the music to resume. Tamsin saw her grandmother comforting the tearful bride, whose wedding celebration had been tainted by violence and strangers. Tamsin felt some remorse over the ruined festivities, but knew that her apology would not be accepted. The bride and her closest relatives had often shown a wary suspicion of Tamsin.

She turned away. William stood watching her, the firelight flickering over his face. She glanced away and bent to pick up the fallen silk, wrapping its softness around her left hand.

She knew she should thank him for helping her. But she only wanted to run from him, ashamed that he had seen the flaw she had tried to hide. She whirled and hurried toward the bonfire.

An instant later, she felt long fingers grasp her left hand. The silk fell away and floated to the ground.

"Evil eye," William muttered. He pulled on her hand and started through the clearing. "Evil eye! Casting a curse! God in heaven, lass, what were you thinking!" His fingers were warm and strong on her skin as he yanked her with him.

Too stunned to answer, overwhelmed by the sudden touch of his hand on hers, Tamsin tried to pull away. He did not slow down, tugging her in his wake. Some of the gypsies stopped and stared after them.

"I didna take you for a foolish lass," William continued in an irritated tone. "But that was a silly performance indeed." He stopped and glared at her. "Do you know what you've done?"

"Nay," she said hotly. "I dinna have a hint of it!"

"Well, you'll soon find out, when Jasper Musgrave puts out a summons for your arrest and accuses you of witchcraft."

"He wouldna," she said. "Anyone can see Arthur is a fool."

"He is. But so is Jasper. He will believe Arthur, if the lad reports this. And be sure he will." He shook his head, looking down at the ground as if in thought. His fingers remained firm over her misshapen hand. She flexed it in his. He did not flinch, did not even lessen his hold.

She wondered if he was so caught up in his anger with her that he did not even realize that he held her left hand.

"Well," he said finally, resuming a fast stride through the camp, "we'd best go back to Rookhope as quick as we can. Likely 'twill take more than a fortnight to sort out this tangle. I'll have to bring word of it to your father. He'll want to be warned that Musgrave may have another charge to lay on your head."

She stumbled after him. "But—but—"

He glanced over his shoulder. "What?" he asked impatiently.

"I—I dinna want to go to Rookhope," she said. The fire of her previous protests had faded, replaced by pure amazement. He had not looked in abhorrence at her hand. He held it in his, even now, his fingers curled around the wedge, warm and firm against her palm.

No man, other than Archie and Cuthbert, had ever held her left hand like this, cradling it casually, warmly, as if it were the same as any other hand. She stared at him as they walked.

"What is it?" he asked, stopping again to look at her.

"You . . ." She searched for the words. "You dinna seem disturbed. . . ." She paused.

"By what? Your hand?" He lifted her left hand, lowered it, did not let go. "I am no superstitious blockhead, like those two fools who just left us."

"You . . . dinna think 'tis a sign of evil?" she asked faintly.

"Evil? Nay." He sounded impatient as he tugged her along. "And I doubt you know aught about laying curses either. But Jasper Musgrave will think it. He'll have his rope around your bonny, foolish neck again, unless we can prevent it."

"What should we do?" she asked. She felt stunned, so relieved by his casual reaction to her hand that she could scarcely think about any other matter.

"I will have to consider it before I can say. Come on."

"Where are we going?" she asked breathlessly.

"To Rookhope," he said, as they reached the wagon. "Get your gear."

He let go of her hand and pushed her toward the wooden steps. At that moment, the door flap parted, and Nona peered out at them. Her face shifted into a toothless grin.

"Now that I think on it," William drawled, "I wouldna put a thorough curse beyond your grandmother's talents."

"Tell the pretty man," Nona said in Romany, looking at Tamsin, "that he should not be so familiar with you unless he intends to wed you. Your grandfather told me all that was said among the *gadjo*. Everyone here has seen him touch you in a courting manner, and we assume he intends to marry you."

"*Kek,* no, Grandmother, it is not as you think—"

Nona pointed a thumb at William. "I like this pretty man well, and I see his lusty desire for you, clear in his summer-sky eyes. But I tell you that your grandfather is furious. He has found a gypsy man who will take you in marriage. And then you go and give yourself to the pretty *rya*!"

"Please listen. It is not what you think."

Nona was too intent on her course to listen. "But I say, it is good that this beautiful *gadjo* wants you in his bed!" She smiled. "I will tell your grandfather that he will be a good husband for you, this one, strong and rich! His leather doublet is very fine, and his metal armor costs much gold. And he has a good heart too, though troubled—I saw that in his hand." She shook her long finger. "But you must tell the pretty Scotsman that he cannot touch you again until we celebrate the marriage!"

"What is she saying?" William asked.

Tamsin, startled, looked up at him. Embarrassment and shame, for her own shortcomings and for her grandmother's boldness, burned in her. "She says dinna touch me again," she translated. As she tried to stifle her agonizing embarrassment, anger rose in its stead. "She says"—she walked up the steps—"that you will have naught but bad luck forever if you touch me!" She nearly gasped at her own absurd answer.

Anger and gratitude grappled within her. He had taken her hand without fear. The warmth and pressure of his touch had shocked her at first. And though the feeling was deeply welcome, it confused her. His fingers against her palm felt like sunshine on shadowed ground. His unhesitating touch brought a kindness so simple and poignant that she wanted to cry.

Instead she had lashed out at him. She stumbled past Nona into the dark interior of the wagon. She could not help but glance back. Nona smiled at William, who looked astonished.

"Pretty *rya*," Nona said, although William could not understand her. "She will be a good wife to you."

William smiled at Nona and peered past her into the wagon. "Tamsin," he called. "Come out. Bring out my armor and my gear, if you will, and come out. We must set out for Rookhope." He waited. "Tamsin Armstrong!" he said with more force.

Nona crowed with delight. "*Avali,* yes," she told William. "This is good! Shouting for her! Tell her what you want of her! Show her your passion! At last, a strong man for my strong girl! You are unafraid of her strange little hand!" She shouted it out for all to hear. Some of the Romany walking nearby paused to look toward the wagon.

"Grandmother," Tamsin hissed. "Stop that! I will explain this to you, if you will but listen!"

Nona pointed at William, who, not understanding a word of what went on, gave her a somewhat bewildered glance. "You stay here with us, *rya*, and we will have a wedding for two couples, eh! I will tell my husband not to worry, for we have found a good man for our Tchalai!" She turned and grinned at Tamsin.

"This man does not want me!" Tamsin said.

"Look at him," Nona said, wiggling her brows. "He does."

"Tamsin," William said, catching sight of her behind Nona. He spoke through his teeth, as if deeply exasperated. "Come out of there, lass! And tell me what the devil is going on here!"

Tamsin stood back in the shadows, her cheeks hot with shame. "My grandmother likes you," she said in brisk summary. "But go away. I willna go to Rookhope with you."

She heard him swear under his breath, saw him remove the hat he wore and shove a hand through his hair, heard him swear again, then saw him wince at the forgotten pain in his arm. Nona folded her hands on her belly and grinned.

"Just give me my gear," he said. "I'll sleep in the camp somewhere. We will talk in the morning, you and I. And be assured I willna leave without you."

Tamsin's temper, barely controlled, sparked further. She did not even know what she was angry about, but she followed the hot impulse that hurtled through her. She picked up his helmet and tossed it over Nona's shoulder through the doorway. William ducked, but managed to catch it. The rest of his gear followed when Tamsin dumped the bundle down the steps.

Nona rubbed her hands in utter delight. "Yes, yes," she crowed. "This will be a good match indeed!"

William gave Nona a distracted smile, oblivious to her meaning. He scowled past her at Tamsin, who kept in the shadows behind the door flap. Then he stalked off toward the trees.

Nona turned to Tamsin, looking elfin and delighted. A moment later she hurried down the wagon steps, coin necklace jingling, and called out for her husband.

Tamsin sank down to the floor of the wagon and put her face into her hands. Within moments, hot tears of frustration and embarrassment trickled into her palms.

Chapter Thirteen

If your hand you hallow,
Good fortune will follow,
I swear by these ten,
You shall have it agen,
I do not say when.
　　　—Ben Jonson, *Masque of the Metamorphosed Gipsies*

Dawn bloomed cool and fragile, a faint lifting of the sky. Tamsin woke beneath the wagon and crawled out to stand in the chilly air, holding the blanket snug around her shoulders. Although darkness lingered, she could hear the murmur of voices and an occasional barking dog, and smelled bacon cooking somewhere in the grove.

Campfires sparkled like golden stars in the morning mist. The Romany had begun to stir after a brief rest, moving slowly through the soft shadows, whispering quietly while they tended to their families and to the horses raised and trained by the Romany band.

When her grandparents had returned to the wagon last night, Tamsin had feigned sleep beneath the wagon, and they had not disturbed her. Across the clearing, William Scott had slept beneath an oak tree. Tamsin had glanced often in his direction, but he appeared to sleep soundly, while she had tossed and turned.

She watched as some of the women prepared for the wedding celebration. Soon the entire camp would walk to the place where her grandfather, as the Romany leader, would perform the marriage. Feasting, music, and dancing would complete the day.

Tomorrow, Tamsin knew, her grandfather would lead his people on a journey to another part of Scotland. John Faw had promised to heed the warning that Tamsin had brought to him. They would be protected from King Henry's plan if no Romany could be found to be bribed or threatened into compliance.

She turned and walked toward the stream on the far side of the trees, glancing toward William Scott as she went. He sat beneath the oak tree, pulling on his long boots. He looked up at her, his gaze cool blue in the dawn light, and nodded to her. No doubt he expected her to be ready to leave for Rookhope soon. Although her heart seemed to leap, she hurried past with a curt, returned nod.

At the stream, a few women collected water in buckets, but no one spoke to her. Perhaps they recalled that she had brought poor luck with her last night, she thought. Tamsin kept apart from them as she rinsed her face and hands in the cold water and ran damp fingers through her tangled curls. When she headed back, a quick glance showed her that William now stood beside his horse, readying his gear to leave.

Ahead, John Faw emerged from his wagon and waved to her. He held some food in a folded cloth and beckoned her forward.

"Tchalai!" he called. "Good morning." He offered her a flat oatcake and crisp bacon, still hot. She thanked him and ate, standing beside him. He modestly averted his eyes, as was proper, until she finished.

"Grandfather," she said. "Thank you for coming to my aid last night."

"We defend our women," he said gruffly.

"I am sorry that I brought trouble to my cousin's wedding."

"The *gadjo* are to blame for that. You did nothing wrong . . . though your behavior is not always that of a proper Romany girl," he added. "But then, you have learned *gadjo* ways."

"Scottish women do act with more freedom than Romany women," she said. "I know you think I behave poorly at times—"

"You have a boldness in your nature that is not of Romany making. Romany women are modest and obedient." His glance was like a grim scold.

"Is it boldness, grandfather, or independence?"

He grunted. "The Scots make much of this independence," he said. "It is good for men, and unseemly in women."

She sighed. Although she loved and respected him as much as she did Archie, her grandfather abided by strict Romany rules of behavior, and imposed restraints on her that Archie had never done.

Her grandfather was, in some ways, Archie's opposite; her father was big and loud, full of humor and affection, while her grandfather was a small dark man with a reserved temperament.

"I only think of your good, Tchalai," he said. "I have always defended your presence among us, though others wanted you cast out as an infant. But Nona and I kept you with us after . . . the one who gave you life went away." He glanced down. "You look much like her."

She knew that. Archie sometimes mentioned it, and spoke of her mother with tenderness, while her grandfather would not even utter her mother's name. Like Nona, he would not allow his grief to lessen or to heal.

"I am grateful, Grandfather," she said. "You and Grandmother have always been kind to me, have always loved me. My mother would be glad to know that I have been cared for by both families."

He looked away. "The Romany do not give up their precious children easily," he said. "When your father took you, we hoped you would return to us, not only in the summers, but someday to marry a *Romanichal* and stay with our band."

She hesitated, choosing her words carefully. "I am not certain that is best for me," she said. "I am happy to spend time both with the Romany and with my father, as I have always done. Marriage—to anyone, Romany or Scot—would change that."

"Life changes," he said. "Life moves, as the Romany do, from place to place. It is time, now, for you to move on. Time for you to wed." He paused. "I have decided to tell Baptiste Lallo that you will be his bride."

Tamsin's heart plummeted. "I have not agreed to that! I do not want to wed him!"

He held up his hand to silence her. "He would be good to you. Baptiste has lost his wife. He needs a woman to tend his fire and his children, and to give him what a man needs from a wife. And I want his guarantee that there will be no more trouble between our bands."

Tamsin shook her head. "It is wrong to use me to buy peace for this band."

"I decide what is right for your marriage. The Romany people have lost the goodwill of both the English and the Scottish crowns. Our bands must support one another with better loyalty."

"I cannot do this. I will not."

"No *Romanichi* refuses her elders as you do," he said sternly. "Soon you will stand in the heart circle with Baptiste and say a vow to take him as your husband. And you will go with him to his wagon. Baptiste has agreed to join his band to mine. Tchalai, I do what is best for you, and for all of us."

"This is not best for me!"

"Your father has given you too much freedom. You are a Romany, born among us. I let you go with Armstrong to learn your *gadjo* roots. I thought if you knew their ways, their language, you would be safe from the persecution our people suffer. But I always planned that you would come back to the Romany."

"I am Scottish as well as Romany. I do not want to marry this *Romanichal*."

He watched her. "Would you marry a Scot?"

"My mother did," she said. "You allowed it."

"That one . . . ran away with Archie," he said, which Tamsin knew. "But he earned my respect. He loved that one." He narrowed his eyes. "Your grandmother says you wish to wed the Scottish *rya*. Is this true? Has he made a marriage promise to you, as those *gadjo* men said last night? Is that why you refuse my wishes?"

She looked away. "He would not want such as me."

"Nona says he does want you. Your grandmother likes this man. I do not trust most *gadjo* men, but I think he is a good one, like his father. Like Archie." He frowned at her. "Do you want this man?"

She stood silently for a long moment. She could hardly explain to her grandfather that in the last few days, she felt as if her heart had been caught fast and sure, by a simple act of fate. As if she had no control, no say in the matter, she felt drawn inexorably to William Scott. She had begun to want him with all of her foolish heart.

"I would rather wed him than Baptiste," she said cautiously.

John Faw rubbed at his chin, frowning. "What would your father say about this Scottish man? Does he know him? Would he approve of him as a husband?"

"He knows him." She paused. "And he would approve."

"Tchalai," he said thoughtfully. "I am your elder and the leader of this tribe. I will give you a choice. You may choose Baptiste, or the *rya*."

She stared at him. "Choose?" she echoed.

"You shame your grandmother and me if you refuse Baptiste and stay among us unwed. You must take a husband, and soon."

"That is no choice. I do not want to wed anyone!"

He threw up his hands. "I should banish you for your impudence and disobedience!"

"Banish me?" she repeated. The Romany punishment of exile was a serious one. Although she did not believe that her grandfather meant that, she felt hurt by the suggestion.

He sighed. "I will do that if I must. Obey me," he said. "Bring happiness to your grandparents. Marry one of these men. It is a fair offer I give you."

She shook her head. "You do not understand—"

"If you love this *rya,* then I will let you go with him." He looked down. "I will grant this in memory of your mother," he said. "She . . . would want your happiness."

She knew what it cost him to say those words, and her heart went out to him for the effort. But she saw that he imposed yet another rule upon her even as he tried to be lenient.

He looked at her. "It is time for you to settle with a home and family. Make your decision."

Her heart pounded. She could not easily yield to such authority. She had too much of the independent spirit of which John Faw thought so little. Nor could she agree to marry either man. One was unthinkable, the other unattainable.

"I cannot do this," she said quietly.

"What will you do? Live in your father's stone tower? The *gadjo* life will not bring you happiness, for you are a wanderer in your heart, like the Romany." He looked past her. "Nona! Come here and tell the girl to listen to me!"

Her grandmother came down the wagon steps and hurried toward them, skirts swinging, coins and chains jangling. She halted between her husband and granddaughter.

"I have heard enough from inside the wagon," she said. "The whole camp hears this, though they look away to give us privacy!"

"Tell her she must choose her husband," John Faw said.

"The Scotsman wants her," Nona said. "I have seen it in his eyes. Husband, you must offer him a horse. Two horses. He has a big stone house and land, and much gold. What does Baptiste have but two crying children and a cooking fire to be tended?"

"If she marries into the Romany, she can settle the dispute between the Faws and the Lallos," he said.

"The *rya* is a good man," Nona said. "Rich and beautiful. The Romany would benefit from one of ours married to such a man."

"Please," Tamsin said. "Leave the matter be."

"Show me your palm, Tchalai." Nona grabbed Tamsin's right hand, spreading the palm open. "I have looked here many times, but let us look again. See, girl. Your heart line is etched and slanted—you hide a sensitive nature behind your boldness."

Tamsin nodded. She too had examined the lines in her own palm, and knew what was there. John Faw leaned close, peering with interest at her hand while Nona spoke.

"Ah, but love and good fortune await you . . . you are capable of great, deep love. See, the heart line is strong, and curves down. A caring, loving heart." She examined the tips of Tamsin's fingers. "But here, see—how much doubt you must conquer before you can find your happiness. Many lessons. If you are not ready for those tasks, the rewards of love will not come to you."

"My fortune is to be alone. I have seen that for myself."

Nona shook her head. "You are afraid to see the joy that is here for you. Look at this thin line"—Nona tapped the swell of flesh below Tamsin's thumb—"see how it runs alongside the life line. That is a special mark, Tchalai, the line that tells of a love that is fated to be, like a twin of your heart."

Tamsin leaned forward. "It is faint and broken. I thought it was just a meaningless line."

"It is faint and broken because you deny your own heart,"

Nona said. "You insist no one wants you. But you must find this man chosen by fate to be your love. Your heart needs to find this man."

"Chosen by fate?" Stunned, Tamsin stared at her grandmother. She had looked at her own palm often, but she had not recognized the line of a twin soul. Perhaps, as her grandmother had said, she did indeed deny her own chance for happiness.

"Chosen by fate before you were born," Nona said. "It is plain to see, here in your hand."

Chosen by fate. The words echoed in her mind. She fisted her left hand, thinking of the tiny cut on her wrist, and wondered again at its meaning in her life.

"Good fortune can appear or disappear with the choices we make," her grandmother said. "You have a loving heart. I see marriage for you, and great happiness. But only if you make the right choice."

"Baptiste," John Faw said.

"The pretty Scotsman," Nona said, frowning at her husband.

"Stop!" Tamsin shook her head.

"Look at your other hand," Nona said, taking her left hand. Tamsin immediately placed her right hand over the left wrist. Nona tapped her left palm. "There."

Tamsin, Nona, and John Faw all leaned forward, heads bumping together. "The right palm always differs from the left," Nona said. "Here, your left holds the qualities granted to you at your birth, and the right shows the changes you have made by your deeds and your thoughts. Look!" she said, tapping the skin.

Tamsin looked. A line ran inside and parallel to the strong, curved line of her life. "The line is much stronger here than in your right hand. You are fated to have a deep and lasting love." She smiled. "But you must take the chance when love comes into your life." She shrugged. "Or you will have nothing."

John Faw took Tamsin's forearm to pull her hand closer. The movement exposed the cut on her wrist. "What is this?" he asked.

"The mark of a marriage promise!" Nona cried.

"I—I—it was an accident," Tamsin stammered.

"But the pretty Scotsman shares the mark. I saw it on his hand last night when I tended his wound!" Nona clapped her hands.

"Husband, I told you! She did make a promise with the pretty *rya!*"

"Why did you not tell us?" her grandfather demanded. "This is not a betrothal. This is a marriage you have made. You promised yourself to this man, and said no word to us!"

Tamsin sighed. She leaned close and explained, as simply as she could, what had happened between her and William Scott in Musgrave's dungeon. Then she tried to explain why she had kept silent.

"Fate has decided this marriage for you!" Nona cried. "You thought he would not want you? You thought we would not approve?" Nona grinned. "We approve!"

"If you want him," John Faw said, "we approve."

"But the union was an accident! We did not mean for it to happen. I was not certain it was significant."

"It is," John Faw said. "If you do not honor this, you will bring much bad luck upon you, and him, and this entire family. You will have to undo the marriage bonds by Romany tradition also, and divorce him, if you are displeased."

"But it was not intended by us," she said.

"Fate has decided this marriage," John Faw said. "Such a sign cannot be ignored, or all our luck will change for the worse."

"Your grandfather is right. Fate has chosen your love," Nona said. "The *rya* also has the special mark of a twin heart. I saw it! What a joyful day, a day of weddings for two couples!" Nona turned around. "Where is my grandson by marriage? Let me embrace him!"

"No!" Tamsin pulled at her grandmother's arm. "Please—no! He does not know! You cannot tell him this!"

"Was he asleep, or drunken? How could he not know?"

"He does not . . . understand what this means," Tamsin said hesitantly. "He is not of the Romany, after all."

"Then we will tell him!" Nona turned. *"Rya!"* she called.

"No!" Tamsin cried. "You must not! Promise me you will not tell him!" William Scott would not put credence in a slip of the knife, fated or not.

Yet her grandparents welcomed the accidental marriage as a miracle of fate. Tamsin was sure that William Scott would see it as insignificant, even a nuisance. She could not allow her grand-parents to tell him. That she must do herself, and carefully.

She looked up and saw him approach with his straightforward, confident stride. He wore his armor and helmet, and his horse stood saddled at the edge of camp. Her heart bounded within her to see him, but she turned away.

"Promise me you will say nothing of this to him yet," she said to her grandparents. "Let me explain it to him."

"She is undecided, I think," John Faw said. "Divorce the man properly if you think it a mistake. Then marry Baptiste, who wants you."

"The *rya* wants her," Nona said. "Are you an old fool, not to see that? Go explain this to him," she told Tamsin.

William came closer. "Are you ready to ride out, Tamsin Arm-strong?" He watched her, his eyes a bright and piercing blue. She wanted to trust him when he looked at her like that, with patience and kindness in his eyes.

"Ride out?" John Faw asked. "Will you take her to your stone house?"

"Aye," William said. "She agreed to it once. Tamsin, did you tell them about our arrangement? The pledge?"

"The pledge?" She stared at him, knowing exactly what he meant. She had not told her grandparents about the legal pledge arrangement, for they would not have understood that easily.

"Ah, the pledge," John Faw said. "She told us, *rya*." He smiled. Tamsin nearly groaned. She knew her grandfather spoke about a wedding pledge.

"Pledge," she croaked. "I told them, aye."

John Faw murmured a translation to Nona, and she grinned in delight.

"Allow me to apologize for the trouble I brought here last night," William said. "Please offer my regrets to the bride for the disturbance. I hope it brought no bad luck to anyone."

"Unlike a *gadjo* to speak regrets to a Romany," John Faw said. "You owe us no apology. May good fortune be yours, *rya*. We will see you very soon. We will come to Rookhope and camp on your lands."

William clasped the old man's hand. "Of course you are welcome on my property. If you are ever in need of a favor, call upon me."

"We will. May good fortune follow you," John Faw said.

William murmured thanks, then turned to Tamsin.

She looked away. Fate had taken a firm hold over her life since the moment she had met William Scott. She had to go with him now. Her grandparents expected it. To see their joy at the news of her accidental marriage made her feel humble. She could not take that pleasure from them.

A long sigh slipped from her. She would go with Scott even if she had to stay in a dungeon. Perhaps, she thought, she could beg a gentle confinement in his tower. At Musgrave's castle, he had said that he did not agree with imprisoning women. Perhaps he would just lock her in a room for two weeks. She could endure that.

If she stayed at Rookhope Tower, she could find out what Musgrave wanted with the Romany and her father. That way, she could better safeguard them from Musgrave's black scheme.

"I will go with you," she said.

He tipped a brow as he looked at her. "No protests?"

She turned away from her grandparents so that only he could hear her. "A fortnight only," she said softly.

"You might want to stay longer," he murmured. "We dinna know what Musgrave will do after Arthur tells him what happened last night."

She nodded. So much had happened, just now, that she could scarcely think clearly. Much more would happen before the day was done, for she had yet to explain all of this to William Scott, who would likely be rather displeased.

She swallowed hard, and turned away to embrace her grandparents. She looked back at William. "I—I will fetch my horse and my gear," she said. "I will meet you outside the camp." He nodded.

She spun on her heel and ran, tears stinging her eyes.

Chapter Fourteen

Some help some help my guid lord she said
Some help pray gie tae me
I am a leddy that's deeplie in love
An' banish'd frae my ain kintrie.
　　　　　　—"Lord Thomas and Lady Margaret"

Tamsin had disappeared among the wagons. William scanned the camp quickly, but saw no sign of her. He looked at her grandparents, who watched him with odd smiles on their faces. He returned a hesitant smile, not sure what they were all so pleased about. He was glad that Tamsin seemed willing to leave with him. He had not looked forward to convincing her.

He cleared his throat. Neither John nor Nona spoke, although the gypsy leader had fastened a deep stare on him.

"Safe journey to you," John Faw finally said.

"My thanks. I am grateful for your hospitality."

John Faw folded both arms over his chest and bowed solemnly. "We are grateful to you, *rya,*" he said. "Very grateful. Keep our granddaughter well and safe."

William nodded. "Be certain of it, *rya,*" he replied.

John Faw leaned over to Nona and translated. She looked up at William, and he was surprised to see the sheen of tears in her onyx eyes. She chattered something to him, and turned to climb the steps of her wagon, waving a hand at him as if she wanted him to wait.

"What did she say?" William asked John Faw.

"She wants to give you a gift," he said. "It is fitting."

Puzzled, William said nothing. Perhaps gypsies customarily gave gifts to strangers upon departure. He waited, and Nona returned to hand him a folded piece of green silk.

"It is a neck scarf, such as our men wear," John Faw said. "She wants you to have it. It was given to us many years ago, when Nona and I were young, by the king of France, when we traveled through that land and performed music and dancing to entertain his royal court. They liked us well there."

William unfolded the scarf, a rectangle of deep green silk embroidered in gold thread. The color gleamed like melted emeralds in the dawn light. "Thank you," he told Nona. An idea occurred to him. *"Merci, madame,"* he said in French. "I am honored by this beautiful gift."

She smiled and began to chatter to him in French. "You beautiful man," she said, grinning, "let me see my gift on you!" He took off his helmet, and she looped the green silk around his neck, knotting it loosely at his throat. Patting his arm, she seemed on the verge of tears.

"Ah, now you look like a Romany man," she said, and grinned.

William touched the silk folds. "I wish I had a gift to give you in return," he said.

"You have already given us a great gift," John Faw answered in French, so Nona and William could understand him. "We will be in your debt forever. Fate has chosen you."

William hesitated, then smiled, deciding that the Faws must be grateful for his help last night. Perhaps too they were glad that he intended to keep watch over Tamsin. Archie Armstrong had been similarly grateful to him. She must be wilder than he had thought, William mused.

With tears in her eyes, Nona bowed and folded her hands in farewell. At that moment, William heard the rhythm of approaching hooves. He turned to see a dappled gray horse loping through the encampment, and stepped back as it headed toward him.

Tamsin rode with reckless grace, back straight and hips supple, skirts flying over her knees, her hair floating out like a black cloud. With scarcely a look toward him, she streamed past and headed out of the camp. When she reached the edge of the moor, she urged her horse to a fast gallop.

William started forward, but glanced back at her grandparents. John Faw pointed calmly toward the moor. "Go," he said. "Follow her. She is your trouble now, William Scott."

He crossed the grove at a run. Within moments, he mounted the bay and rode out of the camp.

Mist hovered on the moor in low, fragile clouds, and the hills seemed translucent in the increasing glow of dawn. William guided the bay over the moor at a leisurely pace. Tamsin rode far ahead of him on the gray horse, but he felt no urgent need to catch her. Easy enough to keep her in sight, he thought, and let her ride off whatever strong emotion had powered her bold departure from the gypsy camp. He would not lose her out here.

She crossed the moor and headed toward an earthen road that skimmed along the wide base of a hill. William followed, the bay's rhythmic stride fast but relaxed. He did not need to push the horse or pursue the girl. The gray would tire soon enough at that pace, he reasoned. Soon or late, the girl would have to pull up.

He watched her ride, hair flying out like a black banner, her skirts high over her long, slim legs. He watched the grace and power that seemed natural to her, and wondered what caused her distress. She seemed to run from something, he thought. Last night she had possessed the courage to stand up to two men who mocked her. Now she behaved as if she lacked even the courage to face him.

He rode at a steady lope behind her, thinking of last night, when he had seen her hand exposed for the first time. Neither shock nor disgust had been his reaction, though Tamsin seemed to expect both from him. Surprise, perhaps, and curiosity, for he knew that she hid some flaw in that hand. He expected to see scars or the traces of an old injury.

What he had seen, finally, was no more than a harmless variation of nature. His heart had gone out to her in sympathy, as he had felt before with her. Tamsin seemed to have a singular capacity to melt the guards around his feelings, no matter that he endeavored to always show himself as cool and unmoved. None but his daughter had that effect on him.

Tamsin seemed to believe that her hand represented some mark of inferiority, even a sign of inherent evil. He could not share even the smallest part of that view. Years of tutelage at the king's side, and his own preference for studying scientific and medical treatises, had made him immune to common superstitions.

Seething fury had rushed through him when Arthur and Ned had mocked and threatened her. William had been about to confront them himself when the girl began to brandish the hand like a weapon. A foolish but courageous act, William thought, touched off by her fiery, impulsive nature. But then, he mused, true bravery often required a touch of madness to fuel it.

He glanced ahead. The road met another track, and continued past a wide crossing to disappear between two steep hills. Tamsin headed for the crossing. Once there, she slowed and circled the horse, glancing back at him.

William remembered when he and Archie had chased her over meadows and roads in the Debatable Land. Then too, she had stopped at a crossing. He wondered if she looked at another of the strange gypsy marks.

This time, she took neither of the roads. Instead, she urged the horse up one of the hillsides, a gradual incline that led to the ridge where William and his cousins had ridden last night. Reaching the peak of the hill, she halted the horse.

William hoped she intended to wait for him and accompany him along the drover's track that topped those hills. He headed after her.

At the crossroads, he stopped, as she had. In the center of the clearing, a cluster of stones was arranged in the shape of a heart. The design was not the same as the scratchings and pebbles that had led him to the gypsy camp, and to Tamsin.

Here, the heart was much larger, a wide heart-shaped space outlined by smooth stones as large as bread loaves. This was no secret sign etched in the dust for other Romany to see, he thought. The heart was a permanent thing, for the stones had been there a long while, half sunk into the earth.

He looked toward the hilltop. The horse and rider were silhouetted on the high crest. Tamsin sat motionless, her back straight, her dark hair billowing out, as if she watched him. In the pearled light of dawn, a delicate mist seemed to surround her.

He guided the bay up the hillside, wondering if Tamsin would bolt as soon as he came near. But when he attained the peak, she sat still. Except for the rippling motion of her hair, and the horse's tail and mane, they might have been an equestrian statue, he thought, like those proud, elegant statues he had once seen in the city of Rome when he had traveled there on a mission for King James, several years past.

He halted, sidling the bay beside her mount. Tamsin did not look at him, though her horse acknowledged his with a soft whicker. Tamsin's silence and stillness seemed to ask the same of William. He said nothing, and waited.

He studied her elegant profile, the slim, graceful lines of her body, the dark, tendriled mass of her hair. She had a fiery kind of beauty, he thought. She was unlike the women he was accustomed to admiring at court. Without the enhancement of textiles and jewels, she had a natural loveliness, simple, strong, yet delicate. But what he found most fascinating about her was not outward.

A flame burned within her, in the heat of her temper and her quick moods, in the lithe, agile style of her movements, in the low warmth of her voice. Most of all, he sensed it in the spirit that brightened her eyes, like pale green crystals lit from within.

Her silence was profound, not a gentle peace in keeping with the dawn, but something darker, tinged with sadness. He did not know why she sat and waited on the hilltop, but he would not disturb her, or the quiet atmosphere, with mundane questions.

He looked outward. The land spread below the hill in a wide vista of misty moors and heather-coated hills, greens and purples softened to pale hues by the fog. To one side of the moor, the gypsy campfires twinkled like morning stars.

After a few moments, he noticed movement there, and squinted his eyes to see the gypsies walking over the moor. All of them, men, women, and children, seemed part of the procession. Soon they came to the same road that he and Tamsin had taken. Through the early mist, they headed toward the crossroads.

"They are going to the heart circle," Tamsin said before he could ask. Her tone was subdued, as if the bright spark within her burned low.

"Heart circle?" he asked. "In the crossing?"

She nodded, lifting her right hand to point. Her left hand was hidden once again in the black glove, and she gripped the reins with it. "Long ago, the Romany people put the stones there. 'Tis where many Romany marriages are made. Betrothal promises are made there too. Romany bands travel to this place just to hold weddings here."

"Is it the custom to marry at dawn?" The sky had lightened further, but the gloom of night still clung in the shadows.

"In the Romany way, dancing and feasting take place before the wedding vows, not after. On the last day of the celebration, the oaths are taken before the night ends." She glanced at him briefly. "The bride and groom would have said their vows last night, but the wedding was delayed."

"Do you want to join them to attend the wedding?" he asked. "I will wait, if you wish."

She shook her head. "I will watch from here. The bride and her close kin willna want me among them." Her voice was flat, lacking emotion. She sat the horse with simple ease, her back straight, her head proud on her long neck. But he glimpsed something fragile in the depth of her eyes.

"Then we will watch from here," he said softly. "If you dinna mind the company."

She did not reply, her gaze intent on the scene below. The gypsies came toward the crossing and surrounded it. William watched as John Faw walked toward the center, staying outside the heart itself. He addressed the Romany, and then beckoned. The bride and groom came forward and stepped into the center of the heart. Faw tied their hands together with a red cloth.

William gave Tamsin a questioning look. "My grandfather, as the leader of the Romany," she explained, "will ask them to say their vows there. He binds their wrists together to symbolize the union. Then . . ." She paused.

He saw the glint of a blade. "What . . . ?"

He heard her take a long, quavery breath. "He . . . makes small cuts on their wrists. They allow their blood to mingle, and speak their pledges to each other. 'Tis all that is needed to seal a Romany marriage."

A thought flashed and was gone, so quickly that he could not catch it. He watched the bride and groom. The earthy sincerity of the simple ritual touched him deeply. John Faw released the hands of the bride and groom, and they spoke. Then the whole group began to wend back toward the camp. Voices joined and lifted in song as they walked.

" 'Tis done," Tamsin said.

"I wish them well," William said softly, half to himself.

Tamsin opened her mouth as if to speak, but looked away, her lip and chin quivering. "I must tell you something," she said at last. He frowned, narrowed his eyes, sensing that whatever she had to say was a burden for her. He waited.

"I spoke with my grandparents for a long while before we left the camp," she began. "You likely heard some of it, for we raised our voices."

"I noticed the dispute," he answered. "But I did not understand the language."

"My grandfather wanted me to wed a man of his choosing," she said. "He wanted me to stand in that heart circle with a Romany man, someone who has offered to wed me. I refused. My grandfather was very upset with me."

"He seemed pleased enough by the time we left," he said, though he felt a surprising sense of jealousy simmer within him. He did not like the thought of her wed to someone else. The thought startled him, for he had no claim to her himself. "The argument seems to have been resolved," he added.

She bowed her head, her dark hair sliding forward. "That is what I must tell you," she said. "The resolution. My grandfather wanted me to wed. If I didna choose a husband, any husband, he threatened to banish me from the Romany."

"Banishment?" he asked. "Exile?"

She nodded. "A Romany who is cast out can never go back, unless forgiveness is given. I didna think he would do that to me in truth," she said quickly, "but he mentioned it, which proved how angry he was, how frustrated. How much he wanted me to marry. I couldna . . . I couldna bear to be banished," she said. "It frightened me to hear him say it. I dinna live with them most of the year, and 'tis true that many of the Romany dinna welcome me. But my grandparents' wagon is my home, as much as Merton Rigg is my home. I need to be free to come and go there, to be welcomed at my grandmother's fire, as I have always been." She stopped, drew a breath.

"I understand." William felt a twist of sympathy. "I know what 'tis like to be taken away from kin and home, lass. Believe me, you dinna want to endure that."

He had been thirteen years old when he had been taken from Rookhope by force and put in the custody of the crown as a pledge for his disobedient Scott kinsmen. He was a man before he saw his mother and his siblings again.

He looked out over the blanket of mist lifting from the moorland. He remembered the cold ride through the glen on the day that his father had died, and felt, once again, the keen pain of that forced parting. The awful loneliness of it, which he had never lost in all the years since.

And then he remembered, like a companion image, the sight of Archie and Tamsin Armstrong, together on a horse at the crest of a hill, like the hill he and Tamsin were on now. He recalled their silent salutes to him, and the way they had watched him, like an honor guard, a gesture of respect. He felt a new rush of gratitude for their gift of friendship—and love—at a time when those had been torn from him.

He drew a breath. "Have you decided to wed this Romany man, and so stay within the circle of your grandfather's band? Is that what you wanted to tell me?" he asked.

She shook her head vehemently, tears pooling in her eyes. She wiped at them with the back of her bare hand. "Nay," she said, her voice cracking a little. "I didna agree to wed him. I could never do that. I agreed . . ." She gulped then, and covered her mouth with her hand, holding back a sob.

He wanted to reach out to her, felt an overwhelming urge to touch her, hold her, not presently for the lust that seemed to flare whenever he was near her, but to comfort her. But a hand, a shoulder to lean upon, a word or two while she cried, would not ease the hurt and confusion she felt. He knew that.

And he knew too that she was too proud, too strong, to allow herself to lean on him. He sat his horse beside her and watched as a tear slipped down the honey curve of her cheek. He fisted a hand, tensed his stomach against the wrenching in his heart, so intense was his urge to take her into his arms.

She brushed the back of her hand over her cheek and lifted her head proudly. Then she lifted the reins and guided her horse down the long slope. William followed, stilling his horse at the empty crossing when Tamsin did. With a sigh, she dismounted and went to the heart circle. After a moment, he climbed down and went to stand beside her. He saw the glint of more tears, blinked back.

"Tamsin." He stepped close, unable to stop himself from reaching out, resting his fingers on her shoulder. "What is it? What happened between you and your grandparents?"

She turned her head away from him, but let his hand stay. He felt her heat sink into him, felt her hair drift soft over his skin. He sensed regret, even guilt, within her.

He wanted to help her in her distress, in return for that long-ago day when she, as a child, had made a gesture of such simple sweetness that it had settled soft in the niche of his heart like a dove roosting, and had never left him. Now, as he stood with her, linked to her only by the touch of his palm to her shoulder, he wanted to give something much greater in return for that old, tender gift. He wanted to repay her and her father somehow, and found, simply, that he did not know how.

"My disobedience in refusing Baptiste shames my grandparents," she said. "My marriage, my obedience, would give them great joy. Such things are of enormous importance to the Romany. I want you to understand that." She drew a breath.

"I do understand," he said. "Is there some other man you can marry, then, and still please them?" The words sparked a dark jealousy in him once again. He admonished himself for it, yet could not deny its existence.

He was surprised to hear a soft, tiny laugh escape her lips. She stared down at the heart-shaped circle. "My grandfather has tried to find me a husband. My father has tried even longer. No man has ever wanted me, or offered for me, until this Romany."

"Dinna tell me no one wants you, lass," he said. He watched her in the rising light of dawn. "I would think many men would want the chance to wed such a bonny, bold lass as you."

I want you, he thought suddenly, the certainty of it so strong, so fierce, that he nearly said it aloud, astonishing himself, and stopped the words as they formed.

" 'Tis well known that no Borderman, and no Romany either—until Baptiste Lallo—will have the daughter of Archie Armstrong," she said. "None want a half gypsy, with but half . . . half a hand, to wife." She shrugged as if to dismiss all of those who thought so. But when she tipped her head a little, he saw the hurt in her eyes.

"Then your father and your grandfather havena asked the right man," he said quietly.

She laughed, rueful and humorless. "My father has asked near every man he meets," she said.

"He hasna asked me." His words were quiet, impulsive.

She caught her breath. "You?" she asked. "What . . . what would you have said to him, had he asked you to consider a lass such as me to wife?" She turned her head and looked at him.

In her eyes, as lucid as light shining through green glass, he saw hope, and fear, and fire. He glimpsed the flame that was so essential to her being, diminished by the rejection of so many. The vulnerability he saw in the depths of her eyes tugged at his heart.

He wanted no part of extinguishing her spirit. As much trouble as she had been to him, as much trouble as she yet might be, he admired her spark, enjoyed it, wanted it to flare again.

The elusive thought that had escaped him earlier, while he had watched the gypsy wedding, suddenly returned with startling clarity. The realization that came with it bloomed and grew, opening with possibility. Within an instant, a cool sweat broke over him, and his heart began to pound.

He had not answered her yet. She looked away, let out a long sigh, and began to walk toward her horse.

"Tamsin," he said.

He must be mad, he told himself. One night with the gypsies had thrown him into a state of utter lunacy. He need say nothing to her of his wild thought. He need offer only sympathy, and give her a boost up into her saddle, and take her to Rookhope for a fortnight as arranged. That was the safe path.

He did not want the safe path, this time. He knew that, and did not know why. And suddenly did not care.

"Tamsin," he repeated. He walked toward her.

She turned, her brow creased slightly, and waited.

"I would have told your father," he said, "that I would be honored to be your husband."

She stared up at him, her mouth open slightly, as if she were made speechless, utterly stunned.

"And I would have told him," he went on, "that you and I were already wed."

Chapter Fifteen

Said the youthful earl to the gypsy girl,
As the moon was casting its silver shine
Brown little lady, Egyptian lady,
Let me kiss those sweet lips of thine.

—English Gypsy Song

" 'Tis true, is it not?" he asked. "You knew about this."

A blush spread into her cheeks, and she lowered her eyes. *Aye,* he thought, *she knew.* She would have known from the first. He wondered if her heart pounded as his did.

He stood watching the dark crown of her head, and waited for her answer. "I knew about it, aye," she finally whispered.

"Then what happened between us in Musgrave's dungeon was . . ." He wanted her to finish his thought. He wanted to be sure.

"There was no intent between us. 'Twas an accident." She kept her head lowered, as if she could not look at him. "You wouldna want me to wife."

"Apparently I already have you to wife," he said wryly.

"But we are not truly wed, by Scottish custom."

"Are we," he asked, "by Romany custom?"

She nodded, swallowed. "My grandfather regards it as a marriage," she said. "He—he knows about this. So does my grandmother. They said it was no accident, but a marriage made by fate between us, bonding us together. They are sure 'tis destiny." She glanced up at him with a slight grimace, as if she expected him to protest, loud and sure.

He only huffed out in surprise. "Marriage by fate?"

She nodded, miserable. "My grandfather saw the wound, and Nona had seen yours. They regard the accident between us as greatly significant. My grandparents respect incidents of fate. They say 'tis the presence and the will of . . . what the Christians call God, and must be honored as such."

"They think us wed?" He frowned. "That explains their behavior toward me. And explains this," he said, touching the green silk scarf at his throat. "Your grandmother gave me this as a parting gift."

"A wedding gift. She likes you well." She glanced away. "They think we are wed, by accident, by fate, by . . . by choice as well. They think we came to want it, when it happened."

"You let them think that," he said. "You didna correct them." He did not accuse her, rather tried to sort out the puzzle as she revealed it.

"My grandfather said that we would bring much ill luck to ourselves, and to the Romany, if we went against the will of fate in this and regarded it as mere accident. He thinks it has far deeper meaning than that. My grandmother agrees with him. She looked at my palm, and saw proof there. She says 'twas meant to be." She shrugged a little, and circled her fingers around her left wrist, rubbing there, an unconscious motion.

"You told him that you wanted me," he said, frowning.

"I did," she whispered. "I did. I am sorry. I couldna agree to wed the Romany man. My grandfather gave me a choice between Baptiste Lallo and you." She looked up at him then, eyes luminous in the dawn. "I chose you."

He stared at her. Her honest words touched him deeply, plunging past reason and intellect, becoming a caress for his soul. He felt honored by what she told him, as much as stunned. Tamsin was forthright, and he was sure she was pure in heart. He knew her, somehow, as well as he knew himself, though he had met her but days ago. She played her games, as others did, dealing out fact and fancy like a hand of cards. He had seen her do that to protect herself and her father.

But in matters of emotion, he thought her heart was like his, guarded but sincere. He sensed a companionship with her, felt that he understood her. And he trusted her utterly, deep down in his soul, where loyalty mattered. He had no reason for that except his own strong, reliable gut instincts.

He did not know how she felt about him, or if she trusted him. Nor did he know quite what to do next. He removed his helmet, raked his fingers through his hair, and turned away. He turned back almost immediately to speak, but found he was not ready to express his thoughts. Blasting out a sigh, he stared at the ground.

The implications of what she had said, and thoughts of what he needed most in his life, rushed through his mind like leaves blown on the wind. He needed to catch them, order them. Some of them, he knew, were exquisitely beautiful, and valuable.

"You are angry with me," she said, watching him.

"Nay," he said. "Thinking." He frowned, rubbed his fingers over his temples, sorting, wondering. He half turned from her.

"My grandfather says that if we dinna want this between us, we must go through the ceremony of divorce," she said.

"Divorce?" He cast a long look at her.

"Romany marriages can be undone almost as easily as they are made," she said.

"Do you want that?"

She hesitated. "If you do," she whispered.

"I am asking what you want," he replied quietly.

She drew a breath, looked away, folding her arms over her chest. "If this union is dissolved, then my grandfather will think me free to wed Baptiste Lallo. I will refuse again, and this time my grandfather willna offer me a choice. He may well banish me, for my refusal would shame him, and he must save his pride. He has a fierce temper, and fierce pride," she explained. "So this marriage would help me. 'Tis the only protection I have, either from marriage to Baptiste . . . or from banishment."

She had given him the honest answer he expected. "If we dissolve this marriage in the Romany way," he said, "you would face an even more unpleasant prospect than marriage to me or a sojourn in my dungeon." He drawled the last words, hoping to see the spark, and the sparkle, return to her eyes.

She only hung her head, her hair slipping down like a skein of silken thread. "I knew you wouldna want to wed with me," she said. "I am sorry. This is foolish. 'Tis a problem of my making, not yours. I pray your pardon. You are free of this. I am the one caught here, not you." She stepped back.

He reached out and grabbed her left hand. She resisted, and he pulled, firm and gentle, until she took a small step toward him. Her gloved hand curled tightly over his fingers. He sensed her vulnerability in that slight movement.

"We are both caught by the same act of fate," he said. "You need this marriage, it seems. Or at least the ruse of one."

"William," she said thoughtfully, "what would happen if we . . . kept the marriage in place? For just a wee while, until Baptiste moves on?" She blushed, as if she felt timid.

Her apprehension almost hurt him to witness. She had pride, a bright inner flame, and he would not side with those who dampened that in her. Suddenly he knew, with striking clarity, what he wanted to do. The certainty of it gave him strength of purpose. He pulled on her hand, drawing her toward him, their gazes joined.

"Then I will honor this marriage by fate, if you want that of me," he murmured. "For a wee while, as you say."

A breeze lifted a lock of her hair, swept it over her face. She stared up at him. "You would do that?" she whispered.

He reached out to sift the dark silk of her hair away to see her face, her eyes. "I owe you a debt, lass, from long ago." She tilted her head, a question. "I will tell you of it later. For now, just know that I always honor my debts."

"If there is any debt, 'tis I who owe you," she said. "You helped my father and I, and you saved me from Arthur Musgrave. Twice. But tell me why you would do this for me."

He glanced away, scanning the misted hills. Several practical reasons for this impractical solution came to mind. He wanted to do something more for Archie and Tamsin, in return for an old debt, deeply felt. He needed this marriage himself, to protect his daughter Katharine from Hamilton. Tamsin would be able to avoid the dreaded sentence of banishment from her Romany kin. And Musgrave would not be eager to pursue claims of witchcraft brought by Arthur, if Tamsin were the lady of Rookhope.

All sensible reasons, which he could list for her in a rational manner. What he could not explain so easily was the powerful urge that compelled him forward, that made him persist when he knew there was no truly sensible, logical reason, after all, to do so.

He should just sympathize with her plight, say nothing to her of his, and take her to Rookhope as planned. Instead, he felt as if he walked a path that might be more foolish than cautious. Yet he wanted to proceed.

Impulsive, true, he thought. But his agreement was founded on his sincere wish to help the girl, not from the physical desire that he undeniably felt for her. That, he told himself, he could control. But he could not just walk away and leave her to her predicament.

"Why would you agree to help me?" she asked again, softly.

"I was as much a part of that unwitting marriage as you were," he said. "It has caused a good deal of trouble for you. If letting the marriage stand, even as a brief ruse, will help you solve your dilemma, then I am willing. And," he added quietly, "I find that I have a dilemma of my own. This would help me, as well. I need a wife, just as you need a husband, for a little while."

Her heart thumped like a drum. She stared at him. "You need a wife?" She blinked. "For a wee while?"

He smiled, that quiet lift of his lips that she had come to enjoy, which crinkled and brightened his blue eyes. "Aye," he said. " 'Twould help me to have a wife just now. And I dinna have time to go out and find one."

"But you could choose a noble lady of the Scottish court, and—and have a genuine wife."

"I could. But you, lass," he said, "are far more interesting to me than other ladies I have met. And whether or not you believe it, most of the noble ladies at court wouldna have the laird o' Rookhope to husband now. You are not the only one who has a poor reputation. Of course," he added in a wry tone, "I have earned my poor name, where yours is undeserved."

She shifted her gloved hand behind her out of habit. The warm pressure of his touch seemed to linger there. She had found the courage to ask him to let the false marriage stand for now, but she felt astonished that he had agreed.

"You must need a wife rather desperately to agree to this," she said.

"Not so desperate that I would snatch the next lass who crossed my path," he said. "This marriage came to both of us when we needed it. Perhaps there is some destiny in it."

She nodded, still aware of the heavy thudding of her heart. "Why do you need a wife?"

"There is a certain man who presses me unreasonably and threatens my kin. I had thought to take a year or two to find a wife to suit me. But if I were to bring a wife home just now, 'twill help avert great trouble for my daughter from this man. He is her grandsire."

She blinked at him, confused. "Daughter?"

"Aye. Katharine," he answered. "He wants to take her from me. But I will keep her safe however I must," he said fiercely. She saw the snap of true conviction in his eyes.

"What—what of her mother?" she asked.

"She is dead," he answered. "Her name was Jeanie Hamilton," he added, his voice softening. He must have loved Jeanie very much, she thought. " 'Tis her father who wants custody of our daughter," he continued. "Now I suppose you willna want to step into such a situation, even for a little while."

"It suits us both. I will help you."

"Then 'tis agreed."

She nodded. "My father and my grandparents pressure me to find a husband. I am weary of the search. This will be a relief to me, even for a little while."

"For us both," he said, watching her.

"Aye. We can dissolve this between us as soon as our troubles are lifted. But . . ." She looked away, hesitated. "But I dinna wish to tell lies regarding this marriage, since 'tis half a truth."

"We can say a vow between us, here, in the Romany way, to make it a whole truth. If you wish," he added.

She nodded hastily. Her heart thudded inside her chest. She felt as if she were about to step off a cliff, either to fall or to fly.

"Lass, yonder lies your heart of stones. Do we make a pledge to fix the bond?"

"For a while only," she said. He nodded again.

In the clear light, she saw rosy color seep into his cheeks. She liked that bright window to his feelings, showing that the issue between them affected him deeply. She was still stunned that he had not scoffed at the odd marriage that fate had created between them.

Her heart pounded heavily. She wanted this, so much, and could hardly summon words to express why. A desire to hold on to the moment grew in her. The reasons to keep this union of fate glittered like stars in her heart, tiny, bright hopes.

She had mistrusted him earlier, and did not understand his mysterious and unexplained loyalties—or disloyalties. But he offered her a precious gift of friendship and salvation from a dilemma, when she had expected something far less than that.

"Twelve Bordermen have turned down offers of marriage to me," she suddenly blurted, as if to give him one last opportunity to reject her.

"Then I am the thirteenth man to have the chance," he said.

" 'Tis an unlucky omen, thirteen."

He tilted his head. "In certain matters, I am known to have the best of luck."

"In what matters?"

"Cards," he said. "Games of chance."

"Well, this is surely a game of chance. I too am lucky at the cards. Though not in much else," she added.

"Perhaps we will be lucky together in this."

"The Romany say that I am *wafri bak*—bad luck."

"Lass," he said softly, "I am not a Romany."

"There is one thing more you must know," she said. "My father will be so glad about this that he will declare you his good-son to everyone he meets. And he will demand a priest wedding. That would be much harder to dissolve. A Romany marriage can be ended in a few moments, with the consent of the spouses." She sighed, shook her head. "This may be a mistake after all. I dinna want my father hurt by this."

He leaned close. "Tamsin," he said. She loved the gentle way he murmured her name.

"Come here." He took hold of her left hand and stepped backward, leading her with him, until his boot heels met the stone rim of the heart circle. He tossed his helmet, tucked under his arm, to the ground.

" 'Tis halfway done," he said. "Tell me how to do the rest."

She looked at him warily. "Divorce? Or marriage?"

He gave her that small, patient smile again, and her heart seemed to flutter. "Time enough for the other," he said. "We will make it binding."

"But we willna be wed by Scots law," she said.

William turned her hand in his, rubbing his thumb along the healing mark on her wrist where his blade had cut her. "By old Scots law, lass, we will indeed be wed if we commit to it in good faith, between the two of us. If we keep it a year and a day, the marriage is made firm. It can be broken at any time before that. So we have a choice, by either custom."

"We will have no priestly vows said over us," she said. "And we willna tell my father."

"If that is your choice, aye."

"Nor shall we live as man and wife," she said softly.

"I must be a madman to agree to any of this," he muttered. "As you wish. It shall be a marriage between friends."

" 'Twould be poor of you to dishonor me when we ask but friendship of one another," she said, sliding him a glance.

"Naught will happen between us that you dinna want," he said. "Believe me." He was deeply serious. She wondered if she had offended him.

She regretted, then, that she had suggested that, and regretted more his acquiescence. Something washed through her, a hot, insistent rush of desire that made her want to touch him, and feel his touch. She wondered what it would be like to be held in his arms. But she had spoken the rule of their mock marriage and would not relent now.

He pulled gently on her hand and drew her inside the heart circle. "What is the custom?"

"There are several," she said. "Perhaps a betrothal promise will do for us."

"Aye. The marriage first, the betrothal second." He smiled. She did too, laughing reluctantly.

"Take off your neck scarf," she said.

He lifted a brow in surprise, but undid the knotted scarf and drew it off, holding it out to her.

"Put it 'round my neck," she directed, "and take the ends, and then say the vow you wish to make. 'Tis the Romany way to make a betrothal promise."

He frowned slightly as he lowered the scarf behind her head, catching it gently against the back of her neck, drawing the ends forward. The silk was wonderfully soft, still holding the warmth of his body, the subtle scent of him. It settled like a ring of heaven around her neck, easing the memory of the rope she had worn not so long ago.

"Now say whatever comes to your mind," she said. "Fate made the marriage between us. If you listen, fate may give you the words for the betrothal."

He nodded, his eyes crystal blue, deep in thought. Then he twisted his fingers in the ends of the silk, shortening the scarf, slowly drawing her toward him.

Her gaze, wide and earnest and made vivid green by the emerald scarf, never parted from his. She was as bright and as pure as a candle flame, and she waited upon his words with a patience and a trust that touched him deeply.

He paused, searching for words. The sun slid upward and began to dissolve the veils of mist around them as they stood in the heart circle. And he knew, as if the sunbeams burned away the mist of his doubt, the vow that was needed between them.

He pulled on the silk until she was but a breath away, until she tipped back her head to look at him. Still he held the scarf taut, catching her close and sure within its length.

"I give you my loyalty, Tamsin Armstrong," he murmured. "I will respect the marriage of our shared blood and shared promises." He felt the depth of her silence as she listened. "I give you my heart as your friend, my hand as your guardian, and my name as your husband. Whatever you need of me shall be done."

Her lips parted, her eyelids fluttered, opened again. His heartbeat surged within him. He was held as fast by that delicate green gaze as she was by a fragile bit of green silk.

"And I give my loyalty to you, William Scott." She nearly whispered the words. "I respect the marriage of fate between us, the sharing of blood and promises. I give you my heart in friendship, my help as your wife, forsoever long as we agree. Whatever you need of me shall be done."

What swept through him in that moment had in it a power like lightning, possessed the rhythm of thunder, filling him, slipping through to the core of his being.

He wound his fingers in the scarf, pulling her even closer, so that her breasts pressed against him, though he could not feel that softness through steel. She tilted her head back, and the morning light burst full over her face.

He saw her with greater clarity than he had ever seen anyone in his life. In her translucent eyes, he glimpsed her vulnerable soul. He realized, despite the wilder elements in her nature, just how innocent she was, just how pure.

He knew then that he had made a true and binding promise. The words he had spoken were a flawed reflection of the power he felt between them, greater than that of friendship formed from necessity. He wondered, suddenly, what he had done. This did not feel at all like a fleeting agreement.

He intended to honor what he had said to her, for so long as she needed it of him. What had happened at this crossroads had spun him like a leaf in a storm. In the first moment of settling, he did not regret what he had done.

Just as in a game of cards, he had taken a chance, gambling what he had on a bright bit of luck. A marriage made by fate had fallen into his path when he was greatly in need of a wife.

The pledge needed one last thing to complete it. He lowered his head and touched his mouth to hers, a kiss like the graze of a feather, dry and soft, meant to be the sealing of a pact.

But she moaned, a little whisper of sound, and the pulse of his need, and her own, pounded through him with undeniable force. He angled his head and kissed her deeply, releasing the silk to plunge his fingers into the cloud of her hair, shaping his palms to her head.

Her right hand came up to touch his jaw. He dropped a hand to her waist and held her against him, knowing that she wanted to be in his arms, and that he wanted her there. He moved his mouth over hers, brushed his thumbs along her cheeks, and felt her lips open in tentative welcome.

She pulled back. " 'Tis done," she said breathlessly. " 'Tis made, this . . . marriage, this friendship that we have pledged."

"Friendship, if you wish," he said. He felt a bit short of breath himself, and curiously muddled.

"Is that what friends do, then, at the royal courts?" Her eyes twinkled, and her lips were still dark pink from the kiss. He laughed softly, and she did too. He liked the sound of it.

He gathered the scarf in one hand and stepped back, tying it about his neck once again. "Pray your pardon," he said. "I meant just to seal the pact with a chaste kiss."

"That wasna chaste." She still smiled, a little.

"It started out in that manner," he said. "I swear it." He took her arm and guided her out of the stone heart. "I promise you, 'twillna happen again."

She pushed slender fingers through her hair, as if befuddled. "What shall we do now?"

"We'll go to Rookhope," he said. "As we had planned."

"And then? Will you put me in your dungeon?"

"Ah, now, would I ask my wife to sleep in my dungeon?"

She tilted her head. "Will you let her have your fine bed?"

He pinched back a smile. "If she wants it."

"Aye, she does," she answered crisply. "You may have a pallet elsewhere." She flashed him a winsome smile, so charming that it might have broken any man's heart. It stirred his like wind through the trees, fresh and pure.

She turned away to walk to her horse, and he could not help but notice the sway of her hips beneath her skirt. Without asking for his assistance, she grasped the horse's mane and placed her foot on a rock in order to climb onto the horse's blanketed back. William stepped toward her and bent to scoop his hand under her narrow foot, boosting her easily onto the horse.

"So that is the way of it," he said, patting the horse's muzzle as he spoke to Tamsin. "The poor beleaguered husband must sleep in a cold corner, while the wife takes his fine, soft bed. I have wed myself a princess."

"If you dinna like it," she said, "we can dissolve the marriage whenever you wish—after my grandfather has told Baptiste Lallo to find himself another woman to scrub his pots and wipe his children's noses."

"And how do we dissolve our marriage pact?"

She cocked a brow at him. "That depends on whether we have a kind parting or an angry one."

"Kind, surely, having done such a favor of friendship for one another this day."

"Then we break a clay pot between us," she said.

"Easy enough," he said. "And angry?"

"We would face one another over the body of a dead animal, say our grievances, and go our ways."

He looked at her in dismay. "Like a hare or a bird?"

"Oh," she said, "like the body of your best horse." She lifted the reins and turned her mount to ride away.

William watched her, aware that a grimace soured his face. He walked to the bay and rubbed the gleaming red-brown shoulder.

"Dinna fret, lad," he said. "Dinna fret. For your sake, I will be careful and courteous to yon lass."

Chapter Sixteen

"Both in a tune like two gipsies on a horse."
—Shakespeare, *As You Like It*

"My grandfather wanted to give Baptiste two horses and some gold coins as a dowry for me," she remarked, as they rode side by side later. She slid him a careful look.

A smile played at his lips. "He obviously preferred Baptiste to me. All I got was a neck scarf."

"Ah," she said. "The finest Oriental silk, embroidered by a princess of France and given to an earl of Lesser Egypt. My grandmother prefers you to Baptiste. She would never have given *him* that particular neck scarf." She tilted her head as she looked at him. "I think I too prefer you to Baptiste."

"And all the while, I thought you didna want to come with me for fear of my dungeon," he said.

Tamsin liked the way he kept his smiles low, so that the humor shone brighter in his clear blue eyes. She thought he enjoyed the teasing chatter between them as much as she did. "Ah, well, a fortnight in gentle confinement wouldna disturb me much. You did agree to give up your fine bed to me."

She hoped for another smile, but he grew solemn. "What happens in a fortnight, lass?"

She shrugged, wanting to preserve the lighthearted mood that had existed between them since their impulsive vows. "We shall break a jug and let ourselves free of this agreement."

He did not answer. The morning light glinted off his helmet, shadowing his face beneath. She watched him, noting the clean, balanced line of his profile, the sensuous curve of his lower lip, the slight droop of his eyelids when he was relaxed. His firm jaw-line was blurred by the dark sand of his beard. She remembered its brush over her skin when he had kissed her. At that memory, she touched her hand to her heart, as if to seal in the feeling that stirred through her.

The smoke of the fire that they had created inside the heart circle had cleared, and left her wondering just what she had done. She suspected, by William's long silence during the ride, that he wondered too. But she wanted only to live in the present moment. She liked riding with him at this leisurely pace, she enjoyed resting her gaze upon him, and she liked the teasing tone between them. He surprised her with as quick a wit as her father, though quieter and more wry.

She felt comfortable in his company, as if she had known him for years, as if she understood him like brother, friend, lover. Though she was unable to reconcile those impressions with what she had learned of him at Musgrave's castle, she told herself that he likely had good reasons for the secrets he kept, and for the motives that did not look wholesome on the outside.

He was capable of kindness and generosity, and had a strong regard for friendship. That in itself bespoke a loyal man, one to admire. Whatever she discovered of him, she would not forget that he had given her his friendship and his loyalty when she had needed help.

She had never had a truly close friend. His pledge to her had tugged firmly at her heart, and helped explain why she had followed through with this arrangement. Perhaps that bond would be enough later.

She glanced at him, and received one of those slow, quiet smiles. Her heart faltered, and she knew that a bond of friendship would never be enough.

By the time the sun shone high and bright overhead, her stomach rumbled with hunger and her bruised leg ached from riding. Tamsin was glad to see William raise his hand and point ahead. "There, on that rise," he said, "sits Rookhope Tower."

She shielded her eyes with her gloved hand. In the distance, a gray stone tower rose above a walled yard. Massive and block-like, made up of two main structures joined together, the keep had a machicolated parapet and a grim, nearly windowless facade. Set on a swath of cleared land surrounded by ditches, the site was protected on three sides by forestland and bare slopes. The fourth wall faced a deep chasm, a slash in the land.

"A strong tower," she said. "And difficult to breach."

"Aye. Rookhope is one of the strengths of the Border," he said. A flock of small black birds rose out of the forest and flew past the tower like a dark veil. "Ah, see there—some of the rooks for which the place was named centuries ago, when the first castle was built on this site."

"Rooks are called gypsy birds, did you know?" she asked.

"I have heard that, aye." He laughed low, as if to himself. "So the laird of Rookhope brings a gypsy bird to his nest."

She knew he made a pun. "Burd" was a Scots word for lass. "Aye, 'tis fitting," she agreed.

"Bluebonnets, just there," he said, as they followed the road, which she saw wound closer to Rookhope, "are called the gypsy flower." He gestured toward the blue blossoms on long, slender stalks that formed airy clusters along the edge of the earthen tract and sprinkled patches of color throughout the meadow. "They grow in abundance here. Named for the way they spread so freely over the land, taking root and sprouting where they will."

"They're bright and bonny, those gypsy flowers," she said.

He turned his head, and below the shade of his helmet brim, his gaze swept her up and down. "Aye," he murmured, and looked away. "I visited a gypsy camp with King James once," he said. "Though it was another band, not your grandfather's. I would have recognized him, and he me, otherwise," he said.

"King James visited my grandfather's band too," she said. "I was with them once when he came—I remember a very young man with long red hair and a lanky shape. He wore the guise of a beggar. He was alone, I think, though he came to see my grandfather at other times too. Certainly you werena with him. I would have remembered you," she added softly.

He shrugged. "I am near enough to the next man," he said. "Dark and tall. There are many like me."

She shook her head. "Your eyes are like those flowers there, bright blue. The color sparks, even from a distance."

He watched her for a moment, then unwound the scarf from his throat. "And yours," he said, "make this silk look dull."

She felt herself blush. He wound the cloth around his upper arm, tucking it with the nimble fingers of one hand. "How was it you traveled with the king?" she asked. "I know you were a friend to him, but I . . ." She hesitated. "I heard that you were a prisoner of the crown in those years."

He did not seem to mind that she knew that about him. "My father was hanged for a thief," he said. "And I was held as a pledge for my kinsmen. I was kept in a dark cell until they knew what to do with me. At the time, the earl of Angus had the young king under his thumb in captivity—a bored and intelligent lad greatly in need of a companion. I was given quarters near the king and allowed to share lessons and leisure time with him."

"Educated with a king?" she asked. "Fortunate, indeed."

"I suppose so," he said. "Though I would have traded it all for the life that was taken from me." Tamsin tilted her head, listening, waiting, but he said no more about that. "Even when James gained back his own freedom at the age of sixteen," he went on, "I didna acquire my own freedom legally until James granted it me when I was twenty. After that, I lived at court, and accompanied the king on his progresses about the country. I did a great deal of traveling myself, on errands for the crown."

"You stayed with the court after you were released?" she asked. "You didna go home to Rookhope?"

"Occasionally, but my family was no longer there," he answered. "The tower was held for me by kinsmen sent by Scott of Buccleuch, the chief of our name. My mother and my sister and brother were at Brentshaw, with my stepfather, Robert Maxwell, but I didna care to go there. So I lived wherever the court happened to be—at Edinburgh, Falkland, Linlithgow, or Stirling—or I stayed at a house I own in Edinburgh. Last year my mother was widowed again, and she wanted to go back to Rookhope with my sister, who is also a widow. Then I too chose to live at Rookhope," he said. "My daughter is in their care."

"Your kin are important to you," she said.

He nodded. "Aye." A curt answer, but deep pink stained his lean cheek, and a small muscle jumped in his jaw. Family, she realized, was essential to him. As were his private thoughts, for he said no more.

"After your confinement ended, you traveled with the king of Scotland?" she asked. "That must have been truly exciting."

His smile was rueful. "Aye. In my way, I have been a gypsy." He glanced at her.

"You went a-wandering?" she asked.

"On errands for the king, aye. I have been to England and Denmark, and to France, Italy, and Germany as well. And everywhere I went, lass," he added thoughtfully, "I saw traveling caravans of gypsies along the roadsides and in the fields, and at market fairs."

She nodded. "The Romany travel everywhere on the Continent, and in the eastern countries too, I hear. They are in great numbers in England and Scotland, although the English now are beginning to deport shiploads of them to Denmark. My grandparents came from France and traveled to England when they were young, wandering up into Scotland," she said.

"They havena traveled out of Scotland, then, for a long while," he said.

"They will stay here so long as they are welcome, I think," she said. "The Scots are more tolerant of the Romany than most other places. They have some freedom here to govern themselves."

"Have you been elsewhere?" he asked.

"Only in England, of a moonlit night." She smiled. "When I was small, I lived with my grandparents and spoke Romany and French. My father brought me to Merton when I was about six years of age. His grandmother—Mother Maisie—was there to help raise me, but I didna speak Scots or any English at all. Da hired a male tutor who spoke French to teach me Scots. I learned more than Scots from my dominie, for he also taught me to read English and Latin, and taught me some arithmetic too."

He glanced at her. "An educated gypsy lass? Unusual."

"You were educated with a king. We are both unusual in our education. And in our wandering natures, I think. Tell me about your journeys with the king."

He shrugged. "The most exciting moments were the times I accompanied him on his secret tours. He liked to go about his country disguised as a beggar or as a farmer. 'The Goodman of Ballangeich,' he called himself then. We found trouble at times, especially in the inns, where there were often fights over gambling or Border matters. I dragged him to safety once or twice, when no one knew that they wrestled or argued with the king of Scotland. The more he went about, the more his disguises were for naught," he said with a fleeting grin. "The Scots are a canny lot. Some would say, 'Ho, there goes the king again,' as he went by in his rags."

She chuckled. "Did you visit gypsy camps with him?"

"Aye, though I didna visit your grandfather's band myself. James mentioned an Egyptian earl named John Faw, who once cured his horse of a sickness, for which the king was very grateful. He must have meant your grandfather."

She nodded. "He did. He met with my grandfather a few times, even invited him to bring his troupe to the royal court to perform. Three years ago, when my grandfather brought his band to Falkland Palace, the king wrote out a note of privilege and safe conduct for him."

He frowned. "Was that your grandfather's band? I heard about the performance—many were impressed—and the writ."

"Then you know what came after."

"Aye, the king issued another writ a few months later. He took away the privileges of the first, and declared that all gypsies must leave the realm of Scotland. He seemed in a temper over it, as I recall."

She nodded. "The Romany are condemned by England and Scotland both now, and so they go back and forth across the Border to avoid deportation and persecution in both countries. My grandfather was hurt by King James's betrayal of friendship."

"James had a fickle nature. Why did John Faw lose favor?"

"My grandfather hit him," she said.

William lifted his brows. "Hit the king?"

"About two years past, the king came to the camp guised as a farmer. He was drunk, for he had come from an inn where he had been dicing. When he came to the camp that night, he fondled one of the women in a rude manner. My grandfather hit him over the head with a bottle of wine that the king had given him."

William blinked his astonishment. "John Faw was lucky—he might have lost his life for such a deed."

"Perhaps he was saved because King James regarded him as an earl among his own people. And he had great respect for my grandfather's skill with horses. The king even consulted my grandmother about his future."

"Did she predict long life and good fortune? James had neither, in the end."

Tamsin stared at the blue flowers that lined the roadside. "She saw the truth, before anyone else," she said. "She knew that the king would come to an early death. I know she warned King James of ill health. But sometimes a heeding is for naught. Sometimes fate is too powerful a force."

"Fate," he said, "works its will with many."

"Aye." She glanced at him, feeling somber. "So now the king is dead, and his wee daughter has the throne."

"A teething bairn on a monarch's throne is far more trouble than you can imagine."

" 'Tis well for the Romany," she said. "The Scots Privy Council canna be bothered with them just now, and my grandfather still has King James's writ of safe conduct. He uses it freely. Many Scots dinna know about the second writ banning us, so that he still gains privileges for his people." She tilted her head. "Have you seen wee Queen Mary?" she asked curiously.

"Aye. A bonny bairn, and a mighty difficulty for Scotland. Henry of England hovers over her cradle like a vulture."

"She has many who will protect her," she said.

"She is safely tucked away at Linlithgow, but I for one would feel more at ease if she were at Stirling Castle. Our infant queen needs a fortress 'round her, I think." He frowned.

"I visited Falkland Palace once," Tamsin said. William looked at her with surprise. "The king invited my grandfather's people to dance and play music one summer three years ago. I went with them. The noble ladies wanted their fortunes told, and I helped Grandmother to read palms and cards. I saw the queen, so tall and lovely, and the king with her, magnificently dressed. The palace was huge and beautiful, with tapestries on the walls, and glass windows, and velvet on the chairs. I saw fine gear everywhere, and grand ladies and lords." She looked at him. "I didna see you there, though. I am sure of it."

"I avoid the grander celebrations, as a rule. I prefer smaller gatherings." He glanced at her. "Such as we have at Rookhope. After supper of an evening, we gather for games and music. You will enjoy that, I think."

She glanced away quickly. The thought of meeting his mother, sister, and daughter suddenly terrified her. "I am not used to such things," she said cautiously.

"You said that you play at the cards," he said. "You will do well with my family. You will see."

"And what shall I see?" she asked. Frightened by the prospect of meeting his family, loath to show her fear and trepidation, she let anger rise in its place. "What will you tell them? 'This is my wife, such as I will keep in my dungeon?' Or, 'This is my prisoner, such as I will keep in my bed?' How do you mean to explain me to them?"

" 'This is Tamsin Armstrong, our guest,' " he said calmly. "Just that."

"Ah. Just that. 'Twillna last long, this marriage, will it?" She looked away, shoving back the mass of ringlets that fell past her shoulder. The summer day was warm, and her tartaned plaid had grown heavy. She untied the cord that fastened it and let the plaid fall behind her.

Smoothing a hand over her chemise and worn brown kirtle, casting a glance at her bare feet, she wished that she had a comb, a fine gown, a pair of shoes. William's kinswomen would be appalled by her appearance. She curled her gloved hand in her lap, aware that she feared their revulsion most of all.

"Tamsin," he finally said. "What has stirred your temper? Do you have regrets?"

"Not I. Likely you will soon regret this," she grumbled.

"I willna. But I might regret my promise to keep you out of the dungeon," he growled. They rode along in silence, drawing closer to Rookhope, climbing a track that led up a hillside toward the tower.

William glanced at her. "My mother and sister expect you," he said. "Dinna fret about meeting them."

She looked at him in surprise. "They expect me?"

"Aye. I stopped at Rookhope after I left your father. I had supper there, and explained to my mother and sister that Musgrave wanted you to act as a pledge."

She frowned. "What will you tell them now?"

"We shall see." He was silent for a few moments. "My mother—Lady Emma—and Helen are caring souls. You will be at ease with them, I promise you."

"What of your daughter?"

"You will find her a delight, I think," he said. "Katharine is but a bairn, scarce eight months in the world."

"A bairn?" she asked, amazed. "I thought her much older."

"She was born but two weeks before the queen of Scotland. The queen dowager is her godmother." He paused, then said quietly, "Her mother died the day the child was born."

"I am sorry," she murmured.

"We werena wed," he said. "But the child is mine, and I will keep her. Now that I have a wife"—he glanced at her and smiled, rueful and endearing—"her grandfather will find it more difficult to claim the custody of her." He slid her a glance. "If you come to regret our agreement, do me the courtesy to endure me as your husband until the Court of Sessions reviews the complaint regarding the fostering of my daughter." She heard the same fierce tone in his voice that she had noted earlier when he spoke of his daughter.

"I can endure this as long as you can," she said.

"So be it, then," he said, and slowed his horse as the massive wall of Rookhope loomed above them. He called out, and within moments the iron portcullis slid upward.

He waved her ahead of him, but she shook her head, realizing she wanted him to act as her shield. She followed, her horse's steps echoing on the cobbled stones beneath the vaulting of the entrance. They emerged in a small courtyard with a well in one corner and arched doorways leading to other areas. Tamsin glimpsed stairs and alcoves there.

"Ho! Willie Scott!" She looked up and saw a man coming toward them. Sandie, whom she recognized from the other night, grinned and clasped William's hand. "The arm is better, I see."

"The gypsies tended it for me," William said.

"And I see you tended to this gypsy, since she's with ye." Sandie winked at Tamsin. His eyes were warm brown, and she liked his quick, friendly wink and his honest grin. Accustomed to Bordermen, she took no offense, sure that none was intended.

"Aye, she is with me, and will stay, so watch your manners."

"Yet another lassie at Rookhope," Sandie said, and sighed. "The place is full o' them. Nae that I complain, I like a lassie about the place. Though they do insist on rules and manners, belike. Perhaps a gypsy lass will be less hard on me for tracking my spurs over the floors, or for my rough table manners, hey?"

She smiled. "I promise, Sandie Scott," she said. "I have no household authority here, nor will I take any. And my manners might be far worse than yours," she added.

William dismounted and took the bridle of Tamsin's horse, walking toward the shadowed corridor that contained the stables. Sandie took the bay's bridle and walked with them.

"A fortnight, is that the agreement with Musgrave?" Sandie asked.

"A fortnight," William said. "Then we shall see what comes next." He looked at Tamsin as he spoke, and something in his voice sent shivers throughout her body.

William held up his hands to her, and Tamsin leaned forward, placing her hands on his shoulders, feeling his fingers slide along her ribs, pressing, lifting her. She stood behind him as he turned and handed the reins to Sandie. William began to walk across the courtyard toward the massive tower, beckoning to Tamsin.

An archway on the ground level led to an alcove and a flight of stone steps, topped by a wide landing and a stout wooden door. William climbed the steps and Tamsin followed. The door swung open, and a woman stood silhouetted in the dim light at the top of the steps.

"William!" The woman glided forward, gowned in black, her full skirt belling out as she approached. She held out her hands. "I am so glad you are back. Jock and Sandie told me that you were wounded and had to stop at the gypsy camp—"

"I am just fine, Mother," he said. "My arm hardly troubles me already. 'Tis healing well, I think. The gypsies work some magical cures." He stepped up to the landing with her, leaning down to kiss her cheek. She smiled up at him, then turned to Tamsin with a polite look on her thin, lovely face. Tamsin thought that she resembled her handsome son most closely in the brilliant blue of her thick-lashed eyes.

William turned to Tamsin, holding out his hand to invite her onto the landing with them. "Mother, this is Tamsin Armstrong," he said. "Our guest."

Chapter Seventeen

O where have you ridden this lee lang day
And where have you stown this fair lady away?
—"Earl Brand"

"Lady Emma," Tamsin said hesitantly. She felt awkward beneath the woman's alert gaze, though she saw kindness there. She smoothed her skirt with her right hand, hid her left beneath her plaid, and wished that her bare feet were not quite so dirty as she climbed the steps to the platform.

"Tamsin, welcome to Rookhope." Lady Emma held out a hand, perhaps the most beautiful hand Tamsin had ever seen: pale and slender, fingers bedecked with small sparkling rings, nails polished to shining ovals. She lowered her head and reached out her own hand, aware that it was grimy and a little rough to the touch. The thought of this perfect, beautiful woman seeing her left hand made her cringe with uncertainty.

Cool, smooth fingers slipped over her own. "I hope you will feel at home while you are with us," Lady Emma said.

"Th-thank you," Tamsin said. She was tempted to drop into a curtsy, as she had seen women do at the royal court the time that she had been there. Lady Emma seemed as elegant and sophisticated as those ladies, and Tamsin felt every bit the vagabond as she stood before her.

"Archie's daughter," Emma said, smiling. "I knew your father well when we were younger. William's father thought highly of him." She folded her hands before her and inclined her head. "You look like your mother, lass. I met her once, just after she and Archie were wed. She was lovely and exotic."

Tamsin felt herself blush, and nodded silently. She glanced at Lady Emma and took in the details of a stunning but simple gown of black damask, her head covered in a black hood with a gabled crown and a black velvet veil that spilled to her shoulders. The hair divided over her brow mingled gray with auburn. Lady Emma seemed a pinnacle of elegance, her air of perfection due even more to her gracious demeanor than to her fine clothing.

"Archie's daughter may be here for longer than two weeks, Mother," William said. His gaze met Tamsin's.

"Come in," Lady Emma said, drawing Tamsin by the arm through the doorway. William followed them into a small alcove containing more turning stairs and one doorway that led to the great hall.

As they entered, Tamsin glanced around the huge, dimly lit room, at the polished timber flooring and a high timber ceiling. She noted the whitewashed walls, the high-set windows, and a hooded stone fireplace at the far end of the room with a low, banked fire glowing at its heart.

"Will! You're back!" Tamsin saw another woman hurrying along the length of the room, holding her dark brown skirts in both hands, slippers knocking softly on the wooden floor. She smiled widely and prettily, extending the smile to include Tamsin. The lighting from the high windows and the fireplace cast shadows over her face.

"My sister Helen," William murmured. "Tamsin Armstrong."

"Welcome!" Helen said, her voice musical and warm. "Will said he meant to bring you here upon his return. How glad we are to meet you."

Tamsin nodded a shy greeting as the young woman took her right hand in both of hers. Helen's fingers were warm and strong, well kept, decorated with delicate rings. Tamsin bit at her lip and glanced at the floor uncertainly.

William's kinswomen were kind and gracious, but so well dressed that she felt exceedingly plain and disheveled beside them. She thought they would assume she was like the filthy and untrustworthy gypsies who were mocked in tales and ballads.

"You must be tired from your journey," Helen said.

"Aye, somewhat. My thanks for your kind welcome."

"Where is Katharine?" William asked Helen.

"Sleeping sound," Helen said, looking up at her brother. "She'll wake soon, if you wish to see her, and if you wish to show her to Mistress Armstrong." Helen smiled at William.

When Helen tipped her face upward, Tamsin noticed that the young woman's face, though cream-hued and sweetly shaped, was deeply scarred across the cheeks and forehead. A pit at the corner of her mouth formed a dimple when she smiled, and the scarring that pocked the edge of her jaw extended down her neck to disappear under the embroidered, frilled collar of the chemise that showed beneath her bodice.

Despite the veneer of scars, Tamsin thought that Helen, who seemed close to her own age, was truly lovely. She saw a resemblance to William in the long, slender nose, firm jaw, and full lips. Helen's eyes were hazel and her hair auburn, enhanced by the brown damask gown, and a pretty cap of stiffened brown velvet, fitted to her head in graceful wings that swept down to partially cover her scarred cheeks.

"Oh, Will, did Mother tell you about the letter that was delivered by messenger early this morning?" Helen asked. William shook his head, glancing at his mother. "From Malise's advocate," Helen rushed on. "Mother read it, in your absence, for the messenger said 'twas urgent. Hamilton has filed his complaint in the Court of Sessions, and threatens to take Katharine from us within weeks!"

"He willna," William growled. "Dinna fret." Tamsin saw a hard set in his eyes.

"Tamsin, you must be tired," Emma said, turning away from the others and toward her with a gentle smile, helping to dispel the tension. "We thought that you could share a bedchamber with Helen and Katharine, William's daughter, while you are here."

"Tamsin will take my own bedchamber," William said. Helen looked at him in surprise. Emma's smooth face was marred by a small, puzzled frown. "Those lodgings are private and comfortable," he explained.

"How generous of you, William," Emma said. "We can prepare a chamber for you elsewhere while Tamsin is here."

"Aye." He sighed and shoved long fingers through his hair,

having tucked his helmet under his arm. "Mother," he said. "Helen . . ." He paused, scratching at his head.

The air seemed charged with quiet lightning. He looked at Tamsin then, so directly that she nearly caught her breath at the intimate power, the shared thought, that passed between them. She wanted to ask him to keep silent, not to do this, but somehow she could not speak. He turned to his mother.

"Tamsin and I are married," he said.

His simple statement produced a profound silence. Neither Emma nor Helen made a sound, though both dropped their mouths partly open in astonishment.

"M-married?" Helen finally repeated.

"This morning," William said.

"Wedded just this day?" Emma asked. "You have wed Archie Armstrong's daughter?" Her eyes rounded, the same brilliant hue as her son's, as she stared at Tamsin. "Where? When? Does Archie Armstrong know this?" Emma asked.

"Nay," William said. "Only Tamsin's grandparents know."

"Gypsies?" Emma asked.

"We had a Romany ceremony. A private one, between us."

Emma plainly gaped. Helen, beside her, stared from one to the other. "Without a priest?" Emma asked.

"The Romany marriage will do for now," Will said. "It is similar to a handfasting."

Tamsin said nothing, made no movement, and felt her cheeks grow hot with a blush. She wondered, dismayed, why William had admitted to the marriage now, so quickly. She had not been prepared for that. Helen and Lady Emma seemed displeased with the news, she thought, but were perhaps too well mannered to protest.

She wanted, suddenly, to turn and run from the room. She must have leaned toward the doorway, must have darted her glance there, for William reached out and took her hand—her gloved hand—firmly in his own.

"We decided rather quickly," William said.

"You . . . ah . . . what . . . ah . . . merry tidings," Helen stammered. "How say you, Mother?"

Lady Emma looked wholly shocked, her translucent skin gone a shade more pale. "How . . . wonderful."

"Thank you." William smiled. Tamsin gave a subtle pull against the grip of his fingers. She felt an answering pressure, a refusal to let her flee. He did not look at her.

"Does this . . . does this mean that Tamsin is no longer a pledge for Musgrave, as you explained when you were here earlier?" Helen asked into another moment of awkward silence.

"I suppose so," William said. "Though I dinna intend to tell him that. But I do intend to tell Malise Hamilton," he said in a grim tone. "I have a wife now, which will eliminate a major portion of his complaint of law."

Emma and Helen stared at each other and nodded. Tamsin was sure that they were still stunned to their bone marrow.

William touched his mother's shoulder. "I know 'tis a surprise. I will explain all of it in better form later."

Tamsin thought she saw the glint of tears in Emma's eyes, quickly blinked away. "I am sure you will be happy," she said. Her voice caught on the last word. "Helen, do take Tamsin to her lodgings. Perhaps she would like to rest before dinner. We shall have a bath brought for her."

"I'm certain I have a gown that I can lend you," Helen said. "We are similar in size, I think."

"My thanks," Tamsin said, convinced that Helen and Emma both thought she desperately needed a bath and decent clothing. She shoved at the mass of her hair, and pulled against William's grip again. He let go, but lifted his hand to her shoulder. The simple warmth of his touch seemed like a blessing.

"Go on," he murmured to Tamsin. "I will send Sandie to Merton Rigg tomorrow to fetch your things."

Tamsin nodded, grateful for his considerate thoughts for her. But she knew that her own clothing, even her best gown, would not compare to the finery to which William and his kinswomen were accustomed.

"Come with me, Tamsin," Helen said. "I will show you Will's chamber, where you can refresh yourself. You and Will must be hungry after your journey and your . . . your wedding. Midday dinner isna ready yet, but we shall share some toast with sugar, and perhaps some good Greek malmsey wine, served in the great chamber, where you and I can celebrate that we are good-sisters now, and you can tell me about yourself. Perhaps Mother and Will can join us." Helen smiled, and Emma nodded in silent answer.

"Th-that would be fine," Tamsin said.

" 'Tis Wednesday, so 'tis a fish day, of course, and we have fresh salmon for dinner," Helen chattered as she took Tamsin's arm and tugged her along the length of the room. "Jock and Sandie caught some salmon in the river. Mother will hover over the cook to be sure 'twill be prepared just right. We hoped you both would arrive today in time to share midday meal with us. But we couldna have guessed at this good news!"

Tamsin nodded, feeling overwhelmed by Helen's enthusiasm. She glanced over her shoulder a little helplessly at a grinning William as she was pulled in his sister's wake.

Tamsin stirred a silver spoon through pink, parsleyed slices of salmon and golden onion, cooked in butter and pepper, that lay nearly uneaten on her wooden trencher. Thick chunks of carrots and leeks, and a hunk of bread, wheaten and fresh, sat untouched on the trencher. A silver goblet, filled with wine, reflected the bleached linen tablecloth and the forms of those who sat at the table in the great hall.

She lifted the cup to sip pale Rhenish wine, tart, cool, and undiluted. At Merton, and among the gypsies, wine and ale were generally mixed with water to extend the supply. Rookhope must be a wealthy household indeed, she thought, to serve expensive wines, cooled in cellars and served in silver, at dinner in the middle of the week. This was not even a holy feast day. She had also sipped sweet malmsey while she sat with Helen and Emma chatting in the great hall. And just before dinner, Emma had handed her a cup of a dark Bordeaux wine that she had felt obliged to drink with them.

Conversation continued in a quiet buzz around her. Although she said little, she strove to listen to the discussion of the recent ban on heretical treatises throughout Scotland. She would have liked to have followed it with better understanding, and perhaps comment with acuity, as the others had done. In truth, she knew little about such matters, and kept losing the thread of the discussion.

She knew that she should force herself to eat more, since she had not eaten since dawn. But her stomach seemed tied in a knot. Laughter rippled about the table. She had not heard the jest, and anxiously picked up the wine goblet to sip from it and cover her confusion. The delicious, enticing warmth of the wine slipped past the knot in her center as the food could not, easing her nervousness a little.

"Nevertheless, your brother must be more cautious," Lady Emma said. "He follows the writings of the Protestant leaders on the Continent with avid interest. I wrote to beg him not to purchase any more works—now that such things are forbidden to be imported or sold, or even read, within the realm of Scotland, he needs must be especially wary."

"Geordie is a sensible man, Mother," William said. "He will use good judgment. His intellect is of the curious sort. He wants to understand the twists and turns in the changing fabric of the Church, and he is deciding whether to remain a man of the Church or return home."

"Safer and smarter to be a godly man than a man of God in such times," Helen said. "Men who preached the new ideas have been burned at the stake for heresy. Geordie must be wary, as Mother says."

William sat beside Tamsin on the long side of the table, with Lady Emma on his right. Helen sat across from them, beside Sandie Scott. They ate with good appetite and took part in the conversation with energy, while Tamsin watched and listened, occasionally nibbling and sipping.

"The salmon is delicious," William said, as he sliced into the fish and took another mouthful.

"I hear Scottish salmon are fetching a crown apiece in the English marketplaces," Emma said. "This was free from the river." She smiled at Sandie, who grinned.

"Hey, mutton, beef, whatever you delight after, Lady Emma, are yours for free," Sandie said. "Borrowed from the English, and served by the moonlight talents o' the surname o' Scott."

Emma laughed lightly. "Better I dinna know from whence it

comes," she said, her tone a gentle scold. "Keep your reiving tales to yourself."

"Tamsin, are you enjoying your dinner?" Helen asked. "You havena eaten much."

" 'Tis delicious," Tamsin said. "My thanks. I find that I am not as hungry as I thought."

William glanced at her. "That wine is fair strong," he murmured under his breath. "Try some of the bread, at least, if you are not hungry, or you will be ill."

She shook her head, stubborn and silent. She could not easily eat the bread with one hand, for she could neither cut it nor tear it without revealing her hand to all at the table. She fisted her small hand in her lap and sipped at the wine again. It tasted cool and fresh, each sip sweeter and smoother.

Helen leaned forward. "After you came to live with your father, Tamsin, did you spend much time with the gypsy people?"

"I spent summers with my mother's people. I still see them whenever they come into the area."

" 'Tis a fascination to me." Helen said. "And so, you say you speak their Egyptian language. Can you also tell fortunes, as the gypsy women do?"

"I speak Romany, which was spoken centuries ago by the race of kings and princes from whom the Romany people descend," Tamsin said. "And my grandmother taught me palmistry, and how to read the picture cards."

"Oh! You can read the *tarocchi*?" Helen said. She reached out to lift the pewter jug that held the wine, filling both her cup and Tamsin's as she spoke.

"Aye, I can." Tamsin sipped at the refreshed wine. From the corner of her eye, she saw William watch her with a slight frown. She sent him a little scowl and drank again. He sighed and turned away to answer a question his mother addressed to him.

"We will have our palms read, Mother," Helen said. She smiled. "I would like to see Tamsin read the *tarocchi*. I know there is a game that can be played with the picture cards, but I have never met anyone who could read fortunes in them."

"Nae just the gypsies tell fortunes," Sandie said. "Scots can too. I have an old aunt who divines the future in sheeps' bones, and people have been visiting her for years for her skill. She makes a good bit o' silver doing that."

"It seems much nicer to read the future in picture cards," Helen said. "Tamsin, will you do that for us? Will has a set of *tarocchi* cards—Marie of Guise gave him a bonny painted set for a New Year's gift a few years ago."

"I have them somewhere, aye," William said. "I havena played the games of *tarocchi* and *minchiate* in a long while."

"Perhaps some evening you can look at our palms too," Helen said. She looked excited, flushing prettily, and Tamsin smiled at her.

"I would be glad to do that," she said. She felt a little bubble of air come up, and pressed her fingers to her mouth.

"Eh, I'd rather play at the cards and win some pennies out o' your purse, Helen," Sandie said. "A good game of ombre or trump, nae that fancy tarockie."

"Sandie, where is Jock?" Lady Emma asked.

"He's gone back to Lincraig, and to visit his brother at Black-drummond," Sandie answered. "He and I mean to ride out tonight, if you would be interested, Willie," he added.

Helen gasped. " 'Tis their wedding night!"

"Another night, then," William murmured. "Has some of the livestock been taken from the fields again?"

"Nae lately, we dinna intend to return reiving favors to any rascals just now. Jock has a rendezvous with the lassie he fancies, over on the English side."

Emma sighed. "The Forster lass. Losing his heart to a girl betrothed to Arthur Musgrave isna the wisest thing he has ever done, though Jock has a serious head on his shoulders in general."

Tamsin sat upright. "Arthur Musgrave?" she asked.

"Aye," William answered her. "He's betrothed to Anna Forster, Ned's cousin. But she and Jock met a few months ago, and seem to be taken with one another, though her family has matched her with Jasper Musgrave's son."

"She willna wed Arthur," Tamsin said. She felt bolder of a sudden, and sat straight. "I saw that in his hand. He will lose her to another—but he will find a wife later, and have much happiness, I think. Aye, I think so." She nodded, then scowled. "Though he's a naughty scoundrel, that Arthur," she muttered. "Truly naughty."

Helen gasped. "You foretold that Arthur would lose Anna to another? Mother, did you hear? We must tell Jock!"

"Dinna tell Jock," Tamsin said quickly. "If 'tis his fate to be with Anna, 'twill happen, even though she is betrothed just now. Fate will bring them together, if they are meant to be with each other." She looked up at William and obeyed an urge to smile widely.

William laughed, short and curt, and looked away, rubbing long fingers over his jaw, shaking his head.

"William," Emma said. "Have you spoken to Jock about his fancy for the English lass? He might find trouble for himself."

"He loves the lass, so I have said naught. He is a canny man, Mother. He knows the risks."

"He risks heart as well as life." She sliced her salmon into dainty pieces as she spoke, using her spoon and knife.

"We canna complain, so long as he is happy," William said.

Tamsin, watching Emma carefully, picked up her spoon and endeavored to hold it in the same way, frowning as she concentrated. The handle seemed slippery, and the spoon clattered to the floor. She bent to look at it. William leaned over to snatch at it, handing it to her with a sour look. She smiled her thanks.

"You can leave your spoons out, Willie," she said, and giggled. He frowned, as if he did not think much of her jest.

Someone chuckled. Tamsin looked up, but the others seemed to be eating rather earnestly just then.

"Aye, 'tis true, Jock seems of glad heart lately," Emma said after a moment. She sighed, and dabbed at her mouth with an embroidered napkin. Tamsin lifted her own napkin to her lips in careful, studied imitation, wanting to get the elegant gesture just right. "Though I fear Anna Forster might break his heart before he sees reason," Emma continued.

"She willna break his heart," William said. As he spoke, he moved Tamsin's goblet out of her reach. She blinked at him, though he did not look at her.

"We will have Tamsin look at his future in the cards!" Helen said.

"I canna do that, unless Jock asks it of me," Tamsin said, shaking her head solemnly. The movement made her dizzy.

"I will ask," Helen said.

"Jock will laugh," Sandie answered. "He doesna take wi' gypsy tricks. He'll make his own fate and fortune, that lad."

" 'Tisna a gypsy trick to see fate in our lives," Tamsin said. "Fate works for us all. Fate brought Willie—"

"Tamsin," William said. "Perhaps you might like to rest for a while."

Ready to refuse, she looked at him, and the turn of her head set the room spinning. She set her napkin on the edge of the table, where it promptly slid to the floor. She looked at it in dismay. "I think," she said, "that I will rest for a wee while." She stood. "Lady Emma, the hospitality was delicious."

"She liked the food," William told his mother.

"Tamsin, I ordered a hot bath placed in William's bedchamber for you," Lady Emma said.

"And I chose some gowns and things for you to borrow, if you wish," Helen said. "I put them in your chamber."

"That is kind of you," Tamsin said. One bare foot seemed to roll under her, and she wavered a little as she stepped away.

"Do you want an escort?" William asked.

She tilted her head. "Think you I am a tipsy"—she leaned toward him—"gypsy?"

"Tamsin," he growled.

"I can find your chamber again. Helen took me there earlier to wash my hands. And my feet," she answered in precise tones.

She left the room, holding her head high, bumping her shoulder slightly on the doorjamb as she passed through. She started up the turnpike stairs and found it necessary to proceed slowly up each wedge-shaped step, trailing a hand along the rough, curving stone wall to support herself as she climbed to the next floor.

A door on the landing led to the cluster of rooms that formed William's private quarters. Tamsin walked through the first room, a small library that contained books in cupboards, and a table and chairs. She traced her fingers over the smooth wood of the furnishings as she went through, and opened a door into the adjoining room, the bedchamber itself. Beyond that larger room lay two more, a small antechamber with a cot and a cupboard, and a tiny garderobe.

Merton Rigg was a fine tower, she thought, but its simple layout and serviceable chambers could not compare to the chambers at Rookhope Tower. Both the library and bedchamber had polished wood floors, painted timber ceilings, whitewashed and tapestry-hung walls, and solid, well-wrought furniture. The rooms were dim, since windows were few and small. Candles and wall sconces were abundant and already alight, and a fire burned bright and fragrant in the hooded fireplace in the bedchamber.

She closed the door and walked into the room, grabbing the carved bedpost to steady herself when the room seemed to tilt. Bedcurtains and a canopy draped the carved walnut bed in dark green damask, and embroidered pillows were piled high against the carved headboard.

The floor beneath her bare feet was thick with fresh, matted rushes, and a small, brilliant Turkish carpet covered the flat lid of a wooden chest at the foot of the bed. She noticed that a gown of black brocade trimmed in gold, another of dark blue silk, a cloak, some chemises, stockings, and a host of accessories lay on the bed. She touched the shimmering materials and sighed.

Shoving fingers through her hair, she sighed again, and cursed herself for a fool. She realized that she had let the wine slip her tongue loose at dinner, and had shown herself to lack dignity and simple manners. If the women of Rookhope had thought little of her at her arrival, surely they thought less of her now.

A wooden tub sat on the hearthstone, filled with water. She walked to it, pausing to take off her cloak and skirt. Lifting her chemise high, she stepped into steaming water, fragrant with bay and lavender.

The moist heat eased into her feet and legs, and she stripped off her chemise and let it float to the floor, lowering herself gradually into the tub, which was so snug that she had to sit with her knees drawn up against her chest. As the water surrounded her, she sighed and sluiced it over her shoulders, breathing in the steam, hoping it would ease the headache that had begun to throb in her temples, and perhaps clear away the fog of the drink.

Nothing, though, could rinse away her conviction that she had made an utter fool of herself at dinner.

A dish of soft soap lay on the hearthstone with a stack of folded linen sheets for toweling. She picked up a small cloth, dipped it in the water, and slopped it over her face with a loud, miserable groan.

Chapter Eighteen

And when he came to the ladyes chamber,
He tirled at the pinn;
The lady was true of her promise,
Rose up and let him in.

—"Glasgerion"

William knocked on the outer door yet again. "Tamsin? Are you awake?" Hearing only silence, he knocked again, soft but persistent. Finally he opened the door and crossed the dark, silent library to knock on the door leading to the bedchamber. Silence. He pushed the unlatched door open, seeing only shadows and flickering firelight.

"Tamsin?" He stepped inside the darkened chamber.

He heard a shriek and a splash, and looked toward the fireplace. Tamsin sat in a wooden tub, dragging a cloth over her breasts to cover herself. She stared wide-eyed at him, dripping wet hair framing her stunned, heat-flushed face.

"Pray your pardon," he said, turning swiftly, but not before he saw, in the light of the hearth, the swells of her breasts, and the graceful gleam of her bare shoulders and arms. "I didna think you would be in the bath. I thought you would be resting."

"Well, I am bathing. Even gypsies bathe," she snapped. "I have been soaking the spirits out of my head with hot steam and a stern lecture to myself. Are you come to lecture me, too? Since you are my husband, I suppose you have a right to be here."

"Not according to our agreement," he said, turned full away.

"These are your rooms too. Once you told your mother that we were wed, there seemed to be no question but that you would share your lodgings with me." He heard a series of splashes.

"I will go." He stepped toward the door.

"Stay," she said. "I need you here."

"Stay?" He turned in surprise.

Her back was toward him now, and she raised her hands to work soap vigorously through her wet hair. "Aye. I must bathe and dress for yet another meal—and yet another vat of wine—and I need some help to ready myself."

"I will send Helen up to you, or the maidservant," he said.

She paused in her soaping, hands deep in foamy lather, and glanced over her shoulder. "I canna ask for help from them," she said. "You must be the one, if you want me gowned proper."

He looked askance at her, and raked a hand through his hair. "You want me to do your hair and lace your gown?"

"You are better able to do that than I am," she said, and bent her neck forward to scoop handfuls of water over her soapy hair. "I can bathe myself, but I canna dress quickly or easily in the fancy gear your sister left for me. I would be all night at the task, and still wouldna finish up looking proper." She slopped more water over her head. "And I dinna have the patience for it, just now."

Watching her, he suddenly understood. Her left hand, bared and soapy, worked as efficiently as the fingered right at washing her head; it moved like fingers inside a mitten, scooping water and massaging her hair.

But the more minute tasks of lacing, tying, and buttoning, which an elaborate gown and accoutrements required, would challenge her beyond her capabilities. Indeed, beyond her patience, for she had little enough of that, he knew.

No wonder she wore such simple clothing, he thought. Chemises and skirts, cloaks, no shoes—even breeches, shirts, and doublets were far easier for her, with her independent spirit and small left hand, to manipulate. Elaborate gear required dexterous fingers, and sometimes even a lady's maid for a second pair of hands. He suspected that Tamsin Armstrong had never accepted help from anyone regarding such matters. Until now.

He stood there silently, watching her work at her hair as firelight and water slid over the fragile contours of her bare back and slim arms. The lush swell of her breasts, tucked against her raised knees, hinted at their fullness.

He noticed her bare left hand, half buried in her dark, dripping curls. And he realized that she had not exposed her hand to his family during dinner, or at any time before that. Understanding hit him like a blow to his belly. He knew why she had eaten so little, so that the wine had gone, fast and sure, to her head.

She had not wanted to show her hand.

What a fool he was, he told himself, not to see the agony she must have been enduring. He could have torn bread for her, could have offered her some sliced food from his plate, like a bride-groom might have done, so that she would not have had to sit there and silently starve in order to save her pride.

"Aye, then," he said softly. "I'll help you."

She paused to hear his answer, then went on scrubbing and rinsing. He came up behind her and dropped to one knee by the tub. She started a little to see him so close. William picked up a bucket filled with water that sat by the hearth, and lifted it over her head. He placed a hand on her wet, soaped hair. The fragrance of roses swept up to him, warm and misty, with the steam of the bath.

"You need some clean water," he said. "You will be all night just rinsing that thick Flemish soap out of your hair."

Soap suds edged the tops of her breasts like lace. She covered herself with crossed arms, bending her neck again to allow him to rinse her hair. He poured a shimmering stream over her head, sluicing water and lather away with his hand. Soon her hair gleamed like rain-swept ebony.

She lifted her head and skimmed her right hand over her hair, keeping the left arm tucked over her breasts. Her fingers slipped over his, lingered for an instant. That brief touch was enough to set his heart to a faster beat.

"My thanks," she said, and closed her eyes suddenly, rubbing at her brow. Her left arm, he saw, tucked a wet cloth against her torso.

"Are you well?" he asked. "Does your head ache?"

"A bit," she said. Her closed eyes were shadowed, and her head and face, with her hair slicked back, were beautifully shaped, with high cheekbones and balanced, elegant features. He stared, fasci-nated by the strength and simplicity of her beauty. His body stirred, hardened, his breath quickened. In firelight, wet and naked, she was more a siren than any woman he had ever seen. He was sure that she was unaware of the power of her allure.

But his awareness was certain and keen. Remembering that he had promised to respect chasteness between them, he leaned away, took his hand down, as if distancing himself would lessen the intensity of what he felt. He found it had no effect whatsoever.

"I didna eat much, and had a good deal of spirits," she said after a moment. "I am not used to strong drink."

"I know," he murmured. "I told my mother you were likely more accustomed to drinking watered wine or ale."

She nodded, and a small crease folded between her brows. "Oh, William," she said, covering her eyes with her right hand, the fingers slim and graceful. "I am ashamed."

"Och, lass, no need for that," he said. "My mother and my sister think you are charming and bonny."

"Charming and bonny?" she asked. "They are only being polite, if they said that. They surely think me a disgrace! Dirty, ragged, without manners or decent clothing, fuddled with wine . . . what a wife for the laird of Rookhope, they will be thinking!" She shook her head again, and winced as if her head throbbed. " 'Tis good I am not your wife, in truth."

He threaded his fingers through her hair, combing out the sopping strands, letting the pressure of his fingers linger on her temples. "Och," he said softly. "Helen laughed with delight over how you dropped the spoon and the napkin. She said 'twas like watching a jester's play. And Sandie is quite impressed. He said you were drunk enough to swarf, and yet walked out of the room like a queen. You have only his respect for that exit."

She grimaced. "I canna face them again."

He bit back a smile. "My mother thinks you are a treasure."

Tamsin shifted her fingers to peer at him. "She said that?"

"Near enough. She laughed, Tamsin. I have rarely seen her laugh so well—not at you," he added hastily, when she looked horrified, "but because she enjoyed dinner immensely. She did suggest that perhaps you should eat a little food with your spirits at the next meal."

Tamsin groaned. "Tell them I canna come down to supper," she said. "Tell them I canna come down, ever. Tell them you have decided to confine me to these rooms for Musgrave's fortnight. Oh, William, William—what have I done?"

He liked the sound of his name drawn on her lips like that, the tone rippling through him. "What have you done, Tamsin lass?" he asked gently. "Coaxed a laugh out of my solemn sister? Brought a smile to my mother's lips, and she in widow's black for the second time in her life? Tell me, what have you done that wasna a good thing, truly?"

"Shown myself to be an ignorant tawny and no more than a jest, an ughsome lass who doesna deserve to be wife to a laird," she said bluntly. "They will ask you to show me the door, and tell you to find a suitable lass to wed. Not that you would protest that," she added.

" 'Tis for me to say who should be lady of my house."

She peered at him. "You were displeased with me. I saw those looks you gave me. You were ready to show me the door."

He shook his head. "I think," he said, "that you are every bit the daughter of Archie Armstrong."

"What does that mean?"

"A nimble tongue for a jest," he said. "I would have laughed out loud myself, silly lass, if I hadna felt so stern and eager for my kin to welcome you. But I think they liked you even better swine drunk than if you had worn brocade and laces and slurped your soup dainty-like, with a golden spoon."

While she gaped at him, silenced, he took a cloth from the stack of folded linen and began to rub her head with it, wringing the water from her thick hair. "Let's get you dressed, then. Helen is eager to see if the gown fits you."

"It—it should," she said, muffled under the towel. "We are much of a size."

"Mother suggested that Helen give some of her better gowns and gear to you, and have some new things made for herself."

"Give good gowns to me? Such fine gear, just *given* to me? I . . . that . . . would be lovely."

"I told her 'twas a good plan. As I recall," he said, "you like fine and fancy gear quite well."

She shrugged. "Well enough."

He smiled to himself. "Good. Helen seemed pleased by the idea. She takes such little interest in her appearance that I think my mother was glad to see that spark in her today."

"But she is bonny, and gowned like a princess."

"She dresses plainly, now, compared to what she used to prefer," he said. "And she thinks she is ughsome."

She looked up at him. "Because of the scars on her face?"

He nodded. "She doesna go out unless she must, and only then with full widow's veiling. And she rarely speaks with visitors. I was glad to see that she liked you immediately." He picked up a larger linen sheet and stood. "Ready?"

"Aye. Turn away," she said unnecessarily, for he shook out the sheet, held it out, and turned his head. Soft splashes, a thunk, and then he felt her take the sheet from him. A moment later, he opened his eyes to see her standing beside him, wrapped snug, only her bare shoulders and arms free.

He looked down at her, sensing the moist warmth that emanated from her skin, inhaling the scent of roses. Her skin and cheeks were flushed, her eyes translucent as green glass.

His heart pounded, and his body stirred again, stubbornly, filling as if he were a youth. He cleared his throat. "We'll need a comb," he said, looking at her hair, a mass of fine black tendrils spilling down past her shoulders. Whirling on his heel, he went to the bed and poked uncertainly among the items that Helen had deposited there.

He was not sure what all of the things were, but he did find a comb among them, of smooth ivory. When he turned with it, she was standing beside him, at the side of the bed, holding the voluminous sheet around her and stroking the black gown with a look of wonder on her face.

He had actually seen more of her at other times, glimpses caught of her slim, muscled legs, and the luscious sight of her in that bath. But the knowledge that she was nude and sweet-scented, a warm and welcoming woman, beneath that toweling made him want to tear the thing away and sweep her into his arms.

Dear God, he thought. She stood beside his own bed, his wife. What sort of fool he had been to wed in such a way and promise chastity, he could not begin to tell himself. Lust struggled with honor. He blew out a breath and handed her the comb.

She sat on the edge of the bed and began to slip the ivory teeth through her hair, soon dragging it through with little winces, finally biting her lower lip and muttering in what was presumably Romany, and presumably swearing.

"Give it me," he said with a sigh, and sat on the edge of the bed beside her. He raked his fingers through her hair to loosen the tangles, shaking some of the wetness from it, and then began to draw the comb down in sections, easing the snarls, picking at the stubborn ones with patient fingers.

She leaned back her head and made a little moan. He wished she had not done that, for his body surged. But he went on combing, raking, easing.

"I used to do this for Helen when she was a bairn," he said. "When my mother was busy with Geordie after his bath, and no one else was patient enough to comb out Helen's tangles—her hair is near as curly as yours beneath those wee caps she wears. I would do it for her, and tell her stories while we sat together." He laughed a little at the memory.

"Will," she said, with a half glance over her shoulder, "what happened to Helen?"

"The smallpox," he said. "Six years ago, she and her husband became ill at the same time. Helen survived. Her husband died of the fever. They had been wed but six months."

Tamsin gasped and turned. "Oh, William! How sad! She is a kind and bonny soul, and bears her burden well." She lowered her eyes. "Is that why she hasna wed again—the scarring?"

He set the comb down. "Aye," he said. "That, and because she misses her husband still, I think."

Tamsin nodded, looking down at her hands in her lap. "I can understand why she hides from others. 'Tis sad that she thinks she must, for she is bonny, though she doesna know it. The scars are but small to the eye after a moment or two."

He watched her, lowering his brows in a little musing frown. "Perhaps you can tell her that someday," he said. "She would like to hear it from you."

She shrugged. "Why would my thoughts be important to her?"

He tipped his head. "Why did you not show your hand today?"

She turned away. "You know why." She fisted the hand in her lap, covered it with her right.

"Just as I no longer see Helen's scars when I look at her," he said, "I see no important differences between your left hand, and your right." He touched her left arm. "But you see a difference, lass. You do."

She shook her head, withdrew from his light touch. "Nay," she said. " 'Tisna the same as Helen."

"And why not?" he asked. He picked up the comb and slid it down through her hair.

"No one thinks Helen evil because the smallpox marked her."

He sighed, watching her, the comb still. "Do you think you were visited by evil?"

"I—I dinna think so," she said hesitantly. "Others do."

"Those who are ignorant will think what they want," he said. "Why should you care? You know what you are."

He heard her soft, doubtful laugh. "And what am I?"

"Bonny," he whispered. "Truly."

She tucked her head, and the rippling, damp curtain of her hair slid forward. William saw her bare shoulders bow with the weight of her thoughts, her uncertainty. She said nothing.

"Come here," he said, and stood. He held out his hand. She looked up at him in surprise. He insisted with his palm. "Come here. Give me your hand. I want to show you something."

She gripped the sheet around her and stood, offering her right hand. William, waited, patient and silent, to show her he wanted her left hand.

She hesitated, then switched hands so that her right held the tucked linen snug over her chest, freeing the left, which she held out, fisted, to him. Her eyes were wide and almost frightened.

"Och, my lass," he breathed. "What have they done to you with their superstitious nonsense?" He slipped gentle fingers around her hand and tugged. "Come with me."

He pulled her with him, through the doorway into the library. In the dim light of the single candle burning on the table there, he walked with her to a cupboard and opened it to reveal the books shelved inside.

He held her hand firm in his while he traced a finger along the spines of some of two hundred books, laid flat and stacked two or three high, that he had collected over the years.

While he searched, he saw Tamsin reach out to touch the small wooden globe that sat on the table in a brass mounting. She slid her fingers along the engraved, painted surface, and the globe spun slowly beneath her fingers. She gasped a little in surprise.

"A terrestrial sphere," he explained. " 'Twas made in Germany. I bought it on one of my journeys." She nodded, and touched it again, watching it turn beneath her hand.

Finding the volume he wanted, he hefted it in one hand, keeping her in his grasp, and went to the table with it, thunking it down and flipping the pages until he found what he wanted.

"This is a treatise written by a Flemish physician ten or so years ago," he said. "Here, I want you to look at these pages." He pointed.

She bent forward, her hand more relaxed in his now, her fist open like a flower inside the warm cage of his hand. He wrapped his fingers around the wedge and felt her thumb slip over his.

She gasped as she looked at the two pages that he had spread open. A series of ink drawings, detailing arms, legs, feet, and hands, were arranged on the pages. Some were views of the outer part of the body, and some were anatomical renderings of muscle and bone. All were images of deformity.

"They are all . . . like me," she said, "in different ways. But each one is . . . different." She scanned the text. "I can read the Latin . . . here, it says that sometimes people are born with limbs of . . . of various shapes, out of the norm. And yet they are healthy, and suffer no illness or ill effects . . . all is well with them, and they need no physician to repair or heal them. They are not to be pitied or suspected . . . but should be regarded as healthy beings . . . as part of the wondrous and endless . . ."

" 'The wondrous and endless variety of Nature in all her aspects,' " he translated with her.

Tamsin straightened and stared at him. Then she bent down and read it again, reaching out to touch the text, nearly losing her grip on her linen sheet. She took her hand from William's, bunched the linen in her right, and traced the Latin text with the tip of her left hand, where a small oval nail grew, as pretty as any fingernail William had ever seen.

He watched her, waiting while she read it again and again, mouthing the Latin to herself, whispering her translation. She turned her hand in slow wonder, and studied the images on the page. One drawing was a sketch of a hand somewhat like her own, and she touched its outlines.

Finally she turned and looked at him. "Thank you," she said. "I thank you for showing me this. Who is this man?" She looked at the book again.

"A physician, a scientist, and a philosopher, who is fascinated by the world around him, and constantly studies it to learn from it," he said. "An educated, intelligent, and wise man. Hardly an unusual man, in these times. There are many like him. They reject the fears and the superstitions of the old teachings, and some of the older theories of medicine and science and philosophy, for new ideas. The Church is breaking down, losing its power and its grip over the educated world, while the thinking of good and wise scientists and philosophers, like this man, is changing our world."

She looked at her hand while he spoke, turning it. "Changing our world," she repeated in a whisper.

"Believe that you are beautiful, and perfect in all ways," he said, leaning closer. " 'Tis so. There are many who see that in you."

She lifted her gaze to his, her eyes a clear green tint in the candlelight. "Perfection?" she asked.

"Aye," he breathed, and suddenly could not seem to stop himself from moving toward her. A slight shift of his head brought his mouth down to hers. The kiss was a simple one, tentative and gentle. Yet in that instant, a power swept through him, strong enough to coax his heart out of its careful, willing prison. He circled his arms around her, and drew her close.

The kiss she returned was heated, tasting of the fire that he was sure lay constantly banked within her. She slipped her arms about his neck, pressing the length of her body to his. He hardened, swelled with the strength of a sudden and overwhelming desire. Pulling in a breath, he spread his hands along the supple curves of her back, slanting his mouth over hers.

She made an airy little moan under his lips, and he was nearly undone by the innocent, sincere passion beneath that sound. He pressed his hand to her lower back, until her abdomen, through layers of damp linen, fit firm to his.

But in the midst of the deepening kiss, a promise he had made surfaced like a leaf swirling in a current. He wrapped his fingers around her upper arms and pushed slightly.

She leaped back, as he did, as if they both had been burned. Her breathing was ragged, but his felt torn clean out of him. He stared at her, and she at him. Clutching the linen sheet firmly, she shuffled back, still breathing hard.

"I—I will get dressed," she said, and turned, bare feet smacking on the wooden floor as she fled.

William rubbed his hand over his face and stood there until his racing heart slowed. With deliberate movements, he closed the book and replaced it carefully in the cupboard. Then he walked toward the bedchamber to knock on the half-opened door.

"Tamsin," he said. "Do you want me to call my sister to come up to you?" He heard only silence. "Tamsin?" A few soft grunts, as if a gentle struggle ensued, drifted to him.

"I can do it myself," she said. A few moments later, he heard a little cry, one of clear frustration, bitten back.

"Shall I tell them you will be down for supper?" he asked.

Another long silence, another breathy little grunting sound, another half cry. Something silky and embroidered flew across the room and landed at his feet.

"Tell them," she finally said, "I will never be able to come down, if I have to wear harnesses and tethers and canopies of state. I canna sort these out, let alone tie them decently."

He sighed. "Tamsin," he said. "I am coming in there. And I swear that all I will touch is silk and brocade."

A pause. He leaned a hand against the door, waiting.

"Please," she said, in a small voice.

Chapter Nineteen

Tamsin crossed her arms modestly over her torso as William entered the room. The long, embroidered chemise she had pulled on, cut full and gathered at neck and cuffs, was of a lawn so fine that it was nearly transparent.

She turned away as William came toward her, but he seemed reluctant to look at her directly. She glanced at him over her shoulder. His cheeks were flushed—probably as flushed as hers, she thought—and he stood by the bed, studying the clothes and items tossed about on the green coverlet. He poked at the black gown crumpled in a heap, then picked up a white silk stocking, raising a brow at the thing as he dangled and dropped it.

"If you'll put the gown on," he said, "I'll lace it for you and we'll be done. I think you can put your stockings on without my help."

"I tried the gown," she said. "It doesna fit. Your sister must be thinner than I am, for the lacings dinna meet over my waist or my—" She stopped. " 'Tis too tight. And too long."

He picked up the gown. "Put it on again," he said, and tossed it to her.

She slipped her arms into the sleeves of the kirtle, a bodice with an attached skirt, opened in the front like a coat. She distributed the voluminous folds of the black brocade skirt, and the hem pooled, too long, at her feet. The sleeves were snug at the top, and wide and long at the elbows, the sleeves of the chemise visible.

Grabbing the silk cord laces at either side of the waistband, she tried to tug them together.

"See you," she told William. "They willna meet. I must be wider in the waist than Helen."

"You're slimmer, if anything," he murmured, frowning as he surveyed her. "Something is missing." He poked among the items of clothing on the bed: a cloak, chemises, a gown in dark blue damask, and an odd skirt of plain linen with stiff strips in it and one panel of brocade.

"This goes on first," he said, and handed her the pale linen skirt. "'Tis some sort of Spanish undergarment, with whalebone sewn in it to support the overskirt. A verdugale 'tis called."

She accepted it, staring up at him. "How do you know, when I dinna know such things about women's fancy clothing?"

"If you must know, my good wife, I have undressed my share of ladies."

"Oh." She felt her cheeks heat, and she dove into the verdugale, trying to pull it over her head.

William took it from her and laid it on the floor. "Step into it and pull it up. Take off the kirtle first."

She did, tossing the black brocade on the bed, and then stepped into the flat pool of the underskirt, pulling it up over her chemise-covered legs. The bone hoops sewn inside the skirt clicked and swung. Her chemise slid up, and she shimmied her lower body as she stuffed the chemise under the verdugale.

"Please," William said in a thin, choked voice. "Dinna do that, lass. At least not when I'm watching."

She glanced at him. His cheeks seemed on fire. The pink stains set his blue eyes to sparkling. She thought he was teasing her, but the spark in his gaze told her that he was serious.

Hesitantly, she smoothed the skirt, tugged at the cords that fastened the waist. William did not offer to tie it for her, and though her knot was clumsy, it held. Then she picked up the brocade kirtle and put her arms into it again. The black skirt spilled neatly over the verdugale, giving a conelike effect, the hem just brushing the floor, trailing a little behind her.

Once more she tried to bring the kirtle together at the waist. "'Tis too small, and doesna even cover the underskirt!"

William rubbed his chin. "Perhaps the underskirt is turned around. Here . . ." He slid his hands around her waist.

She took in a little breath at the warm, gentle shock of his hands nearly on her skin, with only the thin chemise between them. Something low in her abdomen seemed to swirl and pool with heat and yearning, just as when he had kissed her.

She could not think about that wondrous kiss, hardly had time at all to dwell on what had happened between them. He bent his head toward her as he tugged, and she looked down at the glossy, dark waves of his hair, wanting to touch that thick softness.

She flexed her left hand thoughtfully, tempted to slide it over his head, wanting desperately to give back to him some small part of the comfort and reassurance that he had given her.

Despite the infinite kindness he had shown her regarding her hand, he had broken the kiss that had happened between them, had looked at her as if he were horrified with her—or with himself. She too had felt stunned by the kiss and, even more, by her body's strong response. She would have given herself to him in an instant had he asked, had he urged. Instead, wholly unsure of his reaction, she had run from the room, unwilling to face him again.

But the tangle of the gown and its many lacings had defeated her. She knew that William wanted her to come down to supper with his family. She wanted to counter her performance at dinner with some dignity at supper, but she needed help to fasten the gown properly.

William's behavior now seemed all frown and hurry, all seriousness. She wondered if she had dreamed those tender moments between them. He said nothing as he tugged at the narrow waistband of the verdugale, pulling it around her a little impatiently, as if he wished to be done with the task. She could hardly blame him for that.

She glanced down. A panel of black brocade, reembroidered in gold thread over the floral pattern, was stitched into the linen. William swung it into view beneath the opening of the overskirt. "There," he said, standing back.

"Oh!" Tamsin said. " 'Tis lovely. But the bodice is still too small." The sides still gapped wider than a hand span over her chest. The sheer lawn chemise bunched there, her breasts shadowed beneath. She covered herself with a spread hand.

William sat a hip on the edge of the bed, and pulled on her arm until she glided forward to stand between his legs. Her heart beat oddly fast, and her breath constricted. She studied him, so close to her in the firelight, as he studied the puzzle of her gown. She thought that she had never seen a man with such quiet, striking beauty.

"Sometimes the bodice laces up the front, and sometimes it laces up the back," he said. "And some ladies wear a bodice piece fastened to the front. That must be it," He rummaged among chemises, stockings, caps, veils, and shoes. A little silver casket, its velvet lining gleaming with necklaces, rings, and earrings, tipped over.

Tamsin hardly looked at what he did. She stared at him, and fisted her hands at her waist. Suddenly she did not care that the gatherings of the chemise might reveal more than modesty allowed. Her mood soured with a bitter trickle of jealousy.

"You know a great deal about dressing ladies," she snapped.

He glanced at her, his hand stilled on the bed. "I know how to undress them," he admitted. "Though nae so much how to dress them again. I leave that to their servant maids."

"Then there have been many ladies in your life."

He tilted his head, watching her. "Enough to acquaint me with women's gear," he said slowly. "Does that fret you, then?"

She lifted her chin. "Nay. Do what you like. You are not, in truth, my husband. And I am not truly your wife. And so none of what you do with women matters a bit." She glanced away, aware that it did matter, a great deal. She stole another glance at him, unable to stop herself.

He lowered his eyelids, which took on the appealing, languid droop that she sometimes noticed when he was deep in thought, or ready to flare out in temper. "True," he said. "We are not wed, are we, but just doing a favor for one another. Here, my lady"— he inclined his head in a mocking little bow—"put this on."

Those clipped words hurt her. She was neither wife to him nor lady of Rookhope. And she was certainly not equal to the ladies he apparently knew so well.

He handed her a stiff black piece, almost square, meant to fill the gap in the bodice. She noticed several ties along the edges. Silently, she held the stiff thing against her chest and began to tie the silken cords, pair by pair, to the bodice.

She turned away. "Thank you. Go now, if you wish. Of course, 'tis your chamber, so you may do what you like."

He sighed. "Tamsin," he said. "Pray your pardon, lass. I didna mean to offend you, but I see that I have."

Her hands, fumbling with the tiny silken ties, stilled for an instant, and she gave him a brusque nod. The bows that she had made slipped loose, and she let out a little frustrated cry, bitten back.

He blew out a breath, reached out quickly, and closed his fingers around her elbow. "Come here, you stubborn lass," he said, and drew her back between his legs, his thighs trapping her, pressing the shape out of her skirt.

"This thing," he said, "is called a busk or a stomacher, and 'tis two squares of cloth over a thin bit of wood. Hold it there, and let me lace it." She pressed it against her, and he began to work at the laces. " 'Twould seem a tedious thing to wear, like armor covered in silk, but ladies prefer a flattened bosom for some reason. I would rather see something of . . . the endless variety of Nature," he drawled, lifting his brow.

That remark, a startling reminder of his earlier act of kindness, had a simple effect on her. She melted, somewhere inside that she could not quite define. A delicious feeling poured through her, a warm swirl of joy. She stared at him.

He did not look up, tying and tucking the knots. Tamsin felt her breath constrict slightly beneath the firm pressure of the busk and bodice. His fingers were agile and gentle, and he tucked the last laces, his fingers warm where they pressed against the thin chemise just above the tops of her breasts.

She caught her breath, still looking at him. He withdrew his hand. He had not looked at her at all, though she wanted that, very much, even tipped her head to coax it from him.

"There," he said quietly, and lowered his hands. "Lovely."

"Aye, 'tis lovely," she breathed, looking down, smoothing her skirt, belling it out around her. The black bodice was now quite snug, flattening her breasts, smoothing her waist, flared at the hips and full at the hem. The gown created an hourglass shape that was, she thought, elegant and appealing.

But her chemise bunched awkwardly over the bodice, and her breasts were rounded and flattened beneath the busk, their upper curves globing beneath the sheer lawn. William reached out long fingers to tug at the embroidered collar of the chemise. His fingertips trailed across her collarbone as he adjusted the pleatings over her shoulders.

What little breath the tight busk left to her was erased by those gentle strokes. She stared up at him, feeling shivers slide up and down her spine. She felt as if she melted again, deep within the beautiful gown.

"This bit is supposed to be pulled neat, but I'm not certain how 'tis done," he said. Tamsin could feel the chemise twisting about her torso and waist. She bent over and dipped beneath the skirts to pull it down, wriggling as she did so, and then reached up to adjust her bosom. She thought she heard William growl something under his breath.

She straightened, patting the smoothed chemise where it disappeared beneath the bodice. She stepped away to turn in a circle, skirt spinning over her bare feet, and smiled at him. " 'Tis done, I think, and just perfect."

"Not quite," he murmured. "There are undersleeves yet to be tied under those wide sleeves. Then you'll need some bit of frippery and veiling to cover your hair, and silly embroidered gear for your feet, and gewgaws and baubles strung around your neck, and dangling from your ears. When you are decorated like a marzipan confection, then, my lass, you will be considered by many to be just perfect."

She let out a breath. "Oh," she said, her shoulders bowing a little. She balled her left hand by habit, and the long, ruffled cuff of the chemise hid the small fist she made. "There is so much to know of this. I have very simple gear of my own."

She felt a fool again, as when she had taken too much wine. The effects of the spirits still dulled her thinking somewhat. How could she have thought that a beautiful gown would make much of her? She had not even known enough to consider her feet or her hair. Nor was she sure what she would do with the little pile of rings that glittered inside the silver casket.

"Och," William breathed out. "I considered you perfect in naught but the chemise." His voice was so low and soft that it seemed to caress her. "The rest seems unnecessary to me. But if it pleases you, lass, then 'tis necessary." He gave her a little smile.

She tilted her head at him. Excitement coiled in her abdomen at his remark, at his hint that he preferred her in the chemise, that he found her attractive and desirable. She wanted to smile, and pinched it back, letting the humor and the happiness shine out her eyes, as she had seen him do so often.

"You dinna like this?" she asked, holding out the skirt of the gown, swaying a little.

He leaned a shoulder on the bedpost and played with a necklace of amber and gold, sliding the delicate firelit beads through his long fingers. "Tamsin," he said in a hoarse voice. "This business of being your handmaiden is too great a task for me. I think you shouldna ask it of me again. I dinna have the stamina it needs."

She lifted a brow. "You have done this for a hundred other ladies," she said, "at court."

He half laughed. "Never a hundred, believe me," he said. He fastened his gaze on her, keen and languid in shadows and firelight. "Come here."

Her heart pounded within the cage of her breast like the hammer of a bell. She wanted to step toward him. But she knew that if she entered the circle of his arms again, even to let him adjust her clothing, she would be lost forever.

She hesitated. His silence, his gaze, pulled at her, and she resisted. Her heart urged her forward, and fear held her back.

"I thank you," she said, looking away, settling the folds of her gown around her. "I am sure you are eager to be free of this frippery and foolishness. I will finish myself and come down to supper soon. I must comb my hair, and decide which wee cap I like best, and which of those bonny necklaces, and find stockings and shoes—" She stopped, aware that she was chattering, aware that he stood now, staring down at her.

"Aye. You can do the rest without difficulty."

"I can," she said, and snatched a pair of stockings and garters from the bed. She sat on the floor in a wide jumble of black brocade, and stuck out one bare foot and ankle to slide on the white silk stocking.

"Grant mercy," William muttered, and walked to the door.

She watched him leave the room, his body long and hard and lean in the black breeches and pierced leather doublet and shirt. He was right, she thought. She felt a little foolish in such fancy gear. She was accustomed to simple clothing, which he, too, seemed to favor. But the brocaded gown, despite its fastenings and constraints, felt pleasing as it surrounded her in a shining pool of elegance. She felt almost beautiful in it. And she liked too the look she had seen in William's eyes when she had spun before him.

She yanked on the silk stockings, and clumsily tied ribbon garters just below her knees to secure them. Then she stood and rummaged in Helen's generous pile, choosing the amber and gold necklace that William had fingered, and looped it around her neck. She tried to cap her head in a black crescent-shaped hood edged in pearls, from which a black velvet veil cascaded, but she could not make it stay. And the black shoes, when she found them, were strange, tiny slippers with no backs, just a shell for the toes, elaborately embroidered.

She was nearing complete frustration with the cap and hood, unable to fit them over her hair, when she heard voices in the library. William's low drone and Helen's lighter voice murmured together.

"Tamsin," William said. The door opened a bit, and he looked inside. "Come out here, if you will."

Curious, but feeling shy, she padded to the doorway in stockinged feet and wildly curling hair, the gown swinging around her. She went through the doorway into the candlelit library.

William stood there with Helen, who smiled past William's shoulder and gasped with delight when she saw Tamsin.

"Oh! I did wonder if the black was too somber for you," Helen said. "But I vow, you glow like a jewel in that gown! 'Tis bonny on you! Will, what do you think?"

He glanced at her over his shoulder. "Bonny," he murmured.

Tamsin smiled and put a hand to her bare head. "I thank you for your generosity, Helen," she said, and stepped forward.

William stepped aside then, and Tamsin saw that Helen carried a small child in her arms, an infant, swathed in creamy silken garments. The child sucked a fist and stared at her as she came forward, round blue eyes and dark curls glittering in the warm light, cheeks blooming pink, a fat hand waving.

"Tamsin," William said, "this is my daughter Katharine."

Tamsin smiled. "Katharine," she said, making her eyes wide at the child, coaxing a drooling smile in return that made William and Helen chuckle. "Oh, Will, she is bonny."

"Aye," he said. She glanced up at him and saw him grin.

Helen shifted the child in her arms. "Would you like to hold her? After all, she is your daughter too, now that you have wed William."

Tamsin froze. She had not considered this when she and William had made their marriage arrangement. He had hardly mentioned the child, except to explain how imperative it was that he take a wife to keep his daughter safe in his custody. She glanced up at him again, a frown forming. He only nodded.

Helen leaned Katharine toward Tamsin. The baby came into her embrace in a wave of warmth and softness, a scant weight in her arms, delightful and comforting. She adjusted her hold on the child and swayed as if by instinct, patting the little back, savoring the sweet warmth in her arms.

Katharine stared at her, unblinking and calm. Then, without warning, her face crumpled and she began to wail. Tamsin jiggled her and shifted her to her right arm, patting the tiny chest with her left hand, unsure what to do. With a fast lunge, Katharine grabbed Tamsin's left hand, which was buried in the silk folds, pulled it up to her mouth, and began to suck.

Mortified that her hand was exposed—even worse, in the infant's mouth—Tamsin tried to pull away, sure that Helen would feel revulsion. Katharine's grip was intense, her mouth hot and earnest on the tip of the wedged hand. Tamsin looked up at William, almost pleading. He lifted his brows and shrugged.

Helen stood beside her and stared at Tamsin's hand, its odd

shape fully exposed, but for the tip captured inside the baby's mouth. Tamsin wanted to cringe, wanted to run, but stood, and held the child, and helplessly let her devour her hand.

"She does love to suck on all our hands," Helen said. "She is teething fierce." She smiled, her cheeks dimpling, hazel eyes sparkling. "I hope you dinna mind."

Tamsin felt tears rise, and swallowed them down. She looked at Helen and smiled. In that instant, the imperfections in Helen's skin seemed to vanish. To her, Helen was surely the loveliest woman, and the kindest, she had ever seen. " 'Tis fine," she said. " 'Tis fine. Let her suck on . . . on my hand if she likes. She's a bonny wee bairn."

"We think so," Helen said. "She's a good wee lassie."

"Aye so," William said gently. "Come here, my bonny Kate, you've harangued Mistress Tamsin long enough." He slipped his long fingers around the child's middle and drew her up and out of Tamsin's arms. Katharine reluctantly detached from Tamsin's hand, and turned to her father with a coo like a dove.

Tamsin pulled the ruffled cuff of her chemise over her hand. Though she was amazed that Helen, like William, did not seem to be bothered by the sight of it, she could not get used to such acceptance so easily. She was more comfortable hiding the hand, as she had always done. But her throat felt constricted with tears, and her heart seemed to swell with a sense of gratitude, of tenderness, toward all the Scotts of Rookhope.

Helen smiled again. "You look lovely, Tamsin. I am glad I chose that black and gold for you, and the indigo gown I left for you should do just as nicely. Would you like some help with your hair, and in choosing a cap? I have others, if the ones I lent you willna do."

"I—I—" Tamsin stammered, so overwhelmed by the woman's kindness that she struggled against the tears until her lip wobbled. "Nay, thank you, Helen, all the gear is lovely. I can finish the rest myself. I will be down for supper shortly."

"Good. Mother will be pleased to hear that you are feeling better," Helen said, and grinned as if she and William and Tamsin shared a delightful secret. She turned to leave the room.

William looked down at Tamsin, his eyelids relaxed, a gentle gaze. His daughter leaned against his shoulder, eyes closed, peacefully sucking on her own hand. With a fingertip, William reached out and traced the outline of Tamsin's jaw, tipping her chin up on his knuckle. The warmth of his touch seemed to flow from her chin down to her toes. She looked up at him through a sheen of tears.

"The endless variety of Nature," he murmured with a slow smile. His thumb grazed her cheek, while his gaze rested on hers. Tamsin closed her eyes for an instant, breathing in his touch, his kindness, his nearness. She hoped that he would stay, would bend down and kiss her as he had before. But he let go, and turned to carry Katharine out of the room.

Tamsin stood in the middle of the library for a long while, absorbing the tears that burgeoned within her, absorbing new thoughts, new ideas. She turned finally, skirt whispering on the rushes, and saw the table behind her, where the small wooden sphere sat on its brass mountings.

She reached out with her left hand and smoothed her palm over its engraved surface, tracing the tip of her wedged finger over the outlines of the lands of the earth, watching them spin slowly beneath her touch. She felt as if her own world, the small, personal, insignificant sphere of her existence, had somehow tilted, and righted again, and now whirled under a new sun. And she knew then that nothing in her life, or within herself, would ever be the same again.

Chapter Twenty

She came tripping down the stair,
And a' her maids before her,
As soon as they saw her well-far'd face,
They coost their glamourie ower her.

—"The Gypsy Laddie"

"How wicked of Musgrave to insist on keeping a lass prisoner as a warrant for her father's obedience," Lady Emma said. She bent over an embroidery frame as she spoke. A flaming candle in a sconce beside her chair gave a glow to her profile. "Pledging is common enough in Scots law. But an Englishman, keeping a Scots lass!"

"Mother, we know that Jasper Musgrave has a cold heart," Helen added from her place on the floor of the great chamber, where she played with Katharine.

" 'Tis why I told him I would keep Tamsin at Rookhope for the duration of the pledge," William said, seated near the fireplace.

Emma cast him a quick glance as she worked. "But you didna expect to marry her at the time, you said."

"True," William answered. "That came about later."

She slid the needle through the fabric with nimble, capable fingers. "William," she said. "What did bring it about?"

He paused. "Fate."

"Ah." Emma seemed to want to say more. But she nodded and went back to her work.

He wanted to tell his mother more than that, and would, eventually. At supper not long ago, he had explained only the essentials of the marriage to his mother and sister in Tamsin's absence, for she had not come downstairs, although they had waited supper

for her. William had reminded Lady Emma and Helen that he
needed a wife in order to keep Katharine safe at Rookhope.

Although he simplified the matter, he had explained that he
thought Tamsin Armstrong attractive and agreeable, and, as the
daughter of Armstrong of Merton, suitable to be lady of
Rookhope. His kinswomen had agreed politely, but he had seen
tears gleam in his mother's eyes, and he wondered at her
thoughts. She had voiced only quiet approval.

"You said that Archie Armstrong and Musgrave had some dispute over reiving," Emma said after a few moments.

"Aye." He sipped sherry from a small cup of German-made
glass, green as Tamsin's eyes. "Those two squabble constantly."

"As if Archie Armstrong would be obedient," she murmured. "I
knew him well, years ago. A big, blond, handsome man, with a
kind heart and a blunt manner of speech. And a fine way with a
jest, which sometimes got him into trouble."

William smiled. "Aye, that sounds like Archie."

Hearing the light chime of the baby's laugh, he glanced at his
daughter, who sat on the floor with Helen. Katharine looked up at
him, her gaze curious and calm. He smiled, and she made a soft,
excited sound, looking away with a wobbly turn of her head.

"Your father loved Archie well." Emma sighed. "I do recall that
Archie and Musgrave always hated each other, even then."

"Apparently not much has changed," William said.

"What hold would Musgrave have over Archie, and what interest could you have in either of them?" Emma asked. "I sense intrigue in this matter."

"Mother, I canna say more. But be sure that Archie willna
make any of this easy for Musgrave."

"Good," Emma said. "And you must promise to be careful."

William nodded and watched her rhythmic, steady stitching. An
air of calm seemed to surround his mother. He felt a sense of ease
in her presence that he rarely found with others.

He sighed and slouched in the large chair, sprawling his
stockinged legs before the hearth fire and glancing around the
room. The great chamber was a small room, despite its name,
with glazed windows, sturdy oak furniture, timber paneling, and
floorboards strewn with rushes. Turkish carpets of red and blue

covered the tables, and chair cushions and draperies of dark red lent the room the warmth and brilliance of a deep-hued jewel.

In his childhood, the great chamber had been the quiet, cozy heart of Rookhope. Most evenings, after supper in the great hall, William and his parents and younger siblings had gathered around the hearth in this chamber for games, stories, music, and conversation. Seated in the chair that he now sat in himself, his father had taught him to play chess, draughts, and card games. Sprawled on the hearthstone, William had listened to stories of reiving adventures along the Borders, exciting and even comical, from his father, and from kinsmen and guests, including Archie Armstrong of Merton.

He remembered listening with avid attention, wanting to grow to manhood the equal of his father. He had dreamed of becoming as skilled, as witty, as bold and courageous as Allan Scott, the notorious Rogue of Rookhope.

But those dreams, and the loving, secure world where he had been nurtured a rogue's pup, had been destroyed on the day of his father's unjust and horrible death. In the years following that devastating event, Rookhope had been captained by Scott kinsmen, Emma had lived elsewhere with her younger children, eventually marrying a second time, and William had remained a prisoner of the crown. He had come back to live at Rookhope only last year, after his mother and sisters had asked his permission to reside here once again.

William watched his sister and his daughter, heads close together, laughter soft and lovely. He sipped from his cup, and felt tension flow out of his muscles as the heat of the sherry flowed through his body.

Nothing, though, could erase the tautness from his soul. He still felt like an outsider with his own family, in his own home. He watched the love and companionship around him as if he observed it through a glazed window, or as if he watched a mummer's play. He enjoyed the spectacle, but always stayed at a distance from its center.

Years spent apart from his family, and deep hurts never healed, he knew, were at the root of the remoteness in his heart. He could not change that any more than he could alter the facts of his father's

death, or Jean's. He could only sip at the love his kinswomen offered him, as he sipped at strong, good wine—slowly, cautiously,
never filling himself all at once.

"Tell me about Tamsin," Emma said, her voice easing into the
quiet. "Is she as stubborn as her father? She seems, in her own
way, as much the free spirit."

"The daughter is like the father in some ways. She ran off when
I was escorting her here, as I told you the other day, for she didna
care to be held in my dark, terrible dungeon."

Helen laughed outright. Katharine blinked up at her and gur-
gled.

"Dungeon, indeed. I suppose you let her believe that!" Emma's
silver needle flashed, drawing black thread.

"I did," he said. "She set my temper off like a matchlock."

"Ah," Helen said. "And so you married her." She grinned.

William twisted his mouth awry and said nothing. Emma
chuckled, and he glanced at her. Firelight flickered over her face
and warmed the wings of her hair beneath her black gabled hood.
She narrowed her eyes over her work and pressed her teeth to her
lip like a young girl. The years had been a strain for her, William
knew, but age had only enriched Lady Emma's appealing beauty.

Helen supported Katharine with a steady hand and glanced at
him. "Perhaps 'twas your grim manner and ogre's temper that
caused her to run off," she said, teasing. He returned a brotherly
grimace, as he had done when they were very young.

"An ogre, am I?" But he thought to himself how bonny Helen
was in firelight, hazel eyes dancing, auburn hair smooth beneath
the crescent-shaped headdress. Early widowhood had subdued her
inner sparkle, and the scars on her face had made her ashamed of
her appearance. She had finally ceased to wear black constantly,
but claimed she would never wed again, and that she would stay
at Rookhope for so long as her brother let her.

William would let her stay forever, of course, but he wanted
her to be happy again. He saw the loneliness that lingered in the
shadows around her eyes, and felt its twin in his own eyes. He
and Emma and Helen had shared sadness, tragedy, and some happiness too. Love and pain bound the three of them together, like

the interwoven vines and flowers in Emma's elaborate stitchery work.

Perhaps that was why, he thought, he had so impulsively agreed to this ruse of a marriage rather than risking a genuine union with Tamsin or any other woman. He had experienced much hurt in the past. Yet he yearned for love, for solace and passion in his life. Despite his instinct to protect himself, this time fate had managed to catch him fast in its design.

As William mused, and watched his daughter and his sister, Katharine yanked at the rope of pearls that dangled over Helen's stiff bodice, causing Helen to gasp and pry the little fist loose. William leaned forward, elbows on knees, and looked down at his daughter, whose lip quivered as she fretted the loss of the necklace.

"What think you, sweet Kate? Am I an ogre?"

Katharine brightened, leaned over, and slapped her hands on the floor, launching into a strong crawl despite the impediment of her clothing. William held out his hands and scooped her up, setting her bundled behind on his knee.

"There, I didna scare her," he told Helen.

"She adores you," she said.

"Da-da-da," Katharine burbled. William sifted his fingertips through the fine brown curls that escaped her silk cap, her head a warm fit to his palm.

"She's saying my name now," he murmured, touched.

Helen and Emma both laughed. He looked at them, puzzled.

"She says that to me, to Mother, and even to Jock and Sandie," Helen said. " 'Tis all she says."

"Most bairns make that sound at this age," Emma said, as she outlined the shape of a flower in black thread. "She doesna mean you, William, when she says that. Not yet, at least."

"Oh," he said, a little disappointed. Katharine grabbed at his hand and strove to suck on his smallest finger. He watched her, bemused and fascinated, though warm spit trickled down his hand. He thought of Tamsin, who had relinquished her hand to Katharine with great trepidation. His heart had gone out to her, watching that.

Thinking of her now, he glanced toward the door again, as he had done often in the last hour. He wondered if she still struggled with the niceties of her female gear, or if she struggled with embarrassment, and had decided to stay away.

Katharine gave a faint little growl and renewed her voracious, noisy sucking on his finger. "She's more like a puppy than a lass," he drawled. Emma and Helen laughed.

Katharine's grip on his heartstrings was as fierce as her grip on his hand. A sudden, ferocious urge to protect her thundered within him. If Malise Hamilton attempted to take her from him, he thought, whether on paper, in court, or by forcible means, William would fight to the death for her.

He would die for any one of them, he thought, glancing at his kinswomen. But he would not admit aloud to them the intensity of his feelings, or his need to see them safe and content. He was no poet, no composer of songs, to lay his feelings out on parchment, fileted like a fish.

Whenever he was with them, he stayed quiet, smiled some, and listened attentively. His love for his family was heartfelt and strong, though he seldom expressed it directly. But his yearning for a love of his own, hidden behind his calm exterior, was even more profound.

The memory of that tender shared kiss with Tamsin rushed unbidden through him. He frowned slightly, wondering at the unexpected power of that moment.

"I remember Tamsin's Egyptian mother," Emma said suddenly, startling him out of his thoughts. "I met her once. A beautiful creature, though very young, and strange in her ways. Archie adored her. But I never knew that he kept her bairn with him. I thought the gypsies took the child with them."

"They did, but Archie took Tamsin into his home years later . . . at about the time that we left Rookhope," he said. He recalled an image of Archie on a horse in a flurrying snow, with the dark-haired child in his lap. The sight remained vivid and precious. "I saw her with Archie, the day that I left here with Malise."

"You never told me that," Emma said softly.

"I didna see you for years after that day," he reminded her. "I suppose I forgot to mention it." Silence followed, as if none of them knew what to say next.

Katharine stopped gnawing his finger to look up at him. William loved the innocent calm he always saw in her round blue eyes. She had Jeanie's eyes, dark as blueberries, rather than his own lighter hue. At times, the shape of those eyes, a tilt of that brown-curled head, would bring memories of Jean flooding back to him. Most of all, he remembered her laugh, rich and melodious. He wondered if Katharine would have that same laugh as she grew.

Katharine went back to his finger as if to a feast. "This child should be fed more often," William said.

"She is in a fit of teething." Helen stood and lifted the infant from his hold. Katharine began to fuss, mouth wide, eyes clenched. "I'll find her wetnurse. Margaret will be in the kitchens, eating again, I vow, or flirting with the cook's lad. After she feeds, I'll rock Katharine in her cradle myself this even, I think." She snuggled her close. "Sweetheart, come with me. Bid farewell till morn. William—if I dinna see you again this even, felicitations on your marriage, and tell Tamsin the same. I think it a wonderful surprise." She smiled down at him, and he nodded his thanks. Helen left with the child.

The room seemed dimmer, somehow, in Katharine's absence, as if the sun had gone behind a cloud. William settled back and watched his mother at her stitchery: vines and flowers in black thread on linen, which he knew she called Spanish work.

"This will be a fine piece, when 'tis done," she remarked.

"What is it? Table linen?"

"A cover for a bolster. I have done two like it already, on cushions in your own bed. Did you never notice?"

"Nay," he admitted sheepishly. "Pray pardon."

"I doubt you would have noticed a change in there unless we had moved the bed clean out," she said mildly. "Ah, but now that you have a wife in your bedchamber, 'twill be different."

He saw a little glimmer in her eyes. Lady Emma was sedate by nature, but she had never been prim. As the wife of a notorious reiver, years ago, she had brought dignity and elegance to the household, yet always retained an earthy honesty about her.

"Perhaps," he said, and cursed himself for a schoolboy, for he felt a blush rise in his fair skin, and knew she had seen it. He cleared his throat and sipped at the sherry.

"You shouldna be down here with me, William," she said, as she turned the embroidery frame to clip at threads with tiny silver scissors. She set the piece upright and threaded the needle anew. " 'Tis your wedding night," she added.

William sighed, passing a hand over his eyes. He had nearly forgotten that, for he did not feel married, and in truth was uncertain of the status of this unusual union. "Tamsin said she would be down when she finished dressing," he said. "She must have changed her mind."

"She may be waiting for you to come to her," Emma said. She lifted a brow and slid him a glance.

"She might," he said. Only if she was stuck fast in her clothing, he thought. He realized that he was reluctant to go up the stairs to his own chamber. In the midst of that impulsive pledge at dawn that morning, he had promised chastity and he was determined to honor that. But his new bride, who was not his bride, made his body and his blood burn with an inner fire.

"I am glad you decided to wed, though 'twas sudden," his mother said. "I do fret about Malise Hamilton's intentions. Your marriage will weaken his cause against you. At the least, I feared that you might wed one of his choices for you."

"My wife is my own choice, and none of Malise Hamilton's matter," he said.

"Promise me, William," she said. "Promise me that he willna take our wee Katharine." He heard a tremor in her voice.

He stared at the last drop of sherry in his cup. "So long as I have breath in my body," he murmured, "she is safe."

Emma sighed in relief, and went back to her needlework. William stared into the flames in the hearth. Moments later, he turned, as Emma did, when the door of the chamber creaked open.

A shoe appeared first, skittering over the threshold to slide and halt by William's chair. A little soft curse followed, and then Tamsin entered the room, stumbling slightly.

Emma gasped, a faint sound of surprise. William simply stared.

He had seen Tamsin in the black brocade gown already, but now she looked different, changed somehow. Perhaps it was the subtle, flickering firelight that warmed her skin, or perhaps it was the gleaming touches of gold embroidery on the black fabric. He was not certain what was different.

He only knew that she seemed to glow. The sight of her drew the breath from him for an instant, and filled him with a rare, comforting, wondrous sense of joy.

He smiled, a small, private lift of his lips, and watched her with hungry fascination. He could hardly take his gaze from her. The shimmering black and gold heightened the dark honey and rose tones of her skin, complemented her dark hair, and enhanced the luminous green of her eyes. She looked slim and graceful, but the gown and accoutrements were not the sum of her beauty. Indeed, when he began to notice the imperfect touches that revealed her recent efforts with the gear, her charm increased a hundredfold.

She stepped toward him with a small limp, missing the shoe that she had inadvertently kicked off. He bent down and picked it up, a tiny, impractical black and beaded thing, and held it out to her silently.

Her cheeks flushed pink in embarrassment. He noticed that her black hood, a pearl-edged crescent that framed her face like wings, was askew, with curls slipping loose at one side, the velvet back veil crooked. Her false undersleeves were uneven, her silken cord belt sagged, and one pale stockinged foot peeked out at the hem of the gown. Amber beads further warmed her skin and brightened her eyes, and she had kept her own golden hoops in her earlobes.

"Pray pardon," she murmured, taking the shoe from him. She dropped it on the floor to slip her foot into it, and wobbled, losing balance slightly as she did so.

"Sit down, Tamsin," he said quietly, indicating the empty chair beside him. "Never mind the slipper. 'Tis a silly thing, and will only trip you again."

She looked at him in relief, sat down in a shush of skirts, and kicked off her other shoe.

"Tamsin," Emma said, rising from her seat to come forward. "You are more beautiful than I could have imagined." She reached out, and Tamsin offered her right hand, which Emma clasped. "I am so pleased that William brought you home as his wife."

Tamsin stammered her thanks. "Pray your pardon, Lady Emma," she went on, "for the shock of our marriage. And also for my rude misbehavior earlier."

"I will happily recover from such a shock. And you were refreshing at dinner, never rude," Emma said. "But now you have missed supper, and must be hungry."

She shook her head. "I just ate. Helen saw me in the corridor, and took me to the kitchen and gave me something from the stave-off cupboard. Bread and cheese, and some ale. Watered ale," she added.

Emma nodded. "Good. Now, I know you are both tired, and . . . ready to take to your bed for the evening."

William glanced at Tamsin. She lowered her eyes, her blush darkening her cheeks.

"Before you go," Emma went on, "I want to give you a wedding gift. I hoped I would have this chance to speak to you privately." She went to a cupboard and took out a wooden box. Holding it in both hands, she sat and placed it in her lap.

William straightened, uncertain what to expect. He had never seen the carved wooden box before. Beside him, Tamsin had joined her hands together nervously under the cover of her long, ruffled cuffs. She flicked a glance at him and looked away, biting at her lower lip. He understood her apprehension and her guilt. Their marriage might not be one of the heart, but his mother believed it, and had given them her enthusiastic approval.

He cursed himself for a fool. If he had thought this whole matter of marriage and false marriage out—which he had not adequately done—he would have realized that his mother and sister, too, would be enchanted by Tamsin. As he had been.

This marriage of convenience might not be so simple to dissolve after all, with so many hearts charmed by a gypsy lass. He frowned, beginning to suspect that his own heart had not only been charmed, but taken outright.

Emma opened the carved lid of the box and gazed at its contents, which William could not see. She furrowed her brow and seemed unable to speak for a moment. Then she took a velvet pouch out of the box, closed the lid, and looked at William.

"My son," she said, a little formally. "I have kept this coffret for years, wanting to give it to you someday, yet never certain when to do so. Now I think the day has come. You have brought me so much joy this day, more than you can know, by wedding the daughter of Archie Armstrong. 'Tis fitting to give you this now, as a wedding token from me, and from your father." She handed him the box.

"My father?" he asked, stunned. He smoothed his fingers over the lid, hesitant to open it.

"That coffret holds some things that belonged to your father, which I know he would want you to have. I put them in there myself, in the days following his death and your capture. I have not looked in there until now."

William opened the lid with trembling fingers, feeling almost as if he did not want to look inside. He glanced at the items, touching them reluctantly, briefly: a pair of leather gauntleted gloves, a flat, dark blue woolen bonnet, a plain leather coin purse; some folded parchments, a small dagger in a tooled leather sheath, a few coins. A faint scent wafted up, of leather and spice, and something intangible and achingly familiar. Memories began to pour through his heart and his mind, and he shut the lid quickly, as if to seal the images inside with his father's belongings.

"I thank you, Mother," he said, keeping his hand on the lid of the box. His throat felt tight. "I will look at them carefully later. I appreciate it, very much," he added.

Tamsin touched his sleeve with her fingers, warm and brief, and full of a quiet, reassuring strength. She did not speak.

"I took some of the things from his pockets, and from his body, myself, when . . . when they brought him to me, afterward," Emma said. "I wanted you to have them, now that you are wed, and already a father, so that you will remember what a good father he was, what a good husband. I didna want you to forget him."

"I could never forget him," William said, soft and fierce. He pressed his lips together, fisted a hand. He glanced at Tamsin, then looked away from the sympathy in her eyes, feeling his cheeks heat, his jaw tighten.

Emma handed him the velvet pouch. "He would have wanted you to have these too. As I do."

He held out his hand, and she spilled the contents into his palm. A few pewter buttons, a round silver pin set with a garnet, which he recalled seeing on his father's cloak, and two gold rings rolled into his hand: one large, set with an emerald, the other small and delicate, with an emerald and tiny pearls.

"I cut the buttons from his jack the day I dressed his body for burial," Emma said. Her voice was like fine steel, thin and strong. "I took his cloak pin, which has been worn by the lairds of Rookhope for generations, and I took his marriage ring, and mine, and put them away." She paused, drew a long breath, went on. "Now I want you and Tamsin to wear the rings that we wore."

William looked away, his heart thudding hard within him. He heard Tamsin's soft gasp, and he took her hand briefly, a quick grip, released it. He knew that she felt the remorse, the hesitancy, that he felt. And he knew that neither of them would speak now, for fear of hurting Emma irrevocably.

"I know your father would have been pleased that you chose the daughter of his best comrade for your wife," Emma said. She leaned forward and picked up the rings in her slim fingers.

William saw tears shining in Emma's eyes, saw her lip quiver. She stood before them while they sat and stared at her in silence. Tamsin tipped up her head to watch Emma, a stunned look on her face. William felt like Tamsin's twin in that moment, equally stunned, wondering, as she must, just what they had done.

Emma held out her hand. The rings, small and larger, gleamed in the palm of her hand. "Here, my dearlings," she whispered. "May they reflect the unending love that exists between you, as they once did for Allan and me." A single tear slid down her cheek. She placed the rings in William's hand.

William hesitated, staring down at the swirled bits of gold and jewels. "Mother . . ." But he did not have the words he needed. He did not have the courage, or the cruelty, to tell her the truth.

He held out his hand to Tamsin. She looked at him with wide, almost frightened eyes. Then she stretched out her right hand, letting the left lay uncovered, palm up, in her lap.

If Emma was startled, if she had any reaction at all to the sight of Tamsin's hand, she did not show it. William blessed her silently for her grace and compassion. She smiled down at them and stood by, hands folded, tears gleaming, while William slid the little gold ring on Tamsin's third finger.

With trembling hands, Tamsin then slipped the larger ring on his finger. She looked at him, her eyes filled with tears. And he wondered at the powerful force that swept him along on a course that he might never have taken on his own.

Emma smiled. "Och, Will," she murmured. "Kiss your lass. You've wed her by gypsy means, and you will of course wed her before a priest, as soon as we can summon one."

Tamsin's eyes widened. William leaned forward and touched his lips to hers, closing his eyes, lost for an instant in the sweet, warm pressure of her mouth against his.

"I wish you joy of each other," Emma said, her voice thick with tears. "And I bid you good night." She turned and fairly fled from the room.

William looked at Tamsin. She still held his hand in both of hers, as if she had frozen in astonishment.

"I think, my lass," he murmured, "that fate isna yet done with us. We are caught fast, once again."

She let his hand go, and stood. "Aye," she said. "Caught in a wicked falsehood!" With a little smothered sob, she too picked up her skirts and ran.

William sighed and rubbed his brow, and looked down at the floor, where Tamsin's small beaded shoes glimmered in the firelight. He scooped them up, then stood and picked up the wooden box, heavy with memories more than belongings, and left the room.

Chapter Twenty-one

But had I wist, before I kissed,
That love had been sae ill to win,
I had lockt my heart in a case of gowd,
And pinnd it with a siller pin.
                                                —"Waly, Waly, Love Be Bonny"

Tamsin was pacing furiously when she heard the iron door latch give way. The door to the bedchamber swung open and William entered, the wooden box under one arm, her shoes dangling from his fingers.

"I should have locked the door," she muttered, and swung away, skirts swirling, to continue her frenetic circular course.

"I have a key," he said mildly, and shut the door. "Tamsin, I didna know my mother would do that."

"I feel like a sneakbait thief," she said, without a pause in her pacing. "As naughty a rascal as you."

He did not reply, and walked to a table to set the wooden box on the walnut surface. Turning, he offered the shoes to her.

"I canna wear them," she said. "My feet are too large." He dropped them to the floor, letting them thunk, the action revealing his irritation. Tamsin scowled at him, heart pounding, temper surging. He turned an impassive face away, went toward the hearth, where a low fire smoldered, and began to unbutton his doublet.

"Dinna think to sleep in here," she said. Her gown swept the corner of the bed as she turned again in her circuit.

"I'll sleep in the antechamber," he said. "No one need know but us." He stripped off the doublet and slung it over the back of a chair beside the hearth, and sat, in shirt and breeches. He leaned his elbows on his knees and stared into the fire.

"So you want your mother to believe we are not only wed, but are fallen in love," Tamsin muttered as she walked.

"She has concluded that on her own," he said.

"And what are we to do about it?" Tamsin asked. "She is devoted to the idea that we are wed, now—that we belong together, Merton and Rookhope! And you have done naught to dissuade her! What will she do when we announce our intention to divorce according to Romany custom?"

"She willna like that much," he murmured, and leaned back in the chair, resting his jaw pensively against his fist.

"I didna want to let my father know about this," she said, fisting her own hands, "because I know he wants this too. I didna want him to be sad when we dissolve the marriage, as we agreed. But I didna think about your mother, or your sister, for I didna know them! You never told me you planned to tell them about this marriage. You just did it, and surprised me as much as them."

"I had to tell them," he said quietly.

"Did you never think that they too might be upset by what will come later, between us?"

He sighed. "I was a fool, and you may berate me for it. But hey, lass, remember this," he said softly, his calm voice a counter to her own anxious tone, "they are deeply upset about Malise Hamilton's efforts to take my daughter from us. And that is precisely why I told them. This marriage is a comfort to them. I just didna think how much of a comfort it might be," he added, shoving a hand through his hair.

She began to speak, but subsided, understanding why he had agreed to their impulsive marriage. The thought of anyone taking Katharine out of this loving home was unbearable to Tamsin too. Had the child been her own daughter, she would have snatched at any hope of protecting her. She huffed out a breath and resumed circling in the middle of the room.

"This is foolish," she muttered. "So foolish!" Her cap and veil slid sideways, and she tore them off, flinging them on top of the clothing piled on the bed as she went past. Her hair spilled over her shoulders in curls and waves, and she shoved its thickness back ineffectively. "What could we have been thinking, to agree to such a lackbrain scheme?" She knew why, rationally, but her temper needed to emit steam.

"As I recall," he drawled, "we thought about helping one another. The solution suited us both. You needed to avoid a gypsy husband, and I needed a wife quickly."

"Aye," she said angrily. "A false wife in a fine gown, to fool a fancy lord of the royal court!"

"I will do what I have to do to protect my daughter." Quiet words, but she heard the anger flare beneath.

"Aye, even take a troll to wife," she snapped, turning. One of her full undersleeves slid down, and she yanked at the ribbons that attached it to the gown. Inadequately knotted by her earlier, the pieces came loose easily, and she threw them on the floor.

"Tamsin, you are hardly a troll," he said. He slouched, relaxed, in the chair, but she saw the tension hardening in him. It matched her own. "You are as beautiful as any court lady," he said. "More so."

She huffed doubtfully, her mouth tight with anger, her back turned to him. Her heart pounded as she realized how much she wanted him to mean those words. But she could not accept that he did. "I know you need a wife for the nonce," she said. "But such ready compliments willna gain peace between us. I didna mean for this arrangement to hurt anyone!"

"Nor did I." He sighed and ran his fingers over his brow.

She pulled at the silken belt and the amber beads, and pooled them on the coverlet. The exquisite emerald and gold ring glittered on her finger. She examined it for a moment. She had never owned a ring before, and loved this one not only for its beautiful design, but for the meaning that it held for Lady Emma. She slid it off and turned toward William.

"Take it." She held it out to him. "I feel like a thief."

"Keep it for now, lass," he said. "For my mother's sake."

She hesitated, and slid the ring back on. "Only for her sake," she said stubbornly. "Not for yours." Her heart beat oddly as she said that.

"As you will." He stared into the fire again. His composure in the face of her ruffled temper had a calming power, but she would not give up her anger. She wanted to shout at him. She wanted to release the heat of her embarrassment. And she wanted to, and could not, satisfy the sultry, steady fire that his glances stoked in her.

She whirled away and folded her arms. "Lady Emma said she wanted us to wed before a priest," she said. "What will you tell her? That you have a mock Romany marriage, and will keep to that so long as it suits—but a fortnight or so?"

He turned the larger gold circlet on his own finger. "Marriages have been made on less," he said thoughtfully.

"Marriage!" She looked at him. Her heart pounded hard now. She had misheard him, she told herself. He did not mean to offer her true marriage. Surely he meant only to sustain the ruse for his benefit and convenience. "You would have me stand before a priest, now, to make marriage out of this mockery? I willna enter into a church-made marriage to avoid an embarrassment!"

"Tamsin . . ." He sighed. "I willna brangle with you. When you calm your temper, we will discuss this."

"Then I bid you good night, for I only wish to brangle," she said stiffly. Her breathing felt tight, constricted by the flat, hard busk. She began to pull at the tiny laces that fastened the side pieces of her bodice.

She knew he stood, and thought he would go into the antechamber to sleep on the narrow cot there. Ignoring him, she pulled at the small knots he had made, biting her lip over the difficulty. She was very tired. Her head was foggy and ached from the wine she had overdone earlier. Her hands fumbled, and she finally yanked at a knot with a yelp of frustration.

William touched her shoulder and turned her around firmly. "Let me do that," he said. "You will tear the ribbons and my mother will have to repair the gown. She will think I tore it off of you to ravish you. And then what will we tell her, hey, my lass?"

His voice was mellow, soothing her when she preferred to rant. His long fingers were at her waist, nimbly undoing the laces. Her heart quickened and she felt the curious melting sensation that he had awakened in her before. Each time, it seemed more intense.

She scowled at him. "You wouldna want to ravish me."

"Aye, I would," he said mildly. She stared at his head, at the dark waves that fell, thick and silky, over his brow.

"What?" she asked breathily, as if he had knocked the air, and the anger, out of her with those gentle words.

His fingers eased up the side of the bodice. Her breath returned as the busk was loosened, but faltered again with the movement of his hands. "I said," he murmured, "that I would like to ravish you. Very much."

She stared at him. He looked up, the spark in his gaze so direct that she felt, suddenly, as if she flared, head to toe. Surely he heard the thunder of her heart.

"What if I wanted it too?" she asked, scarcely a whisper.

His gaze slid down, up. Without answer, he bent to loosen the other side of the confining busk. In his silence, Tamsin thought that she had made a fool of herself again.

Men were more direct about their physical passions, she knew, from listening to her father's comrades and to Romany men. The lessons of modesty and obedience, taught to her by the Romany even more than the Scots, struggled with her own natural need for freedom, again fed by both cultures, in different ways. Tamsin felt caught between both worlds.

A slow, hot blush flowed up her throat into her face. She had always suffered from uncertainty, thinking herself undesirable, but she had a natural streak of boldness too, when she needed it. The strength of that streamed through her now, overtaking the rest.

Too much wine in her, she thought, then realized she felt the unaccustomed sensation, warm and expansive, of desire. The urge insisted that she discover what passion with this man would be like.

"What if I wanted it?" she asked again, more forcefully.

Still he did not answer. He released the last ties of the busk and tossed it aside. Freed from the flattening confines, veiled by her chemise, her breasts seemed to blossom. William's gaze slid there, and rose to meet hers. His body glided against hers, his fingers slid along her waist. His touch was aching hot through the thin chemise.

Still he did not speak. He sought the ties of her underskirt and freed it. She slid it off, stepping out of the hooped linen, now wearing only the opened black kirtle and the chemise. She wondered if his continued silence, his slow, chaste hands on her gown, meant that he intended to help her undress and no more.

That thought saddened her. But her throbbing heart, and the sultry heat emanating from him, told her that he did want her. And she wanted him.

She looked up at him, standing in the pool of the underskirt, her gown hanging open from her shoulders. Their gazes seemed to touch, sending shivers through her. She leaned in.

With a low growl, he pulled her to him and dipped his head. His mouth slanted hard over hers, taking her breath. She looped her arms around his neck and felt his solid chest against her breasts, linen and lawn between them. His lips were tender over hers, coaxing her to open her mouth to his.

An exquisite craving streamed through her. The first touch of his tongue upon her lips was a luscious astonishment, and she let him dip inside her parted lips, let him taste her, as she tasted him. She sipped at his lips again, drinking in the deepening pleasure of his kisses.

Unsure what would come next, she did not shy from him, but responded to his mouth, loving the warm, sure glide of his hands. She yearned for more of the taste and feel of him, the comfort that his arms, his lips, his body offered her.

His hands plunged into the mass of her hair, his fingers shaping her head as he shaped his mouth to hers. She tilted back, leaned against the bed, half seated now. Her arms circled him, her left hand fisted, her right exploring as she traced the width of his shoulders and the powerful muscles of his back.

When he rested a knee on the bed, she sank down into the luxury of the thick feather mattress and damask coverlet, and lay back. He went with her, and she turned into his arms, feeling as if she had been released from a prison she had not known existed. Hungry for his touch, she opened her lips to him and declared her desires silently, laying her feelings out like jewel-toned cards upon a table, revealing her heart.

He touched the neck of her chemise, where the band fastened with a hook and a thread loop, and undid it deftly. His hand slid inside the generous opening, fingertips gliding over her collarbone and down to graze the upper swell of her breast. Shivers slipped through her, delicate, consuming.

His lips found her throat, his breath warm there, his fingers skimming lower until he cupped her breast in the palm of his hand. She gasped, a quick intake, and arched into his touch, never hesitant, suddenly knowing in the deepest part of her soul that she wanted this, with him, only him.

As his warm palm eased over her breast, her breath suspended. The exquisite sensation echoed in her lower body. When his fingers touched the warm pearl of her breast, brushing, coaxing, she released a soft cry of pleasure and glided her body closer to his, fitting against him through layers of fabric and texture.

He placed small, shivery kisses along her throat and over the swell of her breast, until his mouth took her nipple, drew upon it gently. She uttered a dulcet sound and pulled him closer, shifting to roll toward him, raising her knee, foot upon the mattress. Her chemise slid down her thigh to pool at her hip, and his arm rested warm against her bare leg.

Emboldened by passion, beyond the effects of the wine that only made her languid, she felt as if she grew brighter and more beautiful in his arms. She pressed against him, letting the firm curves of her body plead with the harder planes of his. He growled low in his throat, a deep, raw sound. His hand circled her waist, slipped downward, and touched the most intimate part of her body.

She jumped a little, startled by the suddenness, startled more by the fervor of her own hunger, the fearlessness of it. Moving as if in a dream, floating in a warm sea of exquisite sensations, she arched into the palm of his hovering hand. His touch caressed, dipped, discovered. She gasped, low, breathy, full of longing. She welcomed his fingers, seeking him as he sought her.

He shifted his mouth upon her breast, found its twin, tasted her there, while he explored her with tender fingertips. She moaned in her throat and pulled his head up to capture his mouth for herself. One hand cupped his face, the other slid over his lean, muscled back, her touch thwarted by clothing, searching for an opening, craving the warmth of his skin. She found the heated, hard bulge of him beneath heavy black serge, where he wore no codpiece. Her hand paused there, trembling, and she boldly let it stay.

His breath caught. She gasped a little, for his fingers slipped within her, and encouraged her body to find a rhythm that matched her quickening breath. Pulsing and hot, a light burst suddenly, somehow, within her, in the rich darkness of pure sensation. She lost all sense of where or what. She only felt, and floated, and succumbed. Joy streamed through her, body and soul, and settled to burn in the core of her being, clarified into love. She felt it form, in that moment, and nearly spoke the word aloud.

Her body slowed, weak and fulfilled. She became aware of his lips on hers, his tongue tracing her mouth, gentle, hot. Her hand still cupped over his hardness, and he shifted away, letting out a long breath.

"If you want more of this with me," he murmured, sliding his mouth along her cheek, touching his lips to her ear, while she softened, expanded in her craving for him, "as I want more of this with you, then we have a dilemma indeed," he finished against her ear.

His voice melted her, heat to honey, and she flowed inside for him. Desire, newly felt, had pounded to fullness within moments, dissolving the confines of her body, molding her to him. She wanted more. His body was a strong, hard complement to hers, and she felt as if she were his twin, as if she blended to him like image touching image in a mirror.

"Why," she whispered, sinking into another of his kisses, savoring him, "would that be a dilemma?"

"We would be lost to our fate," he murmured.

"And what is our fate?" she returned, soft, with a kiss.

He pulled back, his hands stilling where they touched her. He rested his brow against hers.

"I dinna know," he finally said. "But 'tis strong. God, so strong. And I canna give in to it. I willna do that to you. Not now." He slipped his hand free of her chemise and sat up.

Tamsin lay back, the black gown shimmering around her. She stared at him and came slowly to her elbows. William kept his back to her, head bowed, hands gripping the edge of the bed.

Her body still throbbed, breathless and wanting. She could not bear the small distance between them. She saw that he preferred that, for he held up a hand when she sat up further.

"Pray pardon, Tamsin," he said, low and soft. "I promised you that I wouldna offend your chastity, and I have. God. You are a temptation to me." He turned away. "No more, I swear it."

She said nothing, just stared at his rigid back, his bowed head. She felt as if she swirled and sank, and somehow ceased to thrive. But she sat upright, her back as straight and unyielding as his. She made no sound, gave no hint that she had just taken a killing blow.

Too many refusals, from too many men. But not one of those rejections—brusque, mocking, disinterested, or polite—had wounded her like this. Not one of those men had more than grazed her fingers in greeting. None of them had touched her heart, and no one had ever breached her soul. Until now.

She had forgotten her fear of his rejection in the bravery of passion. She squeezed her eyes shut.

He reached out a hand to touch her ankle, a tender gesture of apology. But she could not bear it. Quickly, so that he could not touch her again, she got up and walked to the hearth. The beautiful black gown hung open on her, and her hair billowed around her shoulders. She folded her arms over her breasts, over the chemise he had opened and had abandoned.

"Tamsin." William walked toward her. "Let me explain."

She gave a little laugh, turned away. "What need is there for that?" she asked in a flat voice. " 'Tis obvious. You dinna want to take me, as a man takes a woman, though I would have been foolish enough to give myself to you." She drew in a breath. "But if I had, you might have felt obliged to wed me. Why should you take a gypsy, a poor reiver's daughter to your bed, when you can be free to love noblewomen, beautiful women—perfect women—whensoever you choose, and yet have a wife to your name!"

He was beside her in two strides, his fingers like iron around her upper arms. He spun her and held her in his grip, looking down at her, his eyes brilliant even in the dimness.

"Stop," he said. "Those are not my thoughts. I tell you, I canna be so harsh a judge over you as you are over yourself."

She gazed up at him, her chin high, her shoulders tense. "I am accustomed to hearing that men dinna want me."

"You have learned to hear naught else," he growled.

She looked away. "But now, when I gave something of my heart to you, I find that you dinna want me either. That . . . hurts." Her voice dissolved, recovered.

He swore, a low rumble, and pulled her to him, wrapping his arms around her, cradling her against him, though she kept stiff. "I want you," he said. "Oh, God. I want you so much it frightens me." He pulled back, framed her face in his palms, gazed intently at her. "And I am not accustomed to that. I want you so much that I am half mad with it."

"That much?" she asked, a breathless whisper.

His rueful chuckle rang in the core of her body. "I have known you for days only, and yet you are already like a fire in my soul."

She blinked, hearing him utter thoughts that could be her own, feeling as if her life had shifted on its axis and now spun in a new direction. To be desired so intensely by this man, whether from lust or something more, thrilled her beyond measure, took her back to the glow of love that she had felt only moments before.

And then she realized the danger of it, as he had already done. She saw where this could lead, and she bowed her head. "I feel that too," she whispered. "What are we to do?"

He sank his brow against hers and closed his eyes briefly. "We each flame like a brand when the other is near. That brings happiness to some, but it destroys others. The fire between us is fast and hot." He paused.

"And you think 'twill burn out," she finished.

He sighed, pulled back. Though he kept his hands around her upper arms, he put a layer of air between them deliberately. "I have learned to be wary of passion like this," he said. "I have felt it before, and I have been . . . consumed."

She glanced down. "I see," she said. "You loved Jean. You loved Katharine's mother. Naught else will compare to that. I . . . I pray your pardon." She stepped back, and he let go.

That release, and his silence, seemed to her an affirmation that he kept the memory of another close. He had given his love to another woman, and she had borne his child. Tamsin's heart cringed with anguish.

She wanted to ask about Jean, and yet did not want to hear his answer. She had endured enough hurt for now. Nothing would change the love he had for the mother of his child. She felt a stab of jealousy.

"Tamsin," he said, and sighed. "The vow we made was of loyalty and friendship. I willna dishonor that."

She gazed into the fire, where embers glowed red beneath the ashes. "Is it dishonor," she asked, "or honor, to obey this feeling between us?"

He stood behind her. "A good question, my lass, and one I canna answer."

"You desired me, just now," she said in a flat voice.

"I still do." His hand rested on her back. "But I willna give in to it further. For your sake, and for mine."

"And because we have agreed to dissolve our false marriage."

He was silent for a long moment, his hand still and warm on her back. "Too much, too fast, can hurt us both, and hurt others. We dinna know the nature of this fire between us, or what fate has planned for us. 'Tisna always a good thing, to be pulled by fate."

"So you think it best to resist that fate," she said.

"Aye," he answered quietly. "For now. Until we know what fate wants of us. I dinna want to hurt you," he said, his voice dropping to a heartfelt rumble. "I dinna want that."

But he had hurt her already. She only nodded. He had wisdom and patience, taming his passion rather than surrendering to it. Her own impulses were hot and quick, her passion impatient. He was her mirror in some ways, her teacher in other ways. She had learned much from him this day.

She sighed, realizing how exhausted she was, in body as well as emotions. Her life, her feelings, had changed since she had met William Scott. She felt new emotions burgeon within her, like flower buds straining to come forth. She yearned for sleep, hours of it, even days of it, to absorb all that had happened.

She pushed her hair back in a weary gesture. "I am grateful to you," she murmured.

"Grateful?" A breathy, skeptical laugh. "For what?"

"I thank you for wanting me, even if only in lust," she said quietly. "And I thank you for your kindness and your patience regarding my . . . my imperfections." She turned and went toward the bed. "And I bid you good night."

She began to fold the clothing and items that lay strewn on the coverlet. William crossed the room and paused by the narrow door to the antechamber to look over at her. She sensed his glance, heard his sigh, and felt the pull between them. But she did not look up.

The room seemed empty and cold after he had gone. She felt a hollowness within, and knew that a space had opened in her heart that only he could fill.

Chapter Twenty-two

O well I love to ride in a mist
And shoot in a northern wind,
And far better a lady to steal
That's come of a noble kind.

—"Hind Etin"

Led by thin bands of moonlight, silent and swift as ravens, they rode over hills and moorland until they reached a wide, flat river. William halted on the grassy bank in the cover of some birches, his horse quiet but for a breathy snort. Sandie and Jock stopped beside him. The three men waited without speaking in the moonlit screen of the trees.

Across the rippling water, a slight figure emerged from the darkened forestland beyond the riverbank. A girl, in a gown and hooded cloak, strolled to the bank. She stopped, looked around, then tossed three stones into the water. Each one made a distinct, soft splash in the quiet.

At that agreed-upon signal, Jock turned to his cousins, tipped his helmet in silent salute, and urged his mount forward into the river. The horse waded swiftly, parting the calm surface in arrowed, shining waves. Jock guided the horse up onto the opposite bank.

The girl ran forward, cloak billowing back, hood slipping down to reveal red hair bound in a coronet of braids. Jock dismounted and took off his helmet, his blond hair silvery in the moonlight. He stepped toward her and opened his arms, and she seemed to melt into his embrace. They formed one gently swaying silhouette, as if they had never been two separate beings.

William glanced away, felt his heart turn at the sight. His own emptiness, his own loneliness, seemed more keen than ever before.

"Hark you," Sandie murmured. "He is lost, that lad. Lost."

" 'Tisna lost," William murmured. " 'Tis found."

"Aye, found an English lass, he has, and we'll all suffer for it." Sandie, like William, looked out over the dark moor. Then shook his head beneath his sloping steel bonnet. "She's an English Forster, betrothed to Arthur Musgrave," he muttered. "That wedding is set for tomorrow, Jock says. We will all have trouble o' this, I tell you."

William watched the darkness with a wary gaze. He rested his gloved hand around the thick wood of the lance that jutted up from his saddle loop. "We will weather the trouble, man," he reassured his cousin. "Jock loves the lass. That alone is worth any amount of bother. Few have what they have found—be they English, Scots, or Egyptian." The last slipped out, and he frowned to himself as he looked out over the dark moor.

" 'Gyptian, aye. You're lost too, laddie, to your lassie's charms, though you seem loath to admit it, even roped as a husband. At least you wed the lass, without leading her kin after you, as Jock is bound to do, for the price of a kiss."

William did not reply, setting his mouth tight as he watched guard over the night, guard over his heart. Tamsin's kiss had bought a piece of that heart, paid already. A lifetime of those sweet kisses, of her love and companionship, would more than equal the value of his very soul. And be a bargain, he thought.

Ten days had passed since he had been so sorely tempted to make that payment in full to her. Ten days of polite conversation, of gaming at cards and draughts with her and the others, ten days of watching her play sweetly with Katharine and endeavor to learn stitchery from Emma. Nine nights on a flat cot in the antechamber, steeling mind and body against the lure of her, luscious and fiery, in his bed.

Desperate, at times, to take her into his arms, he had turned away, walked away, ridden away to shake loose his intense urges. He had not been able to take the risk. Too easy to lose all, he had thought, if he invested heart and soul in her as he wanted, more each day, to do.

Jeanie's death had taken away all that he thought he had, wiped his life clean of hopes, like a storm driving the leaves from an autumn forest. He had gained Katharine, his most precious, and unexpected, treasure. But he had lost his own future. The price of that beautiful child had come high.

He had meant to wait, as he had told Tamsin, to see what fate planned for them. But each day that passed, each night, proved to him that the bond he felt with her was far stronger than simple lust. Pray God that Tamsin felt as intensely as he did. He believed, now, that what existed between them burned with a fine, bright fire. That kind of flame would settle into lasting warmth and keep forever.

He craved her touch, even in passing: shoulder against shoulder in a corridor, hand grazing hand at supper. The sound of her voice, the scent of her, filled his senses when she was near. He listened for her step, for her laughter, when she was not in the room, felt the gift when she arrived, felt the loss when she left. She had captured a part of his soul, and now he wanted to give her the rest.

Yet he hesitated, deeply afraid, beyond all else, that he might lose her. The blaze he had felt with Jean had begun to burn out even before it had been extinguished by outside forces. With Tamsin, then, he waited, uncertain how long he would delay and deny what was undeniably real within him.

He knew, had known almost from the first moment he saw her, that he was falling deeper and deeper into love, like a man might fall into that moonlit river yonder. And be as lost, and perhaps as saved, as Jock was now.

He closed his eyes briefly, remained silent.

"So," Sandie said, keeping his voice low. "I hear Archie Armstrong just sent word to you that he wants his lassie back. You havena yet told the man you've wed his daughter?"

"We'll take care of it soon," William replied.

"Aye, you'd best do that," Sandie drawled.

William blew out a sigh. "I'll escort her back to Merton Rigg in a few days, when Musgrave's fortnight is over. I will keep my word. Musgrave is to meet with us at Merton. I had a post from him two days ago. I assume he sent a rider to Merton as well, since Archie sent a lad to me to arrange a meeting."

Archie had sent no letter, for the man could not write, but he had sent an Armstrong cousin. The lad had said that the laird of Merton Rigg expected them at Merton in a few days, and that Archie wanted "his lass back home and nae arguments about it."

The sharpness of that statement had puzzled William. He wondered if Musgrave had made some other threat to Tamsin, and he wondered, further, if Arthur Musgrave had raised the issue of witchcraft with his father. Soon enough he would find out.

He peered across the quietly flowing river. "They've wandered off somewhere," he remarked. "I hope 'tisna far. I dinna fancy sitting here in England for long."

"Nor I. Jock says he means to find a way to dissolve Anna Forster's betrothal," Sandie said. "I advised him to bury himself a bridegroom or steal himself a bride."

"Jock isna the kind to do murder," William said. "And he willna beg her father to withdraw the lass's hand from Musgrave and give it to him instead. So . . ." He shrugged at the obvious.

"Aye." Sandie sighed. "I hope he doesna mean to snatch the lass this night." He glanced over his shoulder. "But I have a bad feeling, a creeping along my limbs. We should ride away from this place. Where the de'il has the lad gone?"

"Perhaps behind those rocks, there, or among those trees."

"Whistle out, Willie, and let him know 'tis time to leave."

William lifted his face to the night breeze and cupped his gloved hand at his mouth. He rounded his lips and made a low sound, one of many his father had taught him long ago, the call of a night owl. Soft and careful, he bounced the air from his opened throat and rounded lips, an accurate imitation. Soon it was returned by an owl, far off.

He waited, but saw nothing, and did not hear the soft splashing of Jock's horse in the water. He lifted his face and made the call again: three times, silence, then three times more.

"He's kissed his fill, I would think," Sandie muttered. He looked around. "I hope they havena gone off to fondle. I willna sit idly by like a duck in the reeds while they take their pleasure. He ought to say his farewells and be on his way."

"Farewell may be the last thing he'll say, if the lass is to be wed tomorrow. He might mean to make her a bride tonight instead," William said. He called out again, three soft hoots, and stopped. He heard nothing, saw no sign of his cousin.

"We've been on English soil long enough this night, and nae kine nor woolly sheep to show for it," Sandie muttered. "Though if Jockie snatches himself a wife out o' England, that might be booty enough." He grinned.

A bird called out nearby. William held up his hand for silence from Sandie. The call came again, a raven's croak, wretchedly done by a human throat.

"We're not alone," he whispered.

Sandie slid a brass pistol from a sheath on his saddle, and began to load powder into it. William tightened the bay's reins and eased the horse out of the cover of the trees, glancing across the wide calm of the river. Sandie followed.

Jock was in sight once again, mounted on his horse, leaning down in the moonlight to touch Anna's cheek. She reached up and took his hand, and he bent to kiss her.

"Hurry," William urged in a whisper. He too felt the tension that Sandie felt. "Hurry. . . ."

The girl finally stepped away and turned to run along the bank, away from Jock, while he headed his horse toward the water. William heard Sandie breathe a sigh of relief, and he exhaled some of his own apprehension. "Nae bride this night," Sandie said, low.

"I'd wager they've made some sort of plan between them," William said. "That didna look like farewell forever to me."

As Jock entered the water, the quiet night seemed to explode in shouts and hoofbeats and fury. Riders burst out of another wooded area on the opposite side of the river and headed toward Jock. A pistol flared bright and sounded.

Jock wheeled, shouted, cut sideways on the horse through the water. Anna turned and ran back toward him, cloak winging out behind her. The riders thundered in pursuit. Anna leaped from the bank into the water and began to wade toward Jock, who rode toward her.

William reached down and grabbed the small crossbow that

hung beside his saddle and loaded a short, deadly quarrel into its channel. He balanced the weapon on his forearm, and used one hand to guide his horse out into the clear moonlight.

In the river, he saw Jock bend down, and in one sweeping movement, lift Anna to his saddle. She settled behind him and looped her arms around his waist. The horse plunged toward the middle of the river, surging chest-deep. A crossbow bolt whipped through the night, splitting the surface of the water not far from the horse's flank.

Sandie lifted his pistol, sighted, and lowered it. " 'Tis too far, yet. Just let those English rascals come closer, and let them try to fire on our lad again!"

Another bolt skimmed the water. William answered it with his quarrel, skillfully aimed, knowing the crossbow had a longer range than Sandie's pistol. One of the pursuing riders fell from his horse, but the rest came on, entering the water, churning it to white foam.

Jock attained the near bank, water spraying high in the moonlight. William and Sandie turned their mounts, breasted on either side of Jock and Anna, and launched out over the moorland. Four riders—five, William saw in a quick backward glance—reached the bank and began to chase them.

Jock sent him a fleeting grin beneath the shadow of his helmet. "I think her kinsmen have a mind to come to our wedding," he called.

William shot his cousin a sour glance, and leaned forward as the bay picked up speed.

The priest's voice droned on in Latin, the sound thick and hoarse, for he had been sleeping sound but minutes before. William bent his head as much in reverence as to avoid the low-raftered ceiling of the small room. The main chamber of the priest's small bastle house was overcrowded, already containing a table and chairs, and a curtained bed, with rumpled covers, boxed into one wall.

On the other side of a wattled partition, a cow and several pungent sheep had been awakened by the midnight arrival of three reivers and a stolen bride. Snorts and chomping sounds created the only music for the wedding ceremony.

William tucked his helmet under his arm, his chest armor reflecting the red gleam of the peat fire in the central floor hearth. Beside him, Sandie seemed quiet, even meek, as he stood with helmet in hand.

Jock and Anna knelt before the priest, hands joined, heads bowed. Father Thom had tried to deny them admittance to his little house until he saw the lances and crossbows shining in the moonlight, and had heard the names of the laird of Rookhope and the laird of Lincraig. Now he looked grim and sleepy in a long shirt and bare feet, an embroidered priest's cope tossed over his shoulders, as he hurried through the ritual.

William listened to the intonation and watched Jock's and Anna's bowed heads, fair and reddish, in the light of the flaming candles that each held. Their faces looked somber and innocent, their gazes wholly devoted. The priest sketched the symbol of a cross in the air over their heads, pronounced them wed, and hastened to the table to write out the document of marriage.

Jock turned to Anna as she turned to him. He tipped her chin up with his fingers. The kiss they shared was slow and gentle, a cherishing that took William's breath to watch. Their candles, which each held to the side, haloed them in a golden, peaceful light.

William turned away. He ached for that kind of salvation, that kind of abiding love in his own life. He felt the need burning within him, felt it rock him to his soul and throw him out of balance. Equilibrium lay just within his grasp, though he would have to reach out, past risk, to take hold of it.

Jock and Anna had found the courage to take what they needed, no matter the danger. Witnessing that, even more than the marriage itself, inspired him, filled him with a fervent urge to claim his own happiness.

He turned, saw the priest bending over the parchment, heard the scratch of the quill as he wrote out the names of the souls he had united that night. The priest offered him the quill, and William signed his name as witness. He murmured congratulations to Jock and Anna, and turned away.

He went to the door while the others talked and laughed behind him. He kept silent, stayed wary and apart, as was his nature, for in that he had always found a sense of safety. The simple, hurried marriage he had just witnessed had touched his heart, and he did not trust himself to speak. Later he would give them better congratulations, and see that a valuable gift was delivered to Lincraig Tower in honor of the marriage.

He opened the door a crack and scanned the night, making certain that the hills beyond were still deserted. They had ridden far into Scotland before losing their angry tail of Forsters and Musgraves, and before finding the house of a priest who would marry them in haste, for good coin.

William knew that the four of them could not ride on to Lincraig Tower, Jock's home, just yet, in case their pursuers sought them there. The bride and groom would have to find some other place to spend their wedding night. When that was accomplished, William would make his way back to Rookhope. He expected to see morning sun before he slept.

He meant to do all that he could to ensure that Jock and Anna were protected on their wedding night. He felt an obligation, shouldered willingly out of loyalty and reverence, to defend those he loved, those he respected.

What he saw shining between Jock and Anna was so precious, so fragile in its newly wedded state, that he wanted to be there to act as protector. He would step aside when the danger to them had passed.

And then he meant to try to find the courage that he needed to claim love for himself. What he had witnessed tonight, what he had learned about love, and about himself, gave him hope.

Chapter Twenty-three

"O see ye not yon narrow road,
So thick beset with thorns and briers?
That is the path of righteousness,
Tho after it but few enquires."

—"Thomas the Rhymer"

"So Jock and Anna had already agreed to meet later that even, when she had a chance to collect her gear?" Tamsin asked. "The abduction at the river was a spontaneous thing?"

"Aye," William said. "The Forsters and Musgraves came out in ambush, so Jock took her with him then."

Tamsin nodded. She had heard the story already, but did not mind hearing it again, for each telling brought more, and interesting, details. As with most men she knew, William's full story was not delivered in the first telling, or even the second, but the three women at Rookhope had persistently drawn it out of him.

William had returned yesterday at midmorning, dirty, hungry, exhausted, and bearing news of Jock's wedding. Tamsin, Emma, and Helen had heard the essentials of the story while he ate, and questioned him again at supper, after he had slept for several hours. Today, they had asked him about it again, and William had answered their questions patiently.

"What a wonderful adventure! To go against the wishes of kin, all for love!" Helen sighed. She smiled and swept a gentle hand over Katharine's head, capped in silk.

Katharine cooed in excitement, then lurched forward in her walker, a lightweight framework of sturdy twigs and wooden wheels with a canvas sling seat. Her little feet, in leather shoes, shoved across the polished wood floor. William, while talking to his sister, reached out and grabbed the walker to pull it away from the hearth. He sent Katharine gliding toward her grandmother, while the baby laughed.

"Will Jock and Anna be at Lincraig now?" Tamsin asked. She bent over a small piece of linen held in her left hand. She had begun to show her hand more often, set free somehow by the fact that no one at Rookhope was bothered by the sight of it. Now she laboriously stitched over a simple flower design that Emma had painted on the cloth for her. The silver needle, dragging blue silk thread, slipped, and she winced as she pricked a finger.

"Nay. I think they will stay in hiding for several days, perhaps weeks," William said. "The Forsters, and Arthur Musgrave in particular, will still be searching for them. When Sandie was here earlier today, he said they rode to Lincraig last night, stole a dozen sheep, and burned a barn—to light the bridal bower, they were heard to shout as they rode away."

"Anna's kinsmen will have to accept that she and Jock are married," Helen said. "Jock woke a priest that very night. She is wedded and bedded now, and her kinsmen can do naught."

" 'Tis done, true. Sandie and I witnessed the marriage and signed the document," William said. "Jock sent a man to give a copy to Anna's father, along with a letter in Anna's own hand, explaining that she married by choice rather than force. They slept together as husband and wife. Legally the Forsters and Musgraves can do naught, for she wasna abducted."

"They can carry on a blood feud," Emma said.

"Aye. But all this will cool, I think, given time. The Forsters and Musgraves will cease to demand Jock's life in return for the abduction of the bride. But Jock will lose sheep and cattle to them, I will wager, for the rest of his life."

"As we all do, who live in the Borders," Emma said. "Naught to fret over . . . unless lives are lost," she added quietly.

Tamsin listened, frowning over the linen, dipping the needle in and out of the cloth, her stitches too large or too small, too tight or loose. She bit her lip in concentration, and bit back the urge, once or twice, to utter a round oath or two. Lady Emma and Helen had facile hands at stitchery, but she did not think she would ever master it. Her left hand was too clumsy, and her right hand was too impatient.

She looked at William, thinking how handsome he looked in the pale light that poured through the high-set glazed windows of the great chamber. The daylight was gray and thin, but pure enough to make William's eyes seem more brilliant a blue than the gypsy flowers that Tamsin so cautiously stitched. She had asked Lady Emma to sketch the flowers on the linen, for she had thought to give William the finished piece to use as a handkerchief. But she was sure that her current effort would not be good enough to give to him.

She did not think she would have a chance to attempt another hand cloth for him. William had told her earlier that he had heard from both Archie and Musgrave, and that he planned to take her back to Merton Rigg that evening. The scheme that Musgrave had put into motion, at King Henry's orders, would begin its spin now, and take them all into its heavy current, like the pull of a mill wheel. She and William had found some respite at Rookhope, but the turn of that wheel was inevitable.

And she did not know, when all was done, what would happen to her, to William, or to the mock marriage that had become so important to her.

Rain beat at the windows, a soothing sound, and mingled with the mellow drone of William's voice as he continued to talk to his mother and sister. Tamsin stitched, and listened, and tried to keep her more vexing thoughts at bay. She watched Katharine with a careful glance, as did the others, as the baby rolled curiously around the room, touching things tentatively.

For years, she had thought that, if she ever married and settled in a household, she would miss the freedom to wander that she had enjoyed as one of the Romany, miss the boldness she was allowed as Archie Armstrong's daughter. But she had freedom at Rookhope, stemming from gentle acceptance and love.

Though she had feared the restraints of this sort of life, she was able to be herself here. That gave her a sense of salvation and contentment. Having come to love that, she would have to give it up.

But there was something missing in this peaceful atmosphere.

William had not approached her privately since their first night at Rookhope Tower, either in daylight or at night. Helen helped her with her clothing and her hair now, at William's suggestion after the first day. And his sister and mother were often with her, since they had quickly included her in their tasks and in their leisure moments.

At night, William found ways to avoid her, even in their chambers. He would enter the room at a late hour, after he thought she was asleep. Too often she lay awake in his luxurious, lonely bed, and heard him cross the room, floorboards creaking, to enter the antechamber.

Sometimes, she would hide her face in her arms and cry herself to sleep, longing to feel his arms around her, yearning for his kindness, for his love. Befriended and accepted for what she was at last, she felt lonelier than ever. Her marriage to William was not real. And she realized how much she wanted that bond with him.

But she was afraid to reveal her thoughts and needs to him. Another rejection, even in the gentle way he had, might destroy her utterly. The courage that passion had given her once, in his arms, had disappeared. Her doubts had overtaken her again.

But she sensed a change in him since he had returned from his adventure with Jock and Sandie. He seemed warmer toward her, catching her glance more often, smiling more. She loved the intimate, subtle lift of his lips that sent shivers all through her, and gave her a fragile hope. Perhaps her imagination created that interest in his eyes. Her yearning and loneliness would find hope in whatever morsel he offered her.

The needle stuck her and she swore, drawing the startled gazes of the others. Blood beaded on her finger, and she sucked on it, blinking at William, Helen, and Emma. William pinched back a smile and turned to spin Katharine in her walker. Her delighted giggles brought smiles to everyone for a moment.

"Tamsin, you've worked hard at that lovely piece," Emma said. "I will show you how to decorate the flower petals, if you like. But put away the cloth for now, dearling, and come do the *tarocchi* for us. I know you read the picture cards for Helen the other day, but I wasna with you, and would like to watch it done."

"Aye, if you please," Helen said. "Read them for William."

Tamsin hesitated, feeling William's gaze upon her. "If she wants, 'twould be fine," he murmured to his sister.

"Aye, then." Tamsin went to the table beneath a window.

A patterned carpet covered the table, with an ivory gaming box on the bright, soft surface. She opened the box, which contained four packs of cards in pouches, bone dice, and stacks of wooden draughtsmen and counters for various games. Tamsin chose a pouch of heavy black silk and closed the lid.

She sat on a small bench, slid the cards out of the silk bag, and began to sift through them. William drew up another narrow bench and sat opposite Tamsin at the table.

"So," he said. "Do you want to play a game first? We will need a third player. Twenty-five cards each, trumps counting highest. Silence is the rule of play, and honor is all."

Tamsin knew he teased her a little. She laid the cards face up on the table and skimmed her right hand over them to spread them out. "We can play later," she said. "These cards can also show one's life . . . and fate."

"Ah," he said. "So honor is still the rule of the game."

"Aye," she breathed, knowing he spoke with a double meaning that Helen and Emma, listening, would not understand. She touched the bright cards by their edges and glanced at William. "But if you would rather play the game itself, we can do that."

"We've played enough games," he murmured, his gaze steady, his meaning, again, clear only to her. " 'Twould be interesting to have you read my fate." He rested his forearms, folded, on the table. "Go to, then, lass."

She nodded, his close presence making her head spin a bit. His knee bumped hers under the table and lingered there. She wondered suddenly if she would see her own fate along with his in the lay of the cards.

"These are beautiful," she said, as she winnowed them into piles and mixed them again. "I have seen *tarocchi* with engraved designs, colored lightly, but each of these is hand drawn and painted." She touched one image, its background a thin layer of punched gold, its allegorical figure painted in saturated color. The parchment was thick, stiffened with clear glue, but she was still wary of damaging the gilded, decorated surfaces.

"They were a gift from a friend," William murmured.

"From the queen dowager herself. Helen told me," Tamsin said. "Marie of Guise must value your friendship highly."

"I value hers," he said. "These were done by an Italian painter. There are trumps—twenty-two picture cards—and four suits—cups, staves, swords, and coins. Different than the French playing cards we use, with hearts and spades and so on."

"The suit cards in a French pack can be used for fortune-telling as well. But these will tell us your fate most clearly. Now you must mix them," she said, handing him the cards. He poured them from one hand to the next. At her direction, he separated and stacked them.

Tamsin watched his hands, strong and gentle and handsome, as he manipulated the cards. When he set them down, he relaxed a hand on the table, so close to her own that she felt the subtle heat. She took the topmost cards to arrange twenty-two of them face-down.

"Three rows of seven each," William observed, "and one remaining. What is the significance of that?"

"The rows represent past, present, and future. The last card is the resolution," she said. "Now hush." He nodded, and although she focused on the cards as she turned each one over, she was aware of his gaze on her, his hand near her own, his knee against hers beneath the table.

She sighed as she slowly revealed the cards and began to speak about what she saw there. The *tarocchi* images created a story, as they often did, and this tale did not surprise her.

In the rows of past and present, she saw a childhood of security, a home shattered by tragedy; an intelligent, sensitive lad beset by grief and fear, protecting himself from hurt; finally, an educated, sincere, sensible man of achievement and wisdom and passion, grown cautious despite the love around him. Then more tragedy, more hurt, and the further retreat of his heart, even in the presence of a loving family. When she overturned a card of hope, of new beginnings, her heart pounded softly. But it was followed by a card of doubt and fear.

She explained what the cards disclosed. As she did so, she felt a better understanding and a greater sympathy for him.

William listened, his forefinger crooked over his mouth, his eyes shadowed by a frown. Helen and Emma drew close to watch, their expressions somber.

"Cups show harmony and joy in the home," Tamsin said. "There is much of that in your life, earlier, and in the present. But these cards, in the past—the Hanged Man and the Tower—show devastation, and a new direction." She went on, aware of the silence among the others.

"There is strife here, and change. This card, five coins, says you feel . . . excluded from the warmth of life." She saw Helen and Emma nod soberly. William's face remained impassive.

As Tamsin detailed the other cards, caught by the story they told, she marveled at how precisely the cards had arranged themselves in William's sure hands. He had put something of himself, his heart and hopes and fears, into the cards as he held them. Only then, she knew, could the cards speak the truth and mirror lives and emotions.

All the while, she felt keenly attuned to William's silence. She turned over the last few cards, all but one.

"Ah, the Lovers," Emma said. "A man and a woman, with an angel looking over them."

"But it doesna usually signify an actual pair of lovers," Tamsin said. She glanced at William, whose blue gaze pierced her. "This card, when related to the cards around it, indicates a choice." She looked at him again, though it took courage to do so. "You face a decision. The right path will transform you. But that frightens you."

He glanced away, but she knew he understood and perhaps agreed with her. She moved to the next card. "The Magus. You seek wisdom, the truth. You have more wisdom than you know, and the power to change others around you. The power too to change your own fate . . . if you wish it," she added softly.

He nodded, listening silently, his fingers over his mouth, a gesture, she thought, of skepticism. "And this one," she said, as she turned over the last card in the row of the future. "Ah. The Fool." She frowned. "You have some confusion with regard to some matter in your life, a matter of great importance, for this is a powerful card. 'Tis a card of fate. Let fate guide you, the cards say."

"That figure signifies the force of fate?" he asked.

"Aye," she said softly.

She had not influenced the cards by her manner of mixing or laying them out. Nona had taught her well and thoroughly. She expressed only what the cards themselves told her, by virtue of their symbolism and the way in which each one reflected and enhanced the meaning of other cards on the table.

But she knew, without doubt, what issue was addressed. And she did not miss the significance for herself as she looked at the cards in the last row. Somehow, the *tarocchi* counseled her with the same wisdom they offered William.

"The Fool looks like a gypsy or a vagabond to me," Helen remarked. "Clothed in rags, with a walking stick and a sack."

"Aye, the wandering soul, open to guidance, and chance," Tamsin answered. "William has something of that in him." Her hand trembled as she touched the final card. "This may show us what direction fate would lead you."

He laid his hand over hers. The sudden touch, the warmth, startled her. "Nay," he said in a quiet voice. "I dinna want to see it. If I have a choice to make, I will do it on my own, without fortune-telling. Without fate," he added in a near whisper, to her alone.

Tamsin nodded, unable to speak. She knew the choice he faced involved her and the uncertain matter of their marriage and their attraction to each other. The cards had shown aspects of William's life and his character. Yet each had mirrored her own life and feelings, too.

The final, unknown card made her apprehensive. What if it showed a shattering between them, rather than a joining? She was afraid to look, and glad he had stopped her.

"Well enough," she said. "We will leave it as 'tis."

He nodded, and kept his hand over hers. The heat of his touch seeped into her bones, into her blood. She turned her hand in his, palm to palm, thumbs linking, a natural gesture for a wedded couple. Emma and Helen smiled at them.

"Amazing," Helen said softly. "Much of that seemed to describe William's life. Tamsin didna purposely choose those cards, nor did William, for they mixed them well. Chance decided which cards were laid on the table."

"Or fate," Tamsin murmured, watching William. He lifted a brow, a quick gesture of admittance that fluttered her heartbeat.

"So much of the past and present seemed true," Helen said. "But William has already made a choice guided by fate. He married Tamsin impulsively."

"Aye," Emma said. "And wisely." She smiled. "A wonderful game, Tamsin. I would like to see more of that, another day."

"Will, has Tamsin looked at your palm?" Helen asked.

"Aye, once," he said. "She saw a man of honor, as I recall. And I think she questioned that honor." He smiled at her, a patient smile that crinkled his eyes and seemed to pool affection there. She smiled in return, tentatively, yearning for him to care for her as much as she cared for him.

"Let me look again," she said. He turned his hand, which still held hers. She smoothed her fingertips over the grooves etched in his palm. "Aye," she said. "I see honor, intelligence, a strong love for family, good health. A tendency to stubbornness, but a fairly calm temperament."

"Health, wealth, the love of a good lass, the vanquishing of all my enemies," he murmured. Tamsin scowled at him playfully, for she heard the teasing in his voice.

"What about love?" Helen asked. "Do you see marriage there? Can you match it in your own hand?"

" 'Tisna so simple as that," Tamsin said. "I see several loves here," She frowned. "But they cease after a certain point, and the line shows one strong, intense attachment."

"As it should be," Emma said. "Tamsin, 'tis you there in his hand."

She was not so sure she agreed. That deep-cut, heartfelt line could mean Katharine's mother. She saw a mark that signified the advent of parenthood, near the sign of that love.

Tamsin slid her fingertips over William's palm, savoring the feel of his quiet power under her hand. She caught sight of a minute, finely cut line, and looked closer.

The tiny crease ran parallel to his life line, identical to the one that she had in her own palm. The line revealed that he had a twin for his soul, a love that was rare and sure.

She caught her breath, wondering if, indeed, they were meant to be together. She remembered that her grandmother had been certain that they belonged with each other.

But free will could change whatever was in their lives. The choices made in a lifetime could alter the lines in the palm. Those tiny marks of destined love could mean tragedy as well as joy. Even fated love was not always found, kept, or claimed.

Her heart beat hard as she slipped her hand from his. That minor parting felt like a small rent in the fabric of her life. She wanted to repair it by placing her hand in his again. But she folded her hands in her lap.

William inclined his head, his gaze steady on her, a gleam of bemusement showing there. "My thanks, Tamsin lass. 'Twas entertaining."

She nodded, knowing there was more truth than play in what had happened. She began to gather the cards. William rose from the bench and spoke softly with his mother, who asked him about Jock and Anna's plans following their wedding. Helen chased after Katharine and lifted her out of her walker, which stirred the child to noisy fussing.

"And why," Emma said, "if you went to a priest's house to witness Jock and Anna's wedding, did you not invite the man to come here to Rookhope? I am most anxious to arrange a marriage within the Church for you. Gypsy vows will do, I suppose, but I want to hear Christian blessings spoken over you."

Tamsin felt her cheeks flame. She did not hear William's murmured reply above Katharine's cries, but thought it sounded casual and noncommittal. Some of the cards slipped from her hands and scattered on the floor. She bent to pick them up.

"Tamsin," Emma said. "Helen and I are going to put Katharine down for a rest, and then we will sit in the great hall to have some muscatel before supper. Join us there, dearling."

Tamsin nodded. "I will."

"I must ride out to talk with some of my kinsmen and tenants," William told his mother. "With the Forsters and Musgraves angry at Jock, all those of our surname should be wary after dark." He looked at Tamsin. "I will be back by supper, or shortly after that. Later this evening, before set of sun, we will ride over to Merton Rigg to see your father."

"Aye," Tamsin said. "I have packed my gear."

"Packed?" Emma asked. "Will you stay at your father's for a while? I know you mean to meet with Archie and with Jasper Musgrave, but I hoped that you would come right back to us. But of course, you must tell Archie about your marriage, and he might want you to stay with him for a few days. Then I want to see you two right back here." She smiled and reached up to pat her son's shoulder.

William glanced at Tamsin as he left the room. That flash of blue was enigmatic and powerful. She could not tell if he agreed with his mother or if he meant to leave Tamsin at Merton Rigg forever, a discarded mock wife.

Helen and Emma followed him out, and Tamsin sat alone at the table, gathering up the rest of the picture cards and slipping them into the black silk pouch.

Her hand lingered over the last card, still facedown on the table. She hesitated, then turned it over, revealing the Star, an image of a woman holding a golden starburst.

"Ah, Will," she whispered sadly. "Hope and salvation are yours, if you would but choose that path." Happiness waited for both of them, she thought, glittering bright and full of promise, like the little picture she held.

But William had not wanted to see the final card. Perhaps he already knew what direction he would take. She feared that he would decide to turn away from her, and from their marriage. The *tarocchi* had hinted that the fool in him, the gypsy part of his soul, struggled with the wise man.

Chapter Twenty-four

One gentle Armstrong I doe ken,
A Scot he is much bound to mee;
He dwelleth on the border-side,
To him I'll goe right privilie.
                    —"Northumberland Betrayed by Douglas"

The rain softened as they left Rookhope for the brief ride to Merton Rigg, and soon changed to a mist that haloed the rising moon. Hillsides thick with heather became a sparkling silver carpet touched by moonbeams. Tamsin sat her gray's back quietly, watching the countryside, marveling at its silent beauty.

"There will be few reivers out on such a night," William murmured, looking up at the sky. Lavender lingered there, since darkness came late on Scottish summer nights. "Too soft, this night. The rain will come down again, I think, before long. We may be the only reivers out here, lass." He sent her a brief smile.

She touched the sleeve of her old leather doublet, knowing he referred to the male clothing she wore for the journey back to Merton Rigg. Her own gear—breeches, boots, shirt, and doublet—would do, she thought, since she was about to return to her old life.

With reluctance, she had left Helen's beautiful things behind, folded carefully in the great wooden chest in William's bedchamber at Rookhope. She had placed the delicate emerald and gold ring on the table in William's room, though tears had pooled in her eyes to do it. When she had dressed, she had paused over her black leather gloves, the left one shaped for her hand, and then had tucked them away. The freedom to use her left hand without shame would remain one of the finest gifts she had gained at Rookhope.

Her only remembrance of the elegant things she had worn at

Rookhope was in her hair, which Helen had arranged in a coil of braids at the back of her head, interwoven with green glass beads and covered in a silken net. She had left it undisturbed, covering it in the rain with a flat woolen bonnet that she had among her own few things, which Sandie had fetched from Merton Rigg a fortnight past.

"Will Musgrave be at Merton already, think you?" she asked.

"He might be. His note to me said that he intended to meet with all of us this night. I'm sure he sent Archie the same word. 'Tis late enough now that they could be waiting for us to arrive."

She nodded and rode on. The route to Merton ran along a drover's track that skimmed the tops of rainy, heather-covered hills. After a few minutes, she noticed that her horse had slowed to a walk, as if the gray expressed Tamsin's reluctance. Aware that she might lose William as soon as they reached Merton, she would not have minded had the ride lasted forever.

The bay horse slowed too, and Tamsin glanced at William. He rode with a straight back, one hand casually on the reins, the other resting on his thigh. The space between their horses was less than an arm's length, and every so often their thighs or knees would brush.

"Tamsin." His quiet voice startled her out of her thoughts. "A message came for me late today."

"I saw the messenger arrive, with his blazoned pouch and arm patch, so I knew 'twas civic business. You spoke to your mother about it afterward, but you didna mention it to me. I thought it none of my matter, so I didna ask."

"It is your matter. I wanted to tell you later, when we could be private. I had a letter from Hamilton's advocate."

She glanced at him in alarm. "What did he say? Please God, the court willna let Hamilton take Katharine!"

"The judges of the Court of Sessions reviewed his complaint against me, and found it unworthy of their time. They refused to even summon me for an interview. They consider the child to be in suitable custody—"

"Oh, Will!" Tamsin exclaimed, turning to him in delight. " 'Tis wonderful! Now Hamilton has no complaint against you!"

"No legal complaint," he said. "Aye, 'tis wonderful." He smiled, but seemed subdued.

" 'Tis good to know that Katharine will stay with her kin at Rookhope." Her heart plummeted a little, for she knew that she would not be there with them.

"The judges accept that Katharine is in good care," he answered. "The advocate wrote to me that the court approves of her situation, since her father, as they said, is known to be a friend to the late king and the queen dowager."

"Did the news of your marriage help, too?" she asked.

"I never sent word of that," he said.

She stared at him. "You never told Hamilton or the advocate about the marriage?"

He shook his head. "Apparently my position in the royal court—my reputation—decided the case in my favor. Just as one can be found guilty by repute in Scots law, they found me deserving by repute, I suppose." He smiled, flat and bitter. "Ironic, that."

"Then you didna need the marriage after all," she said, feeling somewhat stunned.

"I didna need it." He watched her. "But it did serve to protect you from a poor predicament, and for that I am glad."

"I—I am happy that this has ended so well for you," she said. Her voice faded. She felt outside that circle of happiness now, despite her genuine joy for all those at Rookhope.

"The advocate informed me that Malise has submitted another complaint for the rights to property Katharine inherited through her mother," William said. "My friend Perris Maxwell will act as my advocate and draw up an arrangement of rental and the sharing of profits. Malise can oversee the land, so long as the deed remains in my daughter's name. 'Tis what Malise has wanted all along, that property. I hope to hear little more from him."

"I am glad 'tis over," she said again, wishing she could be more glad, in truth, than she was. She looked up at the haloed moon, and at the moors and slopes, sheened silver and pewter in its light. She slowed her horse to a near standstill, wishing she could put off the moment she dreaded, the complete dissolution of their arrangement.

"Tamsin," William said. She glanced at him. He too had slowed his horse, and now circled to face her, stopping in the middle of the drover's track, as she did. "Do you want this ended between us?" he asked.

She lifted her chin slightly. "We agreed to end it when we were free. You are free now." No words had ever been so hard for her to say.

"Am I?" A statement, more than a question.

"Aye." She could not look at him. " 'Tis what you wanted."

"And you? Are you free?"

She sighed, knowing that she would never be free of the hold he had over her. "Not I," she murmured. "But if you wish to end the marriage in the Romany way, as we agreed, we will do that in the morning. If you wish," she repeated, desolate.

He sat silent, scanning the hills. After a moment, he took off his helmet, set it in his lap, and raked his fingers through his tousled hair. " 'Tis true that I didna need the marriage, after all," he said. "But I need it now."

She stared at him. "You need it?"

"I do." He watched her.

"Do you have . . . some other dilemma?" she asked.

He sighed, half laughed. "Must I say it out plain to you?"

"Aye," she breathed. "Say it plain."

"Stay with me," he said.

Her heart surged. "Stay?"

"Aye." He shifted the bay closer. William's knee touched hers, and he leaned toward her. "I have thought about naught else these two weeks," he said. He reached out and tilted her chin toward him with gentle fingers. "Truth to tell, I thought I might go mad with wanting you, and yet keeping my distance."

She sighed, closed her eyes, opened them again. But her hopes tripped over her fears. She told herself she had misunderstood his meaning. " 'Tis the fire of lust that makes you speak to me so."

"Lust," he murmured, "is a paltry flame compared to this." He brushed his thumb over her jaw. "There have been times in my life, I admit, when I mistook lust for love. But now, after these weeks with you, I know the difference between them." He moved closer, until his hand curved around her waist and his breath grazed her cheek.

"They are very close in nature, I think, lust, and . . . and love," she said, her heart pounding fiercely.

"Aye." His lips traced over her skin, and she began to melt under that warmth. "One is a fire in the body," he murmured. "The other is a fire in the soul."

"Ah." His lips were so close to hers that her breath caught within her. "And which am I, for you?"

"You," he whispered, "are all to me, and more." His mouth found hers, and his arm encircled her, curving her into him across the small space between their horses. She looped an arm around his neck as the kiss deepened, lengthened. The misted, moonlight night surrounded them in silence like a blessing.

She drank in another kiss, and another, like water drawn from a newfound well, endless and plentiful. He sat back, his fingers sifting over the curls that wisped loose along her brow, and smiled at her, that small smile that she loved.

"Tamsin . . ." He framed her face in his palm. "I canna let you go now. Fate may have brought us together, but since then, you have taken hold over my heart. I dinna think, in truth, that I ever wanted the dissolution of the marriage."

"Nor did I," she said breathlessly, and circled her arm around his neck again. The horses faltered at the sudden movement, and William took her arm to balance her.

"Ho," he said. "You'll fall into the heather."

"Fall with me," she murmured, and leaned forward to kiss him, feeling him smile beneath her lips. His easy laugh, his joy, flowed into her. "Heather makes a fine bed for a gypsy and a reiver to share," she said, her breath quickening at her boldness, at the thought of what she suggested.

"My lass," he said, looking down at her. "My sweet, bonny gypsy. Hold on. I willna bed you now, in heather and moonlight, no matter how much you tempt me."

"Will you not?" she asked, wishing he would.

"Not when we could be in our soft, warm bed—if you will lend it back to me."

"I will," she answered lightly.

He smiled, but then grew somber, tracing his fingers along her neck, where his touch sent shivers through her. "I would bed you properly, my love," he said. Her heart danced at that, and at the deep, true sound of his voice. "But first we will make the marriage complete, with vows said before a priest."

"As your mother wants," she said, nodding.

"As I want," he said. He drew her into his arms gently, and she rested her cheek on his leather-covered shoulder, surrounded by his strength. "When I witnessed Jock and Anna say their vows before a priest, when I saw the love between them, I knew then that I wanted the same with you."

"You said no word of it when you came back to Rookhope," she said. "You could have come to me and swept me away, like Jock did with Anna. I wouldna have protested."

He leaned his cheek against her brow. "I was afraid, I think," he murmured.

"Of me?"

"Something within myself made me pause, waiting for the suitable moment, perhaps. But when you looked at the *tarocchi* cards, you made me think, made me burn to tell you."

"Was it what the cards revealed about fate?" she asked.

"Fate, aye," he said, kissing her brow. "Even more, 'twas what you said about doubts and fears, and having the power to change my life. I wanted so much to tell you my feelings then that I almost took you in my arms in front of my mother and my sister."

"Instead you ran out, with some talk about tenants."

"Aye. I rode about my lands and thought it through. Tamsin, I have never been a cowardly man, or hesitant in my life," he said. "But you have taken me down like a rogue in the night, ambushed me, spun me around."

"Until you chose the right path," she said.

"You showed me the way I needed to go," he replied.

"The way you needed most to go, I did too," she said, and lifted her face for a slow kiss that spun her like a whirlwind. "Fate brought us to this," she said.

"Then let us hope fate will be satisfied that we have obeyed, and leave us be," he answered. "We had best go on to Merton and tell your father."

"This news will please him well," she agreed, smiling. He lifted her left hand in his, the small wedge curving over his fingers, and kissed the back of it as if he kissed the hand of a queen. Then he turned her hand and placed a kiss in the cup of her palm.

Something trembled inside her, and she fluttered her eyes closed. Pleasure swirled through her, along with the poignant, powerful realization that he loved her without restraint, without fears or judgment. She had sought that love all her life, had thought never to find it. Now she had gained it at last, and with the son of her father's dearest comrade.

When she looked at him again, she could not trust her voice to speak. She gave him a trembling smile, the best she could make through a sheen of tears, and lifted the reins. William stepped his horse around to move forward with hers. Then he took her hand again, holding it tight in his.

As she rode beside him, she felt as if the whole of her heart lay cradled in his safekeeping.

"What is that light? A fire?" Tamsin asked after a while, as the drover's track brought them over Armstrong lands. Ahead, the tower of Merton Rigg rose above a mass of treetops, a thrust of dark stone edged in moonlight.

William looked where she pointed, frowning as he tried to discern the origin of a golden light that moved steadily through the trees. "A torch, I think," he said. "We'll know soon."

He wondered if reivers were out, even on such a damp night. The thought concerned him. He urged the bay to a faster pace, while Tamsin rode behind him.

The track sloped down, then up again, meandering along the spine of the hills. William and Tamsin climbed a peak, then stopped to look down, where the view toward Merton Rigg opened wide. The tower rose on a mound of land, surrounded by a wall and ditches in widening concentric rings. Dense woodland formed a dark backdrop beneath the fat, blurred moon.

A bright light, amid a dark cluster of horses, moved along the base of the outer wall. William narrowed his eyes and saw several riders, one of them carrying a blazing torch. The torch fire streamed, glowing hot and yellow, as the men rode around the perimeter of the wall.

They approached the open portcullis, but then rode past it to circle the wall again. As William and Tamsin watched, they came around the outer curve and went around yet again.

"What the devil . . . ?" William asked, half to himself.

" 'Tis my father and some of his kinsmen," Tamsin said. "I recognize the shape of his helmet. He's not holding the torch, though. He's at the center of the group. It looks as if he's got the reins of the horse beside his."

William narrowed his eyes, watching the scene. "Aye," he said slowly. "He's with eight or ten others. They just keep riding around and around. Grant mercy," he muttered, confused by the sight. "They've gone round four or five times since we stopped to watch. And they're going around yet again."

"Are they running a race?"

"No one has tried to pass another. They canna be exercising those horses, at night, in the mist like this. They ride as if they are heading somewhere, yet they only circle the tower."

Tamsin craned her neck forward, straining to see. "Do they have a ball between them, on the ground? Could they be playing at the football, on horses, at night?"

"I misdoubt that," William said. "Has your father ever done anything like this before?"

"Nay." She paused as the group circled past the gate and disappeared again. "It must be a prank," she said. "He likes to annoy Cuthbert sometimes." She shrugged. "I canna imagine what else 'twould be. My father does love a good prank."

"We'll find out soon enough," William said. He rode down the hillside, allowing the horse to walk slowly through the heather. Tamsin came behind him, and within minutes they rode close enough to see the faces of the men riding with Archie.

"They're Armstrong kinsmen," Tamsin said.

William watched as the group came around the curve in the wall again. He recognized Archie at the center of the cluster, and saw a familiar form beside him, huge and cumbersome, though the man's face was obscured. "Perhaps 'tis Musgrave he seeks to annoy," William said. "Look there. Archie has Musgrave's horse by the reins."

"What? If he had Musgrave, he would shut him in a dungeon,

not lead him around the grounds. This looks foolish to me." One of the riders broke away as the group tore past the portcullis and headed around the far curve again. "There is one of my father's cousins. Now we'll learn what game this is," Tamsin said.

The man galloped to meet them, and waved them toward the open gate. William saw a man of Archie's age, rough in appearance, dressed in a jack, long boots, and a dented helmet. Armed with pistols and a lance, he was typical of the Bordermen hard and brave enough to inhabit and ride the Debatable Land.

"Rabbie!" Tamsin called. "What is my father doing?"

"Greetings, Tamsin," he answered. "Archie has a task to finish. He asked me to escort ye and yer friend inside, quiet-like. Keep your voices hushed." He waved them ahead.

"What task could he have?" Tamsin asked quietly.

"He means to go twenty times and more 'round the walls."

"With Jasper Musgrave? Why?" William asked.

Rabbie looked at William. "Be ye Will Scott o' Rookhope, the Rogue's own son?"

"I am," William said.

"I rode wi' yer da," Rabbie said. "And he was a finer man than ye, I have heard. Now get ye inside too, and nae quarrel about it."

"Rabbie!" Tamsin exclaimed.

He waved them both ahead of him. "Through the yett, now. Archie said ye're to go to yer chamber until he comes inside, lass. I am to see that Rogue's Will waits elsewhere."

"Elsewhere? You mean the great hall. I'll wait there with him," Tamsin said. They rode beneath the overhanging iron teeth of the raised portcullis and through the tunnel arch cut in the width of the outer wall. The gate opened on a small courtyard, heavily sloped at one side, where the keep itself loomed huge and massive in the darkness. A few torches, ringed in the mist, spilled pools of weak light over the damp cobblestones.

Another man ran forward as William and Tamsin dismounted. He nodded in response to Tamsin's greeting, and led their horses away. William turned, his glance sweeping the shadowed yard, the huge keep, the small stable and other wooden outbuildings set up beneath the encompassing wall.

While Tamsin spoke with Rabbie Armstrong, William circled a little where he stood. He watched the man walk the horses into the stable, and turned again to see an older man come out of the keep and proceed down the wooden steps that led from the doorway, placed above ground level. He moved slowly, as if with age, and waved to Tamsin.

"I willna go to my chamber like a wee bairn," Tamsin insisted to Rabbie. "I'll stay with our guest, wherever he is to be put. Dinna look so horrified. Ah, there is Uncle Cuthbert come to greet us properly. He will tell us what this is about, if you willna do it."

"Och, Tamsin, be a good lass and do what ye're told," Rabbie said. "Ye dinna want to go where this laddie is going."

"And where is that?" William asked, turning toward him.

"Och, well," Rabbie said. "To the dungeon, then."

William realized that someone stood behind him in the same instant that he felt a heavy blow to his head. He heard a scream, and knew it was Tamsin. He wanted to ask her what was the matter, but the cobbled stones rushed upward to meet him.

Chapter Twenty-five

He's casten him in a dungeon deep
Where he cou'd neither hear nor see;
He's shut him up in a prison strong
An he's handl'd him right cruely.

—"Young Beicham"

Tamsin watched the fire blaze in the hearth and fumed to herself. She spun around as her father and Cuthbert came into the great hall, where she had insisted on waiting. Equally insistent, Rabbie had kept her from leaving the room by standing at the door, a truculent, grim guard. Now he moved aside as the two men entered. Archie crossed the room with a heavy stride, and Cuthbert walked more slowly.

"Da, how could you order William taken down and thrown in the dungeon?" Tamsin cried. "Uncle Cuthbert hit him so hard he went down in the courtyard! Dear God—"

"Eh, he's nae hurt. I just saw him," Archie said. "He's awake now, and there's nae harm done to his bonny face, if ye fret over that. He's shut in a dark cell, where he belongs."

"I thought you had high regard for the son of Allan Scott!"

"I did," Archie said. "But nae more." He sat heavily in a large chair that was angled toward the hearth. "Tamsin, are ye well? Are ye unharmed?"

"Fine," she snapped. "And you?"

"Well enough." He looked at her, and his gaze seemed to soften for a moment. "Yer hair looks bonny, all beaded and twisted-like."

"Th-thank you," she said, flustered. His regard for her, and the simple fact that she had missed her father and her home, confounded her for a moment, despite her anger.

"Is that the sort o' confinement Scott o' Rookhope offered ye? Maids to dress yer hair?"

" 'Twas . . . pleasant there," she said. "I came to care a good deal for his mother and sister, and his wee daughter."

"And him? Rookhope himself? I will hope ye dinna care for that scoundrel," he growled, looking away.

She stared at him, still astonished by his complete change of heart regarding William Scott. She had wanted to surprise him with the news of her marriage. But he was surly and angry, and she could not mention her situation until she saw William, and learned what had happened to alter Archie's opinion of him.

"Ye sent a paltry word to me through Sandie Scott, only that ye were at Rookhope, and thanking me for a bundle o' gear." Archie's tone was petulant and reproachful. " 'Tis all I knew of ye the full fortnight ye were gone."

"I would have sent a letter, but you dinna read. I didna hear from you either," she added.

"Busy," he said, "with that foul list. And with learning about Will Scott and Musgrave. Fiends all."

She fisted her hands on her hips. "I dinna understand this. Why do you say that? And why did you order Will Scott put in your prison? A fortnight ago, you thought rather differently about him!"

Archie glowered at her, but she saw a hint of sadness in his eyes too. "A fortnight ago, I thought he was like his father in more than his bonny face! I had him taken down because he's a scoundrel," he growled.

"No more than you! Less, in fact!"

"Hah! Ye were the one told me he was a ruffian, when I wouldna believe it. But ye've changed yer song, I think." He turned away to scowl into the fire. "And I want to know why," he muttered.

Tamsin rounded on Cuthbert. "How could you hit Will like that?" she demanded.

" 'Twas the best way to get the task done," Cuthbert said, seated in a chair near her father. His thin face and silver hair reflected the firelight as he turned to look at Archie.

"This is foolishness! I want him taken out of that dungeon!"

Tamsin said. Archie stared into the fire and ignored her. "Then I'll do it myself!" She stomped toward the door.

"Rabbie," Archie said.

Rabbie, waiting by the door, stepped forward and took her arm. He pulled her back toward the hearth, where he pushed her down on a bench by the table. She shrugged his hand away. Rabbie stood nearby, arms folded over his chest.

"Ye willna go to him," Archie said. "I suspect there's been enough o' that at Rookhope."

"What has happened, Da?" She felt confused and frightened. "Why did you hurt Will? And what have you done with Musgrave?"

"Jasper's in the dungeon too," Archie said. "English side. We put Rogue's Will on the Scots side, just to be safe. I want nae Border treason on my head when all is done."

"What do you mean to do?" she demanded.

Archie sighed. "Pour us some wine while ye sit there, lass," he said gruffly. He gestured toward a clay jug that sat on the table beside a stack of wooden cups. "And have some yerself. 'Tis watered. Ye have nae head for the stronger stuff, nor ever did."

Tamsin huffed a little in exasperation, but turned to pour the wine, handing a cup to her father. Rabbie and Cuthbert each took a cup too, but Tamsin did not fill one for herself.

"Now what of William?" she asked Archie impatiently.

Archie frowned, looking into the fire. "I was wrong to trust that lad," he said. "And I am rarely mistaken about a man's character. I liked him well and thought him the equal o' his father. But ye were right about him, lass." He took a sip, and paused to shake his head.

"I was right?" Tamsin asked, bewildered.

"He is a treacherous sort, as ye tried to tell me when first ye laid eyes upon him. I've proof o' that now. He and Jasper Musgrave are involved in a heinous scheme."

She gasped, and felt a sensation like falling, like losing strength suddenly. She had hardly thought about Musgrave's scheme, or William's role in it, for days. The newborn flare of her feelings for William, and her growing affection for his family, had taken all of her attention. She had relied on a blithe trust that William and Archie would work that matter out. How foolish of her, she thought now.

"Heinous?" she asked hesitantly.

"Wicked," Archie said. "But this night, I've seen to the matter myself. They're both in my dungeon, and there they will stay. It may be I'll hang them myself," he mused.

"Hang them!" Tamsin stood, knees trembling.

"Or it may be, I'll let the Privy Council do that. See ye," Archie added, "Jasper doesna know he's in my dungeon." He smiled slyly, glancing at Rabbie and Cuthbert, who grinned.

Cuthbert leaned toward Tamsin. "Musgrave thinks he's in the hands o' the Privy Council," he said. "We'll have a confession out o' him soon, that sneakbait! Yer da is a canny man!"

"I dinna understand," Tamsin said faintly, sitting again.

Archie rubbed his hand over his jaw. "We captured Musgrave when he was on his way here. Riding alone, the auld fool, because Arthur was too drunk to come wi' him."

"And that was yer da's doing, too," Cuthbert crowed.

"Tell me what happened!" Tamsin demanded.

"Arthur Musgrave told us his father's plan, and 'tis a naughty thing indeed," Archie said. "We had to stop Jasper from completing his scheme. So we ambushed him, bagged his head, and tied his hands. I didna speak, for he knows my voice. We rode him all over the territory, and then came here and went round the walls till we were nigh exhausted."

"Why would you ride around the tower?" she asked.

"To make him think he was on a long journey!" Cuthbert said.

"We went around Merton Rigg for hours," Archie went on. "Rabbie told Jasper that he was the regent himself, and that Jasper's wicked scheme had been discovered. Hah!" He sat back, grinning. Cuthbert hooted with laughter, and Archie and Rabbie joined him.

Tamsin gaped at them, then stared at her father. "You have Musgrave down in the dungeon, fooled into thinking he is somewhere else, under the custody of the regent?"

"Aye," Archie said, grinning. "He wouldna be so frightened if he knew he was at Half Merton! He pleaded for his head to stay on his neck, he did!"

"Begged mercy of the Scottish regent—me!" Rabbie said.

"Hoo! Hoo!" Cuthbert guffawed. Archie and Rabbie slapped knees and punched shoulders and laughed with him.

Tamsin folded her arms over her chest and glared at each one in turn. "Swine drunk," she said. "How else would you come up with such a prank? Jasper Musgrave has been a naughty scoundrel, aye, but this is a cruel trick indeed!"

"We're nae drunk," Cuthbert said, recovering. "Well, nae that drunk." Rabbie snickered, and Cuthbert grinned again, but quickly went serious under Tamsin's stare. "We had but some July ale at an inn in Kelso."

"And we paid good coin for it," Rabbie said. "Arthur Musgrave downed enough ale to make a dozen swine drunk."

Archie sat straight, his demeanor more serious. " 'Tis how we learned about Musgrave's scheme. We were out collecting the signatures for the list—"

"The list of Bordermen willing to help King Henry?" she asked.

"Aye," Archie said. "We saw Arthur Musgrave bemoaning himself, cupshot and alone. We sat down and ordered more ale and let him think we were his comrades. He's just lost his bride to Jock Scott o' Lincraig, who stole her away and married her himself. A neat trick, that. And a fine reiver, I've heard. I thought to approach Jock one day about taking ye to wife, lass. Too late."

"Aye, too late," Tamsin said decisively. "Go on."

"We bought ale for Arthur until he was as fou as any man I've ever seen. After a while we learned a good bit from him."

"And what does any of this have to do with William Scott?" Tamsin asked. "I want him brought out of that dungeon. If you dinna do it soon, I will do it myself, I warn you."

"Lass," Archie said, "listen." He looked at Cuthbert and Rabbie, who had grown as solemn as Archie. "Archie Musgrave said that his father and William Scott are part of a plan designed by King Henry himself, the greatest scoundrel in all England."

"What plan?" Tamsin nearly shouted out of frustration.

"Jasper and Will mean to snatch our wee queen out o' Scotland and give her over to King Henry's custody," Archie said.

Tamsin stared at him, stunned. "That isna true," she said after a moment. "That canna be so."

"Has Will Scott told you different?" Archie asked.

"He's told me naught. But he wouldna do such an awful thing." She folded her arms to show her conviction. But her gut spun uncomfortably inside. Why had she not pressed William for better answers to the puzzle of Musgrave and his scheme? Had she trusted him in that matter only because he drew her to him, like a lodestone luring a bit of iron?

"Arthur said Will Scott agreed to help Jasper, and accepted a price of three thousand crowns," Archie said.

"Surely Arthur was lying," Tamsin said.

"A man that drunk doesna lie easily," Cuthbert said.

"But Mary Stewart is but a bairn! William has a daughter just her age! I canna believe he would agree to abduct a child, and his own queen!"

"Believe it," Archie snapped. "She willna be harmed, Arthur swears it, just taken over the Border into English custody. Arthur thinks that I am art and part in this scheme, too, and Cuddy and Rabbie with me," Archie said. "He told us that Will Scott fell from good regard at court, but that he can still get close to Queen Mary, so he agreed to help the English—for coin."

"Nay," Tamsin said in quiet, desperate denial. "Nay. He wouldna do such a foul thing."

"Political dealings," Archie said. "Power. Many Scots want King Henry to take over the realm o' Scotland. This country is poor, and lacks a strong leader. Some Scots want to give us up to the English for the sake o' comfort, and hang Scottish freedom. Rookhope must be one o' those disloyal bastards."

"All those years at court," Cuthbert said. "I told ye years ago, Archie, 'twould ruin that lad."

"Aye." Archie nodded. "Tamsin, the English pay coin and land to Scots who help King Henry's cause in Scotland. Henry wants the wee queen raised at his court. He's pestered the Scots Privy Council, who agreed to betroth her to his son, but they willna allow her to go to England until she is at least ten years old. Henry wants her now."

"So he devised a scheme to take her," Tamsin said.

"Exactly. We couldna allow this to go forward, once we learned of it," Archie said. The other men nodded.

"We had to save our wee queen," Rabbie growled.

"So we took Musgrave, and we took Will Scott too," Cuthbert said. "We'll let the regent know we have 'em. 'Tis over, Musgrave's sorry scheme."

"What frets me is that Jasper said we were too late to save the queen," Rabbie said. "He said the attempt was already begun."

"Nae without the gypsies, or without my list," Archie said. "Jasper didna know he was talking to me, after all."

"William canna be art and part in this," Tamsin protested. "Arthur lied—he would do anything to ruin Will's good name."

"Good name!" Archie burst out. "He doesn't have that wi' me any longer!"

Tamsin stood. "I'm going down to ask Will about this."

"What makes ye think he'll tell ye the truth?" Archie asked.

"He will," Tamsin said. "I know him."

"Sit," Archie ordered. "Rabbie, go fetch the lad. I want to hear this too." Rabbie nodded and left the great hall, his booted feet echoing.

Tamsin sat and rubbed her fingers over her brow, curling her left hand into its customary fist. Waiting, tense with dread, she could not look at her father.

Archie went to the table to sit beside Tamsin. He took a pack of cards out of the leather purse strapped at his belt, and poured them from one hand to the other with a ruffling sound. Then he began laying them out in suits, a game with himself that he called "patience," which she knew he played when he was troubled about something.

The silence was broken only by the crackle of the fire and the flutter and snap of the cards. Tamsin leaned her head on her hand and watched Archie lay the cards in neat rows. Not so long ago, she had arranged the *tarocchi* for William. The cards had shown no dishonesty in him, she thought. Had the cards been correct—or wrong?

"There is one thing more that we learned about Will Scott," Arthur said after a while. "Did ye know that at court, they called him the 'bonny laird'?"

Tamsin shook her head as she rubbed her creased brow.

"Hey, Cuthbert," Archie said. "Sing for us."

"Sing?" Tamsin looked up, confused.

Cuthbert cleared his throat and began to sing in a voice that was true, but thready with age.

> The bonny laird went to his lady's door
> And he's twirled at the pin.
> "O sleep ye, wake ye, Jean my lass,
> Rise up and let me in."

Tamsin listened, watching Cuthbert. A shiver went through her. Jean, she remembered, had been the name of Katharine's mother. She turned to stare at her father.

"Ye'll want to hear the rest," he murmured, glancing at her.

Cuthbert continued the song. Tamsin frowned. The melody and the story were similar to other ballads that she had heard growing up. Her great-uncle was fond of singing them. He had collected a chestful of black-letter broadsheets of current and old songs.

Now she heard the tale of a handsome laird and a young lass, the daughter of the laird's enemy. The laird convinced the girl that he loved her, and then got her with child, all to gain revenge on her father, who had hanged his own father.

> "O Jeanie, what ails ye?" her father spoke.
> "Does a pain cut in your side?"
> "I have nae pain, but a lover's gift,
> And my laird must wed me betide."

Archie snapped down a few more cards while Cuthbert sang. "That wee bairnie that Rookhope fathered," Archie murmured. "He seduced the mother a-purpose. She was a Hamilton. 'Tis a muckle popular song now, going about in broadsheets, and they say 'tis true. Rookhope was sent from court in disgrace. Did ye know that?" he asked. "Did he tell ye?"

"Nay," Tamsin whispered. "He never told me any of this."

"Well," Archie said, " 'tis a good thing I got ye away from him. And to think that I wanted ye to wed that lad!

"Never," he continued, laying out cards with fierce precision while he spoke, "never would I let ye wed a man who would mistreat a lass so poorly. Thank God I got ye away from him before he worked his charms on ye."

Tamsin bowed her head while Cuthbert began another verse. When the door of the great hall creaked opened, she could not look up, even when she recognized the step of the man who approached the table. Cuthbert stopped singing.

"Sit, Will Scott," Archie said. "I'm sure you'll want to hear this song. Go on, Cuthbert."

"I've heard it before," William said calmly.

"Aye? And what would you tell us about it?" Archie said.

Tamsin looked up then. William sat on a stool a few feet from the table. His face was pale and drawn, his eyes shadowed, jaw tight. He wore shirt, breeches, and stocks, his boots and doublet cast off somewhere. His hands were joined in front of him by a ring of knotted rope.

"Sing, Cuddy," Archie growled.

> Fair Jean went to the wood one day,
> And took with her some silk
> She leaned her back against an oak
> And bathed her bairn in milk.

> "O daughter, my daughter, what do ye hold
> So close under yer cloak?"
> "I'm weak, so weak, and dyin'," she said,
> "For I leaned against the oak."

Tamsin thought of the young girl, betrayed by the man she loved in an intimate and cruel way. She did not want to believe that William had caused such a tragedy. Yet she could not stop imagining him with his arms around a shadow of a girl who carried his child in her womb.

Cuthbert went on with the song. The last verse rang out, thickening the tension in the hall.

> The bonny laird rode to his tower o' stone
> Wi' his bairn upon his knee.

"Ye'll never see your grandsire again
For he is mine enemy."

Tamsin caught back a sob. "Tell me," she said, looking at William. "Is it true?"

He looked at her steadily. "In part."

"Which part?" she asked.

"I want to know, Rookhope," Archie thundered, "how ye could do that to a lass! 'Tis said that this song is the truth, and that ye fell from royal favor on account o' what ye did to her, and she a lady-in-waiting to Mary o' Guise herself."

William said nothing. He stared at Archie, his face set. But Tamsin saw fury in his eyes, blue as the heart of a flame. She felt her own anger build in waves, until she wanted to stand and scream at all of them—her father, her kinsmen, and William. She felt as betrayed as Jeanie Hamilton, as devastated. Ripped apart in moments, while Jeanie had suffered far longer.

"And why," Archie went on, "did ye take English coin and agree to snatch our poor wee queen from her mother's arms?"

William blinked slowly. "I see," he said after a moment, "that you have divined all my secrets."

Tamsin stood. "Tell me this isna so!" Her heart slammed in the cage of her breast. "Tell me you didna ruin that lass out of hatred for her father!"

He watched her through long-lidded eyes. "I loved her," he said. "But I ruined her. And she died because of it." He looked away.

"Oh, God," Tamsin whispered. "Oh, God."

William stared at his hands. Though rage and pain twisted within her, Tamsin sensed the inner struggle he felt, and her sympathy stirred. No matter what he had done, she did not think she could stop loving him. But she did not know that love could hurt so much, like a stone at the fragile center of her heart.

Tears slid down her cheeks. She wanted him to tell her that it was all lies, all of it, that he had never done this to Jean, or been involved with Jasper Musgrave. But she saw the acknowledgment in his face.

"And Queen Mary?" Archie demanded.

William looked up at Archie. "I have given my word not to speak of that matter."

"But apparently ye know o' that matter!" Archie roared, slapping the table. The cards jumped.

"I do," William said.

"Damn yer soul!" Archie shouted. "I wanted to love ye like a son o' my own! I thought ye were the man yer father was, and he the finest o' rogues! Ah, God. Ye're low scum, indeed." He shoved heavy fingers through his hair.

Tamsin stepped away from the bench and went toward William, her knees trembling, tears wetting her cheeks. She saw him close his eyes briefly, as if in silent anguish.

"Why?" she asked. "Why?"

He looked at her, his gaze a penetrating blue, sharp enough to slice her heart. "Tamsin," he murmured, "trust me."

"I did trust you!" she said fiercely.

"What!" Archie said. "Rookhope, if ye laid a hand on my lass—" He pounded his fist on the table.

William closed his eyes again. The fold between his brows hinted at restraint, at regret. Then he looked at her. "Trust me," he repeated quietly, fervently. Tamsin could not shift her gaze from his power.

"Tamsin, get away from him," Archie snapped, rising to his feet. Cuthbert and Rabbie came forward to flank her father.

"Dinna trust him, lass," Cuthbert said.

"Oh God." She stared at William, clutched at her middle. "What should I do? My father tells me this foul news of you and Musgrave—and then I heard that ballad! You say the song is true. You know of the scheme. And now you want my *faith*?" Her voice rose to a shout. "How can I give that to you? Oh, God! And I want to give it to you—curse you!"

She spun away, saw the cards laid out neatly on the table. With an angry sob, she swept her hand through them. They scattered at her feet like bright leaves.

"What I want to know," Archie growled, "is what else ye've given this spoiler!"

"Naught!" she shouted at her father. "Naught!"

She saw the clay jug on the table, and something slammed

through her like lightning. She grabbed the jug, turned with it, lifted it high, and smashed it at William's feet.

The crash resounded through the hall. The pieces skittered in all directions, and wine sloshed over the floor and splashed William's legs. His gaze never wavered from her face.

"Mercy o' God," Archie said slowly. "I know what a broken jug means to a gypsy."

"Aye! So does Will Scott!" Tamsin spun on her heel and ran to the door, yanking it open.

"Tamsin!" she heard William call. Archie echoed him.

She slammed the door hard behind her, its force relieving only the smallest part of the grief and anger that churned in her.

Chapter Twenty-six

Westron wind, when wilt thou blow?
The small rain down can rain
Christ, if my love were in my arms
And I in my bed again!
                    —Anonymous, early sixteenth century

Clay shards lay scattered at his feet like the bits of his heart. William nudged at them with his toe and looked up. Archie and his kinsmen stared at him as if he had just committed a murder. In truth, he felt as if he had been slain himself. The dark wine at his feet spread out like lifeblood.

"She broke the jug between ye," Archie said. "I am nae fool. I know what it means. I had a Romany wife, and a Romany wedding. What else has happened between ye? Speak, man, or die sitting there." Rabbie, when Archie spoke, put a hand to the hilt of his sheathed dirk.

William took a breath and looked at the ropes wound around his wrists. The sight of rope had always twisted his gut, choked his heart. The knots, his isolated seat in the center of the room, the men staring at him, the hole blown through the center of his being, all seemed familiar.

He had sat like this in another chamber years ago, bound, questioned, shattered numb after the loss of someone he loved. But he had been a lad of thirteen, incapable of fully understanding what had happened to him.

Somehow the loss of Tamsin's trust and love had the same devastating impact as the death of his father, or the moment when he had been torn from his mother's arms and taken away. For a moment, he did not know how to proceed, how to endure. He only stared at the splinters of clay, the wine stains, at his feet. He breathed in and out, existence without thought or emotion, a little space of recovery.

He was not that wounded lad anymore. He had survived. He had grown, like a young oak with a slashed limb, past the damage. He was stronger despite it, and because of it. He would survive this too. Somehow.

When he had entered the hall, while the old man quavered the song, he had seen Tamsin first. She was beautiful, so necessary to him that he felt the ache of that need in his soul. He saw the hurt in her eyes, and felt her anger cut into him. The ropes, interrogation, roused old anguish. The song twisted him further, like another rope tugging him where he did not want to go.

But the most surprising blow he had taken—before Tamsin had finally shattered him—had been the hurt and the disappointment he had seen in Archie's eyes, beneath the man's understandable anger. He had not realized, until then, how much Armstrong's respect meant to him.

Archie was the last remaining link with the rogue that his father had been, the rogue he himself had dreamed of becoming. Armstrong seemed an embodiment of Allan Scott's respect, even his love. William wanted desperately to preserve that link to his father.

The questions, the accusations, the suspicions had made him retreat behind silence. Now he saw that he had been wrong to do that.

Pride and protection had their place, and were instinctive to him. But truth and openness were needed here, in good amounts, offered like a balm for the pain he caused, and felt himself.

He had to begin somewhere. The best place, he knew, was with the most essential truth of all.

He lifted his head. "Archie Armstrong," he said quietly. "I love your daughter."

Archie's face paled. "Well, I see she's divorced ye," he said calmly, though his hand clenched the hilt of his dirk.

"Aye," William murmured. "I thought to wed her proper, with a priest, but she doesna want that now. She's made that clear."

"Ye've been busy this past fortnight." Archie sent him a hard glance, green as glass.

"Somewhat," William said. "Not as busy as you might fear."

He waited for Archie to darken with rage, to shout or burst into violence. But he stood there, a gruff giant, shoving his fingers through unkempt, straw-colored hair, scratching at his whiskers, looking suddenly bewildered.

"Ye love her," Archie repeated. "Ye love her?"

"I do," William said. He sighed, reached up with his bound hands to rub at his brow. "God, I do. You dinna know how much." He lowered his hands, looked at Archie. "The lass torments me, and that is heaven's own truth. I swear it."

"Sweet Savior," Archie murmured, watching him. "By God. I believe you. On that matter, at least." He blew out a breath, raked his hair again. "But I had better hear the rest of it, man, and quick."

"I'll give you the truth on all of it," William said. He gazed evenly at him. "I trust you well, Archie. Otherwise I would tell you naught. But I'll tell you, and you alone."

Archie looked at his comrades. "Go see to our other prisoner. Bring him some ale and bread, for I stand by hospitality, even if he doesna know I'm his host."

"There is one thing you will want to know first, before you send men down to Musgrave again," William said.

Archie turned. "Aye? What?" he demanded.

"I spoke with Musgrave before your man came to fetch me here, across the gap between our cell doors," William said. "He was groggy and not so coherent as he might have been. I suppose you hit him hard, as you did me—"

"What did he tell ye?" Rabbie asked.

"He assumed, since I was in the dungeon too, that we have both been taken by the regent. I didna tell him different." He lifted a brow. "Now, why would he think that?"

"I might tell my sins to ye, when ye lay out yer sins to me," Archie growled. "Go on."

"He thinks we're both in the custody of the Scottish crown, and sure to be hanged on the morrow," William continued. "But he is down there cackling with joy that he's outwitted the regent and any who would stop his king's plan."

"And why warn us, man?" Archie asked. "Is it but another piece in Musgrave's game, that ye're art and part in?"

"That," William said, "I will explain later. For now, you had best be aware, before anyone else talks to Musgrave, that he claims to have already set his plan in motion. He told me that he tired of waiting upon a list of Borderers and gypsies that he might never see—I couldna answer him yea or nay on that matter. He says he's already gathered the help he needs." William gave Archie a hard stare. "He says he's paid coin to some gypsies and rascals who are on their way, even now, to do what they've been paid to do."

"And what," Archie said in an ominous tone, "is that?"

"We were all too late, Archie. The queen is in danger," William answered.

"Jesu!" Archie turned to Rabbie. "Go question him, Sir Regent, and find out what the de'il he's done."

Rabbie and Cuthbert both nodded and left the room quickly. Archie stepped toward William, crunching over broken shards of clay.

"Now, then, Rookhope," he said, folding his arms. "Speak."

William lifted his bound wrists. "No ropes while we talk."

Archie frowned. "Shall I trust ye enough to set ye free?" he asked. "I have been cursing myself for trusting ye wi' my daughter. But I'll give ye a chance to explain first. Only because o' yer father."

"We dinna have much time, Archie, if Musgrave told me the truth," William said. "You had best take the chance that what you heard of me is wrong. Take the risk that I am what you think I am."

"What are ye, then?" Archie narrowed his eyes skeptically.

William paused. "I am my father's son," he said.

Archie sighed, long and hard. He slid the narrow dirk from the sheath at his belt, and came toward him to slice through the ropes, casting them to the floor. "Speak, then."

William leaned forward and quietly began.

She sat on her bed in the dark, curled inward, knees up, head in the circle of her arms. No candle illuminated the room. The peat fire in the hearth gave off a musty odor, and provided only a reddish glow. A candle stood on a table near the bed, but Tamsin did not light its cold wick.

She had not opened the shutters of the window either. The moonlight had been replaced by rain and rumbling thunder. A downpour pattered against the shutters and the roof overhead, for her chamber was on the uppermost level of the tower.

Enveloped in darkness, she let her tears flow. Sobs gathered and rolled through her like the storm, dredging deep, bringing up old pain, and cleansing it with the new. Emotions thundered through her and diminished, leaving her empty and exhausted. She lifted her head and wiped her face on her sleeve, and sat quietly.

Her marriage to William was over, ended in anger and mistrust, a love found and let go too soon, scarcely begun. She felt as shattered and irreparable as the jug she had destroyed at his feet. Calmer now, she feared that nothing could restore the damage that both of them had done through secrets and temper.

William's secrets, had they been revealed to her earlier, might have changed her willingness, but not her feelings. She had no choice but to love him. He was a part of her now, part of her blood and her soul, inseparable and elemental as heat and light to flame. She could exist without him, she knew that. But she would cease to thrive.

She looked at her left hand in the shadows, opened the palm, saw the blush of the reddish light on the uniquely shaped wedge. William and his family had taught her that she could show her hand without shame. That one small liberty was a finer freedom than any other she had known.

William's complete acceptance of her, his delight in her, his quiet love for her, had given her the power to begin to see her loveliness, rather than her flaws. She was changed now, irrevocably. She could not return to her former self. But without him, she did not want to advance to the future.

Thunder sounded again, and lightning flashed. Though weariness pulled at her, she stood and went to window, opening the shutters to look out at the deluge that obscured the night. Mist wet her face, and the wind gusted through the opening.

What she had heard, had said, had done this night, tumbled through her mind. Desperate to hear William's explanation, she lacked the strength to confront him, for she was drained by anger and shock.

Seeing him would only bring more pain to both of them. She had not missed the anguish in his eyes. By now, William would be back in the dungeon. She would not try to see him until morning. By then, perhaps she could control her tears, and steel herself against the torrent of love that she still felt for him.

For now, she only wanted to crawl into bed and give in to the numbness of sleep. The rain drummed heavily as she turned and unfastened the hooks down the front of her leather doublet. When she had removed her boots, stocks, and breeches, she stood in her long linen shirt and fingered its torn hem. William had cut into the cloth to make a bandage for her father the night that they had been in Musgrave's dungeon.

She remembered how generous and gentle he had been then. His various kindnesses to her had taught her to be kinder to herself, his patience with her helped her to be more tolerant of herself. Compassion was part of his nature. She could not understand how, or why, he had hurt Jean Hamilton in order to revenge himself on the girl's father.

Trust me. His desperate words repeated in her mind. *Trust me.*

Oh, God, she thought, she wanted to believe in him. In giving him her faith and trust, she had found better faith in herself.

And in losing faith in him, she lost it in herself. The two threads of their existence were bound together, twirled around one another like strands of silk, each separate, yet forming together a stronger, more beautiful cord.

She wanted to believe William innocent of wrongdoing, but he had admitted to his involvements with Jean and with Musgrave. She should have stayed, she told herself, should have asked questions, and listened, and tried to understand. But she had let her temper undo her, and undo what existed between them.

Weary and worn by her thoughts, she lifted her hands and began to tug at the fine silken net and the pins that held her hair in place. She hardly knew where to start to take it down, once she freed the net and ivory pins. The braiding seemed like the last tie to the happiness she had known at Rookhope. But all of her hopes had collapsed. She would not cling to the reminder.

Her left hand was clumsy and slow. She tangled more than she unraveled, and soon muttered a few impatient curses.

The rain pelted the roof overhead. A loud rumble of thunder, followed by a crack of lightning, made her jump. Her fingers could not undo a stubborn knot of hair, and she pulled at it. Overcome by fatigue and frustration, she covered her face with her hand and sobbed.

"Hey, lass, come here," William murmured behind her, his voice blending with the thunder. Her heart surged. She whirled.

He gathered her into his arms even as she turned. She went, stunned and willing, her anger suddenly small beside the love that surged within her, melting her resistance. He tucked her to him while she cried her misery against his chest.

"Ah, God, Tamsin, I am sorry," he whispered into her hair. "Forgive me—" His lips soothed over her brow and eyelids, finding her cheek and the shell of her ear as she tilted her head.

She meant to pull away and ask him what, and how, but she turned her face to him, and was lost to the blessing of his mouth over hers. *Just for now,* she told herself, and let him erase her fears, her hesitancy, with his lips, his hands, the warmth of his arms. She succumbed to an onslaught of kisses, seeking and giving.

A thundercrack and a burst of rain startled her, jolting a path through the haze of passion. She gasped and pulled away, and a moment later shoved at him.

He stepped back, palms out for peace. His gaze was steady through the dimness. She stared at him, her breath heaving, as his did.

"How did you—what did you—how—"

"Sit down," he said firmly, taking her arm to guide her toward the bed. She went there, sitting, drawing the coverlet over her knees. She watched as he sat an arm's length away, the mattress sinking with his greater weight.

"How is it you are here, and not in the dungeon?" she asked, folding her arms over her chest, over her wildly beating heart.

"Archie suggested that I come to your chamber," he said. "We have been talking in the hall. I told him the truth."

"And what truth was that? About Jean Hamilton? About Musgrave, and the wee queen?"

"Aye, all that. More than that," he said, watching her.

"What more? He knew what the smashing of that clay jug meant," she said, frowning. "How did you explain it?"

"With a simple truth," he murmured. "I told him that I love his daughter."

She stared at him silently. The rain sheeted outside, and thunder rumbled, fainter now than the thud of her heart. She said nothing, nearly afraid to speak.

"I told him," William went on, "that I am tormented for love of his daughter, and that I am saved. That I am a stronger man now, for knowing her, than I was before." His gaze locked with hers, steady and bright, even in the shadows. "She is part of me, and I am part of her. She is the fire inside my soul, and I hope that I am the fire in hers. I know that I flare her temper, at least," he added in a dry tone.

"You told him all that?" she whispered.

"Not all," he murmured. "Some of that is only for you to hear."

Again that surge of the heart, as if her soul stretched out, yearning to touch him. She wanted to throw herself across the space between them and sink into his arms. But she only tilted her head and looked at him, cool and calm. "Do you mean this?"

"Tamsin," he said, and sighed, looking down, brushing a hand over the linen quilted coverlet. "You humble me. You push me. You fill me, and now you've shattered me with that cursed jug. I've lost your trust, and I dinna know how to gain it back."

"There is only one way," she said. "With truth."

"All that I have ever told you, or will ever tell you, is the truth. I have never lied to you. I never will."

"I knew naught of Jean, or Musgrave, or this awful plot—"

"You didna ask. I would have told you."

"And Musgrave, and the plot?"

He looked at her steadily. "I promised the queen dowager that I would do secret work for her, in the interest of Queen Mary. I wasna free to tell you, or your father, why I appeared to be Musgrave's comrade in his scheme. I knew what you thought, but I couldna correct it then. What Archie heard from Arthur Musgrave is exactly what the Musgraves believe of me. What I want them to believe."

"You have been acting as a spy for the court?" she asked.

"Madame the Queen Dowager wants to know what threat King Henry poses for her daughter. I hoped to thwart the English plan, once Musgrave revealed his next move."

"But my father has stopped Musgrave," she said.

He shook his head. "Musgrave has outwitted us. He has sent some others to do the task, while Archie was collecting his list, and while I kept you for a pledge and awaited a meeting. I was mistaken. I should have gone to him earlier. I should have—" He fisted a hand, thumped it on the bed in frustration. "There is little time, now, perhaps none at all. I must leave soon and try to discover this, try to stop it. But I couldna go," he said, and looked at her intently, "without telling you this. Without seeing you. That is a weakness of mine, I think. That I must have your trust. Your faith. Your love," he murmured.

She stared at him, her heart beating, her emotions racing. Her left hand rested on the quilt, and William reached out to curl his hand over hers, caressing her thumb with his, sending shivers through her. She wanted more, but stilled the wildness that urged her toward him. She had to be sure.

"Musgrave means to abduct the wee queen," she said calmly. "And you have never been part of that?"

"Do you truly think that I would do such a deed?"

"I . . . didna want to believe it. But the others said—"

"Believe anything you wish of me, but dinna think I would let harm come to a child. Or to my queen."

"Oh, Will," she whispered. "Pray pardon—" Her voice caught. "I was wrong to assume, just because others insisted. I panicked. I was torn between my father and kinsmen, and you. They confused me—told me things about you—"

"Just trust me," he said fiercely. His hand gripped hers hard. "I would never allow harm to come to Mary Stewart. And I didna seduce Jean," he said firmly.

She paused, knowing that her faith would only be full in him again when she knew the whole of that. "When I heard the ballad, I felt as if perhaps I didna know you, as I thought I did."

He sighed, let go of her hand. She sat back, watching him. "That song is no harbinger of truth," he said.

"The ballads can tell stories of what goes on at court, and in the Borders, and within clans," she said. "I have heard them all my life. I know they are often true."

"Some are quite true, aye," he said. "And some are naught but gossip. The one about Jean and myself is mostly rumor. Few know the truth of it."

"Tell me," she said quietly.

He drew a foot up to the mattress, rested his arm on his knee. "You know I was taken from my family, the day my father was hanged. Malise Hamilton took me away. For years, he and the earl of Angus watched over me like hawks, their prize prisoner, the pledge that bought obedience from some of the fiercest Bordermen, the riding name of Scott."

"Aye," she said. "I knew some of that."

"I hated Malise," he said bluntly. "I resented him as a lad. When I became a man, I ignored his power, and gained my own place in King James's court. And I didna shy from troubling him then. He had a daughter," he added. "I met her only a couple of years ago. She was . . . breathtaking. Beautiful, sure of herself, full of laughter. She became one of Madame's ladies. A court poet said Fair Jeanie Hamilton was a red rose among pale lilies."

Tamsin curled into herself, hearing that. "And so you fell in love with her," she said.

"I had loved other women, but I didna know then what love truly was," he said. "But Jeanie took my heart like a thief. And she made me laugh. Ironic, I think, that the daughter of my enemy showed me how to laugh again."

"She must have been lovely," Tamsin murmured. She felt very unlovely, herself, in that moment. "And she must have loved you very much—the bonny laird."

"She once said that she made it her cause to vanquish the bonny laird. And she did. I played the fool for a petty queen, and I didna see it. We trysted often. She craved jests and laughter, wine and merriment . . . and she craved bonny lairds, apparently."

Tamsin resisted a rush of jealousy. She lowered her head and sat in the dark, and thought of that beautiful young woman. She felt too aware, then, of her small, strange hand, her sagging braids, her ragged shirt.

A poor half gypsy could not compare to a fine lady, she thought, but that bedraggled gypsy loved the bonny laird more than anyone ever could. The thought gave her some courage. She raised her head and looked at him.

"I should have had more sense," he said. "I blame myself."

"She was part of it too," Tamsin said. "And she was beautiful, perfect. You loved her."

"I lusted for her," he said quietly. "I didna love her."

She tipped her head in wonder. "You didna love her?"

"I thought, at first, that I did. I even thought about wedding her, and risking her father for a good-father. But I soon saw that she lacked devotion and loyalty. She wanted laughter and dancing, gambling, heady sensations. She would never have been a faithful wife. She didna love me, but she desired me, as I did her. We were lovers, but I wasna her first. Nor was I her only lover, as I found out."

Tamsin stared, shocked. "Is Katharine . . . your daughter?"

"Jean said so. And when I look at the child . . . aye, she is mine. I know it."

"You didna marry her when you learned she was with child?"

"She never told me," he said. "I was away, on a mission to Flanders, gone for months. We had parted, for I had discovered that there had been others. When I returned to Scotland, she had left court in fear of disgrace. She went to her father's castle. By the time I learned of the child, 'twas too late."

"Too late?"

"Her father kept her confined, but she hadna been well, so she didna protest. When she told him who the father was and asked him to summon me, Malise grew furious. So she escaped in the black of night, near eight months gone with child, and rode to Rookhope with hopes of marriage."

" 'Twas a foolish thing to do," Tamsin murmured.

"She was a foolish lass, in some ways. By the time she came to our gate, she was already laboring. My mother and sister delivered Katharine, a hard birth." He shoved a hand through his hair. "I sent for a priest. But Jeanie died before he arrived. She lost her lifeblood," he added. "She didna deserve that."

Tamsin sighed, sat forward, reached across the gap between them. She touched his arm, rigid muscle beneath the linen of his shirt. "Dear God, Will."

" 'Tis why I have Katharine, and Malise doesna," he said. "She was born in my house, my own daughter. I allow him to visit her, though it bothers my mother to see him. I willna deprive him of Katharine, or her of a grandsire. He does love her, I think. But she will stay in my safekeeping," he added fiercely.

"And the ballad?" she asked. "How did it come about?"

He shrugged. "Who can say? Some clever poet—the court is full of them—who knew us, who heard the rumors that I used her to hurt her father, but who never heard the truth. People love that sort of tale."

"And you have lived with the rumors all this time?"

"I canna stop them. I wouldna try."

"Surely you want the rumors to end, so you can gain back your reputation."

"I would rather mine be ruined than Jean's," he said. "She was well loved at court. Let them think the bonny laird disgraced her. I willna spoil her memory with the truth."

"Ah, Will," she said. "I think you did love her."

"I am grateful to her." His voice thickened suddenly. "She gave me Katharine."

Tamsin felt her own throat tighten, felt tears prick her eyes. She nodded, unable to speak, filled with sympathy, with a love that was so strong, now, that she could neither suppress nor withhold it, and never would again. She uttered a small sob and held out her hands to him.

William reached out and pulled her into the circle of his arms, while the rain sheeted outside, and a roar of thunder rolled past the window. But in the midst of that torrent, Tamsin was where she wanted to be, needed most to be, at last.

Chapter Twenty-seven

O gin my love were yon red rose,
That grows upon the castle wa'
And I mysell a drap of dew
Down on that red rose, I would fa'.
    —"O Gin My Love Were Yon Red Rose"

She felt like paradise in his arms, sanction for his sins, a warm, graceful pledge of forgiveness. He had longed for this, for her, and thought he had lost it forever among the spilled wine and clay shards in the great hall. Gratitude, relief, and a flooding of love, pure and real, swept through him. He wrapped her in his arms, dipped his head, and sought her mouth, kissing her until they were both breathless with wanting. He drew back and framed her face in his hands, their breaths in tandem.

"Tamsin," he said, his voice husky. "I canna repair that broken jug. 'Tis beyond hope, that. But let me try to piece back together"—he lingered kisses over her brow, her eyelids, her mouth again—"your heart, and mine."

She sobbed in answer, and looped her arms around his neck, bringing his head down to hers. She melted into him, the curves of her body fitted to his where she draped over his lap, and leaned into his chest. He lost himself in the comfort of her kisses, while hands soothed and sought, and all he did, she did, stoked the fire that blazed sure and hot within him.

He wanted far more than comfort or benison now, the need so strong that his body ached and pulsed for her. He exhaled, and took her arms to put her away from him a little, both seated on the bed, heads leaned in together.

"Tamsin," he said. "I willna stop, given another moment of this with you."

"Dinna stop," she breathed out. "Please. Unless . . . you still want to beware lust?"

He sighed, caressed her back. "I wouldna beware anything with you . . . but the occasional jug." She huffed a laugh, and leaned against him.

"I need to leave soon for Linlithgow Palace," he said. "Musgrave sent his agents out after the queen, before Archie caught him. I dinna know who Jasper has sent or what he's done. Pray God I can find out from him and get there in time."

"Listen to the storm," she said. "There will be no one riding out tonight. Tomorrow will be soon enough."

"And what if tomorrow is too late?" he murmured.

"Ah, then, I willna interfere with what you must do." She sat up and put her hands on her tangle of braids, and the beads that sparkled in the low light. She tugged, wincing, a gesture of stubbornness with a hint of dismissal.

William sighed, watching her. He lifted his hands to her hair and silently took over the task from her. She bowed her head a little, dropping her hands into her lap as she sat cross-legged in front of him, the coverlet spilled across her legs.

"You dinna need to help me," she said. "I will manage."

"I know," he said. " 'Twillna take long, this."

"Go, if you must. 'Tis one lesson you have taught me, Will Scott," she said, her head bowed, the words hushed.

"And what," he asked, drawing a length of beads out of her hair, feeling another braid give way, slipping like heavy silk over his hand, "is that lesson?"

"Lust willna wait," she said. "But love is patient, and keeps its fire forever."

"Oh, God," he whispered, closing his eyes, bowing his head. His heart slammed within him, his soul felt as if it stirred, awoke. He drifted a rich kiss over her mouth, and went back to his task.

With calm hands, he unraveled another braid, spilled a handful of beads onto the quilt, clicking in the darkness. Tamsin sat serenely while he sifted his fingers through her hair, loosening it, freeing the curls, combing his fingers through the thick, glossy, silken masses as they escaped their confines.

He did not know how he kept at the task, when his body surged and his heart pounded. But somehow what he did was a prelude of what he wanted with her, for her. With patience and caring, he knew he could set her free along with the braids. He wanted her loose from the limits she had placed on herself, so long ago, with her conviction that she was undesirable, less than perfect. When she came into his arms, he wanted her to feel beautiful and cherished.

He left a slow trail of kisses at the side of her neck. Then he unwound a long strand of shimmering beads, coiled around a thick skein of hair. "Females are far better architects than anyone credits them," he remarked. He threaded out some single beads and loosened a coronet of braids.

She laughed, a sultry sound that shivered through him.

"You, my lass," he said, as he pulled out the last few ivory pins and tossed them away, so that the whole of her hair spilled down in a dark, thick curtain, "are beautiful."

"Oh, aye, a half gypsy who canna even do her hair or dress proper," she said. But her voice was light, and without the accusation and bitterness he had heard there at other times. She closed her eyes and moaned low in her throat as he winnowed his fingers through her hair. His body pulsed. He made himself wait. He would wait forever for this woman, he thought.

"You dinna need to wrap yourself in damask and beads, or busks and hoops. Not for me. Though you look bonny in such gear," he murmured, and rubbed her temples until she shivered, moaned again.

He took a handful of loosened tresses, fragrant with roses and rain and woman, and wound his fingers in it. He tugged until her head tilted back. Her eyes were closed. He set his lips to the soft creases that ringed her long, arched throat.

"Mmm," she breathed. "But I want to wear such gear. I like it. For myself, see you."

"Ah, then do so," he said, laying her back gently on the bed. His body throbbed with need. "But that gear will come off when we are in our chamber, my love," he whispered, his hands slipping over her shirt, grazing the firm swell of her breasts, the flat plane of her abdomen, the long, lean curve of her thigh. "I know how to undo whatever you've done."

She smiled and lifted her arms and pulled him down for a slow kiss, opening to him as he licked the contour of her lips and delved inside. Passion washed through him like new wine, raising his heartbeat to match the drum of the downpour outside. He pulled her closer, rolling with her, sinking down into the feather-bed and the pillows.

She worked her fingers at the ties that closed his shirt at the neck. "I am not so skilled at that as you," she said, tugged, and drew the shirt off of him. He tossed it away and took her into his arms, warm against his bare skin. Her fingers fell to his waist, pulled the drawstring there. "But I know how to free you when I want too."

Her hand slipped over serge, taking him by surprise, cupping the rigid part of him so that he filled and swelled under her brief touch. He groaned, took her wrists in his hands to pin her gently, resting on one knee to gaze at her through the shadows.

"Bold lass," he said, kissing her ear. She writhed a little, and he thought he would burst, having hardly begun to love her. He kissed her mouth, drawing away so that she arched toward him, eyes closed, waiting. He slid her shirt away, revealing the supple length of her body, gleaming and splendid.

Too late, he thought, to respect chastity until they were wed properly. Far too late, for he was lost, burning now to meld his body to hers. He sank down to kiss her lips, trailing his mouth over her throat, down over her breasts, perfectly globed, peaked and waiting. He tasted her there, savored her, and she moaned softly.

She swept her left hand over his hair, along the curve of his jaw, let it roam the planes of his shoulders and chest. Her touch was warm, gentle, timid. He knew, from her earlier boldness, that her shyness was due to the hand itself, and not due to how she felt toward him.

Reaching out, he captured her left hand in his and laid his lips to her palm. She seemed to go still in his arms. He kissed her hand again, and put it to his cheek, and looked at her through the shadows. The ruby light showed the glint of a tear slipping down her cheek. He kissed it away and smoothed back her hair.

"You are perfect," he whispered. "Dinna ever think otherwise. I see no flaws in you, only what is fine about you."

She gasped and pulled him to her, wrapping her leg over his, gliding her torso along his until he thought he might go mad with wanting her. "No flaws?" she asked, leaving kisses along his jaw, finding his mouth while she spoke.

"Only a temper," he breathed out, skimming his hand down her body. He found the soft place between her legs, dipped inside, where her inner folds were slick, heated, waiting. She sucked in breath and moaned. He touched her hard, touched her soft, until she arched and whimpered and pulled him to her. He felt her climb to her release and let go, and she grasped at him again, at the drawstring of his breeches, shoving at his confining clothes.

He helped her to free him, then slid his leg over her, laid his lips over hers, pausing, though it cost him will and strength to do so. "We are not wed," he murmured. "You know that."

"We were, once," she said against his mouth, her breath ragged. "I am sorry that I undid that. We'll wed again."

He groaned, low. "How?" he breathed. "When?"

"Now," she whispered. "Here."

And she pulled him closer, spread and opened and surged upward as he glided toward her. A pause only, while his heart thudded. But he knew, utterly, that what existed between them was unlike anything he had known before. Faith and love were strong and pure, here and now. The walls that he had constructed around himself vanished in that instant.

She made an impatient sound, drew on him. Gentle and slow, she took him into her, catching her breath as she surged past the brink. He slid into the lush welcome she offered. Something unexpectedly poignant, something whole and complete, seemed to surround him. He closed his eyes, sank into her.

She made an exquisite sound of surrender, of triumph. He echoed, raw and ecstatic, savored, thrusted, and felt her tremble around him. The lightning took him over, and he knew it flashed through her. He knew then, somehow had always known, that she was the bright, elusive mirror of his soul, rediscovered.

He sighed, and heard the rain again, heard the thunder. He felt her shift beneath him, separate. He kissed her, made a vow to himself that this would never be undone between them.

A little rest, he thought, just for a bit, would help them both. He nestled with her, pulled the coverlet over them, and felt sleep overtake him. It lured her too, for she went still and peaceful in his arms with scarcely a word.

"Oh, God," he said, a little while later. Dim light, cool, moist air, the trill of a lark, poured through the small window. The light streamed silvery over Tamsin's sleeping face. "Oh, God. How long have I been here?" He sat up, shoved back his hair, yanked on his shirt, his breeches, his stocks.

"Will?" Tamsin sat up. He glanced at her sleepy eyes, tousled hair, naked body, sheened and lovely. He leaned over and kissed her, tender and quick, and she reached for him.

"I must go," he murmured. "Where are my boots—ah, still in the dungeon." He shoved his hair back, which fell insistently over his eyes. "I meant to talk to Musgrave and ride out. Damn," he swore, and stood to tighten his waist string, tuck in his shirt. "I need to hurry. God," he said, "dinna do that. You'll stop my heart."

She stood, slim and perfect, and let her shirt fall over her like a cloud, silhouetted by the window. "I'm coming too," she said. "Wait until I dress."

"Stand there like that, and we'll go nowhere but back to the bed," he growled, his voice hoarse with sleep. She smiled and came forward into his arms. "You'll stay away while I talk to Musgrave," he said firmly. "Come down and say farewell to me shortly. And if Archie has food about, can you find me some? My thanks. Sweet heaven, you are a bonny creature." He kissed her mouth, kissed her hand, gave her a little shove toward the bed. Ignoring the protest she began, he pulled the door open.

He ran down the turnpike steps in stockinged feet, while the castle slept around him. He passed the great hall, empty but for a gray, tranquil light, and headed down another set of stairs into the bowels of the tower, where the dungeon lay like a dark, sprawling beast.

*   *   *

"Wake up," he said, prodding Musgrave with his booted foot. William stood back, watched Musgrave rouse, grunt, shift on the straw floor of the small, dark cell. "Wake up!" He fisted his hands at his waist, legs widespread. Booted and in his leather doublet, wearing his sword and dagger, he was prepared to ride out as soon as he found out whatever he could. Just outside the open door, Rabbie Armstrong stood, bleary with a few hours of sleep, holding a torch and William's steel helmet.

Musgrave sat and leaned against the wall, his belly huge, his shoulders bowed, framing the width of his chins. The chain linking his manacled wrists clanked as he wiped the back of his hand over his eyes and looked up.

"Eh," he said. "Did they let you go, then? What are you doing here, dressed to ride out?"

"I'm free," William said. "Tell me what the hell you've done, Jasper. I need to know."

"Confessed, did you? Damned Scots," he grumbled. "And if I confess, think you the regent will let me go? I misdoubt it. Oh, but they let their own damned Scotsman go."

"Confess," William said. "Admit what you've done, and tell the details. They'll let you go back to England. I'll put my word on it."

Musgrave slid him a piggish, disbelieving look. "Did you tell them you're a loyal Scotsman, after all? Typical rogue, turning tail for the other side when it's convenient."

"Who did you bribe, and where have they gone?" William demanded. He stood firm, laid a hand on the hilt of his dagger.

Musgrave stared up at him, and something dawned in his eyes. "Damn you," he said. He heaved himself to his feet with a long grunt, wavered there. "You've sided with the regent! King Henry will be furious to learn of this disloyalty after your promise to me! What did they pay you? We'll double it! We need a man inside the court! Name your price, and ride to England to claim the coin for the deeds we want done!"

William strode forward and grabbed Musgrave's wrists, shoving them upward, causing the chain to choke him, pin his bulk against the wall. "I side with no one," William said, "but the little queen of Scotland."

"Fool! Back a warrior, not a nursling!" Musgrave rasped. "Join those who have already ridden to claim the little prize for Henry. If I were you," he said, "I'd turn in Archie Armstrong and his damned gypsy chit. I told their names to the regent myself last night. Do the same. They'll be taken down, soon, for their disloyalty. If I have to die, Archie will go down too."

"If you tell me what I want to know, and tell me quick," William growled, "you willna die. You'll be taken back to England."

"On whose authority do you say that?" Musgrave asked.

"My own," William said through his teeth. He shoved again, holding Musgrave's hands apart, so the chain was taut. Musgrave sputtered, colored, flexed his heavy hands. "You once stood by and let a rope be put around a woman's neck. Feel that hell for yourself, now," William said, and held the chain tight.

Musgrave gasped, writhed, flailed with clumsy feet. William avoided him without even looking down. "You think naught of taking a bairn from her mother's arms," he said, glaring at Musgrave, rage boiling. "My queen is but a helpless nursling, aye. And my sword arm is hers. Do you hear me?"

Musgrave nodded, rolling his eyes. "You betrayed me," he rasped. "You're naught but a spy!"

"Tell me," William rumbled, and held fast. "Tell me who you sent, and when, and what they mean to do! Or I swear to you, this chain will free you from this life."

"Arthur found them!" Musgrave gasped out. "Arthur found them, gypsies who read his fortune and were traveling north. Lolly Fall, he said the name was. A tawny and his brood. I sent my own men, paid well. They've gone to Linlithgow."

"Why? To what purpose?" William said, teeth clenched.

"The—the tawnies will dance and juggle, and my men will snatch the babe. 'Twill be blamed on the gypsies when 'tis done. No one will notice my men—dressed in gypsy garb—and the clamor will be to hang the wandering vagabonds when 'tis discovered."

"And the wee queen will be away to England," William said.

"Aye. Safe, she'll be. Not harmed." Musgrave stared at William, face purpling, hands clenching at air.

"Why did you want gypsies and Borderers from Archie Armstrong?"

"King Henry wants a list of anyone willing to take coin for loyalty," Musgrave said. "He needs men to support his army when he invades Scotland. Soon."

"I thought as much. And gypsies?"

"My own plan, that," Musgrave said. "Gypsies, to steal the little queen. And if they will not do it, fine. Gypsies to take the blame. Paid cheap, and hanged. No loss."

"Bastard," William bit out, leaning into the chain.

"Let me go," he begged. "God, let me go. I am a loyal man. I act for my king—you act for your queen. We are alike, you and I. Loyal to our own. Gave my oath to Henry—let me go—"

"I should let you choke on your own sins," William growled. He let go of the man's wrists, stepping back so quickly that Musgrave lost the precarious balance of a great body on small feet, and fell, heavily, to his knees.

"You said they'd let me go," Musgrave gasped. "Tell the Regent. You have sway with him—"

"You'll be taken back to England. You have my word on it." William turned and strode to the door, fury fueling his breath.

"One thing, Scott. You are too late," Musgrave said. "Too late to stop them! Henry will have what he most wants—the reins of Scotland in his hands!"

William said nothing. He yanked the door wide, stepped through. Rabbie glanced at him with wary eyes, locked the door, and followed William up the turning steps into the gray light of dawn.

William strode up the stairs with rage and purpose in every slam of his foot, jaw set, lips tight. At the top of the steps, on the wide landing outside the great hall, he saw Tamsin and Archie waiting. She was dressed in a simple brown kirtle and low boots, her face somber, hair loose and wild and dark. Her eyes, like green glass, were windows to her fright as she turned to him.

"William . . ." she said. He glanced at her, silent and grim, and turned to Archie. Rabbie went past them, muttering that he would ready William's horse, and left through the outer door.

"He's sent his own men, and hired gypsies, to go to Linlithgow to steal the queen," William said. "I must go."

"Gypsies!" Tamsin stepped forward. "What gypsies?"

"Lolly Fall," William said, and shrugged.

"Faw? I have an aunt, Nona Faw—" She frowned.

"I dinna know who 'tis. But they've gone already, he says." He pulled leather gauntlets out of his belt, yanked them onto his hands, and lifted his helmet to settle it on his head. "I can stop them, if I can get to the palace before they do."

"Through the hills there is a quick way north. Ride like the very de'il," Archie said. "I'll explain the way. I'll stay here and guard my prisoner. Take Rabbie and some o' the rest, stout Armstrongs at yer back."

"No time to summon anyone," William said. "And you need Rabbie, your regent, here, to talk to Musgrave. I gave him my word he'd be taken back to England."

Archie lifted a brow. "Did ye, now?" He shrugged. "But ye didna say when, nor where, hey?"

"Nay," William said. "But soon, I'd think. I'll tell the regent— the real one. Musgrave will be seen to, at the gates of his own castle. Better than on your own soil."

"Hey, laddie," Archie said, smiling slowly. "Ye forget ye're in Half Merton Tower. I can move Musgrave to Scotland or to England just by shifting him right or left in that dungeon doon there." His smile spread to a grin.

William laughed reluctantly. "You auld scoundrel."

"If you tell Jasper, he'll know he's at Merton," Tamsin said. She handed William a hunk of bread and cheese wrapped in cloth, and he took it from her with a nod. "You dinna want him to know that."

"Oh, I'll let him go, when I please," Archie said. "Wi' my list clutched in his hand."

"The list of Bordermen?" William headed toward the outer door, where stairs led down to the courtyard. Tamsin and Archie went with him.

"Aye, a list o' Bordermen who have sworn to me they'll never support King Henry," Archie said. " 'Twas the only list I could gather. Think Musgrave will pay for that, hey?"

"He just might have to," William replied. The courtyard was rain-washed and cool in the soft light, and he strode fast toward the stable, where Rabbie was saddling the bay.

"Will, I'll come too," Tamsin said. "Wait for me." She stepped toward the stable.

He grabbed her arm. "Nay. Stay here." She shook her head, tried to pull away. He was loath to let her go, and circled his gloved hand around her arm, gazing down at her. "Farewell," he said. "I'll be back in a day or so. I promise."

"I'll go with you. You need me."

"Aye, I need you. I'll admit that to all and sundry," he said in a wry tone. "But I want you to stay here."

"I willna stay here, and do stitchery for you, and mend your stocks," she said. "And I canna cook, nor do my hair up!"

"I would never ask any of that from you," he murmured. "Just stay here for the nonce, and out of trouble."

"But I can speak Romany, and reason with gypsies, and I can ride as quick as you can."

"Aye, she can do that," Archie said, nodding.

William shot him a glance. "She's your daughter, man. Keep her here and out of danger, for love of God."

Archie watched them, arms crossed, a little smile on his face. "I canna tell her what to do," he said. "I did hope ye might try to tame her, though. Ye're just the bonny rogue I've been searching after. Ye do mean to wed her proper, hey!"

"Aye, I'll wed her proper, any way she likes," William said, giving her a steady gaze. "But I willna cross her. Unless there's danger involved. As now," he added through his teeth. Tamsin scowled up at him. "She has a good arm for a jug. I'll keep out the way."

"Aye, that's the thing to do," Archie said, smile in place. "Her mother had a good arm for a jug too. Threw a few at me, over the little time we were wed." He scratched his head. "Ye learn to catch—or to duck," he mused. "And I didna mind wedding her again, each time." He grinned at William.

Tamsin jerked her arm free and glared up at them. "This is not a jest, either of you! I can help you, Will. I can turn the Romany away from this scheme faster than you can. And I can find them, if you canna. Let me try. Please. Or I'll follow you," she added, folding her arms.

"She'll do that," Archie said.

"Lolly Fall," she said simply. " 'Tis Lallo and Faw. If my grandfather is involved, he's got a scheme. I must go."

William finally nodded. "Aye, then, you must. But hurry. We dinna have much time for you to ready yourself—"

"Done." Rabbie stepped forward with the bay and Tamsin's dappled gray, both saddled. "I knew our lass wouldna stay here while her laddie went off to the gypsies. Tamsin, there's packed food and a plaid for ye, do ye need it."

Tamsin smiled at Rabbie, gave her father a quick embrace, and ran to the gray. She stepped her booted foot into the stirrup and vaulted up, settling her skirts around her legs.

William nodded to Archie, and mounted the bay beside her.

Archie stepped between their horses, spreading his arms to grab both bridles, looking from his daughter to William. "Through the hills, northeast. Tamsin knows the way. Will Scott," he said. "Keep my lass safe."

"I'll do that, Archie," he said, gathering the reins.

"Aye, I knew that ye would. I knew it, years back, when ye were but a bit lad, and she a bairn in her granddame's arms."

William stopped, looked down. "Years back?"

"After Tamsin was born, and ye but barely out o' yer skirts, I first thought to match ye," he said. "I had a bonny daughter, yer father had a braw lad. Allan liked the plan. When Tamsin was six, we decided to fix the agreement to wed ye when ye were grown. We meant to put it down in ink. But . . . Allan died soon after. The day I fetched Tamsin from her gypsy kin was the day they took him down, and took ye away from Rookhope."

William felt chills along his spine. He glanced at Tamsin, whose eyes were wide, filled with her own wonder. He could see that she had not known it either.

"That day, Archie . . ." he said quietly. "That day, I saw you and Tamsin, sitting on a hill. You waved at me, both of you. I never forgot. Ever." He fought the constriction in his throat. "I always felt that I . . . that I owed you for that good farewell."

"You owe us naught for that," Archie said. " 'Twas all we could do then, watch ye go. I would have snatched ye back from them, if I could have. We lost ye too, that day."

William nodded, swallowed, touched deep in his heart by Archie's love and respect for him.

Archie beamed, looking from one to the other. "Now I see ye together, as I always knew ye should be. Like a twinned pair, ye seemed when ye were wee, alike in looks, in temper, in yer way o' seeing the world. Fate took ye away from us, lad, and the loss o' yer father saddened me greatly. Still does. But fate was kind to us, see, and brought back the bonny rogue meant for my lass. Tamsin, I told ye this was my dream, to see ye wi' him."

She smiled. "Then fate has finished its task for us."

"Nae till that bonny wee queen is made safe," Archie said. He stepped back, letting the bridles go. "I'll wager only you two can see that task done. Fate knows that, see. Perhaps 'tis why ye've been brought together, to save that wee bit lassie that our country needs and loves, hey. But you, Will Scott . . ." He looked at William, frowning. "See you keep my lass from harm."

"I will see to it. Come ahead," William told Tamsin. He gathered his reins and turned his horse, and heard her close behind him as they thundered through the gate.

Chapter Twenty-eight

On we lap and awa we rade
Till we cam to yon bonny ha'
Where the roof was o' the beaten gould
And the floor was o' the cristal a'.

—"The Wee Wee Man"

They rode fast and hard, with short breaks to breathe the horses and to make quick meals from the food Rabbie had included. The morning mists faded, and the sky shifted from cloudy to blue and back again throughout the day. The hills were thick with heather and green, the lochs and rivers were bright, and Tamsin longed to slow down and admire the beauty of the views. But she and William swiftly passed through, turning what should have been a leisurely two-day journey into one long, demanding day.

She saw no hint of Romany presence, no distant camps on the hillsides or in woodland groves, no *patrin* signs scratched in the roads as they galloped past. She wondered if they were indeed too late. The Romany hired by Arthur Musgrave might have arrived at Linlithgow already.

The little queen might be endangered even now, she thought, or stolen outright. She understood fully William's need to press on, and did not complain.

By sunset, they arrived in the small town below the palace of Linlithgow. On a wide green hill above, the stone walls of the palace gleamed rosy and smooth. William dismounted at the base of a cobblestone hill, and Tamsin did the same. Glad for the chance to stretch her stiffening muscles, she walked her horse slowly upward to the gates beside William.

"Oh! 'Tis lovely!" she said. The south gate was flanked by

round towers and decorated with carved and painted armorials. To the left, she saw a wide, calm loch extending behind the palace, surrounded by meadows and low hills.

"Aye, 'tis a beautiful place," William said quietly. She remembered that he had spent much time at Linlithgow. Here too he had first loved Jean Hamilton. At that thought, she sighed. Then she remembered the manner of their loving the night before, and an echo of that joy rushed through her. She glanced at him shyly. He sent her one of the low, gentle smiles she loved.

A guard came forward. "Rookhope, sir!" he said. "Welcome! Ye're just in time to see the merriment."

William frowned. "Merriment?"

"Some Egyptians have come to court, to offer singing and dancing, and the telling o' fortunes. A long while has passed since this palace has seen such gaiety. Some o' them are just inside the courtyard, sir, and the rest are in the great hall, I do think. Ye'll hear the music when ye go inside." He waved them through the gate. They walked the horses through the gatehouse tunnel toward the open inner court.

Tamsin gasped. Pink evening light poured into a courtyard that was open to the sky and faced on four sides by high, windowed walls. An ornate stone fountain dominated the center of the court, its basins and spouts dry.

Around the courtyard, she saw Romany—nearly three or four score, she realized as she glanced around. Some talked and lounged, while others danced, performed tricks, or played music. Still others had set up makeshift market stalls, using small carts or blankets thrown on the ground. They offered an array of baskets, cloths, cakes, rope, horse trappings, and metal goods. A few of the men repaired kitchen ware and horse gear brought to them by palace servants. In a far corner, some Romany men showed horses for sale, discussing them with palace noblemen.

Elegantly dressed men and women walked among the Romany as if at a market fair, observing, bargaining, murmuring. At each corner, royal guards stood in red and yellow livery, their halberds relaxed in hand while they watched the activities with interest.

On the circle of grass around the fountain, a Romany man juggled leather balls in the air, while two young girls performed acrobatic dancing, leaping over one another. In a corner, a woman in a head scarf and a shawl bent over the offered hands of two noblewomen. Three men played a viol, a cithera, and a drum, while a young woman sang in the Romany language. Beyond them, a man performed feats of sleight-of-hand while a few courtiers watched in amazement.

Tamsin and William stood beneath the south arch and stared. The walls seemed to echo with music and chatter, and more music emanated from open windows on the eastern side of the palace.

A page ran forward and took their horses, leading the animals toward the stable to the right of the entrance. Tamsin stood gazing at the scene. She recognized many of the Romany in the courtyard. When William glanced at her, she nodded.

"This is my grandfather's band, and many others, perhaps Lallo's people too," she said. "Why would Grandfather take a bribe from Arthur Musgrave? I warned him, and he promised that he and the band would wander far out of the Borders until danger of that had passed."

"This *is* far out of the Borders, my lass," William murmured.

She bit her lower lip and nodded. "I dinna see him here."

"The guard said that some of the gypsies are entertaining in the great hall—up there, in the eastern wing. John and Nona might be there."

"Perhaps," she said. She clung to the shadows beneath the entrance arch, hesitating. Two facets of her existence, old and new, met here: the Romany world in which she had been born, and the realm of the nobility of which William was so much a part. Her father's world, of reiving and small lairdship, lay somewhere in between. She had hoped to be able to enter William's world to please him.

But when she looked at the Romany, so familiar to her, and then looked at the refined noblewomen who strolled among them, she was unsure of herself once again. Standing here in a plain gown, with undressed hair, she was more a Romany lass than a noblewoman, after all. She glanced at William, and saw him look anxiously toward the windows that faced the palace walls.

"You go ahead," she said. "I know you want to go inside. I will stay here and find my grandfather."

William frowned. "If you find your grandparents and discover the truth of Musgrave's plot, I want to know. I will come to look for you. But if we havena found each other by darkness, then meet me in the northwest block, there." He pointed toward an inner corner. "Take the stair to the first level. You'll find a corridor with a tall window overlooking the loch. Wait there for me."

She nodded. He leaned down in the shadow of the vaulting and kissed her, swift and hard, with an underlying tenderness that made her sigh. Then he strode across the courtyard at a half run, cutting through the crowd. He spoke to a guard and entered the east wing, vanishing inside an archway.

Tamsin stepped into the courtyard, nodding to those she knew from her grandparents' band. Some greeted her, others ignored her. In the far corner, she saw Baptiste Lallo near the Romany horses, talking with some gentlemen. She deliberately wandered that way.

Lallo stopped talking to stare at her. A young Romany woman initiating speech with a young man would be immodest, but she slowed near him and caught his gaze. She paused as if lost.

He came toward her. *"Romanichi,"* he said. "Romany girl. What are you doing here? Your grandfather said you married a rich *gadjo.* Is he one of the *rya* in this place?"

She looked at him, his face dark and gaunt, but pleasant, his eyes large and black above an inky mustache. He smiled, showing pale, well-formed teeth.

"Oh, that *rya* is not with me," she replied in a half-truth. "I am here to find my grandparents. Have you seen them?"

He frowned at her. "Did you leave the man?"

"I broke the jug between us," she said.

"Ah," he said, nodding. His eyes gleamed.

"Where is my grandfather?" She looked around the courtyard.

"He has gone with some of the others into the palace. I will take you to him. Follow me." She did. He strutted with animal grace, swaying his shoulders from side to side, swinging his arms. She saw some Romany women look at him with interest.

Baptiste spoke with a guard, explaining that they were with the players who had already gone to the great hall. The guard stepped aside to admit them to the stairs that led upward.

"Baptiste Lallo," she said, as they climbed. He turned. "What is going on here? I have only just arrived."

"We were invited to this place," he said. "I myself was given the invitation by a *rya* who paid me in advance for our services. The queen of this land wants singing and dancing and entertainment. And we, of course, are the best," he boasted.

"The queen of this land is an infant," she said.

He shrugged. "Then her mother must have requested our presence. We have been juggling and dancing and playing music since this afternoon. We will soon be packing up to leave the palace, for the guards have told us we cannot stay here past dark. I know your grandmother has made some good silver telling fortunes today. I myself earned good coin by selling two of my horses. My horse are the finest."

"I am certain of it. Have you seen the baby queen?"

"I saw her," he said. "She is not pretty, for she is pale as milk, and thin, with hair the color of copper." He paused on a small, circular landing to wait for her. "My own children are plump, nut-brown, and smart. You will like them, Tchalai. You must come to my wagon to meet them. My mother cares for them now, but she is old and irritable." He smiled as she stood beside him. "Now that you have left that *gadjo,* you will be eager to wed a Romany man, a real man. Myself."

She looked away to discourage him, for he looked at her as if he already owned her. "Which way is the hall?" she asked. She heard music, buffered by stone, and was uncertain of the direction.

Baptiste stepped closer, and she nearly jumped when he took her upper arm. "I will forgive you for wedding that man, since you have divorced him," he said. "I told John Faw that I would take you, even though you were born with a curse, for I think you are a fine woman. And I keep my word." He nodded. "Your grandfather will be glad to see you have found some sense and left that man, and come home to your Romany family."

She shook off his hand, her heart beating hard, but somehow he did not frighten her. She nearly left him there, but realized that she might be able to learn of the plot from him. He took her arm again. This time, she let him.

"I have missed the Romany, that is true," she said. "Tell me, who invited you to this palace, and paid you to bring the entertainment? Is he here to greet the Romany? I would like to meet such a generous man."

He laughed and leaned close. He smelled of horses, and his hand on her arm was firm. "You have told this man's fortune," he said. "He was in the camp the night of the wedding, when you were there. I chanced to meet him later that night, out on the moor. He and his friend offered me coin and told me to have the Romany here on this day. A gift for the Scottish queen from the English king, they said." He shrugged. "What do I care the reason? Silver is silver."

"Ah," she said. "Is he here?"

"No," he said. "Friends of his are here. They bought garments from me and my mother earlier today, headcloths and cloaks and jewelry. The people of the court like Romany dress, they said. We wear more comfortable clothing than they do, that is true! My mother showed them how to wrap their heads, because they insisted on wearing headcloths and cloaks. They looked foolish when they were done, like old Romany women!" He laughed. "But they seemed pleased with themselves."

Tamsin stared at him, her mind rushing over what he told her, and beyond. Baptiste was either truly unaware of a plot to steal the queen or else he pretended stupidity. "Can you show these men to me?" she asked.

"*Avali*, yes," he said. "We can laugh at them. You and I will laugh much together, Romany girl. I like your smile." He leaned forward and kissed her, his mustache prickly, but his lips surprisingly gentle. She shoved at him.

"Modest?" he asked in surprise. "You have been a married woman. And I will make you happy, I, a good Romany man. Ah, come here!" She ducked into the corridor, and he launched after her. At the end of the corridor, a guard stood before wide doors. She hurried toward him, Baptiste following.

"We are Romany, come to perform," she told the guard in a breathless voice. He nodded, his gaze traveling up and down her body. He said nothing, but opened the door to admit her, then Baptiste, who pounded up behind her.

She entered the room and stopped to gaze at its grandeur. The enormous chamber seemed full of light and color, crowded with people and music and laughter. Well over a hundred feet long and a quarter of that wide, the hall had a soaring, elaborate timberwork ceiling, painted and tapestried walls, huge arched windows, and a tripartite fireplace dominating one wall. The three glowing fires that burned between its carved pilasters were mere sparks in the overall brilliance.

"Beautiful," she breathed to herself, looking around.

Baptiste, behind her, grunted. "Wasting good gold on houses, when they could spend it on horses—and give some riches to the Romany, eh? Look, John Faw is there."

She glanced where he pointed. Across what seemed like a sea of people, her grandparents mingled among a group of Romany in the center of the room. Three girls danced in a cleared space as a crowd of people, both courtiers and Romany, watched.

The girls swirled and undulated in bare feet, with delicate bells ringing on wrists and ankles, and filmy silk scarves floating around them. Men played drums and viols to accompany them, with insistent, driving rhythms that thrummed in the air.

Tamsin looked past the dancers and past her grandparents, who had not yet seen her, to scan the crowd. But she did not see the one face she sought, that of a dark-haired man with sky-blue eyes. She twisted, looking, but he was nowhere in sight.

She turned back to Baptiste. "Show me these men who wear headdresses like Romany women," she said.

He nodded and took her arm, and she allowed him to guide her as they edged their way between people. "There," he said. "Just there, see! Ah, now they disappear again. They were near the little queen and her mother, who are watching the dancers."

"What?" Tamsin raised up on her toes to peer through the throng. A dais was set up along one long wall, with a brightly embroidered canopy draped behind it. Seated on a huge carved throne chair in the center of the platform, a woman in a black gown held a child in her lap. The cleared space for the dancers and musicians extended to the dais itself.

Tamsin shouldered her way to the edge of the crowd. Baptiste followed, his fingers still wrapped around her elbow in a possessive way. She edged nearer the dais, stopping to peer between two women, elegantly gowned and perfumed, who glanced at her and immediately turned their backs to ignore her. In her simple brown kirtle over a chemise, and with her hair loose and wild, she knew they took her for one of the gypsies.

She drew herself tall, standing between them. Their haughty glances made her want to insist to them that she was, indeed, one of the gypsies.

She leaned forward to look toward the dais. The queen dowager, Marie of Guise, must be the woman holding the child, she thought. The woman was tall and slender, splendidly gowned and coifed in black silk and black velvet trimmed in silver and pearls. She smiled and tapped a foot to the music.

The little queen stood on her lap, a lively, pink-cheeked infant in a long, voluminous gown of creamy damask, with a little lace cap over her reddish gold hair. The child was so excited by the music and the crowds that she squealed, waved her arms, and bounced, standing, on her mother's knee while the queen dowager circled her small torso with long, tapered fingers.

Tamsin smiled, watching Queen Mary Stewart, and seeing Marie of Guise's warm pride as she kissed the child's cheek. She thought of Katharine, who often refused to sit, preferring to bounce on straight, stubborn legs in just that way while someone held her. Suddenly she felt an overwhelming urge to find William, to be with him and to help him protect this royal child, just as she wanted to help him keep his own daughter safe.

She glanced past the dais, still searching the crowds for William, but she could not find him in the vast room. The men Baptiste had described did not seem to be about either. Nudging Baptiste's arm, she pulled him with her.

"I must speak with my grandfather," she said over the blare and beat of the music. "And you must show me these foolish men!"

He nodded and craned his head to look over the people; he was not a tall man, but taller than she. "Come," he said, and put his arms around her shoulders, leading her beside him and shoving through the crowd in a confident manner. They wended through the assembly until they approached John and Nona Faw. Baptiste tapped John Faw on the shoulder, who turned.

"She has come back to be with us," Baptiste said. "To be with me! I knew she could not stay away." He sounded proud.

"Tchalai!" Her grandfather took her into his arms, jostling Nona, who turned and uttered a glad cry. Tamsin went into her embrace next, and then stood back. Smiling, she held her right palm up to delay their rapid questions about how, and why, she came to be at the royal palace.

"I will explain," she said in Romany. "But first there is a much more important matter to tell you about. We must find some men who are disguised as Romany." She turned to Baptiste. "They are bad *gadjo,* you know," she said, taking a chance.

He frowned, mustache twitching. "They are stupid to pay silver to wear women's garments. But bad? I am not aware of this. If they are bad *gadjo,* we must keep away from them."

"No, we must find them. Listen,"she said. Baptiste and her grandparents leaned toward her, and she explained, in rapid Romany and simple terms, what she knew. "They are men from England, come here to steal the baby queen," she said. "They disguise themselves as gypsies. I think they will try to sneak the royal child out with the Romany when our people leave here. They mean to blame the crime on the Romany."

Nona gasped, and John Faw scowled at Baptiste. "Did you know any of this?" he asked.

"No, no," Baptiste said. "I would not allow them to harm a child! We must find them. I will kill them with my bare hands!"

"That is not needed," Tamsin said. "We must keep them away from the queen and urge the royal guards to capture them. Come. Show these men to us, Baptiste Lallo."

"I will," he said firmly. She heard his anger, and felt the sincerity of his hand at her elbow. Suddenly she liked Baptiste very much, for his simple pride in himself and his people. Her grandfather, she realized, would never have asked her to marry a man she could not like.

She looked back, and saw that her grandfather followed them, while Nona stayed with the Romany. Baptiste guided them closer to the dais, where Marie of Guise stood, now, to hand the infant queen to another woman, who Tamsin assumed was the child's nurse. Mary Stewart seemed temperamental, fussing a little, cramming a fist in her mouth as her nurse murmured to her.

The women glided off the dais in the company of a man in a green velvet coat and brocaded doublet. The crowd parted, and the royal party disappeared through an arched doorway.

Although the music had stopped for their departure, the Romany performers began again, this time with young male acrobats and jugglers, and the music resumed for the crowd that remained. Tamsin looked at Baptiste, who still searched the throng.

"Ah," he said. "There they are! This way!" He pulled on Tamsin's right hand and half dragged her toward the exit that the queen and her party had taken.

Four men, in bright head wrappings and striped cloaks, shouldered toward that doorway as well. The men murmured to the guard at the door and were allowed to leave. Tamsin and the others approached the guard.

"All 'Gyptians must go down to the courtyard," he told them. "No roaming about the palace." He held the door open. "And we want ye out o' here by dark, ye know that."

Tamsin stopped. "Do you know William Scott, the laird of Rookhope? Has he come by here?"

The guard looked surprised. "Aye," he said. "He came into the hall earlier with Madame the Queen Dowager and Her Grace, but left with Sir Perris Maxwell. Why would ye be looking for Sir William?" He grinned and leaned forward. "A wee tryst, hey? Well, he has that repute. If I see him, shall I say that a bonny gypsy is seeking him?"

"Tell him," she said, "that his bonny wife is seeking him." She flashed the guard a brilliant smile, and saw astonishment flicker in his face. She shook her hair back over her shoulders and glided past him like a queen, head high.

Tamsin, Baptiste, and John Faw hurried along a narrow gallery, its windows open to the music and laughter in the courtyard. The sun had set long since, and the shadows had grown deep. Baptiste took her arm again.

"Wife?" he asked. "Wife to this William Scott? The *rya*?"

"Yes," she said in Romany. "He is here in the palace. I must find him and tell him about these disguised men."

"But you said you broke the jug with him!"

"I did. He did not like that much. Nor did I," she added. "We have decided to stay wed." ·

Baptiste stopped. "But I thought you came back to wed me." The keen disappointment in his voice caused Tamsin to stop too. John, who walked more slowly, caught up to them.

"I am sorry, Baptiste," she said. "If I were free, I might be happy to wed you." Her grandfather gaped at her.

"I truly wanted to be your husband," Baptiste said.

"Be my friend," she said earnestly. "I would like that."

He sighed. "A beautiful woman is like a beautiful horse. Many men are eager to own her, but only one can."

"No one owns me, Baptiste," she said. "This marriage is my wish."

"Beautiful, and strong-willed too." He sighed again. "I suppose I must be your friend." He looked long-suffering.

She smiled, pleased by his support, and pleased too that he considered her beautiful. That feeling, first sparked in her by William, was still new and wonderful.

"Where are we going?" John Faw asked, glancing around.

"William asked me to meet him in that tower over there." She pointed through the window. "We must cross the courtyard."

"This way," Baptiste said. "There are halls that connect. I was up here earlier, walking with a pretty *gadjo* lady."

"Baptiste!" Tamsin said, half laughing.

He grinned. "Did I say I would be a faithful husband? I am far too pleasing to the ladies."

"Then you will have no trouble replacing me," she said.

"True," he said simply, and took her arm to tug her along.

They passed through another wing of the palace, hastening down an open gallery and around a stair into the north wing, running through large, deserted, connected chambers. Each room was decorated with painted ceilings, floor tiles, tapestries, and fine furniture. Their rapid footsteps echoed, and Tamsin glanced around in awe.

"Fine things they have. We should not be here," John muttered. "They will accuse us of being light-fingered."

"All will be well," Tamsin assured him. "But where have those men gone? We did not see the direction they took!"

"If they want to steal the little one, they will go this way," Baptiste said. "The royal chambers are at the end here. My lady friend told me that," he said.

They entered a large, empty chamber, its two tall windows spilling evening light. Torches glowed in sconces, revealing sumptuous decor, and a dais and throne. At the other end, a small alcove housed a locked door. Around a corner were stairs, and a narrow corridor ending in a niche, with a tall window and a cushioned seat in its recess.

"This is where I am to meet William!" Tamsin said. John and Baptiste went down the stairs to look, and Baptiste came back a few moments later.

"We just saw the disguised men through a window in the stair," he said. "They are out in the courtyard, where our people are gathering up their goods to leave this place. Stay here and wait for your man, and tell him the danger." He paused. "Tchalai—he is a lucky man, your *rya.*" He grinned, then turned and ran down the turning stairs after her grandfather.

Tamsin smiled, thankful to have found an unexpected friend in a man she had misjudged. She went into the window recess and sat on one of the cushioned seats to wait for William.

The tall window was cut so high that she could not see over its sill, but beside her seat was a tiny window. She peered out over the peaceful loch behind the palace, watching as swans glided over the water, and birds skimmed overhead, and the last of the light faded from the sky.

Chapter Twenty-nine

"Above all, we must have a care of the little lass your Queen."
—Giovanni Ferrerio, about Mary, Queen of Scots, 1548

"There you are," William said, a little while later. Tamsin turned with a sense of relief at his voice. He came down the corridor, and she moved toward him.

He reached out to take her hand, and then handed her a little cake and a small silver cup with cool wine. "I am glad you found this place," he said while she ate. "I didna see you earlier, and I began to worry. I have been in the queen dowager's apartments. She tells me that she is glad for the entertainment, but didna invite the gypsies herself. One of the guards said the wanderers claim to have been invited and paid."

"Arthur Musgrave paid coin to Baptiste Lallo to bring the gypsies here. But we can trust Baptiste," she added. "I was wrong about him—he is a good man. I am sure he can be trusted."

"Ah," he said. "That makes sense. Your grandfather would surely try to choose a husband whom you could love."

"I couldna love any man as I love you," she murmured, tipping her face up. He leaned down and gave her a tender kiss. "Though I like him. He thinks I am beautiful." She gave him a teasing smile. "William, he knows the men who want to steal the little queen," she said urgently.

"Tell me," he murmured, and drew her toward a corner of the little hall. He leaned a shoulder against the wall beside her, while she explained in a half whisper what she knew about the men Baptiste had seen.

"My grandfather and Baptiste have gone off to find them," she finished. "The men should be easy to recognize in the crowds. They are wearing headcloths and cloaks, like women, though they think themselves very fine."

He smiled. "Excellent," he murmured. "I have just been in the queen dowager's apartments. She will want to know this, but I canna go back to tell her now. These men must be found and stopped."

"We'll go to the courtyard. We can summon the guards to search the palace." She stepped forward.

"Not we," he murmured, putting out an arm, hand flat against stone, to block her passage. He looked down at her. "I want you safely out of this."

"Dinna think to leave me here to wait alone while you run after those men." She tilted her chin stubbornly. "I'll come with you."

"Nay. I have another mission for you," he said. "The queen dowager thought to summon one of the gypsy women to read her palm." He lowered his face toward hers as he spoke, and her resistance began to melt. She tipped her head upward. "I told her I knew the best one for the task. I told her," he said, "about you."

She blinked at him in surprise. "You did?"

"Aye." He trailed his mouth over her cheek, and his voice thrummed deep through her. "She has been concerned that I find a wife. I explained how I came to fall in love with you. She is delighted, and eager to meet you. I promised that I would bring you in to her soon."

"Take me there, then," she said breathlessly.

"My love," he whispered, "there are many places I would like to take you." Her heart pounded at his sensuous hint, but he drew back. "But that will have to wait. I'm going down to the courtyard to find John Faw and Lallo. Go ahead to Madame's bedchamber yourself. 'Tis just down the hall. She is expecting you. The nursemaid and the queen are with her."

"Go to the queen myself?" she asked in surprise.

"Aye." He kissed her then, rich but all too brief. " 'Twill be fine. Look at her palm. And wait for me there, if you will."

"Trysting with gypsy lasses, now, Scott?" a man said.

Tamsin gasped, heart leaping. William turned, standing back, his hand going to the dirk at his belt.

Two men stood at the end of the corridor, both elegantly dressed in velvets and brocades, one younger, with a neat dark red beard and short hair, the other an older, silver-haired man. The older man, who had spoken, frowned as he waited for an answer. Tamsin slid away, but William caught at her left hand.

"What is it, Malise?" William snapped. Tamsin, hearing the name, knew they faced Malise Hamilton.

"I was on my way to speak with Madame," the older man said. "And I saw you with the gypsy lass. Still intent on ruining women? Not that I much care if you disgrace a tawny wench." He looked disdainfully at Tamsin.

"Malise Hamilton," William said. "And Perris Maxwell. This is Tamsin Armstrong, the daughter of the laird of Merton Rigg. You will want to congratulate us. She is my wife." He emphasized the last word.

Perris looked surprised and pleased, but Malise went pale, eyes narrowing. "A gypsy?" Malise asked. "You've given Katharine a gypsy for a mother?"

"Half Romany," William said. "Tamsin's father is a Border laird, and was my father's closest friend. And her great-uncle was Johnnie Armstrong of Gilnockie, the notorious Border reiver."

"Quite a lineage," Perris said, and grinned, bowing to Tamsin. She smiled hesitantly, grateful for his genial response.

"Thieves and tawnies!" Hamilton burst out. "How can you think to provide my granddaughter with such a stepmother!" He fisted his hands in outrage. Tamsin drew back, but William held her left hand fast in his.

"Enough, Malise. You and William have just settled your differences in the courts," Perris reminded his companion.

"We will never settle our differences," William said.

"This is a further insult that I will not forget!" Malise said. He turned and stalked away.

Perris sent William a long look. "Ill-timed," he said.

"Anything with him is ill-timed," William answered wearily.

"He will come to accept this later. He is concerned, just now, because Madame is upset about the matter we were discussing earlier." He glanced at Tamsin.

"She knows," William said. "We can speak freely. And she's just told me that there are some counterfeit gypsies about the palace who we want to find, I think."

"Counterfeit gypsies!" Perris frowned. " 'Tis a crime in Scotland, just that alone, guising as Egyptians."

"I'm sure they've committed more than that offense," William said. He glanced at Tamsin. "Go on, lass. The queen's chamber is around the corner, and down the hall." He lifted her hand, kissed it, let it go. "Tell her who you are. And tell her that I will send a guard to her as soon as I can. The one who was there earlier went off to hear the gypsies and never sent his replacement. This place has been thrown into chaos with so much entertainment. Just what Musgrave wanted, I suspect," he muttered.

She nodded, and watched him stride away with Perris, heard the echo of their footsteps in the turnpike stair. Sighing, she walked slowly along the stone corridor, lagging her steps. When she found the arched oak door that would lead to the queen dowager's chambers, she hesitated nervously.

"Hey, gypsy girl," a man said. She jumped at the unfamiliar voice and turned. Two men, wearing headcloths and striped cloaks, walked toward her. She stared at them in alarm, suddenly frozen by fear.

"Hey, tawny girl," one of the men said. "What is your business in that chamber?"

She watched them warily. "I—I have been summoned by the queen dowager herself," she said, hoping to frighten them away. "She wants a fortune- telling."

"Good," he said, grinning at his companion. "We want a favor of you. There is some gold in it for you." He flashed a bright coin. She stepped back instinctively, and they followed her deeper into the hall, cornering her.

She opened her mouth to scream for William, but the larger of the two men leaped forward and pinned a hand over her mouth, pulling her against him. "When you are admitted to that chamber," he growled into her ear, "we will go in with you. Tell those inside that we are your gypsy kinsmen."

"Nay," she mumbled against his hand, struggling.

He held her tight. "I mean you no harm, and no harm to anyone else. And I am willing to pay you a gold coin to get us into that chamber with you." His breath was hot and fetid.

"Nay!" she shrieked, the cry muffled. She twisted.

"Refuse me," he said, "and I will kill you now. Obey me, and all will be well for you and your gypsy band." He held her so tightly that her breathing constricted and her heart pounded.

The second man pulled a dagger and laid its tip between the laces of her bodice. She felt cold steel prick her through the cloth. Though she tried desperately to think, panic hazed her mind. All she knew was fear, for herself, and on a larger scope for the little queen and her mother.

With cold certainty, she knew her refusal would only bring her death. They would spill her blood and her life out on the stone, here and now, and force their way into the royal chamber. If she agreed and went into the bedchamber with them, she might be able to stop them from harming the little queen.

She nodded. "Let me go."

The man loosened his hand and allowed her to step away. The other man grabbed her upper arm and pressed the point of the dagger into the middle of her back. "Through the heart, girl, if you try to give us away," he hissed in her ear.

She drew a breath and held out her palm. "Give me the coin," she said, hand trembling. She wanted them to think she cared only for that and for herself, and for no one else.

The larger man chuckled low and handed her the gold.

She tucked it into her bodice and went to the door. The men pinned her close, the dagger pricking her back like a bee sting. She raised her hand, fist shaking, and rapped on the wood.

They waited. Tamsin drew a breath, squeezed her eyes shut, and thought of William. Her love for him warmed her, strengthened her. Then she thought of his devotion to the baby queen. A shiver ran through her, bringing with it a surprising infusion of courage, and a touch of indignant fury.

She looked back at the men. "Did you know," she drawled, "that you are disguised as gypsy women?"

They gaped at her, and at each other. She looked away, smug

and satisfied, knowing that remark would have made her father proud.

At that moment, the door opened, and she blinked at the unexpected face that appeared in the gap. Malise Hamilton saw her and glared. "What do you want?" he asked.

The steel point pricked her again. "Madame—Madame wanted someone to tell her fortune," she stammered. "My—my husband told her that I would do that for her."

"Who are these men?" he asked.

"Gypsy kinsmen," she said. She wondered if he heard the brittle, frantic note in her voice.

"You bring your own guard?" he asked sarcastically. "Or do you hope for a handout of silver? You will not get it here."

Beyond his shoulder, she glimpsed a woman holding a golden-haired infant swathed in creamy silks. Tamsin prayed that Hamilton would refuse them entry and bar the door, even if it meant that she would die in that moment. She felt, suddenly, as if the courage that enabled her to knock on that door also gave her the strength to face death if she must. She only knew that she had to save the royal child.

"We are . . . er, gypsy men, come here to delight the wee queen with feats of juggling," one of the men said.

A woman's calm voice murmured something, and Malise nodded and opened the door. Tamsin entered, and the men sidled in with her. One of them gave her a surreptitious shove, and she took another step forward.

"Stay by the door until Madame decides if you can entertain her child," Hamilton told the men. "Madame, the gypsy fortune-teller is here," he said in a sneering tone.

"Ah! William's bride!" Marie of Guise turned near the wide hearth and came forward, moving with a gentle susurration of silks over the floor. She extended a hand.

Tamsin had never thought to meet a queen, or to knowingly bring harm to anyone. She hesitated, frightened. In an awful twist of fate, she had brought danger into this peaceful royal chamber herself. But when she gazed into the queen dowager's calm and intelligent eyes, she felt assured. Her courage and resolve returned.

She bowed her head, made an awkward curtsy. "Madame," she said softly. "I am honored."

"Vraiment, vous êtes belle," Marie of Guise said, smiling. She tilted her head. "You are bonny," she said, with a heavy accent. "Sir William is very happy. I saw it in his eyes when he told me about your marriage."

"Merci, madame," Tamsin said, nodding. The queen dowager looked surprised. "I speak your tongue," Tamsin said in French.

"Très bien," the dowager queen said. "I prefer to use my own language. Come tell my fortune, then. William said that you have a talent for that."

Tamsin glanced about the room, past the huge bed swathed in violet fabric. The nurse sat on the bed with the infant queen in her lap. The child stared around at all of them, sucking her fingers. Tamsin glanced past her, and saw a window with a cushioned seat, and a table with three fat, burning candles.

"Can we sit there, madame?" she asked in French.

The queen dowager nodded, and led Tamsin to the little niche, seating herself in a rustle of silks. Tamsin drew the candlestick closer and bent forward, standing in the niche while the dowager sat and extended her right hand, palm up. Then she took the woman's hand, balancing it on her left.

"How interesting," Marie of Guise noted, still using French. "Did you know that one of King Henry's wives had six fingers on each hand? Queen Anne Boleyn, the mother of his daughter Elizabeth. She was very beautiful, I hear, though she came to a tragic end."

Tamsin paused, startled. "I did not know about the English queen's hands, Madame," she said. "I am grateful to hear it." She traced the lines in the woman's palm with a gentle fingertip and frowned.

"Madame, I see intelligence, a sharp mind, and much graciousness. You are well loved by your people. You love gambling, taking chances, Madame," she said with a smile. "Ah, so much tragedy," she murmured, frowning over the bars that marred the path of the woman's heart, marking pain and loss. "But that is, we hope, behind you." There would be more grief, she saw, but she chose not to speak of it. "A long life, Madame, and good health."

She went on, answering the dowager queen's keen, perceptive questions.

"Madame," she whispered then. "I must warn you of danger."

"Do you see that in my hand?" Marie whispered.

"Non, madame," she said in rapid, quiet French. "Here in this room. Those two men forced me to come here. They are not gypsies. They want to steal your daughter."

"Dear God," the dowager queen whispered. Her hand flinched in Tamsin's gentle grip, but she made no other sign of fear.

"You must move her to safety. Is there another exit?"

"There is," she murmured calmly, as they bent over her hand.

"Take the child out that way," Tamsin murmured. "I will delay them somehow."

Marie of Guise nodded and stood. "What an interesting fortune," she said, her face pale. "I am very grateful to you."

The queen dowager went toward the bed, and the young nurse stood. Marie of Guise took her infant into her arms, kissing the child's flushed cheek. "Malise," she said quietly.

Hamilton came toward her. "Madame," he said. "The gypsies have offered to entertain the child."

"She is tired," Marie of Guise answered in Scots, smiling at the men. "Take my daughter away from here, quickly," she said in French, and handed Malise the infant. He lifted her and turned in one smooth motion, heading for a door in the shadows beyond the fireplace. Marie of Guise took the nurse's arm and they rushed after him, slipping through the doorway.

Tamsin whirled to see the two men start after them, daggers drawn. She ran toward them, and reached up to yank on the bed-curtains with all of her strength. With a heavy rip, some of the curtains collapsed, and she flung a swath of violet across the men's path, entangling their feet.

She spun again, and pushed over a tall, heavy carved chair positioned by the fireplace. As she backed toward the shadowed door, she skittered another chair, and then a stool, over the floor. The men stumbled, hollering and swearing, over the curtains and the furniture, coming nearer. She reached the door and yanked on its iron latch, slipping through and slamming it.

The door led out to a windowed alcove, beyond which was a corridor and turnpike stairs. Neither the dowager nor Malise Hamilton were in sight, but she had no time to wonder where they had gone, or to look for them. She heard the two men thunder out into the hallway in pursuit.

She pounded down the turning stairs, hand sliding along the curved wall, feet nimble on the wedged steps. Breath heaving, she ran through the doorway on the ground level, out into the courtyard, and straight into chaos.

Throughout the court, the Romany were collecting their belongings and moving toward the south gate. Men, women, children, horses, and carts surged toward the arch. The noise, echoing against the surrounding stone walls, was deafening.

Guards seemed to be everywhere, on horseback and on foot, some shepherding the Romany toward the gate, others arguing with them. A group of men, mounted and armed, rode through the court from the stables.

Tamsin fled into the midst of the commotion, turning, searching for William, her grandparents, or Baptiste. She saw her grandmother with Romany kin and ran toward her.

"Where is my husband?" she called out to her grandmother in Romany. "Have you seen him?"

Nona shook her head. "They are rushing us out of here," she said. "They are impatient and rude, for we only brought them pleasure for the day!" She scowled, and then turned to help a woman who was clumsily loading cloth sacks onto a cart bed.

Tamsin spun again, scanning the crowd quickly. She saw Baptiste hurrying through the middle of the court and ran after him.

"Where is William?" she called. "Have you seen him?"

"That way!" he said, pointing. "We found two of the men, but they rode out of the gate. We are going after them. Your *rya* has gone to get his horse, and I will get mine!"

"Wait!" she called, as he sped away from her. "Wait!"

She turned again, and saw her grandfather rushing toward Nona. He explained something to her, pointing toward the gate, then ran toward the Romany men who were handling horses in a corner of the wide court. Baptiste ran there too, and Tamsin went after them, skirts flying high.

She whirled as she ran, still looking for William. Finally she saw him, mounted on a large black horse she did not recognize, riding beside Perris Maxwell on a gray horse. William set his helmet on his head and steered his mount through the crowd, moving toward the gate. She pounded toward him, calling over the din. He turned.

"Tamsin! Stay here! I'll be back for you!"

"Will!" she called, running. "Stop!"

He circled the huge, restive horse and loped toward her. "Go back inside," he said, bending down. "The men we were looking for have left the palace."

"Two of them were in the queen's chamber," she said urgently. "They tried to take the queen. Malise Hamilton and the dowager queen took her safely away, but the men are still here somewhere." She looked around the courtyard frantically, and then saw the two men in headdresses. They merged with the crowd on foot as some of the Romany eased into the arched gate tunnel. "There!" She pointed. "See those two men, in headgear!"

He lifted the reins. "Go inside," he ordered. "I will be back." He turned the horse and galloped toward the gate, catching up with Perris. The men in the head wrappings and bright cloaks had already disappeared.

Tamsin turned and saw Baptiste mounted on a white horse, a spirited stallion wearing only a blanket and bridle. Behind him, John Faw rode another white stallion, a matched, beautiful pair of animals. They guided their mounts toward the gate.

Tamsin stood by the fountain and watched them. After they had gone, weaving their way through the throng, she turned and noticed the mounted guardsmen in helmets and steel chest armor, whom she had seen earlier.

Now Malise Hamilton was mounted on a black horse in their midst. Tamsin wondered if he too rode out after the disguised men. He carried a bundle in one arm, and rode steadily toward the arch. His guardsmen called out to the gypsies to move aside.

Something made her glance upward, then, to the western wing of the palace. There, framed in a pedimented window, Marie of Guise looked down over the courtyard. She opened the lower shutter and leaned outward, waving her hands in a way that struck Tamsin as odd, even alarming. The dowager withdrew from sight.

A moment later, Tamsin saw her framed in another window, and another, as if she ran, stopping to look out.

Puzzled, Tamsin glanced around the courtyard, and saw several guards running from one of the tower entrances, calling for their horses. Then she looked toward the gate, expecting the guardsmen with Malise Hamilton to stop. Instead, they spurred their horses and ordered the Romany out of the way.

Just as Malise passed under the shadow of the arch, carrying his bundle, Tamsin glimpsed a bit of golden hair and lace, and heard the drift of a tiny, angry cry, despite the noise and commotion. She ran forward, craning to see.

Malise carried the infant queen wrapped in a blanket. As Tamsin cried out, running closer, he tucked the blanket over the child's head, completely hiding her, and then disappeared into the mass of horses and people moving through the tunnel.

Tamsin whirled toward the far corner, where some of the Romany horses remained. Their owners quieted the agitated horses. She ran up to one of the men, a distant cousin of hers, and snatched the reins of a glossy black horse from his hand. As her cousin gaped at her, she clambered onto the horse's blanketed back, pulled on the reins, and nudged the animal with her knees.

"That is a valuable horse! Stop, girl!" the man shouted in Romany, as he chased after her.

She reached into her bodice, pulled out the gold coin the disguised man had given her, and tossed it to him. Then she hunkered down and headed for the gate.

The dark interior of the tunnel was densely packed, the echoes of voices and neighing horses shrill and loud. Tamsin edged the black along one wall, calling out in Romany for people to shift out of the way. She glanced ahead and saw Malise and his guard leaving the tunnel. They rode into the dim evening light, and swiftly disappeared down the cobblestone hill that led away from the palace and through the town.

Tamsin urged the black ahead, blocked at one point by a cart that had gotten stuck. The tunnel arch was neither wide nor long, but the Romany seemed unwilling to pass through a few at a time. A massive pair of wood and iron doors normally closed the outer end of the gate, and only one stood open now, slowing progress for all.

Her horse began to buck and shift, and Tamsin feared, for a few moments, that she would lose control of the animal. She leaned forward and patted the muscled neck, speaking in soothing tones, and walked it steadily toward the exit.

When the black finally stepped out into open air, Tamsin breathed out in relief and guided the sidling horse down the gradual slope to the town. The tiny copper bells fringing the blanket and decorating the bridle rang softly in the open air. As she passed the Romany who streamed along the main street of the town, she looked ahead for Malise and his guards, and for William and the others.

At the outskirts of the town, she saw Malise and his companions cutting across a wide moor. The slightest nudge of her legs sent the black sailing after them. She hunkered low and pressed with her knees, and knew she could close the distance.

A few moments later, she straightened, pulling back on the reins, peering ahead. Foolish, she told herself, to think she could stop armed men from taking the little queen wherever they wanted. Perhaps Malise Hamilton took the queen to safety.

Then she remembered Marie of Guise's stricken face in that upper window of the palace. She was sure that Hamilton had not taken the little queen with the consent of her mother.

Tamsin circled the black on the moor, feeling its power, tense and restrained, beneath her. Behind her, the Romany made their way out of the town and toward the moor. Turning, she saw in the distance a group of horsemen riding west toward some hills. Surely that was William and the others, in pursuit of the men disguised as gypsies. Controlling the horse as it sidled, she glanced eastward, where Malise and his guards rode away with the little queen.

For another moment she circled uncertainly, knowing she could not stop Hamilton without help. Remembering the guards who had readied to leave the palace just as she rode out, she knew that the queen dowager must have summoned help, and that Hamilton would soon be pursued. Hamilton's track would not be lost. That knowledge decided her.

She hunkered low and launched the black toward the west, and toward William. Of all men, he could stop Malise Hamilton from taking the queen. And of all men, he deserved the chance to try.

Chapter Thirty

"He is either himsell a devil frae hell,
Or else his mother a witch maun be
I wadna have ridden that wan water,
For a' the gowd in Christentie."

—"Kinmont Willie"

William leaned into the wind as the black stallion, a loan from Baptiste, galloped over the moorland. Perris rode hard at his side, and John Faw and Baptiste Lallo just ahead. The horse was swift, powerful, and nimble, and carried an armed man and weapon-loaded saddle with ease, which, William was sure, the Romany horse was not accustomed to doing.

The four men they had pursued had disappeared among the hills already. He glanced ahead and saw no sign of them. He thought about turning back to find more men and organize a fuller search, when he heard Perris yell to him.

He turned. Perris gestured behind them. William twisted, and saw a horse coming after them, black like his own, streaming through the gathering darkness like a shadow. Then he caught a glimpse of the rider's long black hair billowing out, and her skirts flying back over bare legs. He swore, loud and fierce.

He turned and rode back. "What are you doing here?" he called to Tamsin. "Go back!"

"Hamilton!" she called out, circling her horse around his. "Hamilton has the queen!"

"What?" he said, halting his horse.

She pulled up beside him. "He took the queen," she said breathlessly. "I saw him, after you rode out. He rides with an armed guard, that way—" She pointed eastward. "Madame sent guardsmen after them."

He twisted in the saddle and called to Perris and the others, who had turned to ride back. He explained what Tamsin had told him, and Perris nodded.

"Dear God," Perris said. "I had heard rumors of a second plot to take the queen, a Scottish plot to wed her to the regent's own little son. But I had no proof. Since Malise is bastard half-brother to the regent, this doesna wholly surprise me though."

"If they ride eastward, they may mean to take her to the regent's castle on the coast," William said.

"We must go after this Hamilton," Baptiste said, listening. "The men who were dressed as Romany women are long gone. They did not take the prize they wanted, so what do we care? This Hamilton has the treasure you want!"

"Aye," William said. He looked at Tamsin. "Go back to the palace. We will go in pursuit."

She only looked at him, with a decidedly unconvinced tilt of her head. He saw that she had no intention of complying, and he had no time to argue with her. He simply wheeled eastward, and all of them pulled around and launched after him.

The moon rose white and huge, casting a silvery sheen over the hills and moorland. While the surrounding shadows darkened, William and the others rode near enough to see Malise and his men ahead of them. Perris spotted the queen's guards riding over the moors, and pointed them out to William, then turned and rode back to meet them.

William led the rest onward. All four rode Romany horses, hearty and swift, trained to obey the slightest shift of the rider's leg or hand. Tamsin rode to his left now, and he glanced at her. Despite his concern for her safety, he was glad that she was there.

When she looked at him, he gave her a little smile and tipped his helmet. Then he surged ahead, knowing that she and their Romany companions came fast behind him.

He heard a shout, and looked back to see Perris and the guards riding not far behind now. William waved them all onward.

Within moments, they joined forces with the royal guards. Few words passed between them, since time did not allow it. Command and consent were made by gesture, expression, and intu-

ition. They rode together, swift and quiet, and came on the heels
of Hamilton's guardsmen.

The royal guards cut into them like reivers into a herd of cattle,
splitting them apart, driving them away. Lances and swords
flashed in shadow and moonlight as guard met guard. William
stormed through their center, twisting only to wave Tamsin out of
the way, and to gesture to John Faw and Baptiste to keep her
back.

William saw Hamilton on a pale horse and edged toward him,
hampered by the tumultuous movements of the horses around
him. Hamilton sliced away from the group and took off over the
moorland, his bundle secure in his arms, his helmet glinting as he
repeatedly looked behind him.

William urged his horse after him, clearing past the other
horses at last. He launched out over the moorland, his mood grim,
dark, determined. Within moments, he noticed that Baptiste, John,
and Tamsin rode beside and behind him, their speed in keeping
with his, hoofbeats thudding, quickening his heart to a fierce
pace. The other guards had ridden in pursuit of Hamilton's men.

As he drew nearer, he saw the pale blur of a tiny head, heard a
small cry snatched back by the wind. Fury, desperate and pure,
rolled through him. A profound need to defend and harbor that
small soul poured after it, filling him to the brim with steadfast
purpose. He rode onward, the horse responding to subtle com-
mands.

He did not look to see who rode with him. The thunder of their
combined hoofbeats seemed to shake the very earth.

Then, as the shadows thickened and the moon rose higher,
William felt as if the horse slowed, as if its long, sure strides became less certain. He heard it snort. Sensitive to the horse's sig-
nals, as the black was to his, William glanced down.

The tufted, uneven ground gleamed in the moonlight. Ahead,
where Hamilton rode, the dark shadows of the grasses mingled
with tiny, endless chains of shimmering pools like black mirrors.

Marshland, William thought, and swore aloud. Of course, he
thought, for they rode eastward toward the sea, where the watery,
treacherous bogs that plagued much of Scotland increased. He
pulled up gradually, allowing his horse to pick its way through the

morass. He looked down and saw the horse's feet dipping deeper with each step into the bog.

He called out and whirled to warn the others back. They too glanced down and saw the danger, and hesitated, a few of them retreating to the more solid ground that they had left.

Tamsin rode forward on her horse, a black twin to his own. She looked at him, and he saw that she felt the same resolve that he did. Danger surrounded them, and the earth had its own power to draw them down and defeat them, but they would not stop.

He nodded in silent affirmation when she sent him a pleading look. Together they urged their horses over the soft ground, riding cautiously, glancing down, then ahead. If Hamilton could ride onward, William thought, so could they.

Moonlight created a wide path to follow, turning the watery patches to polished jet, while the tufted ground had a rough texture. The horses moved carefully, while William scanned the gloom, looking for more certain ground.

He saw Hamilton skimming the marshland like a shadow, like a fool, riding too fast, forcing his horse ahead, glancing backward nervously. Then, as William watched, Hamilton's pale horse stumbled, recovered, then stumbled again, floundering, forelegs sinking in the bog.

William pushed the black then, taking the risk, praying that the horse's instincts were as good as he thought they were. He did not look behind him, but encouraged the horse with knee and hand and voice. He kept his gaze intent on the man and child, and the faltering horse, not so far ahead now.

He heard Hamilton's horse neighing as he drew nearer. Hamilton struggled to handle his mount, balancing the bundled child in his left arm. The pale horse floundered again, its back legs sinking now. It lurched sideways, strained to climb out, and tipped rider and bundle into the thick black water.

Behind him, Tamsin screamed. William felt the ground slide beneath his mount's hooves. He flung himself from the horse, booted feet sinking to the ankle, and took a step, dropping to his calf, pulling up, running on. As he crossed the bog, he sank again and again, to the ankle, to the knee, once to the hip, every step uncertain in the oozing mire.

Ahead, the pale horse found solid ground and pulled itself free, loping away in the darkness. Hamilton, though, stayed in the dark slime, shouting out, waving.

"Malise! I am coming!" William called. He was not the only one in the watery part of the bog, now, for he heard shouts and splashes behind him, and turned to see the others dismounting, leaving their horses behind.

He ran on, sinking, rising, until he was covered in muck and wetness, mired and slowed by the weight of his wet clothes and the mud in his boots, which pulled him down with each step.

He was within twenty feet or so of Hamilton now. He saw the man's face in the moonlight, saw the infant's small, pale head. When he heard her thin, angry wail, he felt a rush of relief.

"Malise!" he shouted again. "Stay there! Wait!"

He lurched forward, but fell again, his strength and power working against him now. The thick, porridgy mass began to suck at his legs and hands as he tried to gain a hold. The musty odor was overwhelming. No matter how hard he strained, he could not seem to get closer to Hamilton.

He saw Hamilton struggle too, sunk chest-deep now in a black hole of watery muck. He held the baby high while she cried plaintively. William turned in desperation, and saw the others coming toward him, saw them sink and fall and stumble.

"Stay back!" he yelled. Seeing a rough patch of grass, he rolled onto it, lying on his side. He tried to slither ahead, but felt his hands plunge into the ooze.

"Will!" He looked behind him. Tamsin crawled toward him on her belly. Baptiste and John Faw were behind her, both sunk to the knees, dragging a long, thick, leafy tree limb. Someone must have gone off to cut the thing, William thought gratefully, knowing the branch would be useful.

Tamsin inched closer. "William!" she called.

He began to protest, but realized that she could help. He twisted on the relatively firm bit of earth he had found, and stretched out a hand toward her.

"Come here," he said. He caught her wrist and pulled her toward his little turf island. She slithered up and half sat, leaning against him, both of them coated in slime.

"Tamsin," he said. "You can reach Hamilton and the bairn. You're lighter than any of us here. We're sinking with each step, but you can go farther, and more easily."

She nodded, breathless, understanding. "Could they drown?" she asked. "Can he not climb out?"

"He's sinking," he said, wiping a hand over his face. He had lost his helmet somewhere, he suddenly realized. "He canna find a hold to climb out. We have to reach him soon."

She nodded without comment. Once again, he was struck by her ease of acceptance, by her ability to handle strain and fear. A reiver's daughter, he thought proudly, and rested a hand on her shoulder in a quiet gesture of love, reassurance, and gratitude.

Behind them, Baptiste edged the end of the tree limb toward them. William caught hold of it and got to his knees.

Ooze seeped through his breeches, but the scrap of ground, tufted with long grasses, was secure. He hefted the sturdy tree limb and began to slide its length over the treacherous stretch that lay ahead, hoping to discover, with its far end, another solid place to anchor it like a bridge.

"Will! Will!" Hamilton called out, waving an arm. "Jesu, help me here!" He hugged the infant close to his head as he shouted. She worked an arm free and batted about, screaming. Hamilton nearly lost his grip on her writhing little body, wrapped in wet silks.

"Oh, God," Tamsin said in a choked voice.

"He willna let her go," William said, trying to balance the heavy tree limb.

"He willna let her go." Tamsin repeated the words while William eased the long limb toward Hamilton. The frontmost end hit fluid, tilted, and began to sink.

Tamsin left the turf patch to slip feet first into the bog, while William held one end of the tree limb fast. She slithered forward into black water, breast-high. With one hand on the tree limb, she glided toward Hamilton. At the other end, she strained to lift the limb out of the mire. It was stuck fast, and sinking deeper.

The baby cried, an insistent whimper now. Hamilton's face was pale and stricken, his hands dark with mud as he tried to keep the baby above the level of the bog that sucked him deeper.

Tamsin pulled, futilely, at the tree branch. William slid into the bog with her. The mud sucked at each wading step he took. He sank chest-high in muck. He felt the tree limb jostle behind him, and looked back to see John Faw and Baptiste stabilizing it.

The infant's tremulous wail piped across the bog in an eerie echo. That helpless, frightened sound ripped through his heart. William forgot who the child was, what she represented. He responded only out of his profound need to protect. Even toward Hamilton, in that moment, he felt only the natural pledge of one human toward another in need.

He gave a powerful groan and surged through the bog, breaking its clinging grip on his feet. And found, through some miracle, a firmer base for his step.

He dipped down in the ooze and shifted a shoulder under the tree limb, lifting it free of the mire. He slid it forward, balancing it on his shoulder.

Hamilton reached out to grab the far end. William pushed it steadily closer, balancing, waiting. Tamsin extended her left hand toward Hamilton.

"The bairn!" she called. "Give me the bairn!"

Her hand was clearly exposed in the moonlight, a narrow curving wedge and thumb. William saw that she was not even aware of it, nor did Malise notice.

"Take her!" Hamilton cried. He held the little flailing bundle toward Tamsin. She strained her arms to the length of her reach, and a moment later, swept the child into her embrace. Securing the baby in her left arm, she snatched hold of the tree limb with her other arm and began to shift backward.

William stretched his hand out to touch Tamsin's shoulder. He grabbed hold of the soggy back of her gown and dragged her toward him, while she held the wailing infant, who clung to her neck. He shoved them toward Baptiste, and John Faw, who crouched behind him on the solid, grassy patch.

Once Tamsin and the little queen were pulled to safety by the Romany men, William turned back. He felt a lurch of the tree limb he still held as Hamilton pulled on it. William strained to hold the heavy branch up, his feet sucking down again.

As Hamilton dragged forward along the tree limb, William

stepped back, shifting by increments, like a giant with the weight of the globe on his shoulders. Muck slopped at chest level as he sank farther himself in his efforts to pull the other man free.

Then he felt a slight lift in the burden. John Faw and Baptiste had hold of the tree limb, and now drew it back with steady, reliable power.

"Rya!" John Faw yelled, reaching out to him. "Take hold!"

William stretched an arm back and grasped the man's wrist. The old Romany was like a bull, powerful and compact. He strove to pull him until William felt the bog give up its hold.

Soon he shifted up to sit on the grassy patch, and took hold of the tree limb with the Romany men. Together they pulled Hamilton closer. John Faw and Baptiste slipped away, heading back to the shallow part of the bog.

William turned to watch Hamilton heave himself onto the solid patch. They sat beside each other, breathing heavily, coated in slime.

"Dear God," Malise said. "By hell. I am a fool."

"Aye." William sniffed, wiped his arm over his brow.

"I meant her no harm," Malise said. "I spoke with some Scottish nobles, who convinced me that if the wee queen were to wed my nephew, the regent's small son, things might go well for Scotland, and for the Hamiltons, and for Mary Stewart too."

"Ah," William said. "Is that what this was about?"

"Aye." Malise lowered his head. "We thought to keep her safe, we did, with this plan. Safe from King Henry."

"Foolhardy," William said. "The lot of you."

Malise put a hand over his face. "By God, Will Scott, I owe you my life. And you and the gypsy lass saved our queen."

"The gypsy lass," William said, "is my wife."

"Aye. Your wife." Malise slumped. "Katharine's stepmother."

"She is that." William looked at him. "I've taken bairns from you before, Malise. Your own daughter, and then the rights to your granddaughter. For those, I am sorry. But for this last one, you'll have no apology from me. And you'll face the dowager queen and your government. And your regent." He got to his feet and held out a hand.

"Will Scott," Malise said. "I had no hand in your father's death. I want you to understand that. I confined you, as a lad, because 'twas my appointed task to do that. But I didna hang your father myself. You saved my life this night, and our queen. I owe you the truth, and I will tell you the tale of that day, when we have time to talk together."

William stared at him, numb, exhausted. All he could do was nod. Malise got to his feet, but did not take the hand William offered. He stepped into the shallow part of the bog and made his own way back without a word, as William did for himself.

Ahead, near the two black horses, William saw Tamsin. She waited for him with the infant queen wrapped in a gypsy horse blanket, safe in her arms. William trudged the last few steps toward them. He reached out.

She ran to him with a faint cry of relief. He scooped her, and the babe, into the circle of his arms, profoundly glad to feel Tamsin's slender warmth against him, and content to hear the queen of Scotland squalling indignantly at his ear. Tamsin was laughing and crying all at once, and he smiled against her damp, peat-scented hair.

He laughed again, as she did, wordlessly, breathlessly. While the baby sucked at her dirty little fist, he kissed them both, slimy and sweet and tearful under his lips.

Tamsin looked up at him, and he tipped her chin up with a finger, grazing his fingers along her besmirched cheek. He touched his lips to hers again. She was warm and gentle under his mouth, and she was all he would ever need in his life.

He looked up and saw Perris coming toward them. He clapped William on the back, and then bowed to Tamsin.

"My lady," he said. "Lady of Rookhope. We all owe you an enormous debt. You kept Scotland's queen safe."

"We all did that," she said, smiling at him.

Perris held out his hand. She offered him her grimy right hand, and he kissed her fingers as if she were a queen herself. "I will certainly recommend some reward for both of you," he said.

William saw that Tamsin fisted her left hand, burying it out of sight in the baby's wrappings. He frowned and put an arm around her. Then he realized that she might do that for the rest of her life, out of habit. No matter how often he told her that she was beautiful, or how often he told her that he loved her—and he would do that daily, he knew—she might always keep some of that uncertainty about herself.

"Lovely lass," Perris said. "Fortunate man," he said to William, and smiled ruefully. Then he walked away.

William turned to Tamsin, and lifted the little queen out of her arms, balancing her sweet, blessed weight in the crook of one elbow. Tiny hands grabbed his neck, and a round, warm, silky head rested against his cheek. He hugged the infant to him, and closed his eyes briefly as a powerful flood of love, of simple, endless thankfulness, washed through him.

Then he reached out and took Tamsin's left hand in his, and kissed the small wedge that curled over his fingers, never taking his gaze from hers.

The tearful smile she gave him, lit by moonlight and by her own inner happiness, made her incandescently beautiful in his eyes. And her happiness, he thought, was reward enough.

Epilogue

"There's comfort for the comfortless,
There's honey for the bee,
There's comfort for the comfortless,
There's nane but you for me."
                    —"The False Lover Won Back"

"Nine hardheads!" Archie stared across the table at Tamsin. "You took all nine hardheads again!" He made a sound of disgust and threw his cards down on the table.

Tamsin scooped the pile of small coins toward her. "Be glad you dinna play with better coin than that," she said. "I willna empty your pockets this way, either of you. Hardheads are near worthless." One by one, she dropped the dull, thin coins into a velvet pouch, letting them clink to underscore her victory. She grinned mischievously at her father and her great-uncle.

"There, see ye," Cuthbert said. "She has yer own wicked smile, Archie Armstrong. Och, Tamsin, tell true. How is it ye win at the cards each time?"

" 'Gyptian tricks," Archie muttered. "Fast-and-loose."

"Luck," Tamsin said, frowning at her father. "And skill with re-membering the cards."

"Luck! 'Tis near impossible to play Ombre wi' ye, lass. I've won thrice in all these months o' riding here to Rookhope for a bit o' the cards. But thrice."

"She is good wi' the picture cards," Cuthbert admitted.

"I dinna know why you fuss each time I win," she said. "When you play at the cards with Lady Emma, you never fuss about los-ing. And she is just as good as me, if not better."

"Why begrudge Tamsin a wee bit o' luck?" Cuthbert asked. "The gypsies used to think her muckle bad luck to be around."

"Aye," Archie grumbled. "Bad luck for those who play at the cards wi' her."

Tamsin smiled and stood, smoothing her skirts. " 'Tis late. I must go see to the bairnies."

"Wi' our hardheads?" Cuthbert said. "What are we to gamble wi' when ye've gone up to sing ballads to yer bairnies?"

"If 'twasna so cold, we'd be out riding a raid into England, and nae sitting here at the cards," Archie said.

"My bones are too auld for that, if yers are nae. And 'tisna the merriment it used to be," Cuthbert reminded him, "now that Jasper Musgrave sits in his bed all the day and barely speaks, and eats porridge like a bairn."

"Aye," Archie grunted. "I willna steal livestock from a man who's had an apoplectic fit." He slapped the cards down on the table to mix and restack them. "I barely got Jasper back home to his castle before he took ill, that time I took him by the sly—and I'll remind ye o' my cleverness, for I bagged his head good on the way home, and he never knew 'twas me had him fast for a week. And when the regent sent men to arrest him, we had the news that he was so upset that he had a muckle bad fit, and lost his speech and was put to bed. Now that his son is in a Scottish prison with that Malise Hamilton, I feel pity for Jasper, I do."

"You and Jasper have plagued each other since before I was born," Tamsin said. "I think you both must miss it."

"Aye," Archie said. "But I've other matters to take my notice, now." He wiggled his brows.

"Did ye ask her yet?" Cuthbert said in a low voice.

Archie flushed pink. "Nah."

"Ask her," Cuthbert hissed.

Tamsin pinched back a smile, watching her father glance across the chamber. Lady Emma sat sewing on a bit of linen, and talking quietly with Helen and Perris. As if she knew Archie watched her, Emma looked over her shoulder and smiled. Archie cleared his throat and dropped the cards.

Tamsin glanced around the room, and realized that William, who had left their company a while ago, still had not returned. She wondered what delayed him. She found herself immediately listening for his step, and for his laugh, which had grown louder and heartier, and far more frequent, in the eighteen months since their marriage before a priest.

Archie reached into the leather purse at his belt and withdrew a copper coin. "Look what I have," he said, holding it up so that the firelight glinted on the shiny metal.

"A babbie!" Tamsin said.

"Aye, a babbie, minted in honor o' the wee queen's coronation at Stirling, two weeks after you and Will rescued her from that wicked plot. Rare they are to find, too."

She held out her left hand. He dropped it in the little cup of her palm, and she held it up. "Oh! A bonny wee portrait of our Queen Mary."

"Hah, our lass likes a sparkly thing well, she does. 'Tis that dark gypsy blood in her," Archie said to Cuthbert. He reached up and snatched the coin from her hand. "Ye'll see that again when ye win it from me, lass."

"I'll play Primero, then," she said. "My nine hardheads for the babbie."

"Bah, Primero," Archie said. " 'Tis a bairnie's game!"

"What is a bairnie's game?" William asked over a loud din as he entered the room.

"William! Oh, and the wee rogues! Dearlings, what is the matter?" Tamsin hurried toward William, whose arms were filled with two blanketed bundles. Their twin, dark-haired sons, six months old and wailing to a crescendo, looked around tearfully and hopefully when they heard their mother's voice.

She took one of the boys, Allan, from his arms, and left William to joggle little Archie. "I'm all out of bairnie's games," William said. "I went up the stair, and heard the wailing, and found the poor nurse exhausted. I told her I would take them down here for a bit. And Katharine too, who wanted to come down as well—" He turned around. "Kate? Where did you go, lassie? Ah, there you are!" His voice lifted with delight.

She toddled around the door and peered up at him silently, her thumb securely in her mouth, dark blue eyes wide and staring beneath a cap of thick, dark curls.

"She looks tired," Emma commented.

"Come here, sweetheart, come see the babbie I have!" Archie called, holding out his bright coin. Katharine waddled over to her grandfather and climbed up into his lap. Helen swept forward and lifted little Archie from William, while Emma came and took Allan from Tamsin, the women eager, as always, to lavish their love on the children.

Perris sat down to begin a new game with Archie and Cuthbert, and William took Tamsin's arm, leading her toward the window. They stood looking through the open lower shutter upon a winter twilight, the sky streaked with violet, orange, and indigo, reflected over the snowy hills.

Silhouetted against the brilliant sky, a single oak tree rose from the crest of the hill opposite Rookhope, its bare limbs twisted in a dense, lacy pattern. Tamsin glanced at William and saw that he focused his gaze on that solitary, magnificent old tree, beneath which his father, Allan Scott, was buried.

"He would be glad to know that there are two new rogues at Rookhope now," she murmured. "Allan and Archie. Both dark-haired and hot-tempered, and, I hear, the image of your father. And you," she added, slipping her arms around his waist.

"Ayc," he said softly, nestling her against him. " 'Twould make him glad to know that." He kissed the top of her head, and continued to gaze out at the old oak tree.

"Will," she said. "My father may be asking your mother an important question soon. Did you know?"

"I wondered," he said, and she heard the smile in his voice. "He did hint to me that he might be interested in courting someone, and in marrying again, after all these years."

"I think he has always loved your mother a little, since the days when he and Allan Scott were young rogues," she said quietly. "He once told me he was disappointed that she left after your father's death, and married another man."

"Perhaps she wasna ready, in those days, to be with someone who would remind her so much of Allan Scott," he said. "But now she is ready at last. I would be honored to have Archie for my stepfather—since I have him for a good-father already. If he asks her, I think she'll say aye. She blushes like a lass when he looks at her."

Tamsin smiled. "And have you seen the way Perris and Helen look at each other of late? There is a wedding there too, if I am not mistaken."

"Oh, well," he said. "I always expected that. I dinna know why he's waited so long. Helen and Paris loved each other in the legends, after all. 'Tis fate." He rested his chin on her head for a moment. "Tamsin," he said. "I want to show you something." He reached into his unbuttoned doublet and took out a folded bit of parchment.

"What is this?" she asked, taking it.

"I finally opened the box that my mother gave me, which holds my father's things," he said. "I confess, I didna have the heart to look in there until now. But I am accustomed to being a father myself, now, and I thought 'twas time to . . . visit my father again, in a small way. I didna expect, though, to find that. 'Tis a letter, in his own hand."

She did not open it, sensing that his father's writing hand should remain private for him. "What does it say?"

"He wrote the letter a few weeks before his death," he said. "He put down his wishes in writing."

"A will?" she asked in a whisper.

"Nay," he said. "A statement of his desire that his son and heir, William Scott, thirteen years old then, should wed the wee daughter of his closest comrade, Archibald Armstrong of Merton Rigg. He wrote, there, that this match was his dearest wish."

Tears started in her eyes. "Oh, Will," she said, tipping her face up to rest her cheek against his. "Oh, Will."

His hand came up to shape her head, his fingers slipping over her braided hair. "You know, Tamsin, my lass, what that means."

"Aye," she whispered, turning her head for his kiss. " 'Twas fate between us, all along, from the first."

Author's Note

Two schemes existed in 1543 to abduct the infant Mary, Queen of Scots. The first was the idea of King Henry VIII, who wanted the little queen wed to his son Edward and raised in England. The second plan was linked to James Hamilton, Earl of Arran and Regent of Scotland during Mary's minority, who thought that she should be wedded to his young son. Both plots were in the air just before the queen's scheduled coronation at Stirling Castle, at the age of nine months.

The English scheme ceased to go forward when King Henry's advisors protested. What became of the Scottish plan is unclear, but it is likely that reason prevailed there, also. *The Heather Moon* is a fanciful version of what might have happened had the plans gone a little further.

In 1553, when Queen Mary Stewart was ten years old and living at the French court, the Scottish Privy Council issued an unusual writ, a renewal of privileges granted to a certain band of "Egipciouns," or gypsies, who had previously gained and lost the favor of James V in 1540. Young Queen Mary, in agreement with her mother, who was then regent, along with the approval of the council, extended a safe warrant to a particular gypsy leader and his retinue. It begins: *"To oure lovit Johne Fawe, lord and erle of Littel Egipte."* The hint of affection in the document appealed to my imagination, and became part of the blend of history and romance in this novel.

The word "gypsy" is first used in sixteenth-century England to describe the wandering groups of "Egipciouns" who came to Britain from Europe by the early sixteenth century. The earliest records, from the fourteenth century onward, describe a wandering people, traveling in wagon caravans, who already exhibited characteristics that might today be considered stereotypical.

Even then, they were skilled with horses and metalsmithing. They danced, juggled, and were known for their music, as well as sleight-of-hand tricks and clever scams. And they were renowned for divination, especially palmistry, phrenology, and tarot cards. Early drawings of gypsy troupes show dark-skinned, handsome people with bright clothing, wrapped turbans, earrings, and other ornaments. Medieval legal documents contain accusations of child-stealing, horse-stealing, general thieving, begging, and vagrancy. In most countries, records indicate persecution, banishment, and strict punishment.

In the past, as now, the gypsies in Britain referred to themselves and their language as Romany. Medieval Europeans believed that they came from Egypt, but modern studies of their language and oral traditions indicate that they probably originated in India in the twelfth or thirteenth centuries, perhaps as Hindu outcasts who were banished. They became itinerant musicians and performers, surviving by their wits and talents.

Little sympathy was accorded them in sixteenth-century England, but Scotland showed more tolerance for them. There, the gypsies obtained royal assistance from the crown. There are records of payment to gypsies for entertainments at the royal Scottish courts. Evidence exists of intermarriage between gypsies and Scots from the sixteenth century onward.

When describing palmistry, card games, and *tarocchi* cards, I relied on what would have been known and used in the sixteenth century. Treatises on palmistry were widely available at the time. Although the ancient art was understood and widely practiced by gypsies, it was also regarded as a science and used by many European physicians.

Playing cards and tarot cards were immensely popular in the sixteenth century. *Tarocchi* was primarily a game played for points, and is still popular today. Even in the fifteenth and sixteenth centuries, there are references to gypsies who told fortunes using tarot cards and regular playing cards (a deck of fewer cards, minus the picture "trumps", as they were called then). The card layout used in this novel was current in medieval times.

As in *The Raven's Moon* and *The Raven's Wish,* I used verses from Scottish ballads to introduce many of the chapters in this novel. Wherever possible, I chose the oldest known versions, and relied on the ballad collections of Francis James Child and Sir Walter Scott. Other quotes are taken from contemporary documents and literature.

I sincerely hope you have enjoyed *The Heather Moon,* and found some hours of pleasure, humor, and excitement with these characters. I love to hear from readers. You can reach me through my website at: *http://members.aol.com/KingSL/* or at P.O. Box 356, Damascus, Maryland, 20872 (SASE appreciated).